THE LAST ORIGINAL WIFE

ALSO BY DOROTHEA BENTON FRANK

Porch Lights

Folly Beach

Lowcountry Summer

Return to Sullivans Island

Bulls Island

The Christmas Pearl

The Land of Mango Sunsets

Full of Grace

Pawleys Island

Shem Creek

Isle of Palms

Plantation

Sullivans Island

THE
LAST
ORIGINAL
WIFE

Dorothea Benton Frank

WILLIAM MORROW

An Imprint of HarperCollins*Publishers*

THE LAST ORIGINAL WIFE. Copyright © 2013 by Dorothea Benton Frank. All rights reserved. Printed in the United States of America. No part of this book may be used or reproduced in any manner whatsoever without written permission except in the case of brief quotations embodied in critical articles and reviews. For information, address HarperCollins Publishers, 195 Broadway, New York, NY 10007.

HarperCollins books may be purchased for educational, business, or sales promotional use. For information, please e-mail the Special Markets Department at SPsales@harpercollins.com.

A hardcover edition of this book was published in 2013 by William Morrow, an imprint of HarperCollins Publishers.

FIRST WILLIAM MORROW PAPERBACK EDITION PUBLISHED 2014.

Library of Congress Cataloging-in-Publication Data has been applied for.

ISBN 978-0-06-213247-5

16 17 18   OV/RRD   10 9

For Peter

Sea-Drinking cities have a moon-struck air;

Houses are topped with look-outs; as a dog

Looks up with dumb eyes asking, dormers stare

At stranger-vessels and swart cunning faces.

They are touched with long sleeping in the sea-born moon;

They have heard fabled sails slatting in the dark,

Clearing with no papers, unwritten in any log,

Light as thin leaves before the rough typhoon;

Keels trace a phosper-mark,

To allow old ocean-drowned green places.

—JOSEPHINE PINCKNEY, *SEA-DRINKING CITIES*

CONTENTS

PART THREE

THERAPY CONTINUES

PART ONE

HERE WE ARE

CHAPTER 1

Leslie and Wesley's Present Situation

ATLANTA, SEPTEMBER 2012

Welcome to Saint Magnolia's Wounded Theater. At least that's what I called it. Within these slick walls reside Atlanta's pish-posh team of premier psychiatrists, psychoanalysts, and relationship counselors who specialize in the broken hearts/crushed egos of the privileged and renowned. Their lavish confessionals, perched high above the city, are, well, breathtaking. I was here because my husband, Wesley, insisted this was the only place he'd even consider receiving, as he was loath to say, *therapy*. And as it was on my first visit, the vast waiting area was packed.

Just for the record? *Wesley* needed therapy. *I. Absolutely. Did. Not.*

The circular reception area held a large round workstation of bird's-eye maple. The countertops of deep brown granite were chiseled and polished. Behind them stood two young women who appeared to have fallen from the pages of *Vogue* magazine. Above them hung a chandelier worthy of an opera house that I imagined sailed right to America directly from the lips of the finest glassblowers of Murano. Every square foot of their offices was as beautiful as a session was insanely expensive, leaving me to wonder where exactly was this much heralded recession?

"I'm here to see Dr. Katz," I said.

"And you're Mrs. . . . ?"

"Carter."

"Thank you." She pecked around on what looked like a keyboard from the *Starship Enterprise* and smiled when she found my name among those on his appointment calendar. I was officially entered into the captain's log.

"Please make yourself comfortable in the waiting area. There's bottled water . . ."

"Thanks."

My heels clicked across the beige marble flooring that was shot with veins of black and gold. When the veins of gold caught a stream of afternoon light, they sparkled like the proverbial streets of paradise. Perhaps some people thought all this grandeur was a comfort; you know, they must be good at what they do if they can afford all this? Not me. The whole drama was a grand demonstration of conspicuous consumption and their complete disregard for carbon footprint. I shuddered.

I took a small bottle of cold water from the refreshment station and sank into one of only two unoccupied overstuffed velvet club chairs, unscrewed the cap, and took a long drink. Okay, I'd admit this much, as off-putting as the swank trappings were to me? Well, the chairs were like a beautiful womb, upholstered in swirls of deep purple and olive on a field of smooth ecru velvet. I could've slept in them. No, I could've lived in them. If I thought no one would have noticed, I might have pushed one through the door, down the hall, into the elevator, and somehow with God's grace, I would've smooshed it into the back of my car. Just the thought of it gave me a little thrill, and this was a time in my life when thrills were not happening for me in Atlanta.

In between the chairs were small tables that held magazines on mental health, extreme adventure travel, vegan living, and every kind of yoga. You could tell a lot about the soul of an organization by the reading material in its waiting area. For my money, these particular choices leaned a little to the side of wacko, but, I reminded myself, my son was a granola-boy who had been living in an ashram in Nepal for the last three years while he contemplated the universe instead of completing his MBA. It wasn't like Bertie aspired to climb Everest and then come home and become an adult, not that climbing Everest is a childish thing to do. I'm suggesting *that's* a lofty goal. No, this was something different. He was completely under the spell of all things Hindu, Himalayan, and Tibetan. His current passion was to photograph the people as they went about their lives in the spectacular landscape near the Roof of the World. He was transfixed by the exotic temples and stupas, the smells of burning yak butter candles, and Buddhist monks seated in long lines on low cushions, chanting in guttural tones. He was completely taken by the regular people, their devotion to their faith, and their pilgrimages to Lake Manasarovar. His plan was to sell his pictures to a magazine like *National Geographic* or maybe put together a documentary for PBS with Bill Moyers. I have to confess that while his photographs were out of this world stunningly beautiful, neither of these goals had yet to come anywhere close to fruition. So my beautiful son, Bertie, was still woven into the umbilical cord of his father's wallet.

I have never been able to mail Bertie an additional check for even fifty dollars because my husband had some very deep-rooted and completely exhausting control issues. Therefore, I had lived on a very, very strict budget and never had an extra fifty dollars. All spending had to be justified in the accounting department of Wesley Carter's stingy brain.

This unpleasant detail was one more item on my list entitled *Why Am I Living Like This?* Here's how it went: Bertie called Wes and they made small talk. Eventually Bertie would politely and humbly ask him for some money to hold him over until this deal or that deal came through. Wes pitched a fit about it and then took it out on me for a month or so until Bertie called again. Life as Wes's emotional dumping ground had long ago become tiresome and ridiculous. And odd as this may seem, part of me envied and also admired Bertie's courage to be a nonconforming, unmaterialistic seeker. The only thing he ever spent any real money on was camera equipment. At least he had a passion. Thank God he wasn't selling drugs to make ends meet. Or getting mixed up in human trafficking, which I knew went on in Asia because I had read about it somewhere. But maybe that was Thailand? I can't remember. And wasn't Thailand part of Asia? God, my brain is a piece of Swiss cheese. The important thing is that (a) he had a passion and (b) things could've been worse. And then there was my daughter, Charlotte, who is licensed to sell real estate but somehow rarely closes a deal. We'll get to her.

I sighed hard and looked around. I imagined that this was how ultrahip offices in Los Angeles or New York looked. The large trees and fish tanks with exotic specimens made the space seem less clinical. It was obvious that a team of experts had given this whole environment much thought. The broad strokes of the interior decoration and even the low and warm lighting were designed to soothe the rankled nerves of those who came and went. Equate opulence with consolation, and one step inside these massive vaulted doors should make the most egregious elitists feel better even if the therapy didn't solve their problems. My cynical gut told me that any place that was home to a dozen or so counselors who were *this* busy had to be an outpatient crazy house in disguise.

This was my second session with Dr. Harrison Katz, the celebrity psychiatrist slash relationship consultant. He appeared on all the morning network and cable talk shows to offer his opinion whenever a celebrity couple or a politician got caught cheating or was considering divorce, which would mean about every five minutes. I still had a little time to wait so I looked around to see who was there.

Seated right next to me, just my luck, was a painfully odd-looking woman with baby bangs and white cat-eye eyeglasses who might well have been there to cure Nosy Nellie disease. She kept leaning over, looking at my handbag, my shoes, sniffing so loudly that I wondered if I should offer her a recommendation for a good ENT doctor. It was becoming clear that she was determined to talk to me. She leaned forward and back about four times until finally, she cleared her throat and spoke.

"So I told my therapist that I needed to make some friends. That's why I'm here. To learn how to make friends. He said I need to be more present in the moment and to read people more deeply when I try to engage them in conversation. Do you have any idea what he meant by that?"

"No," I said, deliberately lowering the volume of my voice hoping that she would too. "I'm sorry, I don't." I noticed a small tattoo of a frog on her ankle. The frog's lips were pursed.

"Well, I think it sounds like a lot of New Age blah blah, you know? I mean, how could I be more present in the moment? I'm here, aren't I?"

"Yes," I said quietly, focused on my magazine, trying hard not to make eye contact.

"If I were to read you right now, I'd say you don't want to engage in conversation. Is that right?"

Oh, brother, I thought, this dame's way off her meds.

"I'm just trying to gather my thoughts," I said. "I'm sorry." I got up to look at the magazines on another table and to send her a cue.

Then she called out to me, "So it's probably none of my business, but why are *you* here?"

Really? I should answer this? I walked back to her and leaned down.

"Um, can you keep a secret?"

"Sure!"

"I'm thinking of taking a chain saw to my husband while he's sleeping? And you know, I just wanted to see what my counselor thought. Before I actually *did* anything. You know . . ."

"You're right. It's none of my business," she said, embarrassed. "But you're kidding, right?"

"Of course I'm kidding." I smiled to be polite and said, "Look, it's okay. I'm just trying to organize my brain before I go in there."

"Oh, sure. But my therapist says if you want to make friends, encourage others to talk about themselves."

"That's good advice. Usually."

I smiled at her and thought, Wow, this poor busybody only heard half the message; she missed the part about the right place and time. Maybe her bigger problem was situational awareness. And that frog. And the sniffing every other minute as though she was pulling back the high tide of the Atlantic Ocean. Jeez.

I moved to the other side of the office, picked up a yoga magazine, flipped through it, thinking about my idiotic life. What did Wes expect me to get out of therapy anyway? Unless there was a brain surgeon in one of the offices poised to give Wes a lobotomy, nothing was going to change.

Suddenly, Dr. Katz's door flew open, and a stylish woman of indeterminable age bolted out of his office, wailing. She stopped at the reception desk, announcing that she needed to make another appointment for an immediate emergency private session. Meanwhile, I stood there evaluating her neck and eyebrows and lack of jowls, wondering who her plastic surgeon is because she looks amazing. Not that I'm a devotee of cosmetic surgery, but like every woman over thirty, okay fifty, I think about it from time to time. Okay, a lot. I think about it a lot these days. Then I thought, She's got to be sixty but her face is forty, and somehow it's not stretched tight like a snare drum. She was as skinny as a hanger, which would explain why the dress she was wearing looked so fabulous on her. I recognized it from some ad I had recently seen. Maybe it was Chanel. No matter. Still, she must've spent three thousand dollars on that bit of silk whimsy and lace and at least another thousand on the shoes.

My inner voice piped up to tell me that all the money in the world can't buy happiness, and I told my inner voice she was an idiot. Money might not buy happiness, but not having any was just about guaranteed to make you miserable, unless you had the soul of Mother Teresa of Calcutta, which I did not. I was conflicted about some issues and certain of others.

I heard the brunette receptionist with the goddess ponytail say to her, "I'm very sorry, Mrs. Del Mastro, right now there are no extra sessions available for three weeks."

Well, Mrs. Del Mastro with the amazing face-lift, apparently used to getting her way, was having no part of *no* and proceeded to show the receptionist some tooth.

"Wait a *minute!* How can this *be?* I've been coming here for *years!* I'm in the middle of the biggest disaster of my life . . ." She began to weep uncontrollably. She reached over the counter, violating sacred space, and grabbed a box of tissues. "*Please!* Find *something* for me!"

"Maybe we'll have a cancellation . . . I can call you if—"

"*Cancellation?* My life's hanging by a *thread* and I have to wait for a *cancellation?*"

Then she turned to face me. "Are you seeing Dr. Katz?"

"Who, me?"

"Yes, you! I'll buy your session from you! I'll pay you double!"

I was so shocked that I kind of gasped.

"Triple!" she said. "Please!" Then she did the unthinkable and grabbed me by my arms, giving me a good shake. "*Please! Help me!*"

Apparently hearing the ruckus, Dr. Katz rushed from his office to our sides, speaking to poor distraught Mrs. Del Mastro in the same voice he probably reserved for the criminally insane.

"Come now, Mrs. Del Mastro. Let's unhand Mrs. Carter."

"You don't understand . . ." she sobbed, her comments directed to me. Then she dropped her arms to her side and spoke quietly. "I came home and he was in our *daughter's* bed with two teenage girls, *friends* of our *daughter,* Emily. *Teenagers!*"

"My God!" I said. "What is this world coming to?"

"He's just a *horrible* son of a bitch," she said. "I just want to *murder* him!"

I wouldn't have blamed her if she did. Not one bit.

"Nasty!" I said, offering what I thought was appropriate support.

"Mrs. Carter? I'm *concerned* about Mrs. Del Mastro's state of mind and I was wondering if I might prevail upon your generosity to . . ." Dr. Katz said, winding up for the pitch that I intended to accept. But I was suddenly determined to be compensated for the time I was about to gladly relinquish with just one tidbit of information.

"Can you step over here with me for a moment?" I said to her.

We walked away from Dr. Katz and I whispered to her.

"You can have my time for nothing, but just tell me one thing."

"Yes, anything!"

"Have you . . . you know . . ." I raised my forehead and cheeks with my thumbs and forefingers in that sign language all women over forty speak and whispered, "Had work?"

"Gerald Imber. New York," she whispered back.

"Is that with an *i* or an *e*?" I began digging in my purse for a pen.

"An *i*."

"Thank you. It's time for you to divorce the bastard," I said, scribbling Imber's name on a scrap of paper. "Take all his money. Every last nickel. None of that *divide by two* bullshit."

She stood back, awestruck, and stared at me for a few moments.

"Thank you! I will! You know what? I don't know why I was waiting for someone to give me permission. Of course! I'll divorce the bastard! Why didn't I . . ."

"Because," I whispered, "if you could muster the courage to recognize you needed to get a divorce, our Dr. Katz would go out of business."

"By God, you're right," she said as though her eyes had been opened for the first time.

She smiled a little. The poor woman was exhausted. There was nothing on earth that could surpass the value of camaraderie between women, especially women in crisis.

"See you next time?" Dr. Katz said to me.

"No problem," I said and waved them off.

"No, wait!" Mrs. Del Mastro said and turned to Dr. Katz. "You know what? I'm fine. I know what to do now. So you go on and keep your appointment with Mrs. Carter. And I may or may not return. Ever."

"*What?*" Katz said, clearly shocked.

Mrs. Del Mastro bit her lower lip, self-doubt returning. "I'll let you know," she said and turned to me. "Want to have lunch sometime?"

"Sure," I said.

She reached in her gorgeous orange handbag, pulled out a small case, and clicked it open. She handed me her card.

"Call me," she said. "I think I'm going to have some free time on my hands."

"I will." And I would. We smiled at each other, and she went to the door and stopped. She looked at Katz and said, "I'll call you."

Then she was gone.

Something heavy hung in the air in the next moment as I quickly wondered if Katz would blame me for losing his patient. He did not. Dr. Katz arched one eyebrow and appraised me in bemused suspicion. He could not have cared less.

"What?" I said.

"Nothing," he said. "Shall we?"

I followed him into his office. I sat in the same chair I had last time and waited for him to find his place in his notes. I still wasn't quite comfortable with the idea of someone having a big fat bulging file containing my feelings and thoughts, but at this point it was still a pretty skinny file and I suppose he needed something in writing so that he didn't confuse one patient with another. Anyway, I had nothing to say that was so revolutionary. I was certain he had heard my complaint from a very high percentage of women who came to him for help. The difference between them and me was that I wasn't throwing a fit in the waiting area. No, I had actually done something about it.

"Now, Mrs. Carter, when I saw you last, you were about to tell me about, let's see, you called them *the Barbies* and about a trip to Edinburgh? Let's see . . . ah! Can you pinpoint any conversation or a specific event that triggered your general disgust with the institution of marriage?"

"Well, that's a pretty cold clinical way to put it. I wouldn't say I am generally disgusted with the institution of marriage. I just think that at a certain point in your life you reassess things."

"Like what? Unrealized goals?"

"Maybe to a point, but for me it's more like *just what in the hell am I doing here?*"

"Do you think you might have unrealistic expectations?"

I thought about his question for a moment and had a sudden day-dream of myself as a young woman, dressed in my wedding gown, leaving the church on Wes's arm, rose petals swirling all around us in the air. My heart was overflowing with joy for our future. I was also two months' pregnant with Bertie and had dropped out of college in my last semester to rush to the altar. What was it that caused the first little piece of my heart to die? Was it the overfried eggs he threw in the sink because they had brown spots on the bottom or the fact that I didn't make the bed the same way his mother did, mitering the corners? Maybe it was because I could never remember to rotate the dinner plates or his underwear so that they all became worn evenly. I was trapped with nowhere to run. So was he.

"Dr. Katz? It's a little bit like the chicken and the egg. *That* question is so old it just doesn't matter anymore."

"Then you tell me. What is the question?"

"Well, there is more than one, but let's start with this: Are you giving up way more than you're given to the point that your marriage is so lopsided that it's obvious to everyone? Has your marriage become absurd? Does he actually *care* if you're happy or about even being a part of what makes you happy?"

"Don't you think your husband wants you to be happy?"

"As long as it doesn't cost him any time, effort, or money. Look, I don't think he ever thinks about it or views my happiness or any part of it as his responsibility."

"Okay. What do you think you gave up that was so unfair?"

"Dr. Katz? I gave up everything—my own identity, my ambitions, my self-respect, and I very nearly gave up my own brother. My only sibling."

"How's that?"

I looked at him, trying to decide if I had the desire to continue.

"Because Wes hates gay men. He would not allow my only brother into our house."

"I see. Hopefully, we can resolve that issue in a joint session."

"We won't. There is no solution to it. Wes just is who he is, and nothing short of a miracle is ever going to change that."

CHAPTER 2

Meet Wesley Albert Carter IV

Six P.M. and *boom!* I'm in Dr. Jane Saunders's office, in the chair, ready to spill my guts like a girl. Nice. To say I've come here under stress and duress would be the understatement of the year. For my money? You can take all the shrinks in the world and throw them off a bridge. Who sits around all day listening to people carp and whine? People who can't figure out what else to do with themselves, that's who. They say, *Oh, I'm fascinated by human behavior.* Yeah, right. They take other people's problems and other people's money and they feel better about themselves. *Oh, look! I'm not so screwed up! Oh, look! I'm rich!* Please. Just my opinion. On the other hand, I'd been told by some very reputable people who are very high up in the firm that these guys are the best. We'll see about that.

The one good thing I can say so far about this psychiatrist or whatever she calls herself, a relationship therapist, is that she's punctual, which is good because time is a valuable commodity. I really hate to be kept waiting. It makes me nuts. And she's got great legs, but let's keep that between us. I've got enough trouble as it is. My friend who's a lawyer says if this doesn't go right, this business with Les could cost me big-time.

The doctor came around from behind her desk and took a seat in the chair opposite me.

"So," she said, looking at the paperwork in her manila folder, "Mr. Carter?"

"Please!" I held my hand up and gave her my most charming smile. "Call me Wes," I said, thinking I'd be more comfortable because then this *session,* or whatever it's called, would feel less serious.

"All right, Wes," she said, smiling, "then please call me Jane."

"All right, Jane, it's nice to meet you."

"And why is that?" she asked.

"Why?" I felt my neck get hot. It wasn't exactly a hospitable question, was it? "Well, because I've, I mean, *we've* been told that you and your colleague might be able to help my wife and me get things back like they used to be?"

"Is that what you want, for things to be as they *used* to be?"

"Funny question. Just so you know, I'm only here for the marriage. Going back to how things were would be fine with *me,* but my wife has other ideas."

"Go on."

I thought about it for a minute and realized being here with Jane could be very uncomfortable and I didn't like the hot seat. I was the one who put *other* people in the hot seat. I didn't like to tell strangers what I was thinking. If I'd learned anything in all my years in corporate America, it was that showing all your cards was a bad idea. To tell you the truth, I wasn't too sure *what* Les had in mind in terms of changes she had been looking for from me and the kids. But I'd come here to see this silly therapist, hadn't I? I was trying to fix things, wasn't I? I wasn't such a terrible husband. Still, I decided to dump the blame where it belonged.

"Well, my wife ran off and left me this past summer. And she's pretty much the main caretaker for our granddaughter, so our daughter was very upset." I waited for Jane to ask me why Les left, and when she didn't, it seemed that I was supposed to supply some kind of an explanation. "She said she'd had it with us."

"I see. Was there any particular reason, a specific incident that led to her, as you say, running off? A disagreement?"

"Well, I guess you might say she thinks our daughter takes advantage of her."

"Do *you* think your daughter takes advantage of your wife?"

"I don't know. Maybe in certain situations on certain occasions. Maybe."

"Do you have other children?"

"Yeah, a son. He's been over there in Kathmandu riding elephants with the hippies. Don't get me started on him. Anyway, she's been annoyed with me ever since we got back from Edinburgh a few months ago."

"Go on."

"See, we were traveling with this buddy of mine, Harold Stovall, and his new wife, Cornelia."

"And is Cornelia a friend of your wife?"

"No. Well, actually, I wouldn't say they're *not* friends, but Danette, who is Harold's ex-wife, was, well, is *still* Les's best friend. But let me tell you, Cornelia's a beautiful girl. I mean a *stunner*." I smiled then thinking about the sheen of Cornelia's thick copper hair and those perfectly white teeth of hers. And did her curtains match her sofa? And she had these adorable freckles. Were they everywhere? Harold was a lucky man. The dog.

"I see. Younger?"

"Oh, yes. I'd put Cornelia's age somewhere around thirty-two? Maybe thirty-three."

"How old is your friend Harold?"

"Harold's my age. Sixty-three."

"And your wife?"

"I married a younger woman too. Ha-ha." Jane's facial expression did not budge one inch. This head doctor was a humorless bitch. I could already see that too. "She's fifty-eight."

"Do you think the dramatic age difference made your wife uneasy?"

Oh, I could see where this was headed. Yeah, boy. Unless I said Harold was a total hog from hell for divorcing Danette and marrying a girl from his firm, then I was a hell hog too. I didn't have the energy or the inclination to debate the obvious. Jane's question was my cue to remind her of how it goes in, let's say, *mature* marriages.

"Look, Jane. These things happen every day. People get married, they raise a family, the kids leave home and when that happens? They take a hard look at each other, really see each other for the first time in decades, and guess what? They don't like what they see. You know? That beautiful girl you married is now postmenopausal, things are drooping left and right, she's a little thick around the middle, and she's turned into a harpy."

I watched as Jane Saunders shifted around in her seat.

"A harpy?"

"Yeah, you know. Her life doesn't suit her anymore. But you've got this secretary or colleague, and this girl is young and vibrant and practically a pulsating life force. She's gorgeous and she hangs on your every word and by golly, she thinks you're a god! Yes! A god! You're Zeus hurling lightning bolts from the sky!"

"Zeus?"

"Yeah, Zeus! But! When you come home at night, there's the old ball and chain, wrung out from doing nothing, pissed because you're late and you forgot to call, and your dinner is in the oven so dried out that it's basically inedible. And after you choke your way through another miserable meal of boneless, skinless chicken and mushy broccoli with fake butter and fake salt because your doctor said you should watch your pressure, there she is, asking you to go take out the garbage or change the lightbulbs. I don't have to paint you a bloody picture, do I? This is what you do for a living! Right?"

"Right. I've got it. Tell me about your trip to Edinburgh. What happened there?"

I cleared my throat and tried to refocus.

"Well, it was unfortunate. I mean, what happened really shouldn't have happened. And then the whole situation snowballed into this terrible misunderstanding. I felt bad for Les. I really did."

This was a lie. The truth was that, at the time, I was furious with Les because her stupid accident almost ruined the two days of golf I was supposed to have with Harold. Jane was quiet, waiting for me to continue. I really didn't feel like getting into this because the sequence of events probably wasn't going to showcase my most appealing qualities, but what choice did I have? And what did I really care what this ice cube Jane thought anyway? I was simply going to tell her our story, listen to her advice, and be on my merry way.

"She fell into an open manhole and cracked her arm. I was walking a little ahead of her with Cornelia and Harold, and Cornelia was going on about how much she loves the Dallas Cowboys. So I'm listening to her and thinking, Wow, this girl really knows her stats! The next thing I know we're back at the hotel and Les isn't with us. So I wait and wait and finally I think, What happened here? So I retrace my steps back to the restaurant where we'd just had a huge lunch. When I get there, there's my wife being loaded into an ambulance like a hundred pounds of potatoes. Apparently she knocked herself out when she fell. She had a concussion. And she was kinda bloody. She cut her head and cracked her arm and she lost some teeth, but we have a good dental plan so they were able to fix her up once we got home."

The truth was that Les looked like one of those witches from *Macbeth*; her mouth was disgusting to look at, all swollen and everything with snaggleteeth. I could hardly eat on the plane ride home, not that it was a gourmet meal or anything like that. But it was free and I was hungry. Still, my gut wrenched to look at her.

"Gosh. So what happened then?"

"Well, we went to the hospital and thank God they had an orthopedic doctor and a pretty good plastic surgeon over there. They set her arm, sewed up her head, and kept her overnight, which of course nearly ruined my plans completely."

"And what were your plans?"

"To play the Old Course at St. Andrews with Harold! Why else would you go to Edinburgh? To buy a kilt? I had only wanted to do this *all my life,* but Les has to go fall in an open manhole and break her arm! But once I saw she was okay and was in good hands, I figured why not go hit the ball, right?"

"You couldn't play another day?"

"Are you *kidding* me? I had that tee time set up for *two years!*"

"What happened to her teeth? Would you like a drink of water, Wes?"

I realized I was yelling. Normally I yelled whenever I felt like it and who cared, but now I felt like Dr. Hotsy Totsy thought I had a temper and bad manners to boot. I could see it in her face. She was judging me. I tried to redeem myself with a little backpedaling. And why I was trying to redeem myself to this witch is anybody's guess.

"Sure, that would be nice. Thank you. They fixed up her teeth with temps. But she wasn't eating anything she was so black and blue—lips out to here." I gestured, hoping she'd see some humor in it, but she didn't. She handed me a glass of fizzy water, which I don't like because the bubbles give me indigestion. Despite that little factoid about my esophagus, I took a sip to be polite and smiled at her. "Look, Jane, surely you can understand why I was conflicted." Had she never heard of the Old Course at St. Andrews? Did she live under a rock? I mean, come on!

"Okay. And how do you think Les felt?"

"Well, we had a pretty terrible fight about everything. Les claimed her accident never would have happened if I had been walking with her instead of racing ahead to hear what Cornelia was saying."

"Do you think that's true?"

"No! Wait a minute. Look, I wasn't racing anywhere. She was lollygagging around, stopping, looking in windows, taking pictures of everything in sight with her silly new phone. She wasn't watching where she was going. It wasn't like I pushed her or something."

Jane made a note and looked up at me, slack jawed. I thought she might have accidentally swallowed a hidden piece of Nicorette gum or something and I'd have to jump up and give her the Heimlich, but, thank God, she took a deep breath and finally closed her mouth, writing furiously on her tablet. Now what was *that* all about? Did she think I was a wife beater? Wait a minute!

"Look, I'm *not* a bad guy."

"I'm not here to pass judgment, Wes. Does your wife think you're a bad guy?"

"She never said it in those exact words, but I know she *thinks* it. All she kept saying over and over was, *How could you leave me like that in a hospital in a foreign country when I didn't know a single soul?* I guess it doesn't sound so good, but if you'd been there, you'd understand. Cornelia went and sat with her, which infuriated her. Go figure *that* one out."

"Hmmm," Jane said and made some more notes.

"I mean, Cornelia could've been shopping or sightseeing. I think it was pretty nice of her to give up her time for Les."

"Okay, let's move on a little, to some other areas. How would you characterize your intimate life with your wife?"

"What do you mean by that?"

"Would you say it's robust? Not what it used to be? Nonexistent?"

What? I was now supposed to discuss my *sex life* like this Jane was a medical doctor? The back of my neck broke a sweat.

"Look, it's weird for me to comment on that to a stranger. Let's just say I don't have any problems in that department."

The silence hung between us then like something thick and awful, something you wouldn't want to touch. Something you would have a hard time trying to penetrate. I was plenty uncomfortable.

"Okay, look," I said, "we've been married for nearly thirty years. Things don't happen as often as they used to, and the fireworks in the bedroom pose no danger to humanity, that's for sure." That was a clever way to put it, I told myself. But did this bitch smile? Hell no!

"But you considered your marriage to be a good one up until this incident in Edinburgh? And then, of course, her unexpected departure?"

"Unexpected departure. Humph. That's one way to sugarcoat it. Listen, I'm the last one out of all my friends who still has his original wife."

"Really?"

"Yeah. Shouldn't that tell her *something*?"

"Like what?"

"I don't know! That I still love her?"

"*Do* you still love her?"

"Of course I do! Why would she walk out on me? Was it her hormones?"

"Not at her age. At least it would be unusual if it was. Anyway, we can talk about that next time because our session is ending."

"Next time? You think I'm coming *back* here again? I mean, I have work. I'm a very busy man. I was hoping that you'd listen to my side of the story and give me some advice and we'd call it a day!"

"I see. Well, Wes, here's my advice. I think you're here to save your marriage, is that right?"

"Yes."

"Well, then, if you think you can save your marriage without any help from me or someone in my profession, then all right. But I can tell you from experience, you do not yet have an impartial view of your marriage. You have to come to a place where you can see things from Les's point of view and then you can begin to repair the damage. That takes time."

I thought about what she said for a split second and then decided it was total bullshit. One hundred percent total bullshit.

"You know what?" I said. "I don't beat her. I never ran around . . . well, not too much. She lives in a nice house. She's never had to work for a living. She drives a nice car. I take her to Vegas once a year. Is she crazy?"

"I don't know. Is she?"

This woman, this therapist, Jane was wearing me out.

"Look, I married her, didn't I? I stayed with her, didn't I? What the hell does she want from me?"

"We need time to find that out, Wes. It takes time. Little changes can make all the difference. And it's interesting that you choose Zeus as your avatar."

"Why's that?" What the hell was an avatar?

"Because he's the Greek god known for his many affairs."

A lying philanderer. I knew she had me where she wanted me. I was trapped. The fight went out of me like someone popped my little red balloon. The bitch was right. I had no fucking idea what Les wanted from me that I hadn't already given her.

"Fine!" I said. "I'll see you whenever our next session is."

CHAPTER 3

Les in Dr. Katz's Office

I was back in Dr. Katz's office for Round Three, convinced more than ever that this was an utter and complete waste of everyone's time and money. All I was doing was regurgitating the story of the bravest and smartest thing I'd ever done. Not even an army of mental health workers would ever convince me that leaving Wes had been a mistake.

"Where would you like to begin?" he asked. "I think when we last met you were going to tell me about a dance at your club? The Barbies?"

"Sure," I said. "Okay, so there was the spring dance at our club. Tessa, my great friend, had only been gone for a few months. I was still missing her something awful. We raised our children together, you know? Me, Tessa, and the other ex-wives of all the men at our table."

"Was her death sudden?"

"Yes. When she was diagnosed, she found out she had stage IV lung cancer. And she was never even symptomatic beyond this stupid little nagging cough she had for just a few weeks. She thought it was allergies. Can you imagine the horror of it? She just collapsed, was taken to the hospital, was diagnosed, and was dead in ten days. Can you imagine? It was a horrible, devastating shock for everyone."

"I'm sure it was."

"I don't have a picture of a birthday party or a Fourth of July picnic or anything that involved our children without Tessa and her children right in the middle. We were all very close."

"Maybe I shouldn't say this . . ."

"No, please! Say anything you want."

"Well, it's just that I think sudden death is so hard for the survivors, but I think it's far worse to watch someone you love just waste away. Especially if they're in any kind of pain."

"I completely agree. Poor Tessa didn't even have a chance to be in pain, it all happened so fast. She had a kind of cancer that they said was small cell and very aggressive. I can tell you that her death was a real wake-up call for me."

Katz sat there tapping the eraser of his pencil against his legal pad, waiting for me to drop my revelation on his page.

"Anyway, we were at the spring dance at the club. Paolo, Tessa's widower, was there with his new wife. It took Paolo a whole whopping two months to marry his personal trainer, Lisette, who may or may not be thirty."

"This age difference thing really has resonance with you, doesn't it?"

Dr. Harrison Katz was quickly losing points with me.

"Yes. It does. But my annoyance doesn't stop with the age spread, Dr. Katz. Paolo's swift remarriage was just another sign."

"Sign of what?"

"Really? That wives are so easily gotten over and so easily replaced. We are an expendable breed."

"Do you really believe that?" To his credit, his expression was briefly ever so slightly incredulous.

"Yes, I do. The evidence is all over the place. Men wear us out, either bury us or divorce us, and then they just go get another woman to be their mother."

"Go on . . ."

"So I looked around at these second wives with their fake boobs and their Jennifer Aniston flat-ironed hair and their Michelle Obama toned upper arms and I felt more like a chaperone than a peer. They were all wearing skintight bandage dresses with spiky platform high heels and they had their spray tans and big chunky jewelry. I was wearing, well, something age appropriate, pearls, pumps, a nice dress. I realized over the course of the night that they had plenty of chitchat for each other, but when they talked to me, they deferred as though they were being respectful of their grandmother. That was when I came to what I thought was a rather startling realization."

"And what was that?"

"That I *didn't want* to be there. I really didn't *want* to be there! Worse? I didn't *belong* there! All of a sudden I didn't care. Wes's friends were married to girls who are young enough to be their daughters. I didn't *want* to spend every holiday and weekend for the rest of my life with a bunch of Barbies. These men were Wes's oldest friends, and their *former* wives were mine. These insipid young women would *never* be my friends. Moreover, I didn't *want* them to be my friends."

"Hmmm . . ."

"Hmmm, what? Listen, every time I looked at those men and thought about how much they hurt their families, I got angry. And guess what? They hurt me too!"

"And how is that?"

"Really? You need an answer to that? Look, the self-indulgence of those men, with the exception of Paolo, denies me the company of my closest friends. There will be no more Saturday nights with them. It's all done! Finito! From here on in, weddings will be awkward, baptisms will be awkward, graduations . . . the entire structure of my social life has been undermined by a bunch of men who are afraid of getting old and who think a younger woman will reverse the clock for them. The social life that I had, that I *loved,* is gone! You can't see that? "

"Yes. I do. But it is what it is. Divorce is painful and it impacts everyone, but as you know, half of all marriages end in divorce. It's not unusual."

"Dr. Katz, I'm not campaigning for tougher divorce laws. Quite the opposite. I'm saying my life, my marriage—it all just doesn't make sense anymore. I might have twenty years left to live or maybe twenty-five and I've just come to the conclusion I don't want to spend them in a relationship that has run its course, surrounded by people I don't want to know. It's just stupid. I don't want to be made to feel bad about my age, and I don't want to be anyone's personal slave anymore. And maybe most important, I don't want to spend the rest of my life with someone who feels he's giving me a break by staying married to me. It's just about as simple as that."

Katz sighed hard and made some notes. Obviously, he did not disagree with me.

"What about your daughter and your son? What do they think?"

"It's time my daughter took responsibility for her daughter and for their lives. And my son, as you know, lives out of the country."

"But what did they *think*? You know, about you leaving?"

"My son totally gets it, but then he's basically run as far from Atlanta as he can. My daughter, Charlotte, was surely irked and inconvenienced."

"How is that?"

"Well, she viewed me as her babysitter. Basically, she just dropped my granddaughter off with me whenever the mood struck. She's a real estate broker and when someone calls she has to go to work."

"Sounds to me like *you* may have been the one who was inconvenienced."

"No, not really. I adore my little granddaughter, Holly. She's very easy to make a priority over everything else in my life. But it's not right, you know? She's as pretty as a little girl could be, with curly blond ringlets and eyes so big and clear blue you could swim in them. And she's so sweet! No, Holly is the greatest joy I've known in years!" We were both quiet then, and I was feeling a bit wistful. "I love to read to her, and we love to do all sorts of things together."

I was remembering having Holly for an afternoon last spring, one when we decided to walk around the yard to see what we could find. What a marvel it was to see the world through the eyes of a three-year-old little girl. Every single thing was fascinating to her. We got down on our knees and followed a fat worm crawling through the grass and she giggled the music of tiny, high-pitched wind chimes. When I imitated the worm and his wiggle, Holly wiggled too, and we both dissolved into laughter. In the next minute, she pushed her little nose into my roses and was absolutely stunned by the sweet smell of them as though she had never smelled a flower. *Oh!* she said and inhaled deeply again. She peeled a handful of the petals from a thick bloom fallen to the ground and rubbed them in between her chubby little fingers. *Soft!* she said and rubbed them against her cheek. I could see her in my mind's eye. I must've been smiling then because I lifted my head to see Dr. Katz was smiling too.

"What other kinds of things do you do with her?"

"Oh, everything in the world! We make cookies, we read books, we play dress-up . . . you know, we play simple games like peekaboo and sometimes we color or make things with clay, like little animals. I feel so badly for my daughter."

"And why is that?"

"Because of all she's missing! No matter what I say to her, I cannot make her see all the happiness there is to be gained by having a little girl of her own to love. She doesn't seem to be able to relate except in the most basic ways. To children, I mean. I know she loves Holly, after all she's her own flesh and blood, but I think she sees her as, God forgive me, a burden she'd rather not have. She's the one who ought to be in this chair. Not me."

"I see. And Holly's father?"

"Oh, him? He's gone with the wind. And I thought he was such a nice young man—shows you what I know. Brad was his name. He always dressed so nicely and was so sweet to me. Who knows what goes on between the ears of young men today? In my day there would've been a hurry-up wedding and maybe a divorce later on, but at least the child would have a name and a chance at having two parents."

"Do you think that's a better idea?"

"Yes! Because maybe, just maybe, they'd face reality together and then find the courage to rise to the occasion. Doesn't a child need a father? Think she'll have abandonment issues when she grows up? Besides, why should this fellow get off the hook scot-free? No child support? Not even slightly interested in visitation? I mean, Dr. Katz, don't you think it's morally wrong to bring a child into this world and then walk away like a tomcat?"

"Personally, I agree, but professionally? I'm not supposed to voice my opinion."

For someone who wasn't supposed to have opinions, he had plenty. In my opinion.

"Right. Listen, I know being a single parent is hard on Charlotte. She's still angry with Holly's father and probably always will be, but look! That awful irresponsible relationship produced a beautiful, affectionate little girl who's as smart as a whip! It just seems to me that if Charlotte were more engaged with Holly, she would enjoy her so very much. So much. And here's what I worry about. Pretty soon Holly is going to figure out that Charlotte would rather be elsewhere. That's when the chickens will come home to roost. She'll spend the rest of her life trying to please a mother who can't be pleased and a father who can't be found."

I could hear his brain ticking as he thought to himself, And that's why I'll always make a living.

Dysfunctional relationships kept the lights on in his penthouse.

"Hmmm," he said. "Is that why you left home and went to Charleston? To force her to take responsibility?"

"Maybe on some level, but actually, I went to Charleston, which is where I'm from, to think. And to help my brother, Harlan."

"I see. Tell me about your brother. Is he ill?"

"Not at all. Harlan is a distinguished professor of the Italian Renaissance and he lectures all over the world. And he's the chair of the Art History Department at the College of Charleston."

"I see. Older or younger?"

"Older but only by a few years. Anyway, he was taking a group to Rome for part of the summer and he needed someone to watch his dog. And his house."

"Aha! So his departure for Italy coincided with your departure from Atlanta?"

"Yes, but that's irrelevant because I could have gone to stay with Harlan anytime. We have a really wonderful relationship."

"Tell me about it. Is he an important part of your family? I mean, is he close with your husband and children?"

"Hardly. Wes is a huge homophobe, and he would never allow

Harlan and Leonard to come to the house. Leonard was Harlan's partner for decades. When he died—he was much older—he left Harlan a gorgeous house in the old part of Charleston."

"Leonard died from what . . . AIDS?"

"No. Thank you. Leonard, who was healthy in every single way, had a massive heart attack at seventy-two while doing the Bridge Run in Charleston. He was a marathoner. Why do you assume that if Leonard died, it had to be from AIDS?"

"You're right. It's a ridiculous assumption. I apologize. I just made the fleeting connection that if Wes didn't want them in the house that it might have been because they were HIV-positive. Many well-meaning, uninformed people used to think AIDS was an airborne virus."

"True. No offense taken, but here we are again looking at another chink in the façade of my marriage. Wes just straight up hates gays. My only sibling happens to be gay. Wes hates him."

Silence from the shrink. Finally. I went on.

"So . . . ? It makes it impossible to mindlessly adore my husband."

"Do you think that's what he expects? Mindless adoration?"

"Look, Dr. Katz. No, it's not what he *expects,* but it's what he *sees* when he looks around at his friends."

"I understand."

"Really? Well, I'm glad you understand because I sure don't. I mean, Wes's friends are successful, reasonably intelligent men. What's the matter with them? Do they *really* think that all that fawning over them from their Barbies is sincere?"

"Maybe they don't care."

"Maybe you're right. Maybe they don't care. What a thing to say. Well, how's this? Maybe pretending to be in love leads to believing you're in love."

"Really? Do you believe that?"

"I'm not so sure about a lot of things anymore. Maybe love is a calculated gamble."

"How so?"

"Because you're signing up for a lifetime tour? Maybe it's doomed to fail from the start, and there's nothing you can do about it."

"What on earth do you mean by that?"

My lovely Dr. Katz must've had live-in help around the clock.

"Look, when the husband leaves home in the morning, his wife is still dead tired from doing dishes the night before until eleven thirty, and she looks it. But there she is at six A.M., making his three-minute egg and one slice of lightly toasted whole wheat anyway."

"Wives and mothers usually make breakfast unless they're sick. Don't they?"

"What? *Egg duty?* Hello! The kids are out of the house, and I think a man can boil an egg as well as a woman. But that's not the point and it's not where I'm headed. Unconsciously or not, he all but refuses to make eye contact because his actual scary number age is reflected in her puffy, no makeup face, and he hates to think about the fact that he could drop dead any minute from natural causes."

"Mrs. Carter, isn't that a bit harsh?"

"Nope. Not one bit. And when he gets to the office there's the secretary or coworker or junior partner who's just blown out her hair and got herself all gussied up and she smells like some subtle fragrance that's acceptable for the workplace, something that's not overtly bait. Nonetheless, it is definitely bait. He takes a whiff, compliments her; she smiles and, doing her best to be all innocence even though she's the scheming slut of the world, she thanks him. Demurely. At least as demurely as she can manage."

"Okay, I'm getting the picture now."

"You don't know the half of it. In his mind, the affair is off and running. It's all he can do not to think about her night and day, and what's even funnier is that he thinks the blossoming affair is his idea. What he doesn't know is that she has already memorized his favorite restaurants, movies, music, football team, and the names and ages of his wife and children. She knows that Little Johnny is the class clown but a straight A student and that Little Lulu only wears lavender and wants to be a ballerina when she grows up."

"How does she know all this?"

"Because she's done her due diligence. She's over thirty. Her prospects for a wealthy husband have all but vaporized, and she can't trade on her looks much longer. But she chooses her target because she knows this guy has enough financial assets to give half to the current wife—which assuages whatever modicum of guilt she can muster—and that because he's young enough, he'll still earn enough to give her a better life than she could ever have on her own. She knows exactly when the last child will be leaving for college to minimize the trauma of his divorce. You know, women still only earn seventy cents to every dollar a man earns."

"I'm aware. So continue down this road. Where does it lead?"

"Well, it leads to any number of scenarios, but they all involve a bed."

"And you find this to be . . . what? Appalling?"

"It used to be that *appalling* was the only thing I could think about it. And all that lying and betrayal *is* terrible. But now I'm thinking that maybe those women are doing us a favor! Well, not in every single case, but think about it. If I had just half of all our assets in my name, I'd have much more expendable income than I've ever had in my whole married life! Did I happen to mention to you that I found a bank statement showing we had ten times as much money as I thought?"

"No, you didn't."

"Well, I did. I'll be a very wealthy woman if I divorce Wes.

Maybe life's like that old song by the Beach Boys—'Two Girls for Every Boy.'"

"So is money very important to you?"

"What kind of a question is that? Of course it is! Money gives you the freedom to decide things. To make choices. I could live anywhere I wanted to live. I could spend my time exactly as I'd like to spend it. And I wouldn't have to answer to anyone."

"Do you feel like you have to answer to your husband?"

"Ha! That's a good one! Dr. Katz, my husband thinks he's in charge of everything, including where I go to fill the car with gas and which road I take to get there. If I need a hundred dollars more than what he usually gives me to run the house for a month, he wants an explanation. Can you imagine such a thing? After all these years? Do you know how demoralizing it is to live like that? But does he ask me when he orders new golf clubs? *Custom golf clubs?* What do you think?"

"Hmmm. What about commitment? You know, the *till death do us part* part of the deal?"

"I'm thinking that must have been written into the wedding vows when you died at sixty and before all these men started having zipper trouble."

"That's very funny, Mrs. Carter."

We both knew that zipper troubles were the bedrock of his practice. Why, not one week ago that poor Mrs.—what was her name?—Del Mastro—yes, that's it—wasn't she about to lose her mind in the lobby over her husband's flagrant carrying on?

"Thanks. I've been known to turn a phrase now and then. But Wes thinks my sense of humor is stupid."

"Hmmm." He made a note. "Do you think your husband has zipper trouble?"

"I do not have solid proof, but I don't believe Wes is immune to the world."

"So then is fidelity less important to you now than it was, say, ten years ago?"

"I'm not sure how to answer that, but I'd say that recent events have prepared me to consider fidelity in new ways."

"Go on."

"Well, fidelity is about standing by someone, isn't it? Isn't a marriage supposed to consider the needs of both people?"

"You tell me."

This Dr. Katz was suddenly borderline insufferable.

"Well, I've always believed that it's supposed to be about *both* people and their dreams and needs, and all the stuff of life should get equal billing. It should be an equitable relationship. At least that's what I think."

"And, correct me here, but are you saying that egalitarianism is a concept beyond your husband's grasp?"

Egalitarianism? *Touché, Dr. Katz! A most propitious use of the word, you arrogant ass.*

"By light-years," I said politely. I hadn't been doing the *New York Times* crossword puzzles for years for nothing. "Anyway, I'm telling you all this to demonstrate how the younger women are calculating love and how the older women like me are calculating a new net worth."

"Our time is up, Mrs. Carter, but I wanted to give you something to think about until our next session."

"Sure."

"Do you think it's possible that the death of your friend and the divorces of all your other friends compounded by your accident in Edinburgh may have caused you to emotionally disengage to protect yourself?"

I had to admit I had never considered that as a reason to leave Wes. A gossamer veil of confusion floated up from hell and settled quietly all around me.

CHAPTER 4

Wes in Dr. Saunders's Office

God! Didn't she have kids or a husband or anybody in her life? Where were all the pictures? Nothing but books on analysis on the shelves and photographs of a beach somewhere on the walls. Maybe she shared the office with a neat freak. Or maybe she didn't want me to know anything about her life. Yeah, that was probably it. This woman was pretty buttoned up. She had gone to the ladies' room and I was waiting, wondering how many times we were going to rehash the same old crap before we moved on to some solutions. But then that's what I am—solution oriented. And this Dr. Jane Saunders? Well, the sooner we closed the case, the less money she would cost me. It was just like going to a lawyer, and don't get me started on that whole morass of bullshit billable hours! But I have to say this, and may God strike me dead if I'm telling a lie, she did have amazing legs.

She came back into the office and sat opposite me.

"Thanks for waiting."

"No problem."

She actually smiled, never mind it was the smallest smile that ever crawled across the face of an iceberg.

"So, Wes, when our last session ended, we were talking about how things are between you and your wife. You said that you never ran around *too much* . . ."

"Aw, come on. Did I really say that?"

"Yes, your words. I think this is a good place to pick up where we left off. Do you think your wife is threatened by the new young wives? Or do you think she's worried about you stepping out?"

"Humph. Les isn't threatened by anyone. She *used* to worry about what I thought. Did she look all right? Was dinner okay? Was I happy? Did I need anything? But these days? You'd think she doesn't have a care in the world."

"So there's been a marked change in her attitude?"

"A marked change in her attitude? Yeah, you could say that."

"I see, how would you describe it? Is she, say, hostile?"

"Hostile? Les, hostile? No, she doesn't have a hostile bone in her body."

"Then how *would* you describe her attitude?"

"There's a word for it—gimme a minute, it's right on the tip of my tongue—resolute! That's what she is! Resolute!"

"Okay. And how does this resoluteness manifest itself?"

I took a deep breath and exhaled. "She says she's absolutely not spending every weekend for the rest of her life with a bunch of women she has no desire to know who have no desire to know her. She's talking about the new wives of my friends. She ought to have a little respect."

"*All of them?*"

"Well, yes. One guy is a widower, but he remarried. His trainer."

"My goodness. So do you blame her? I mean, assuming these

women are much younger than she is, do you understand why this might be an uncomfortable position for her?"

"No! I think if she really loved her husband, she'd suck it up. She always sucked it up before now. What's so different all of a sudden?"

"Wes. May I ask you a few questions?"

"That's why I'm here, isn't it?"

"No, actually. But in the interest of moving things along, I need a few more facts. Number one, you're a pretty serious golfer, aren't you?"

"You'd better believe it! I've been playing golf with the same guys for the last twenty-eight years! Weather permitting, of course."

"And how many holes do you and your friends play every weekend?"

"Somewhere between thirty-six and seventy-two."

"And how long does it take y'all to play just eighteen holes?"

"Around four hours if the guys in front of us play on as they should."

"I see, and after a round of eighteen holes, what do you do? Have lunch?"

"Sure! Then we go out and play another eighteen. Why?"

"I'm just thinking that if you're working all week and out many nights and traveling a lot for business, it sure leaves your wife a bit high and dry, doesn't it? I mean, it almost sounds like you spend more time at work and on the golf course than you do at home or in her company? Does it seem that way to you?"

"Look, Jane, Les likes to be on her own. She likes to go see the ex-wives, go to girly movies, shop, be with our granddaughter . . . she has her own interests. I have mine. And I do take her out to the club every weekend and as I told you last week, we go to Vegas at least once a year. Some years we go to the Bahamas. You know, just to mix things up."

"Does she like to go to Las Vegas?"

"I don't know. Of course she does, right? Why wouldn't she?"

Dr. Jane Saunders, the Ice Queen of Atlanta, just stared at me like I spoke Turd instead of English. What was she trying to tell me?

"I think we're ready for a joint session, Wes."

"Fine with me," I said.

Frankly, I couldn't see an inch of progress. I'd pay for one more session and after that? I was already losing interest in this whole charade anyway.

PART TWO

HOW WE GOT HERE

CHAPTER 5

Les—Atlanta, April 2012

All our lives began to unravel last December 31, when Harold sheepishly announced he was leaving Danette at the overcrowded New Year's Eve party at the Piedmont Driving Club, that venerable institution of stone and timber with the most majestic ballroom in town. Lately it was becoming the stage for too many life-changing events. It wasn't the first time that Danette suspected Harold was having an affair with someone, I think, but she had absolutely no idea this one was so serious. They were both a little drunk. Maybe we all were. Well, maybe just slightly tipsy. It was late; we'd been at the club since eight, drinking champagne and wearing silly feathered tiaras with our gowns, and the boys in their tuxedos wore glittered top hats. As we did every New Year's Eve we made ridiculous resolutions that no one would keep, and quietly we all wondered what the coming year would hold, each of us praying for our own private miracles. Good health. Better health. A marriage for this child, a good job for another. This hopefulness was something hardwired into our psyches, that a new year might mean some monumental something wonderful could happen to bring us happiness at a level we had never known. A new year was a chance to start over. Maybe even, just maybe, there would be peace on earth for one entire day.

The orchestra played and we danced and danced, but Lord save me, I couldn't wait until the clock struck twelve so that I could go home at twelve fifteen and take off my heels. Those black satin pumps that I thought made my legs look so good turned out to be individual torture chambers. My throbbing feet were my priority, and then suddenly I was blindsided. What happened next was the last thing in the world I ever expected.

It was around eleven forty-five. We were sitting with six other members we barely knew, a very ancient couple who seemed sweet and two other young middle-aged corporate types and their young Barbie wives. Paolo had stayed home, still mourning and saying he just wasn't up to celebrating anything yet. We didn't blame him really, but his absence made me miss Tessa like crazy that night. I remember thinking, At least I still have Danette.

Harold's cell phone kept buzzing—cell phones are strictly forbidden in the club. He had once been a stickler for rules and propriety. But lately? A silly club rule didn't stop Harold from pulling his phone out and looking at it. Someone was texting him like mad and Danette was becoming suspicious, rolling her eyes in my direction. The next time it buzzed she grabbed it from his hand. Harold tried to grab it back from her, but she slid his phone across the table to me. Before Wes could grab it from my hands, I managed to read a partial text message that involved Harold's tongue and the sender's nether regions. I was aghast. Wes's entire head turned beet red as he read it. As if by instinct he started to sweat and tossed it back to Harold. But Danette caught it and read it, and her expression was one of honest horror. I don't know why she chose that moment to speak up and defend her own honor. She had to know it would become the Most

Talked About and Exaggerated Moment in the History of the Club—well, for 2011 anyway. And why take someone on—especially your husband—in a public place when you know in your heart it could get really ugly? But she'd had just enough champagne to take the chance that a sassy reprimand would put an end to whatever foolishness he was engaged in.

"You know, Harold," she said loudly enough for all of us to hear, "you can't have me and your little floozy too. You have to choose."

Harold cleared his throat, which we suddenly recognized as a harbinger of doom.

"Right now? Here?" he said.

"Yes. Right now and right here," she said.

Without missing a beat he said, "Wes? Would you drive Danette home? I have to go and meet someone."

I couldn't believe it. None of us could. But Harold stood and left, the orchestra started playing "Auld Lang Syne," and Danette dissolved into tears. Wes, in a gallant demonstration of southern gentlemanly manners, moved from his seat next to hers and handed her his perfectly pressed linen handkerchief to dry her tears.

"Come on, sweetheart," he said. "Les and I will take you home."

There have been many moments when I've wanted to kill my husband. This was not one of them. Wes could be a really great guy when he recognized the moment that called for it.

That same night, and perhaps at the same moment, somewhere across town in a romantic restaurant a promising young physician named Shawn Nicholls slipped a two-carat diamond on Harold and Danette's only child Molly's finger and asked her to be his wife. When Shawn brought Molly home, they found us at the kitchen table. I had never seen Molly happier in her whole life, and her young man, Shawn, was just beaming. She didn't even notice that her mother was a total wreck.

"Mom? We have something wonderful to tell you! Where's Daddy?"

"Dad? He's not here. Why don't you just tell me?"

"Actually, Mrs. Stovall, I should have discussed this with you and Mr. Stovall some time ago . . ." Shawn said.

"Is something wrong?" Molly said. "What's wrong? Why isn't Daddy here?"

"Your father and I had a little disagreement, that's all!" She put a smile on her face. "Now tell me! What's going on?"

On hearing the good news, Danette, being made of stronger and better stuff than her ridiculous husband, Harold, opened a bottle of champagne and began filling flutes.

"Harold's not going to ruin everything!" Danette whispered to me and dried her eyes again. "I'm so happy for you, darling!" She hugged Molly with all her might and then turned to Shawn. "We've waited all our lives for a wonderful young man like you to come along! Welcome to the family—such as we are."

Everyone laughed a little, and then she hugged him too. Happiness eclipsed Danette's pain, and optimism ruled the balance of the evening.

"Let me get a good look at that ring!" I said.

It was the first of many important moments that Harold would miss. And it also marked the moment that Danette decided Harold Stovall would no longer have a place in her tender heart. Her daughter was getting married and that was all that mattered for the foreseeable future.

The Little Floozy in question turned out to be Cornelia Street, the thirty-four-year-old buxom redhead who was the assistant to the director of human resources in Harold's law firm. Cornelia, who had tried out for and lost at auditions for every reality show that ever crossed the Georgia state line, was, shall we say, known to be very

ambitious and extremely generous with her favors. (Read: exhibi-
tionist, social climbing, slut of the world.)

Danette cleaned Harold's clock rather smartly and in fact
almost completely. That old saying "Hell hath no fury like a woman
scorned"? Danette embodied the words, but in the way a true lady
would.

Harold quickly married Cornelia on Valentine's Day, exactly
four nights before his daughter's engagement party, which was also
held at the club. At the engagement party we also had the opportunity to meet Lisette, thirty-one, who was Paolo's personal trainer. I
thought I might throw up. Wow, I thought, it took him all of a couple
of months to find a replacement.

Molly, the poor child, had no idea her father, Harold, was getting
remarried. Neither did anyone else. Molly was understandably devastated and could barely maintain her composure, wondering aloud
to anyone who would listen, when would her father stop ruining
her life? And I wondered to Wes, didn't Cornelia know that she was
barely ten years older than Molly?

When indeed? I thought.

I began to think there would never be an end to the bad taste and
timing of Wes's two remaining best friends, others having left for
sunnier climes and younger arms over the years.

Danette decided back in January that she was going to dramat-
ically change her life. Rather than beg Harold to reconsider, which
was what Wes predicted, she invited Harold to get the hell out of
her gorgeous center hall colonial in Buckhead and to go live with his
Jezebel in her tiny one-bedroom apartment in the Allure apartment
complex at Brookwood on Peachtree Valley Road. That would be
NW, thank you. And yes, *Allure*. Harold was too smitten to have any
shame. He bubbled over with a never-before-seen enthusiasm and
couldn't pack and hit the road fast enough.

Freedom from Danette's wrath! Let my lawyers handle it! I want to be free! Free! Take the money! Give her whatever she wants! I'm outta here! Cornelia! My love!

Of course I never heard him utter these actual words, but they were all over his face every time I saw him at the club during the short negotiation period of his settlement battles with Danette. He wanted a fast divorce and didn't even have the decency to show the slightest bit of remorse. All through dinner, Cornelia had her gelled nails all over Harold, and his hand traveled her lap to the point where I wondered when someone from the Ethics Committee would ask them to knock it off. My face was in flames, but Wes seemed not to notice a thing. The next thing I knew we were having dinner with Paolo again but now with Lisette on his arm. Oh, Lord, I thought.

Naturally, after any one or all of these dinners Wes and I would go home and the rest of the night was completely ruined. Well, for me, at least. Wes didn't seem to care that I was so unnerved by Harold's happiness or Paolo's or why. He'd tell me to go to sleep and quit fretting over things I couldn't change. He needed his sleep. He had an early tee time. He'd roll over and give me a slap on my hip, roll back, turn out the light, and begin to snore within minutes. I'd lie there for what seemed like hours wondering if Harold had lost his mind or if I was losing mine.

The sight of Cornelia and Harold together simply made me ill. It was way worse than Paolo and Lisette. Maybe because Tessa was gone.

Listen, I'm hardly naive. I've seen the *Jerry Springer Show*. I knew that people fooled around and had been fooling around since the days of Sodom and Gomorrah. Many of them wound up divorced, but I never thought anything this brazen and embarrassing would happen to Danette. Reality shows were one thing, but Harold's behavior just seemed so vulgar and desperate. And Cornelia was cheap. At least

Tessa was dead. She didn't have to see Paolo cavorting around with gel in his spiked hair.

Having dinner with Harold and Cornelia and Lisette and Paolo was awful. I missed my friends. Hopefully, Tessa was in heaven petitioning the good Lord for Harold and even poor Paolo to get an irreversible case of erectile dysfunction.

But what of Danette on Friday and Saturday nights? Was she home all alone in a sad chenille bathrobe, curled up on a sad sofa, watching a sad movie and drinking straight vodka, getting sadder by the minute? At least that's what I heard Cornelia say to Lisette in the ladies' room when they didn't know I was in another stall.

"Actually, ladies, Danette is not sad or drinking vodka. She's doing great! She put the Buckhead house on the market, sold it for a whopping sum, and bought herself a wonderful craftsman's cottage in the Oakhurst section of Decatur. She's as happy as a clam."

"She is?" Lisette said.

"Well, good for her," Cornelia said.

"You *girls* have no idea what kind of a *woman* Danette is. So, as her best friend of thirty years, I'm going to ask you politely not to run your mouths in public about her because it makes you sound happy that Harold left her, which you obviously are, but that sort of talk is better done in private."

"We're in the *bath*room," Lisette said.

"A public bathroom is not a confessional," I said.

"It's *not* public. This is a *private* club," Lisette said.

"She means we probably shouldn't gossip anywhere we might be overheard," Cornelia said, looking at the floor.

" 'Cause you never know who's in the next stall?"

"Tessa must be spinning in her grave," I said, looking Lisette right in the face.

Lisette was as thick as a brick. I walked out of the ladies' lounge leaving them there, jaws agape and red faced. I thought, Score One for the Home Team, those little twits can kiss it.

It was true. Danette was flush with cash for the very first time in her adult life. She sold all her sterling silver and started collecting mercury glass. She gave all her designer clothes and handbags to Jody's Fifth Avenue, an upscale consignment store, and started shopping at Anthropologie, mixing the deliberate bohemian of their tops and sweaters with her plain pants from Talbots. She began to look interesting in a new way. She got a great short haircut and bought a Prius. I didn't mind the Prius, but to my great disappointment, she refused to discuss Harold or to say terrible things about Cornelia. I had mental steamer trunks filled with catty things I was dying to say about Cornelia. And Lisette! I was like an angry feline with a giant fur ball trapped in my throat and Danette had pulled away the soapbox the same way Peanut's Lucy swipes the football from Charlie Brown. She was determined to be dignified. It was killing me.

"I can't speak for Harold's behavior," she would say. "He's a grown man."

She said things like this a thousand times until I finally got it through my head that if she wanted to tell herself she didn't care, then I should support her and tell my inner yenta to go throw herself in the Chattahoochee River.

This posture went on for some time. Danette was the Queen of Serene, the Soul of Discretion, until, that is, it was time to start seriously planning Molly's wedding. Then she gradually shifted gears, and all conversation moved to a new story entitled "What to Do About That Little Bitch, Cornelia?" And there was a subtitle, "And Lisette."

It was a beautiful day in early April, and I arrived at Danette's new home carrying a take-out lunch from the Brick Store Pub, our new favorite haunt. Danette was in the nesting stage of her new life.

Flowers were coming into bloom all over her front yard, and the new gardens were starting to take shape. Danette was doing a lot of the work herself, and if you could believe what she said, she loved getting dirty in the yard.

I let myself in through the open kitchen door and found her there rinsing a huge copper pot in the sink. You could see your face reflected in the patina. In fact, you could see your face in all her pots and pans that were suspended from an overhead rack above the island in the center of her newly renovated kitchen. Houses that were too clean made me nervous. And Danette, as composed as she appeared to be, had a house where you could literally do surgery. She must have been cleaning to compensate for something. She couldn't fool me. But it was beautiful all the same.

"Hey! It's a gorgeous day out there in Decatur, Georgia! We ought to be having a picnic in the park!" I dropped the bag on a counter, took off my sunglasses, and let my eyes adjust to the indoors. "Lord! We sure do have some sun!"

"Hey, yourself! Gimme a smooch!" she said. I blew her a kiss and she blew one into the air back to me. "What'd ya bring? Just tell me they had the pimiento cheese and I'll die a happy woman." She rehung the pot above her head. Just for the record, until she and Harold got a divorce, I'd never seen Danette Stovall dry a pot in her life.

"I've got food for an army." I began unpacking. Imitating the voice of Rachael Ray, I said, "We've got pimiento cheese with pickled jalapeños to be served up with crostini and EVOO, butterbean hummus presented with pita chips and EVOO, a baby spinach salad with sliced turkey and tahini green goddess on the side for you and a muffaletta for me with balsamic and EVOO. Oh! And a brownie to share. Without EVOO. Ha-ha-ha."

Danette giggled. "You're so bad! What? No soup?"

"You're kidding, right?"

"I'm kidding. You want tea?" She opened her refrigerator and pulled out a pitcher that was filled with iced tea, mint leaves, and lemon slices.

"Sure. I think I could drink the whole pitcher! Want me to put lunch on some plates?"

"That would be great."

"Speaking of great, your *yard* is looking amazing," I said.

"Thanks! I've got a new guy to mow, blow, and go—fifty dollars a week! Isn't that incredible?"

"I'm imagining your old bill in Buckhead was slightly more?"

"Are you kidding? It was like the Rape of the Wallet. But to be fair, it's three acres versus one-third of an acre. You know, I met this guy, he's a landscape architect from down the street, and he thinks we can turn the whole backyard into an oasis—new fencing, a little waterfall, maybe an outdoor fire pit, definitely a barbecue area and lots of seating. He's drawing up a rough plan for me to consider. I was thinking if Shawn's parents wanted to, we could have the rehearsal dinner out there."

"Why not? They're from Vermont! How could they possibly plan the right rehearsal dinner for a bunch of picky southerners from that far away? Now who's this architect? Single?"

"Forget it; with my luck he's probably gay. Brilliant but different. A little quirky but in an exotic kind of way. Anyway, Leslie, it doesn't matter because I'm not exactly looking for a man. Am I?"

"Quirky doesn't mean gay and you know it. And we all need something to keep our coat shiny, don't we?"

"Oh, please!"

I looked over to the table where we had lunch last week, and today it was covered with samples of wedding invitations and notes on Post-its stuck to magazine tear sheets that showed wedding cakes, bridal gowns, and food.

"Oh my word! Would you look at all this stuff?"

"Wait till your two get married. You'll see." She handed me two plates and began putting all her papers back into a cardboard box. "Molly could care less about anything that has to do with this wedding besides her dress. She's in l-o-v-e. She ought to know what I know."

"Amen, sister," I said and sighed and began unwrapping the food. "My kids are never getting married."

"Oh, yes, they will. There's a lid for every pot."

"Whatever, but I'm not holding my breath." We looked at each other and I could see her thinking that what I'd said was probably true. Who wants to marry a young woman with a young child in today's world? It would take a very special man. And my son, Bertie? Marriage, family, and fiscal responsibility were a long way off in the future for him. Sometimes my children's performance in the world was deeply disappointing to me, but what good did it do to say anything? None, I'll tell you. Absolutely none. They had been born belligerent. I was well beyond the begging and pleading years with them and had been reduced to a life of prayer as my only weapon. Thus far the heavenly response has been sporadic. But at least we were speaking. Many families had children in rehab or jail or estranged children and I had much to be thankful for, but still, isn't it awful when a parent has to content herself by lowering her expectations? I had such lovely dreams for them.

And then, as if Danette was reading my mind again, she said, "My momma used to say that if you lived long enough you'd see everything. Isn't that the truth? Gosh! This looks so good! I'm starving."

"I don't know. Maybe."

We sat down and began to eat.

"Know what?" I said with a mouthful. "I still can't believe Paolo married that airhead Lisette. Tessa must be flip-flopping in her grave."

"You know I hate gossiping, Leslie."

"Oh, save me. I thought you got over that."

"I'm working on it. As fast as I can. Is it a sin if I say that I really don't want to see Cornelia at Molly's wedding? Or this insipid little idiot, size zero, Lisette?"

"Gossip is not a sin. Especially when it's just between us. And I've been waiting for you to say something about that."

"And what are we supposed to do about the bridal lunch and showers? Act like what? That we're from California circa 1970 and it's all groovy or something?"

"Well, we could all hold hands and sing 'Michael Row the Boat Ashore,' or how about let's not invite them?" I said. "I don't care if I ever see them again."

"In a perfect world the father of the bride leaves his trampy-looking new wife at home." She took a bite of the pimiento cheese and moaned. "I could eat this stuff until I get sick."

"Me too. Push the hummus over here, darlin'. Thanks." I scooped a tablespoon or so onto a piece of pita. "So the wedding's September eighth or fifteenth?"

"The fifteenth. I booked the club. We're doing the ceremony there too."

"What? No cathedral wedding?"

"I know, I know. I struggled with that, but Molly said, and she's not wrong, that on any given Saturday we could spend an hour getting from St. Philip's to the club because of traffic."

"She's probably right. Traffic is truly miserable these days."

"Not only that, St. Philip's already has four weddings that day."

"Too bad you can't co-op the flowers with the other families."

"Isn't that the truth? The cost of wedding flowers is over the moon. But thankfully Shawn's parents have that bill. So are you getting excited about your Edinburgh trip?"

"I'd just as soon get salmonella as travel with them, but you know

Wes! He's been dreaming of playing St. Andrews all his life. And he can't go anywhere without Harold."

"Men," she said.

"Yeah." We looked at each other for a minute and we could read each other's minds. Danette should have been coming to Edinburgh, not Cornelia. "Tessa had some nerve to die and leave us."

"She certainly did. But you'll have a good time."

"Listen to me, I will not have a good time. I will be miserable. Cornelia and Lisette have bonded and I'm like a third wheel—an *old* third wheel. You have no idea how awful it is to be with them. We can't fill a table at the club for an event anymore, which is actually a good thing because I can always hope that someone my age will accidentally sit with us. But usually it's dinner for six, and frankly, it sucks. Now I get to *travel* with stupid Cornelia too? Wes acts like he's giving me a thrill to take me to Scotland. Oh, big whoop! Not that I have anything against Scotland, but haven't you heard me say for years that I wanted to go to Italy? I mean . . ."

"Les, Les! Stop! Listen, I know you think I'm all torn up about Harold, and at first I was! I miss our lives together—you, Wes, Tessa, Paolo, me, Harold—but it's over, and I'm *really* okay with it. I've moved on! I'm not angry anymore, but that doesn't mean I want to see his insipid face or Cornelia's at Molly's wedding, and God save me from Paolo and Lisette. It's all too ridiculous."

"Well, I sure don't blame you for not wanting to see them. I don't either! But are you really okay?"

"Totally and completely. Because I have to be. Besides, I have a wedding to plan. Did I tell you that Molly asked Suzanne to be her maid of honor? And Alicia is going to be a bridesmaid."

Suzanne and Alicia were Tessa's daughters. We had known and loved them from the minute they arrived in this world at Northside Hospital.

"She did?" My eyes filled with tears. "Oh! That makes me so happy! They've been friends since the sandbox!"

"And she's going to ask Charlotte if Holly will be her flower girl."

"Wonderful!"

"And old friends are a special treasure, aren't they?"

I reached across the table and put my hand over hers, thinking how dearly I loved my friend. Let Harold be a damn fool. Danette would always be my dear, dear treasured friend.

At least that was what I was thinking about until I got home and made dinner for Wes.

We were sitting across the table from each other, and I was recounting my lunch with Danette.

I told him, "And Suzanne, Paolo's daughter, is going to be the maid of honor! Isn't that wonderful?"

"Sure," Wes said. "That's nice."

"So you know I'm going to have to give the bride's lunch the day of the wedding."

"Why?"

"Because it's tradition, that's why. There will be a lot of guests from out of town and then the bridal party and . . ."

"Hold the phone, Les! That's gonna cost a lot of dough!"

"We're not poor people, Wes. We can afford to give a lunch for twenty people. Besides, your granddaughter is the flower girl!"

"Know what? I think it's a good idea if you split it with Lisette."

"What?"

"Yes, Lisette. After all, Harold is the father of the bride, and he's paying for the wedding. And at some point you're going to have to act like you're friends with those two. For the sake of appearances, if nothing else."

"Never. Not in a *million* years."

"Come on, Les. Cut the poor girls some slack. We're traveling with Harold and Cornelia, for God's sake! In like a week we'll be in Scotland with them. You'd better figure this one out!"

"Wes, our *daughter* is five years younger than Cornelia and only God knows if Lisette still goes to summer camp. It's the truth."

"And I bet you think that's funny? Well, it isn't."

He cut a piece of the roast beef and pushed it onto his fork. Instead of eating it, he put his fork down on the side of his plate, tightened his lips, and said, "Then you aren't giving a lunch for twenty people with my money. Unless you want to go out and get a job. How's that?"

"Really? Is this an ultimatum, Wesley?"

"No, you should know better than to be this way. It looks bad for you to be hostile. Do you know what people will say?"

"How am I going to explain this to Danette?"

"Aw, for God's sake, Les, why can't you girls just get along?"

I felt like screaming, *They're girls, I'm an adult, and it's an important distinction. I'm not going to Edinburgh. Screw you and the Old Course at St. Andrews too! And while we're at it, screw Harold and Paolo too!* But I said none of those things.

Did he know how much it was going to hurt Danette if I hosted a bridal lunch with Lisette? Did he care? The lunch, which had just become the *dreaded lunch,* was still six months away. I'd surely find a diplomatic way to tell Danette before then. What choice did I have? If Wes said I had to do something, I had to do it. In fairness to him, he didn't dig his heels in that often. Get a job? Yeah, right. The want ads were stuffed and bulging with jobs for women my age. It was too depressing to dwell on it, but it was all I could think about while I was packing for our trip. The ugly cold hard truth was that the painted corner in which I stood was fashioned by my own hand. I should've finished college like my mother wanted me to do and gone on to do something like become a CPA, a job I could work at while

I was raising our two children. I just really hated it when Wes reminded me that I had no financial assets. He probably had no idea how upsetting it was, and even if he did, he probably wouldn't have cared. In any case, I wasn't looking forward to Edinburgh.

I laid out all my clothes and accessories I planned to take across the bed in Bertie's room. Then I stood back and looked at them—all the sensible shoes and cardigans in case I caught a chill and the tiny umbrella and the collapsible hat to protect my hair in case it was windy or raining—and I thought, Wow. These are the belongings of a much older woman than I considered myself to be. I called my daughter, Charlotte.

She answered on the second ring.

"Hi, Mom! What's going on?"

I told her what was happening and she said, "I *knew* you were going to hate this trip. I *told* Daddy so. And I *totally* don't blame you. Just go to Phipps and buy a bunch of Eileen Fisher! It's a *total* no-brainer."

"I'd feel better if you came along, you know, so I don't buy the wrong thing?" I hated admitting I was insecure about my fashion sense, but I was. Anyone would be next to Cornelia. Charlotte had met her and Lisette and thought they were, in her words, a couple of obvious opportunistic bitches. It was one thing we *totally* agreed on. There was a long pause from her end of the phone. I knew she was thinking that it was rare for me to ask her to do something for me. She was trapped, and she knew it wouldn't be nice to refuse.

"I have to bring my kid," she said with a groan, still angling for a way out.

"Why don't I pick y'all up?" I said, cringing at her unattractive reference to my sweet Holly.

"Nah, then I have to move her car seat and that's a whole big pain. I'll pick you up."

We only lived ten minutes apart so she was there in my driveway before I could even reapply some lipstick. I hurried outside to meet them so Charlotte wouldn't have to unbuckle Holly and then repeat the whole rigmarole of lifting her up into the car, waiting for her to scramble into her seat, and buckling her up again. A three-year-old little girl was not like a bag of groceries you could just pick up and toss into the backseat of an SUV.

"Gammy!" Holly squealed with delight when I opened the door and got in.

"Hey, princess!" I said. I kissed my fingertips, slipped my arm into the backseat, and squeezed her toes. She giggled so spontaneously that I could feel it in my heart. "Hey, darlin'!" I leaned over and gave Charlotte an air kiss.

"Hi, Mom!" She made a smooching noise and smiled. "Okay. Want to start with Saks?"

"Why not?"

We backed out of the driveway and headed toward the Phipps Plaza Mall.

"What's the temperature going to be in Scotland?"

"Probably about ten degrees cooler than here," I said. "And I think it drizzles a lot."

"Okay, so we're looking for things to layer," she said. "Got it."

"You see? This is why I wanted to shop with you. You just know to make a strategic plan and then go for it. I'd be rambling around all day!"

"Oh, I doubt that."

Before long I had an armful of new clothes, all of it on sale, of course, and I was standing at the checkout counter, ready to pay. Between Charlotte and an excellent saleswoman I felt like the choices I'd made took a few years away from my appearance. Shopping had seldom been easier or more efficient.

"Thanks for coming with me and doing this," I said to Charlotte.

"No problem. I don't like to think about those two little *hoes* making you so unhappy."

"It's just a really terrible situation that's never gonna get fixed."

"Well, when they see you in that pink jacket, it will give them something to think about."

"I hope so."

Charlotte and Marcy, the saleswoman, had run all around the store pulling clothes in khaki and black for me to try on. I stayed in the dressing room with Holly and colored in her coloring book. Then once we established the core pieces, they ran around again for accessories and I colored some more. I had scarves and belts and faux jewelry and all sorts of things I probably never would have chosen for myself. And the best-looking pink silk blazer I had ever seen. I hoped Wes wouldn't kill me for spending so much money. But look how much I saved! And then I thought, Really? To heck with that! He could rant and rave until he barked like a fox, I deserved some new clothes from time to time. Did he check with me when he bought a new suit? No. He did not.

"You know what's amazing, Mom?" she said. "The difference in your posture and your attitude when you're all accessorized from head to toe. You're just, I don't know, more sure of yourself."

"You're right. Isn't that funny? But I think that would probably apply to most people. Anybody want to go to the Varsity for a chili cheese slaw dog and a chocolate shake?"

"I do! I do!" Holly said.

"Let's make it quick." Charlotte said. "I'm supposed to show a house this afternoon. Can you take Holly for a few hours?"

"Of course!" I said and knew Charlotte would come in around eleven, smelling like alcohol and that I'd say, *Holly's asleep—why don't you let me just bring her home in the morning?* Then I'd say, *Come sit on the couch by me and let's watch* House Hunters International and she'd fall asleep in five minutes. I'd cover her with a blanket like I always did and I'd go to bed. In the morning, I'd make breakfast, and neither Charlotte nor I would say a word about the previous night. My daughter was a bit of a barfly and I knew it. I hoped with all my heart that she'd meet a nice guy and Holly would have a daddy in her life. But cruising the bar scene was probably not the best way to meet a nice guy. Maybe I'd suggest one of the online services to her—wasn't that how people found love these days?

The following week Wes and I were in our living room, having a glass of wine with Paolo, Lisette, Harold, and Cornelia. We were waiting for our car service to take us to the airport and Paolo and Lisette had come by to wish us a safe trip.

"Boy, it's a good thing we live in Atlanta or else we'd have to change planes." I said this in the direction of Cornelia and Lisette, deciding to make small talk, you know, to set a lighthearted tone.

"What are you talking about?" Cornelia said.

"Well, there's an old saying that if you die and go to hell, you still have to change planes in Atlanta," I said in my most charming voice. And youthful voice too. Yes, I sounded decidedly youthful.

They looked at me as though I'd lost my mind.

"I never heard that," Lisette said and looked to Cornelia. "Did you?"

"No," she said. "What does it mean, Les?"

"Oh, never mind," I said, feeling two thousand years old. "It's a dumb saying anyway."

"Oh," they said, and they began discussing Lady Gaga's latest concert.

Now, just to set the record straight on this one, I'm well aware of Gaga's meat dress and that she was born that way and I even sort of like her music.

Not really. But right there and then I knew it was going to take a lot more than a pink silk jacket to get me through this trip.

CHAPTER 6

Les—Post-Edinburgh

After many visits to the oral surgeon and orthopedist, I was finally feeling and looking almost like myself again. But it wasn't just my teeth that were broken or my left arm, it was my spirit. Of course, Wes didn't notice any significant difference in my mood but—here comes old and lame golf humor—that was par for the course.

It was Wednesday, the twenty-third, right before the spring dance at the club. Danette brought over a pound cake, still warm from her oven. She listened as I recounted (for the fiftieth time) the horrors of the trip over coffee in my kitchen.

"I still can't believe what happened. He actually left you in a hospital in a foreign country and went off with Harold to play golf and thought that was okay? You're kidding, right?"

"No. I am not kidding. And he said the accident was my own fault, that I was lollygagging, taking pictures, and not watching where I was going. Maybe that's true, but there's another truth here and that's that it was a forty-minute walk back to the hotel. So for forty minutes . . ."

"He didn't realize you weren't by his side."

"That's right. That's what upsets me more than anything else. But actually, his judgment sucks all around. Remember when he didn't show up for Tessa's funeral because he had a lunch date?"

"You're right. Awful."

Danette and I looked at each other. The implications of Wes's attitude were so heartbreaking and disappointing. I had been reliving the entire ordeal in my mind. The first face I saw when I regained consciousness was Cornelia's, not Wesley's. Her gigantic boobs were staring at me. This simple fact angered me in a way I had never known. I was beyond furious with him. What if I'd had a serious head injury? What if a decision had to be made and I was unconscious? Would *Cornelia* be making that call? Did she know I was allergic to penicillin? No. I could have been dead and laid out on a cold marble slab in a Scottish morgue with an ID tag on my big toe, but don't worry, Harold and Wes were sinking putts on the Old Course.

Danette sighed deeply and rapped the tips of her fingers on the table a few times.

"Oh, Les, don't read so deeply into this, honey. When it comes to things like this? Men are just like, well, as dumb as a pile of rocks. We both know that."

"No. Wes is many things, but stupid isn't one of them. You know, Danette, I might as well face it. Wes doesn't love me anymore. I don't think he's shown me any real affection in ten years. And I haven't been much better about showing him any either."

"Oh, come on now. You've had a nasty accident and you're surprised that Wes isn't all over you, seeing to your every need? Are you serious? He was *never* that kind of guy. Harold's not either. And to tell you the truth, most successful men aren't very sensitive to the needs of others."

"That doesn't make it right."

"No, it doesn't make it right, but it's the way it is. That's why we need girlfriends. And sisters. Now tell me how you're feeling otherwise. You still sore?"

"Well, my bruises are all faded and the really terrible one here on my cheekbone I can cover up with makeup. My mouth is still sore. Oh, who cares? I don't know . . . I just . . ."

"You've got the blues, shugah! And you're entitled to a good case of them from time to time—we all are. Let's have some more cake. We'll both feel better."

Danette was right. Sometimes cake was the answer.

Since we had arrived back at home from Scotland I had been marinating in a stew of marital discontent. But the silver lining was that my sweet brother, Harlan, had been calling me twice a day.

"Every time I talk to you, you sound a little better!" he said.

"It's because I'm hearing your voice," I said. "Best medicine in the world!"

"Are you, like, up and around and driving and going to the grocery store?"

"Only if I want to eat," I said.

"Wait a second here; doesn't Charlotte go shopping for you?"

"Only on the first day back," I said.

"Oh, and now she can't because she's too busy showing houses that she never sells?"

"Oh, hell's bells, Harlan, she has her own life, you know? Anyway, you don't have to worry about me. Danette's here all the time, and we're a long way from starving. Believe me."

"Well, I can't be there because I have to work, but if I could, I'd be there and cheer you up. And PS, I don't see why you can't convalesce in Charleston. Lord, here I am in this big old house all by my lonesome, except for my ghosts and my little darling! I'd *love* to have you here to fuss over!"

Harlan had an adorable little dog, Miss Jo or sometimes he called her Miss JP, named for the aristocrat who had once owned his home. Josephine Pinckney was her name, and Harlan's historic house was as incredible as Josephine Pinckney's life had supposedly been.

"There's nothing to fuss over. I'm fine, really I am."

"Well, we're just going to have to find an excuse for you to come for a visit, and I think I might have just the ticket. Did I tell you about my summer plans?"

"Nope."

"I can't believe I didn't tell you! But then I've been so focused on your accident and all . . ."

"For heaven's sake, Harlan! Tell me!"

"Well, it seems that I have been asked to lead a group of trustees and donors through the ancient art and ruins of Italy for a month."

"A month?"

"Yes. It's a pretty posh trip—we're staying at the Gritti Palace in Venice and the Hassler in Rome—first class everything. I haven't been there since Leonard and I went to Carnival in Venice years ago. I'm superexcited."

"No kidding! Who wouldn't be? It sounds like the experience of a lifetime!"

"It should be. I wish you would come with me. I promise you'd have a better time than you did in Scotland."

"Very funny. Listen, you could take me waterskiing on the river Styx and I'd have a better time than I did in Scotland. Anyway, I can just see me walking out of here for a whole month. Wes would die."

"Oh, please. No, he wouldn't. Seriously, Les, I'm not leaving until the eleventh of June. So I'm thinking of giving myself a bon voyage party. Why don't you come down and spend the weekend? And maybe Miss Jo would like to see her auntie?"

Miss Jo, my niece in question, was a three-year-old female Havanese with more personality and spirit than you would ever expect to find in a dog that was not in the entertainment business. She had an elaborate bed in every room of Harlan's house and a wardrobe to suit every occasion. With accessories. Harlan and Miss Jo went everywhere together. She probably would be desolate with him gone for a month. If I actually went to his party, maybe I could bring her back to Atlanta with me. Holly would adore having a little dog to play with.

"Well, we'll see," I said. "Let me know when your plans are all set."

Harlan and I hung up, and I walked around the house like a zombie. It dawned on me that I hadn't dusted in a while. My conscience was rattled a little by that so I went to the kitchen and took out my bucket of cleaning supplies, even though my arm was still in a cast and a sling. I wondered what Wes would say if I wanted to go to Italy with Harlan? What *would* he do if I was gone for a month? He could hire a full-time housekeeper, but would she know to rotate his undies? The towels? The dishes? I didn't know whether to laugh imagining Wes's frustration or cry my eyes out because this was my life.

After I gave the living room a straightening up as best I could, I wandered into his study with a dust cloth intending to put a spritz of lemon wax on his bookshelves and desk. I was dusting away when I noticed that one of his lower cabinets was unlocked. They held his personal files, and for whatever his stupid reason was, he kept those cabinets bolted like Fort Knox. Part of me was curious to see what was in there and another part of me—the she-devil who lives in all women—wanted to see if he was hiding anything. I mean, why *were* the doors always locked?

I pulled out a folder from the crammed drawers. Its contents were articles he had clipped from various magazines and newspapers regarding different golf courses, golf clubs, and golf pros. On the one hand I thought, He really ought to widen his horizons—you know, what about taking a wine-tasting course or something? What about sports cars? And on the other hand I thought, Well, at least he knows what he likes.

I replaced that file and thumbed through another huge one. This one was from our bank where we had various accounts, and it held statements going back to 1988. Boring, I thought, but for some inexplicable reason, I pulled out the most recent one and opened it carefully.

How are we doing, Wes? I thought.

For decades Wes had been tucking away money for our retirement, even though his company offered generous retirement benefits. Every year his company gave him stock options and he'd been exercising them and then telling me he wouldn't sell any stock, not one share, because you never knew what horrors we might find in old age. It was true that 80 percent of the average person's health-care expenses were spent in the last eighteen months of the individual's life. At least that was what Wes said and I believed him. Back in the eighties, every now and then he would say to me, *Oh, by the way, I took my bonus money and bought Apple in the IPO for practically nothing a share.* Or he'd mention, *I snagged a huge block of Microsoft today in a killing!* Or Motorola, or Nokia, or Pfizer.

Whatever, I'd think, and I'd diaper a baby or drag a garbage can to the curb or defrost a pot roast. He may as well have been speaking Chinese.

Wes was always very prudent, and not that I had much of a choice, I supported it. Who could argue with prudence? Besides, until I had my accident, I could not have cared less what he did with his money, even though there was barely enough to go around. I recognized that he had some primal need to have control of the family finances, which I thought was ridiculous but not worth fighting about. Now suddenly, post-Edinburgh, I was feeling that his control was maniacal, and I resented his secrecy.

I decided to open the envelope. I wanted to see for myself how our little nest egg was doing. Then I had the breath knocked out of me. To my utter and complete astonishment, it showed a portfolio balance of over twenty-two million dollars at current market value. *What?* That *couldn't* be right. I felt my blood pressure drop and thought I might faint. At first I was positive I was reading it wrong, so I took my reading glasses and planted them on my nose, clucking to myself about losing my eyesight and my mind at the same time. I sat down at his desk and counted the zeros and rechecked the decimal point at least ten times. I was no math whiz, but I began to understand what I was reading. It read two two comma zero zero seven comma three one six point two four. What in the world? How could this be? Why didn't I know this? I knew he was buying stocks and putting money in a fund now and then but twenty-two million dollars?

On that day and in that very moment, the compliant little lamb I used to be died.

It dawned on me like an atomic blast. I didn't *know* about it because Wes didn't *want* me to know about it. And why wouldn't he want me to know? The immediate answer to that, one that made any sense at all, was that Wes was a miserly bastard who didn't even trust his wife of thirty years to know what he was worth. I was pissed, like my momma used to say, in purple, paisley, and puce. Pissed bigtime. Here I was, dusting his office with my arm in a sling because he would only let me have a housekeeper once a month. Here I was driving used cars and watching every penny and worrying about money my whole married life while he was sitting on an insane fortune.

But wait. My heart started to race. How had he come to acquire such an enormous amount of money? Was it stolen? Was Wes in trouble? I could tell no one. I didn't want to be an accessory to a crime. It was obvious to me that Wesley had committed some kind of terrible robbery and eventually he was going to be found out and have to go to jail. Decent people didn't come by that kind of money honestly. It just wasn't possible. Was he selling drugs? Was he an arms trader? Suddenly I was ashamed. How powerful was his need to hoard and why? Why would he risk his reputation and his freedom this way? It was a sickness; that much was certain. Keeping a secret of this magnitude was surely going to eat me alive. I didn't know what to do. I stuck the envelope in my sling and closed his cabinet door. It automatically locked.

Then I looked around his office and our living room and the dining room. The wall-to-wall carpets had been cleaned so many times they barely had any nap left. The dining room furniture was cheap looking. Our living room sofa was from another century, and our mattress was at least twenty years old. The curtains were faded. The only room in the house that looked halfway decent was the kitchen, and Wes had raised so much hell about the cost of the renovation it wasn't worth it to ask to redecorate anything else. But if that money was legitimately ours, why were we living this way? It had to be stolen.

The next day I went to Bloomingdale's and bought a dress to wear to the spring dance that weekend. I was still so confused and nervous that I bought the darn dress at full price, something I had not done in years, and I put it on the credit card I was to use only in case of an emergency. It was a black knit tank dress and a little jacket with pretty buttons. I was so upset that I had spent so much money that I bought shoes and a handbag. Then to top it all off, I made an appointment for a facial and a blowout. Wes was going to kill me. Too bad, Wes, resourceful as I was, I couldn't blow my hair out with one arm.

Saturday night arrived before I had a chance to think about it and there we were at the Piedmont Driving Club sitting at a table for ten. There were Cornelia and Harold, Lisette and Paolo, Wes and me, and two other couples about whom the casual observer might say, "Oh! Aren't those men nice to take their granddaughters to the club?" These were not granddaughters but man-eaters.

Cornelia and Lisette were carefully avoiding any direct conversation with me. Ever since our ladies' room chat, they were less congenial.

After dinner, all the boys went outside to smoke cigars, Cornelia and Lisette were drinking their third cosmos, and I was still sipping my first glass of wine. The other two were sipping their second dirty martinis, comparing their diamonds and how they spent their new husband's money on lingerie, day spas, and shopping sprees in New York. And it seemed that everyone had a Brazilian bikini wax except me. When did pubic hair go out of fashion? I missed that memo.

Lisette said too loudly, "Paolo said he had the *best* time in Atlantic City!"

"Don't you worry about all those hookers?" Cornelia said.

"Nah. Paolo said he would never, *ever* sleep with a hooker."

He didn't need to, I wanted to say, *he had one in-house.*

"Yeah, right. And you believe him? What about you, Les?"

"Wes hasn't been to Atlantic City in years."

"That's what *you* think." Cornelia giggled, leaned into Lisette, and said over the music, "Shhh! See that girl at our table? That Tamara whatever her name is? She used to work for an escort service."

"No!" said Lisette. "No way!"

"Word!" said a very indiscreet Cornelia and fist bumped Lisette. "Saw her on the Internet."

Never mind why Cornelia was surfing escort services on the Internet—probably visiting old friends.

The winds suddenly shifted, and I could smell trouble. I saw Tamara's expression change as she stared a hole through Cornelia. Her friend, Sasha, perked up as well.

"What about the other one?" Lisette said.

"Girls!" I said, knowing these other two were about to explode.

"Big ho," Cornelia said and burst out laughing.

Well, that was it. All hell broke loose. Never mind the club rules, a loud catfight—albeit a brief one—ensued. Cornelia and Lisette were on their feet and the other girls took off their shoes. Tamara and Sasha began to come at Lisette and Cornelia with the obvious intention of trying to stab them in the eyes with their spike heels. Cornelia, who was all muscle, grabbed Sasha with the long hair and yanked on it for all she was worth, coming away with a handful of extensions. Lisette threw her drink in Tamara's eyes, and then Tamara slapped Lisette across the face. Sasha kicked Cornelia in the stomach, which was quite the acrobatic feat given the confines of her outfit. I was so shocked and it all seemed to be happening so fast, all I could do was inhale! Finally, I jumped up and got the attention of the captain of our table and said, "Get my husband! He's on the terrace with Mr. Stovall and Mr. Ferretti!"

There was hair on the floor; vodka, olives, and glasses of iced water were flying through the air; chairs were overturned; and a lot of mascara was running down all their faces. The next thing I knew they had pulled the tablecloth from the table, sending plates and flowers and glasses all over the floor. Cornelia was doubled over in pain, and Lisette was still at it, giving Sasha a solid punch in her jaw. Shrieking and well-composed guests recoiled, gasping in horror and scurrying away like mice.

"In my life, I've never seen anything so *disgraceful*!" said Lynn Bagnal, notorious for her gorgeous pearls and perfect thank-you notes.

Her husband, Scott, the president of the Board of Trustees, was heard to exclaim, "Why, this is the most disturbing thing I know of since McIntosh called Button Gwinnett out to the Field of Honor in 1777!"

"Ladies! Please!" someone said.

"Please! Let's stop this right now!" another man said.

There would be fines levied, memberships would be placed in

jeopardy, and Lord only knows what other kinds of consequences would arise. I could see Paolo and Harold's names on the Wall of Shame bulletin board. This club meant everything to them. Despite the influx of Barbies, the club itself was very conservative. In my peripheral vision, I saw Harold swoop in and grab Cornelia by the arm just as Paolo grabbed Lisette. Wes was huffing and puffing, bringing up the rear, picking up the overturned chairs in his path.

"What happened here? I demand to know what happened here!" he said to me.

"Why don't you ask them?" I said, pointing to Cornelia and Lisette with my good arm.

"You know I hate this kind of thing, Les. It's deplorable."

"It's also deplorable for you to go to Atlantic City and cavort with God knows who and not tell me!" I said this quietly and evenly. I was pretty certain no one heard me but him.

"What?" He was clearly surprised. "That has nothing to do with this! This is *our* club and you're supposed to set a good example!"

"Wesley? Number one, I am not a babysitter; two, I'm not stooping to their level; and three, I had and want nothing to do with it. It's not my problem! Take it up with them."

I turned to get my bag with every intention of leaving.

"Where are you going?" he said.

"I think I've had enough, Wes. Enough of you, your friends, their asinine wives and their infantile behavior. I've had enough of this whole circus to last me for a long, long while."

"We're not leaving yet," he said. "I can't abandon my friends with this mess!"

"Well, you sure didn't have a problem abandoning me in Edinburgh, did you?"

"That was different, Les."

I got very close to his face and said, "Really? Shove it up your ass, Wesley Albert Carter IV. I'm leaving."

And I did. I could feel Wes's fury burning holes in my back as I walked away. I had defied him and I had defied him in the club with his friends theoretically looking on. The truth was that Paolo and Harold were definitely going to be occupied with restoring order and dignity to the remainder of the evening. Maybe they'd take their silly wives in hand and punish them with a big time-out between them and their black American Express cards.

It would never occur to Paolo or Harold that I might walk out on Wes. Not in a million years. I had never done anything like that before. I was Leslie, the Good Wife. The one who never complained too much. The one who let Wesley do exactly what he wanted, no questions asked. The one who seemed happy with what little tokens Wes threw her way. Good old Leslie. We were Wesley and Leslie— wasn't that precious? Well, I wasn't feeling *precious* then and might never feel *precious* again.

Did Wes follow me? No, he did not. This fact did not make me angry. It made me deeply sad. It was another affirmation that it was more important to Wes that he call the shots than it was to explain to me how he wound up in Atlantic City without my knowledge or to understand the depth of *my* fury for once in our married life. Because I left, Wesley would say I had some nerve, that just because the other girls didn't know how to behave themselves, I shouldn't give into my emotions and throw a hissy fit in public. Well, I'd be ready for him if he did say that. I had not thrown a hissy fit or any kind of fit at all. I had just let him know calmly and politely that I knew he was a liar and that I wasn't going to be held responsible for the juvenile behavior of his friends' wives. It was absurd.

I stood on the portico of the club and waited in the night air, which was blessedly cool and not too terribly humid. The doorman had called for a taxi for me. I smiled at him and he said, "Nice night, isn't it, Mrs. Carter?" I think I said something like, "Yes, you can feel summer in the air!"

Strangely enough, I was composed. I felt like a gracious adult woman, sophisticated enough and savvy enough to know when it was time to say *Stop! No More!* So what if I was wearing St. John with Ferragamos with a lowish heel instead of some skintight strapless tube with spike heels that looked like it all came from a catalog for pole dancers? My whole outfit was beautiful. To me and to other women who wanted to look like a lady it was elegant and beautiful.

I was sick to death with feeling bad about not being some hot number with a fake tan, straight hair, and a bald you-know-what. (I still don't understand that last one.) Honestly! Going forward, this world of Barbie wives would only be my life if I allowed it to be my life and I already knew I was done. The door on that entire part of my life was closing, and for no good reason and every good reason it was suddenly fine with me.

I rolled down the window and let the night air play havoc with my fifty-dollar blowout. I felt liberated. It felt very, very good. The taxi driver must have seen me smiling in his rearview mirror.

He said, "Fresh air feels good, huh?"

"Sure does," I said.

"Dull party at the club?" he said.

"Anything but!" I said. "Just not for me, that's all."

"I see," he said.

"Well, it used to be, but not anymore."

"I see," he said again.

My driver was smart enough to know some kind of foolishness was afoot and polite enough not to pry. Sometimes taxi drivers loved to regale you with stories demonstrating the accumulation of their lifelong gathering of wisdom, wisdom gained by hearing and seeing every imaginable thing in the world come to pass right there in their cab. In their minds, all humanity winds up in a taxi at one point or another. Maybe it did.

"Yeah, things change," I said.

He said, "My momma used to say the more things change, the more they stay the same."

I had absolutely no idea how that philosophical nugget applied to my situation.

Then he added, "Me? I'd rather stay home with the wife and watch *Dancing with the Stars*."

Now that made perfect sense. In the strangest and most humorous way, it actually did.

CHAPTER 7

Les Goes to Charleston

On Sunday morning at first light, Wes left to play golf. I pretended to be asleep. I didn't want to hear one word come out of his mouth. No more grief. I didn't even want to hear the sound of his voice. Who died and left him in charge of me? I was thoroughly disgusted with him, his lying, his friends, my daughter, and honestly, I was disgusted with myself. If my son had been in town, I wouldn't have been too happy with him, either. My insides were roiling. Something had to change that very day.

When I heard the garage door roll down with its familiar clunk, I knew he was gone. I rolled over and picked up the business card my taxi driver had given me the night before. I had slipped it under my alarm clock. Joe Sanchez—404-555-5222.

"Call me anytime," he had said. "I'm here to serve."

Yeah, just like my husband. Somehow the story was always about Wes—how he was annoyed, how he was insulted, how he wasn't getting the right amount of homage from his minions (that would mean me and the kids). And then there was his other problem—

appearances. Well, I was all done with homage and putting on the bright smile for the sake of appearances and I didn't feel like being around when the IRS or the FBI showed up to throw him in the Big House. He didn't need me because he sure knew where to find a lawyer (read: golf club), and he knew where praise and glory could be found as well—just ask Cornelia or any of her silly little friends.

My mind was made up. I was headed for the Lowcountry and the company of my darling brother. I needed to smell some pluff mud and to feel Harlan's arm around my shoulder. I didn't plan to drive to Charleston because I didn't think it was wise to take a five-hour road trip steering the car with one hand. But it was not impossible to fill a couple of suitcases with summer clothes and pack my makeup and toiletries in a duffel bag. Besides, I didn't need a car in downtown Charleston. I thought about calling Danette and telling her where I'd be, but I didn't want to drag her into the middle of something that would make her uncomfortable. She didn't need another episode of anybody's domestic drama. And I thought about leaving Wes a note, but I didn't know what to say. Well, there was plenty I could have said, but I decided to let him stew in his juices. Eventually he'd realize I was gone somewhere when he checked my closet and the bathroom.

So I called Delta Airlines and booked a flight to Charleston for early that afternoon and I called Joe Sanchez to take me to the airport. And, of course, I called Harlan.

"You get yourself to Charleston as fast as you can and I'll be waiting for you in the baggage claim, okay? Oh! This is too wonderful! We finally get to spend some time together! And Wes doesn't mind?"

"I didn't ask him."

There was a pregnant pause.

"All righty then! Woo! I'll get to chilling the vodka right away! Miss Jo and I will see you soon!"

The flight from Atlanta to Charleston would take less than an hour, a mercifully short transfer from my tortured internal bedlam to what I hoped would be a slice of peace. I was nervous in one way, but then, as I sat in the gate area flipping through a magazine, a sense of calm overcame me and I was rather proud of my decisiveness. I had discovered a weird strength in the back of Joe Sanchez's taxi. Wes had gone beyond my limit of what I was willing to endure for the final time. I had officially lost interest in his game of charades. Just like that. I felt something phenomenal would have to happen to make me love my marriage or him again. And guess what else? I felt free.

I marveled at the Atlanta Airport and how efficiently it moved tens of thousands of people every day. It was organized chaos on a very grand operatic scale. Funny that I knew tons of people but I never saw anyone I knew there. I could have bought a ticket for Istanbul and the Atlanta airport would surely have had at least three flights there a day. Istanbul. There's a thought. Wes would never look for me there. But would Wes look for me anywhere? Probably not. So here I was, perhaps on a launch pad from one life to another.

We boarded the plane. I was already dreading the phone call that would surely come from him. I could hear him in my head. *Where the hell are you? Just what the hell do you think you're doing?* I was happy when the flight attendant told us to turn off our cell phones. Maybe I'd just leave mine off forever. Well, for the day anyway. Let him sweat a little. I mean, I knew that eventually I'd have to tell him where I was, but for the next few hours while he was chasing that stupid little white ball all over hell's half acre, I'd have some peace. I closed my eyes and tried to nap. Miraculously, I did sleep until I heard the pilot announce that we were to begin our descent.

Our compact fifty-seat plane came down through the clouds and circled the marshes around Charleston as we prepared to land. I love flying in small planes because the experience is visceral, so much more exciting than the Airbus that took us to Scotland. When you hit turbulence, you felt it in every nerve ending. Turbulence combined with bad weather brought about copious prayer and desperate promises while I furiously searched my purse for my St. Christopher medal. As I thought about that I realized I had precious few thrills in my life if bumping around at thirty thousand feet got me excited.

But, my pathetic life aside, I was awed once again by the natural beauty of the Lowcountry. It was impossible not to be impressed and then be drawn into it. The crystal blue water in the tiny streams below sparkled and curled like tendrils around and around until they reached the Wando or the Cooper or the Ashley Rivers. Flocks of snowy egrets roosted in the shallow waters, unaware of the rest of the world. That's what I wanted for myself for even just a little while—to be unaware of the rest of the world. I needed some time.

I managed to remove my compact from my bag, intending to reapply some powder and lipstick so I wouldn't look a fright, and I was surprised to see the scowl staring back at me from the small mirror. When did I become a woman who scowled? When did my eyes become so disappointed? My smile and my eyes had always been my best features. Now I looked angry and defeated. Maybe I was. It had been so long since I'd even thought about what I wanted out of my life, about what would make me happy. God only knew, I was getting very little personal satisfaction from the two children I had raised. And we already know about Wes. How much of all that failure was my fault? Maybe Harlan would help me sort things out. He was good at getting to the bottom of things and making practical choices. Actually, Harlan was brilliant about most things.

We pulled up to the terminal, and the signal *binged* to let us know it was all right to unbuckle our seat belts and get moving. I scooped up my carry-on bag and my purse and stood, hunched a little so I didn't bang my head on the overhead compartment until the door was opened and we began to disembark. A nice-looking man stepped back to allow me into the aisle.

"Thanks," I said.

"Can you manage all that?" he asked.

"Oh, yes. I'm fine, thanks."

So chivalry wasn't completely dead. I smiled and went ahead of him, thinking that was a nice thing for him to do. More men should offer help.

As I took my first step onto the Jetway, there was a powerful change in the air. The humidity mixed with the perfume of salt and the foul traces of fuel was profound. Immediately, I could feel dampness on the back of my neck and each one of my hairs began to rise and expand. The first order of business would be to find a salon and a stylist who could tame my hair back into submission.

I passed the security lines on my left and turned the corner to see Harlan there with Miss Jo. At first I was smiling and then I became overcome with emotion. I dropped my bag and threw my free arm around his neck, planted a big smooch on his cheek, and then I promptly burst into tears.

"My little runaway! A run, run, run, run, runaway!" Harlan sang to me, and I began to laugh.

"Oh, Harlan!"

"What? I don't sound like Del Shannon? Come on, little sister. Dry your eyes." He handed me a tissue. "Let's get your bags. Miss Jo has been stuffing olives with blue cheese all morning!"

I looked down to his charming dog, and don't you know she was wearing a cotton sundress with olives and martini glasses printed all over it. I laughed again and told Miss Jo she was beautiful.

"She thinks you are too," Harlan said. "I'm so happy you're here."

We walked arm in arm to the carousel, and as I pointed out my bags, Harlan whipped them into the air as though they were empty and lined them up on the floor.

"Been spending a lot of time at the gym?"

"Honcychile, it's beach season, you know," he said, pulling another bag off the carousel. "I bought a new Speedo. It's a Pucci print."

"Oh, right! I can just see you wearing a Speedo!"

"Oh, fine. Maybe not. What the heck is in your bags? Rocks?"

"Housecoats."

"Jeepers. Housecoats? Who are you? Ethel Mertz? We can't have that! Truly, I'm working out for my cholesterol. I'm down fifty points! And without eating oatmeal."

"God spare us oatmeal. Ethel Mertz?"

"Yes."

"The housecoats are a metaphor for my misery."

"Got it."

Harlan piled my bags in the trunk of his fully restored 1955 Chevrolet Bel Air. It was blue and white with white leather interior and one gorgeous trip down memory lane.

"You're still driving this land yacht?" I asked.

"Excuse me! This is one of the great American classics!"

"With an AM radio and manual locks?"

"I prefer the past," Harlan said, smiling.

"Know what? Maybe I do too!"

We drove to downtown Charleston listening to the hum of the engine on I-26 and the sounds of the city on the peninsula where we were born and where we grew up. I wondered how I would tell the story to my brother. It was pretty obvious from the amount of luggage I had that I was staying for longer than a weekend. He didn't seem to mind. In fact, I knew he loved company. I thought about Harlan and what his life was like in Charleston. He had so many friends and things he was involved in—everything that had to do with the arts in any way, shape, or form had a place in his princely heart. And he was a marvelous cook, entertaining all the time. He was a great storyteller too. People adored him and loved to come to his house. Harlan was gregarious and so filled with historic facts that we used to laugh and say we were going to put him on a quiz show. Surely he would have made millions of dollars, not that he needed money. Leonard had left him tons, in addition to the house they shared.

We turned off I-26 and began to make our way downtown. Traffic thickened and we slowed to a crawl. By the time we reached the corner of Meeting and Market Streets, throngs of tourists were everywhere, taking pictures and peering through windows of local businesses. It was high season for tourism. Spoleto Festival and its many amazing events brought hundreds of thousands of culture lovers to the Holy City every year as it had for decades. In fact, tourism was one of the more important engines that powered Charleston's economy.

Professional guides dressed as Civil War soldiers driving horse-drawn carriages regaled tourists with stories of the bygone glories of the Confederate South and what it was like to be a true Charlestonian. Harlan and I always laughed as we listened to them because they could embellish a story like no other tour guides the Holy City had to offer. To my way of thinking, the tourists were getting a great bargain, and I suspected that mostly they knew when they were being offered a fish story with a side order of truth. When you looked at their faces, everyone was always smiling, a sure sign of customer satisfaction.

There would be plenty of time for Harlan and me to talk. Plenty of time. As much as Wes's secrets frightened me, I had to tell someone the truth. Harlan was the person I trusted most.

We pulled off the street, rolled through the beautiful wrought-iron gates at 36 Chalmers Street, and came to a stop. In their curls and swirls I noticed for the very first time that the left gate had a J worked into the design and the right gate had a P for, of course, Josephine Pinckney.

"I never saw that before!" I said. "The J and the P, I mean."

"What? Oh! That's because it was overgrown with roses and Lord knows what else! Philip Simmons made those gates."

"Really?"

Philip Simmons had been Charleston's premier wrought-iron worker.

"Yeah, I thought you knew that."

"I probably did. Harlan, I swear, I can hardly remember my own name these days."

"My poor sweet sister! Why don't you take yourself inside and I'll get your bags."

"Thanks. Come on, cutie." I turned to Miss Jo, who perked up and yipped as though she meant to say, *We're home!* We went inside Harlan's beautifully restored ancient town house. I stepped into the small foyer. There stood a small demilune over which hung a portrait of Josephine Pinckney in an elaborate gold gilded plaster frame. On the table sat a small arrangement of fresh flowers, a picture of Leonard in a silver frame, and an Imari bowl where I suspected Harlan dropped his keys. To my right was a small living room, and to my left was the dining room. Beyond the dining room was the kitchen, and farther back was a comfortable den with French doors that led to the garden.

Ahead of me was a gracious flight of steps, each one inlaid with geometrical border insets of blond walnut and deep red mahogany. Each landing had gorgeous inlays of fruit and flowers that must have taken years to construct by hand. I had always thought that Harlan's house had the prettiest interior stairs in town. There were stairs that seemed to hang in midair and others worthy of a Scarlett O'Hara descent but none prettier than Harlan's.

Charleston was chock-full of architectural wonders, to be sure, and every unique detail of her homes was carefully preserved and pointed out when the opportunity arose, but only discreetly and among dear friends, of course. The only thing more important to Charleston than her glorious history was the refined manners of her citizens. Charleston was not a city of braggarts.

Harlan was right behind me with my bags.

"Let's give you the whole third floor. How does that suit you?" He was already up the stairs with two bags, and I followed him with my duffel.

"Fine! That will be great."

I climbed the first flight of stairs and stopped, feeling winded. My heart was pounding. I was awfully out of shape and I knew it. These steps would be good for me. But my initial thought that the third floor would be wonderful to have to myself could have been wrong—it might be dangerous. What if I had a stroke on top of everything else?

"Come on, chickee! Let's shake it up! It's cocktail time!"

"Harlan, it's only three thirty!" I called up the stairs.

"Honey? It's Sunday, and any time after church is cocktail time!"

I giggled, thinking that all over Charleston, gentlemen in linen suits and ladies in Lilly were imbibing mimosas and Bloodys, feeling virtuous for having attended services and a little naughty at the same time.

At last I reached the third floor.

"Moses! Harlan? I sure do wish you had an elevator. Lord!"

"There's no way to attach one to the house without compromising its integrity."

"Still! Mercy!"

I dumped my duffel bag on the floor and huffed and puffed my way over to the window. The room had a beautiful view of Washington Park across the street. Mothers were there with their children, who played among the live oaks, azaleas, and boxwoods. Tourists and natives occupied the benches, enjoying cool drinks and sandwiches. Everyone seemed to be smiling. It was a beautiful, peaceful sight.

"Don't go all feeble on me, Sister! We have company arriving at six."

"What? Who?"

"Oh, just a few friends I wanted to see before I left. So why don't you unpack and I'll meet you in the kitchen? I've been making super cubes all week. Gotta refill my trays." He lifted up my largest bag and put it on the bed.

"Okay, Dr. Cool One, what's a super cube?"

"A two-inch-square ice cube that's hard as a rock so it doesn't dilute your drink."

"Well, that's a piece of genius."

"I'll say it is. Wish I'd thought of it. I'd have zillions!"

"Like Pet Rocks and Chia Pets."

"Exactly. So how long can you stay anyway?"

Harlan eyeballed my luggage and then looked at me with a semi-anxious expression that said, *Just when are you going to tell me what's going on here?*

"I'm not sure. Why don't we discuss that over a cold glass of something?"

"Perfect! I'll see you in a few. Maybe you'll stay here while I'm in Italy?"

"Maybe I will!"

And he was gone, the quick and sure-footed sounds of his shoes on the steps fading until they disappeared.

I opened my first bag and then the closet door. Fortunately, there were plenty of empty hangers, and soon I had emptied the first bag and then the other. All that was left to do was move my toiletries into the bathroom. Harlan had put out beautiful thick white towels for me, and a plush matching robe hung on the hook behind the door. On the little table next to the sink was a cut glass tumbler and pretty containers of cotton swabs, cotton balls, and dental floss picks. The bathtub was wide and deep, and the thought of climbing in for a good long soak seemed like a dream. I picked up the bar of bath soap and inhaled. Verbena. My favorite. Every woman should have such a thoughtful brother, especially one you could run to in times of trouble.

I ran my brush through my hair and then I wound it up into a twist. Although Harlan's house was air-conditioned, heat rises and the third floor felt warm to me. I pulled the chain on the ceiling fan in my room and then in the sitting room next door. There was a sofa and a huge chintz club chair, a desk, and a flat-screen television. There was no reason to go downstairs except for food and human company.

I changed into a pair of pants, a cotton shirt, and flat sandals, ones that hopefully wouldn't slip on the steps, and went to find Harlan. He was, as promised, in the kitchen making a mountain of tomato sandwiches with Duke's mayonnaise and ham biscuits with Mrs. Sassard's Jerusalem Artichoke Relish.

"Wow! Don't you look cool and comfortable!" he said.

"Sweet thing," I said. "What can I do to help?"

"There's tea in the fridge or I can make coffee if you want but I think it's too hot for coffee."

"I'll pour tea. It's gotta be a thousand degrees outside." I took two glasses from the cabinet and filled them with ice and tea. "Lemon?"

"In the hydrator drawer," he said. "There are bunches of slices in a baggie. It just feels like a thousand. You'll adjust to the humidity."

I squeezed two slices into our glasses, added two spoons of sugar, and stirred it all around.

"I know. Come sit with me," I said, sitting down at his kitchen table.

"Okay," he said and covered his platter of food with a clean damp linen towel. "Tell me what's going on, Sister Sue. Tell your big bubba everything." He sat down across from me and raised his glass. "Our momma would die all over again if she saw you so distressed."

"God rest her soul," I said. "At least she had the good sense not to marry Willie. And she was right. I never should've married Wes."

"You had a bun in the oven. It was almost thirty years ago. There weren't that many options and I told her so. Like a million times."

"God, life is so complicated, isn't it?"

"How do you mean, sugar puss?"

"Well, look at Momma, now that you brought her up." We rarely spoke of her because Harlan was a great fan of Momma and I wasn't. "There we were, growing up on Logan Street, South of Broad by a hair."

"Well, after Daddy died, she wasn't going to live anywhere else. It gave her emotional security. You probably don't remember the big house on King Street."

"No, I was too little. But the point is that we couldn't afford Logan Street. She should've moved us out to west of the Ashley or east of the Cooper."

"Are you kidding? She would've rather died than live in the burbs! You know that!"

"Excuse me, so she worked as a *cocktail waitress* in a dive bar on Rivers Avenue outside the gate to the naval base so we could pay the rent and say we had bragging rights on a South of Broad address? Do you see a conflict here?"

"Honey, what she saw was two hundred dollars a night in cash and your Ashley Hall tuition paid in full. It was honest work. You want more tea?"

"No, thanks. If Ashley Hall had known what Momma was doing, they would've thrown me out the front door."

"She was the Merry Widow, hon."

"Carrying on with Willie who owned the bar for how long? And she never married Willie because?"

"He had too many tattoos. I know, I know. It's confusing. But he let her work there until the day she died. He was a good man. Most bars wouldn't have women over forty selling drinks. There's terrible age discrimination, even today."

"You're telling me? That's part of what brings me to your door, Harlan."

"Come on, Leslie, let's bury Momma for the moment and let me have the big story."

"Oh, Harlan, I don't even know where to begin."

But I did begin and over the next hour or so all my worries were laid on the table to be considered, and at last I got to the horrible money business.

"Back up the bus, baby. *What* did you just say? Did you say twenty-two million dollars?"

"Yes. Harlan, I'm just worried sick about it. You and I both know that Wes has *never* earned that kind of money. He's got to be involved in something very bad. I don't care what kind of bonuses he makes or how well the company is doing. It just doesn't make any sense to me."

"Look, who knows?"

"I shouldn't have done it, but I took his bank statement from the house. I have it upstairs. Should I go get it?"

Harlan was incredulous.

"Not now. We don't have time. God knows, but he's a cheap son of a b. He probably invested his First Communion money in IBM. I'll have to give this some thought. There's never been a great love between us, but I don't think he's a crook, Les. I just don't see it." He sat back in his chair and exhaled long and slow. "Do you remember if there were any specific stocks listed?"

"Wes owns a single share of Coca-Cola his great-grandfather bought for his father in something like 1920. Right when the company went into business. And he's got some Apple and Microsoft. Maybe some others. I know he has some money in funds."

"Well, look, if he still has that Coke stock, it has to have split like a thousand times. I'll look it up on the Internet in the morning. I promise, first thing tomorrow. Come on, let's set up the bar and the dining room table. Marge will be here soon."

"Who's Marge?"

"Local talent. She helps me with parties."

"Oh, well, that's good!" I was chewing on my lip, something I'd done since childhood when I was worried. "What do you think Wes will think when I'm not there with his supper?"

"Don't worry so much. You'll get wrinkles. But you *should* tell Wes you're here."

"I can't deal with him. I just can't. And I don't want to."

"Okay. I understand that, but he's going to be very angry, you know."

"How about I don't care?"

"Okay. Do you want me to handle him? I can call him if you like."

"Do whatever you want. I just don't want to talk to him right now."

"All right, in the meanwhile, let's get rid of that ugly old hospital supply sling—I have a big silk Hermès scarf that will look ever so much more Hepburn!"

I giggled. "Which one? Audrey or Katharine?"

"Does it matter?"

It did not.

"And I meant what I said about you staying here. It's only a month."

"I'll really think about it, Harlan. Thanks."

When I went upstairs to change, there was my sundress on the bed. I didn't remember putting it there. Nonetheless, I slipped into it, Harlan changed my sling, a definite upgrade, and with a little makeup I looked so much better. I still hadn't turned on my cell phone because I didn't want to hear from Wes. And I wondered if Harlan called him.

The doorbell began to ring, and soon, from the garden to the living room, Harlan's friends were milling about, telling stories, gobbling up sandwiches, and drinking all kinds of cocktails, the most popular being Dark and Stormys—a mixture of rum and ginger beer—and Manhattans made with rye, vermouth, and cherries. Funny. In Atlanta we mostly drank wine. It looked like Charleston still liked her cocktails. Anyway, our mother always had, and this crowd sure did. There was something very comforting about traditions being honored. And I remembered then that Dark and Stormys were Leonard's favorite drink.

I heard a voice behind me and I knew I recognized it from somewhere in my past.

"Cocktail parties were invented in Charleston, you know."

I turned around and ran right into the smirking smile of Jonathan Ray, my first serious boyfriend. I knew immediately that Harlan had invited him for my sake. As good as he was, Harlan liked being controversial from time to time.

The years had been kind to Jonathan. He was gray around the temples, but he still had a full head of hair and the prettiest blue eyes the good Lord ever gave to a man besides Paul Newman.

"Well, look at you! Jonathan! How wonderful to see you again! And what do you mean cocktail parties were invented here? I've never heard that."

"That doesn't mean it's not true. Thirty years later and she's still the skeptic? Can I freshen up your drink?"

"Sure, why not?"

We stepped over to the bar where Marge was shaking one mini cocktail shaker after another with such enthusiasm I wondered how her elbows could stand it.

Clack! Clack! Clack!

The super cubes banging against the stainless steel made a riotous noise.

"What are you drinking?" Jonathan said.

"Oh, just vodka with a bunch of tonic and a lime," I said.

"I've got one for you!" Marge said. "How about a Georgia Punch?"

"For a Georgia Peach!" Jonathan said. "Perfect!"

"Great! But I'm a transplant, you know," I said and managed a weak smile, thinking that this peach had already been bruised enough.

"Haven't you been there long enough to claim Georgia?"

"Jonathan, when you're born in Charleston, you should know it's impossible to be anything but a Charlestonian. The last thing you want is dual citizenship."

"That's actually comforting to hear," he said.

She handed the frosty glass to Jonathan, and he handed it to me with a napkin. No ring. Wedding ring, that is. Why was I even looking?

"I'll have a Manhattan," he said to Marge.

"Right away!" she said, and inside of a minute she handed the tumbler to him.

"Thanks," he said and turned to me. "So why don't we sneak out to the garden where we can hear ourselves think?"

"Sure, but shouldn't we tell your wife where we're going?"

"Can't do that," he said, with the funniest expression. "She's ancient history."

"Really? Didn't you marry Clare Mullarney? What happened to her?"

We worked our way through the dining room to the kitchen and finally to the open French doors in the den. Then we stepped out onto the terrace where fig ivy climbed the walls and the sweet smells of Confederate jasmine were all over us as though we had walked into a cloud of it.

"Wow? Smell that?" he said and I nodded. "What happened? Well, let's see. We got married, we had two children, she started painting landscapes with a bunch of *en plein air* pot-smoking hippies."

"Nuh-uh. She must have lost her mind to leave *you*!"

"Exactly. She said being married to me wasn't interesting enough. Then soon after painting no longer interested her, she was overcome with an all-consuming urge to go make artisanal cheese in Vermont."

"Yikes. She sounds like my son."

"Oh?"

"He's currently in residence in Nepal, smoking weed with hippies from all over the world. He's a stoner on an international level. I'm so proud." I could hardly believe I was actually saying what I was saying, and then I thought, It's the damn truth, isn't it? Until that moment I had always made excuses for him.

"I thought Harlan said he was a photographer for *National Geographic*?"

"I think he'd like to be one, but so far? No go."

"Too bad."

"It's okay; he has an IV right into his father's wallet. It keeps him in clean water for his bong. So what happened to your wife again?"

"So I just told her, fine, she should go make cheese, just leave me the kids. I was in my third year of medical school. She said I was a workaholic."

"Well, here's another nice mess you've gotten me into, isn't it, Ollie?"

"What?"

"You never watched *Laurel and Hardy* when you were a kid?"

"Oh, right! Right! *Now* I get it! Nice one!"

"Yeah, nice lead balloon, but continue." My face was flushed. I was so embarrassed. Maybe Wes was right about my sense of humor—it was pretty dumb.

"Well, she left me the kids, I raised them, my mother helped, God bless her heart, and it all worked out okay. When my grandmother passed away, she left me her house out on Sullivans Island. Remember that house?"

"I surely do! We spent as much time with her sitting around that kitchen table as we did walking on the beach. She was a great lady."

"Thanks. Yeah. I love to remember those days with you. Anyway, my daughter's married to a dentist and they live out in Portland. She teaches first grade and my son's doing his residency in sports medicine out in San Diego."

"Really? Weren't you in sports medicine too?"

"Yeah, I actually run it for the Medical University. I treat all the big athletes in the Southeast."

"Really?" Why was it when men made their careers sound grandiose it was okay, but if a woman had said the same thing she'd be bragging?

"Yep. I had hoped that when my son graduated, he'd come into my practice and eventually take it over. Now I think I'm going to move out there, maybe live in Napa."

"Ah, Napa. Is he married?"

"Not yet. And I wasn't going to bring it up, but what happened to your arm?"

"Oh, this? I sort of fell in an open manhole in Edinburgh last month. It's just a crack."

"How in the world did *that* happen?"

"It's a long story. But you never remarried?"

"Not so far. There have been sort of a long series of women who came and went, but between my practice and my children I was too busy to get serious."

"Oh, come on . . ."

"Okay, there was Blanche, but she had five children."

"Five children. I'd run like hell."

"I did."

We both laughed. I looked at him and thought, Oh boy, here comes the chemistry, racing across the decades like a freight train. I was just as physically attracted to him as I had been when we were teenagers. But I pulled in the reins of my imagination with the thought that he probably had fifty Barbies in his life and couldn't be less interested in me. I needn't worry that he would do or say a thing that was inappropriate. Jonathan wasn't that kind of guy. Maybe he had a big ego, but he was the consummate gentleman.

"So where's Wesley?" I was surprised he remembered his name. "See? I kept up with you through Harlan."

"Wesley is in Atlanta."

"What's he doing there?"

"Hmmm." I looked at Jonathan's wristwatch. It was seven thirty. "Right about now? Probably scratching his head."

"Why's that?"

"He wants his supper and I'm not there to serve it to him on bended knee."

Jonathan stared at me in concerned amusement—if there is such a thing.

"Aha! You went AWOL?"

"Yep."

"First time?"

"Yep."

"Well, you know what? I never liked Wesley anyway."

"You never met him. But that's not to say you'd like him if you did."

"I wouldn't like him. I'm sure of it. Wesley is a stupid name."

"I don't like him much either. Hmmmm."

His eyes traveled every inch of my face. "I know this sounds very cliché, but how is it that you haven't changed a bit? You and Harlan have those crazy hazel eyes that look like magic, and your dark hair has a bit of silver here and there but it's beautiful."

"Oh, Jonathan. You're so funny."

"No!" He smiled wide, charmed by my protest. "It really is. Show me a woman your age who still has a great figure like yours. I mean, dang, Les, you look really great! I always said you should've been a model or something."

"Oh, Jonathan. What a silly thing to say."

"No. It's not. My eyes aren't liars, and you know doctors are notoriously unflattering."

"If you say so then." I giggled like a sixteen-year-old girl.

"So Wesley turned out to be an insufferable bastard?"

"Yep, pretty much."

It was incredible that I was telling Jonathan these things. I was normally extremely discreet. But where did being *discreet* ever get me? Nowhere. And besides, even though I hadn't seen him in almost thirty years, Jonathan Ray knew my heart. There was and had never been any point in playing games with him. We had known each other at that rare, sweet time in our lives when we were in our childhood one day and on the next day our childhood was a million miles behind us. The only problem was that I went to college in Atlanta, met Wes, got married, and never lived in Charleston again. Everyone thought I'd wind up married to Jonathan. But even if I had wanted to, I couldn't very well marry Jonathan and then give birth to Wes's child. Talk about bad taste?

"So what are you going to do?"

"I'm going to give my life a lot of thought. That's why I'm here. To think."

CHAPTER 8

Wes's Great Annoyance

I was starving when I got home. Thirty-six holes is a lot of walking even with a golf cart and all I had for lunch was a BLT. The house was dark and I could feel it, funny how you can feel it, there was no life. At first I was annoyed because Les knew I was expecting dinner. She *always* made dinner on Sunday nights. But then I got scared. Her car was in the garage. What if she was lying on the floor upstairs dead? What if she had another fall, like maybe she had a brain tumor or something that was making her lose her balance? Jesus! So I ran all over the house looking for a dead body, praying that she was just unconscious. I ran from room to room and she wasn't there. I started getting really nervous. What if someone broke in the house and kidnapped her? You know, like a botched robbery or something and they didn't mean to but they took her as a hostage because she'd seen their faces? I ran to the silver closet. It was locked up tight as a drum. I found the key in the kitchen drawer and unlocked it. Everything was there. Well, for as much as I could tell.

What in the world was going on here? I checked her jewelry

box. I couldn't tell if anything was missing or not, well, it's not like she ever had anything of real value worth stealing anyway. She was never the whaddya call it, the *bling* type. No, Les liked good leather and nice perfumes. At least that's what I always bought her and she never complained.

I decided to call our daughter. There was probably a simple explanation and I was getting all riled up for nothing.

"Where's your mother?" I said to Charlotte. "Is she with you?"

"No, Daddy. I haven't seen her all day. Why?"

"She was supposed to be home and she isn't. That's all."

"Is her car in the garage?"

"Yeah."

"Did you try Danette?"

"No. I don't even know if I have her number. Do you know her number?"

"Look where Momma keeps her cookbooks. There's a plastic-covered list on the right-hand side of the shelf. Everybody's phone number is on there. The plumber, the electrician . . . you know."

"Okay, I'll go look."

"Don't worry. I'm sure she's over at Danette's talking and she probably lost track of time. Or maybe they went to a movie."

"Okay, you're probably right."

"Call me back, okay?"

"Yeah, sure."

We hung up and I went to look for Danette's phone number, but even as I found it and dialed it I had a lousy feeling in the pit of my stomach. And it wasn't just hunger pangs. I have the kind of guts that know when trouble is coming. I can smell it a mile away. I mean, to be honest, it was one of the reasons I was so successful.

She answered on the third ring.

"Wes Carter here, Danette. You got a minute?"

"Well, Wesley! What a surprise. Howdee do to you! You think I forgot your last name?"

"Look, Danette, this is a serious call. Sorry if I didn't use the right hello." I wanted to say, *Now I know why Harold dumped you,* but I didn't. "I can't find Les and I was just wondering if she's with you."

"Nope. I haven't seen her since last week. What's going on?"

"Oh, nothing. I'm sure she's fine." I paused for a moment. "We were supposed to have dinner at the club," I lied. "Maybe I just missed her in the dining room. Okay then. Um, thanks. You okay?"

"Yeah, I'm fine, Wes. Thanks for asking. You?"

"Good. I'm good. Okay, so if she calls, will you ask her to call my cell? I'm gonna go back up to the club and look for her."

"Sure. I'm sure she's fine, Wes. She's a big girl."

"Right. Okay, thanks then."

We hung up, and I thought about how Danette wanted to nail me for announcing myself with my last name. It was how I talked all day long at the office. I'd answer the phone and say, *Wes Carter.* So shoot me, you tired old hag. One good thing I had to say about Les was that she never played the Gotcha Game with me. She was real decent about all that kind of BS.

I jumped in my car, turned on the Sinatra station on my satellite radio to calm myself, and drove back to the club as quickly as I could. Inside I checked the bar. Maybe she was waiting for me there. There were a dozen or so people milling around but no Les. I stopped to talk to the bartender.

"Hey, Louis? You seen my wife tonight?"

"No, sir, Mr. Carter. And I've been here since noon."

"Okay. Thanks."

Just where the hell was Les? I decided to have a beer and a burger and think it through. I drained my current beer, went to the grill room, said hello to a bunch of people as I passed them and they all asked for Les. *Where's Les? How's Les?* I said, *Oh, she's fine.* It was a rare occasion that I ever came to the club without Leslie at night. It felt weird. I took a seat at the bar under the huge flatscreen overhead. The Braves were playing. Nothing like a good ball game.

"What can I get for you, Mr. Carter?" Jack the waiter said.

"I think I'll have that bacon cheddar burger. Medium. With fries. And I'd like an Amstel with a cold mug if you've got it."

"Sure thing."

"Thanks. What's the score?"

"Braves are ahead by two."

"That's the way we like it, right?"

Okay, number one, I know she was really irritated last night. Why Cornelia and Lisette had to rumble with those girls I don't know. I just thought Les should've stopped them, that's all. What did she say? That she didn't want to be their babysitter? But she's older and she ought to have been able to finesse that one. What made her so mad? I thought I was paying her a compliment. Okay, to be honest, I think I raised my voice a little because I was disappointed that it seemed like she just sat there sipping her white wine and watching the crazy train roll through town. Maybe she's trying to give all the young girls enough rope to hang themselves. Maybe this behavior has to do with her loyalty to Danette and I guess she probably still misses Tessa. Maybe it's because I said she should have that party with Lisette. Who the hell knows how women think?

I do know this now. After the disaster in Edinburgh, she sure doesn't love Cornelia and she probably never will. Lisette either. She's probably threatened by them. I mean, there's Cornelia with that flaming red hair of hers, and over there is Lisette with a body that ought to be illegal. And there's my Les. She's almost twice their age, and to be blunt, the bloom is way off her rose next to those girls. There's just no nice way to say it. It's the truth. I mean, Les has many redeeming qualities. She's the mother of my children and she's been my good and loyal companion for all these years. She's extremely dependable all around the board. But she ain't no looker anymore. Not to me anyway.

So we had a little disagreement last night in front of the world and she took a cab home. I guess that was pretty unprecedented. Yeah, come to think of it, it was the very first time she'd ever done anything like that. And now she was nowhere to be found. Could she have left me? Why would she do a crazy thing like *that*? Maybe she left a note? Maybe I missed something?

I signed for my meal, drove home, and turned on every light in the house. First, I went over every inch of the kitchen and the laundry room for clues. That's where she was half the time, so I might have found something there, but I didn't. Maybe she left something on my desk? No, she did not. I went upstairs and looked in the closet where she stored our luggage. It looked to me like a suitcase might have been missing, but I wasn't sure. How the hell should I know how many suitcases we owned? It finally dawned on me that I should check her closet to see if there were clothes missing. Now, do you think I could really tell? There was so much stuff jammed in there you'd have to be a forensic expert to figure that one out. But it was possible. There were some empty hangers on the floor and it seemed like there were fewer shoes.

So. She left me. Just like that. She left me? Really? No warning. No note. No nothing. I called her cell again and left a stronger message.

"Les? It's me. Look, I don't know what kind of a game you're playing and I don't care. I just want to know that you're all right. Just call me and tell me where you are or else I'm calling the police!"

That ought to put the fear of God in her. Let her worry that the police are out in the streets looking for her. I poured myself a nice big scotch, a single malt reserved for special occasions because this might be one, turned on the television, and got comfortable in my recliner. People could say what they wanted about recliners but I loved mine.

My cell phone rang. It was Charlotte.

"Did Mom turn up?"

"No, but I'm sure she'll call soon."

"Did you check with the hospitals and the police?"

"No, no, honey. Don't worry yourself. If she doesn't show up tonight, I'll check with them in the morning. I'm sure she's fine. Probably blowing off steam at the movies."

"Steam? Did y'all fight?"

"No, no. Just the usual silliness between married couples. Nothing to be worried about."

"Okay. Did you call Danette?"

"Yeah, she said she hasn't seen her, but for all I know she's sitting there with her drinking white wine spritzers."

"Well, okay then. If you're not worried, I'm not going to worry either. I called her cell and she didn't pick up."

"Me too. That's why I think she's at the movies. Go on to bed, sweetheart. Tomorrow's Monday. Big week ahead."

"Okay, Daddy. Love you."

Soon I was watching the third episode of *Law and Order* in a row and my eyes started getting heavy.

The sun woke me up. My back was killing me and my head hurt. No wonder! I slept in a chair! Now whose fault was that? Thanks, Leslie. Whenever I fell asleep in the chair, I could always depend on her to wake me up. But she wasn't there so I got a backache out of the deal.

I went right to the kitchen and made a pot of coffee. Then I threw a couple of slices of bread in the toaster and cracked an egg into the frying pan and turned on the gas. I went outside to get the paper and when I got back, breakfast was ready. Well, the egg was all stuck to the pan for some reason—I probably should've put some butter in there or something—and the toast was cold, but the coffee was strong and I didn't really care about the rest of it. I just ate the toast and a banana and downed a lot of coffee and thought to myself that I had done pretty well. I threw the dishes in the sink and went to take a shower.

So I was standing there under the hot water in my altogether and it occurred to me that there was no one to do those dishes or to make the bed except me. Crap. Les *knew* I hated coming home to a house that wasn't spotless. What was the name of that housekeeper she used sometimes? I made a bet with myself that it was on that list where I found Danette's number. I'd just call her and ask her to clean up and maybe leave me something for dinner. Maybe a roasted chicken. Great God! It was already seven thirty. I had to get to the office. I had a calendar packed with back-to-back meetings all day! Classic Monday. Les might think it was okay to shirk her duties and go run all over hither and yon, but I had a business to run.

As I rode the elevator up to the executive floor where my office was, I thought about Les's cream puff brother. I'd bet the ranch she's there or that he knows where she is. They were thick as thieves, those two. Now here's a good one to show you she's no saint either. Les knows that I can't stand to be in the same room with that brother of hers and she still goes to visit him and asks me if he can come here. She knows how I feel about homosexuals, and still she tries to force this totally unwanted family relationship on me. This has been going on for *thirty* years. You'd think she'd get the message, right? But she asks if he can come for Christmas and I say absolutely not and she gets mad and I'm the bad guy. Go figure.

"Morning, Gina," I said to my secretary as I went through the door.

"Morning, Wes. Coffee?"

"Nah, I'll get it myself. Hold my calls for a little while, okay?"

"Sure! How was your weekend?"

"Uneventful," I lied. "Played some awesome golf though. You?"

"Saw a new movie. Nothing special."

She was probably lying too. But what were we supposed to say? *Oh, my wife left me.* And she'd say, *Oh, I got my heart broken by my twentieth boyfriend.* No way. That's why I liked Gina. She kept her personal business to herself.

"Oh! Danette Stovall called. Should I get her on the line for you?"

"No, that's okay. I'll call her later. Thanks."

I went into my office and closed the door behind me.

I was going to suck it up and call Harlan. He needed to know that his sister was missing, and if she is there, I needed to know that too. Surely he would tell me if he knew. I looked his number up in my files, took a deep breath, and dialed it.

Just when I thought my call was going to go to voice mail, he answered.

"Harlan? It's Wes."

"Yes, I saw that on my caller ID. How are you, Wes?"

"Well, I've been better. Listen, Harlan, steel yourself, man, I've got some very disturbing news to tell you."

"What?"

"Les is missing. You haven't heard from her, have you?"

"Yes. She's right here. She's fine."

"Well, can you put her on the phone?"

"I'll ask her if she'd like to speak to you. Hold on." I knew he covered the phone with his hand, because I could hear muffled conversation in the background. Then he came back on the line. "Wes? Leslie is very upset right now and feels like it might be better if y'all spoke another time."

"What? Did she say that? You listen to me, you little weasel, you put my wife on the phone with me this very instant! Do you hear me?"

"Or what? There's no reason to resort to vulgarity and threats, Wesley. Sticks and stones, you know. Hold on."

There was another muffled pause, and then I heard Les say, "I said I don't want to talk to you now, Wesley." And then she hung up.

She disconnected the call! Was she *insane*? I am her husband of almost thirty years and she hangs up on me? Just what the hell was going on here? What did *I* do? Did I walk out on her? No! I was the abandoned one and *this* is how she treats me? I sat there looking at the phone, feeling my blood pressure rise until my ears were pounding.

My phone rang again and it was my secretary.

"Your daughter's on line two."

"Thanks," I said and pressed the flashing light. "Charlotte?"

"Yep. Did you find Mom?"

"Yeah, it seems that your mother decided to take a little trip to visit your uncle and decided not to tell anyone."

"Wow. That's not like her at all. Did you talk to her?"

"Nooooo. It seems she doesn't want to talk to me right now."

There was silence from my daughter's end of the phone. Then she spoke.

"Dad? Did you two have a fight?"

"We don't fight, Charlotte. But sometimes we don't agree on everything."

"Yeah, that's sort of how it is with me and Mom too." There was a pause and then she said, "Do you want me to call her and talk to her?"

"Right now? I don't really care. I'm plenty pissed, if you must know."

"Oh, great. Maybe you should go to Charleston and see what's going on, Dad. Don't you want to know?"

"Are you kidding? Right now I'm thinking about cutting off all her credit cards and closing her bank accounts. And you think I should go see what's wrong with her?"

"Oh! Dad! That's terrible! Look, we both know that ever since the Edinburgh fiasco she ain't been the same."

"Like that was my fault? I waited all my life to play St. Andrews and she almost ruined the whole thing!"

"Yeah, well, I think Mom has a different point of view on that one."

"It seems like all of a sudden she's got an opinion about everything! Since when did I ask for all these opinions?"

"Daddy. You know I love you, right?"

"Of course. You're my daughter." What kind of a question was that?

"Look, sometimes? Well, you can be a little rough, you know?"

"No, I *don't* know. In this particular instance, your mother is dead wrong. Just because we disagree about a couple of things doesn't give her the right to spend money to waltz herself down to Charleston without telling anybody where she's going. It's not nice. She could've been dead in a ditch for all I know."

"Yeah, and you, Harold, and Cornelia would already be back at the hotel."

"What's that got to do with this?" Oh, she was a smarty-pants today, this one.

"Nothing, Daddy, just that you aren't exactly Mr. Sensitive all the time."

"Maybe. But being all gooey inside didn't get me where I am today either. I've worked hard all my life to give your mother and me and you kids everything I never had. This is how she thanks me? With this kind of disrespect?"

"All I'm saying, Daddy, is that she must've felt pushed pretty far for her to break out and do something like this."

"Pushed? Your mother? You gotta be kidding me! You can't push that woman one inch!"

"Really? Okay, you're a cupcake and I'm the Queen of England. I love you, Daddy, but sometimes . . . ?"

"Sometimes what?"

"Sometimes you just don't get it."

CHAPTER 9

Les Steps Out

The morning after his party, as he promised he would, Harlan tried to make sense of Wes's bank statement. A lot of low whistles and *Holy Mother*s came out of his mouth as he read and reread what was in front of him. Finally, he turned on his computer and went to the bank's website and this was all before we even had breakfast. I rewarmed his coffee several times and asked him if there was anything I could get for him and he shook his head, shooing me away.

"Give me ten more minutes," he said three times. "What's Wes's birthday?"

"Why?"

"I need a password."

"March sixteenth."

Click! Click! Click! Click!

"And his social security number?"

I recited it to him.

Click! Click! Click! Click!

"That was too easy. I'm in! Wish me luck!"

"Happy hacking!" I said.

I busied myself with the *Post and Courier,* browsing my horoscope, the obituaries, and the arts section. I opened the French doors to the garden and stepped outside, thinking I'd work the crossword puzzle in the fresh air. The old Kennedy rocker looked like the perfect place to ponder the name of the northernmost tributary of the Ohio River—six letters—so I rocked back and forth on the uneven ancient bricks, clacking in a broken rhythm. The tiny Carolina wrens were chirping their morning song and I was completely charmed by them as they darted in and around the branches of Harlan's beautiful pink crape myrtles. But I was not fooled into believing that this slice of paradise would last for very long. The weather was getting warmer by the moment and soon Charleston's sweltering summer would be here. I hated to think about it. Finally, after the paper was read, I went back inside and exhausted every morning talk show. At last Harlan appeared at the kitchen table, collapsed in a chair, folded his hands in front of himself, and smiled as though he had discovered the true meaning of life.

"More coffee?" I asked.

"No, I think it might just be time for a little something stronger. Is there any champagne left over from last night?"

"Really? I can look."

"No. I'm kidding. I'm already caffeinated up to my ears. You'd better put that paper down for a moment."

"Oh, God, Harlan. Is Wes going to jail?"

"No. He might go to hell but he's not going to jail."

"So what's the deal?"

"The deal is that it all looks perfectly legitimate to me, but here's what baffles me. This statement is in your name too. Didn't you realize that?"

"What? How could that be? I mean, am I liable too?"

"You need to get all that criminal stuff out of your pretty head right this minute. It's very frustrating to me. You do not comprehend what this means."

"Give me that," I said and took the papers from him. "Okay, it's legitimate, you say?"

"Yes, I found a website that says one share of Coca-Cola stock bought in 1920 would be worth almost five million dollars today."

"No kidding? Wow. Five million dollars? That's *ridiculous*!"

"Isn't it? Now, he inherited that, so there might be some legal quibble about whether half should be yours or not."

"But half of the rest of it is actually mine? For sure? Definitely?"

"Yes, ma'am. I'm no lawyer but I can tell you, should you decide to make a new life for yourself without Wes, you are worth either eleven million dollars or eight and one-half million dollars. And then there's the value of your home and its contents and whatever else he might have stashed in the Cayman Islands that you'd have to discover, of course."

"Holy smoke, Harlan. Either way, it's a darn fortune."

"And either way, cupcake, it's a fortune that you had no idea even existed."

"Yeah, that's pretty screwed up, isn't it?"

"Screwed up in a *very* major way, if you ask me and you did. *You*, my dear, are a very wealthy woman."

I started getting angry. "A wealthy woman who has never owned a new car. Who cleans her own house. Who rarely buys anything at regular price. Even chicken. I mean, I've been clipping coupons for ages. Well, now I get them on the Internet."

"It makes me like him even less," Harlan said. "*If* that's humanly possible. Not that there's anything wrong with getting a bargain."

"Agreed. Harlan, can you help me think of any reason in the world he's been keeping our bank statements behind a locked cabinet door?"

"Well, in my experience, when people lock things up, it's because they don't want anyone to see them."

"Of course. That's the logical answer. It's so strange."

"And because they have control issues. I think it's always been important to Wes to believe he's in charge of the world. You know, the *Atlanta Mastah of the Universe*? To me? It's tiresome, really, because if you decided to pull the plug on him, it wouldn't take the worst lawyer in Atlanta five seconds to figure out you are entitled to half. Almost thirty years of marriage? Two children? No, baby, you're entitled to half of everything."

"Jeezaree."

"And right about now? He's got that fact in his very odd meerschaum pipe, the one that's an old dude's head, and he's smoking it. Does he really still smoke that thing?"

"Not really. Harlan, my head is just spinning."

"I'll bet. Tell me what you're thinking."

"I'm thinking that for the last three decades I've scrimped and saved for everything I wanted outside the puny household allowance he gives me. And about how demoralizing it was to ask him to give me a little more now and then. I mean, if I needed an extra two hundred dollars, he'd practically have a breakdown."

"Sugar, I mean this in the most respectful way, you could've gone to work. Even Momma went out and got a job."

"Oh, please! Doing the most inappropriate thing she could find. She embarrassed me all my life."

"You should really let that go, Les. Sure, it was embarrassing sometimes, but she had chutzpah!"

"Well, you know perfectly well Wesley wouldn't allow me to work! He wouldn't even hear of it! My chutzpah would make him look bad, like he wasn't man enough to support his wife and family. You know he was always very old school. I had to stay home with the children—which didn't go so well now that I look at them. I really was a terrible failure at motherhood."

"Don't say that!"

"The truth cannot be denied. I wasn't cut out for motherhood. And by the time they were in college, I was already in my forties! Who hires a woman in her forties who didn't even finish undergraduate school? If Wes ever heard about Momma and Willie, he'd flat lie down and die."

"Maybe you should tell him. Then the entire enchilada would be yours."

"Harlan? You are a devil! But how we kept all that from him and his Bible-beating parents is still a miracle. I thought then that it was probably because they lived in rural Pennsylvania and didn't ever travel."

"Maybe that's true, but it's also true that sometimes perfectly reasonable parents just give birth to knuckleheads. Look, I'd be the last person on this planet to criticize you or your choices. That said, I have to say that I think living with Wes must be the most frustrating and unsatisfying arrangement I can imagine. I'd kill myself."

"Unsatisfying? Whoo-hoo! That's a good one! Who thinks about *that*?"

"Wait a minute. Are you going to tell me you don't think you're entitled to some kind of satisfaction in your marriage? Emotional or otherwise?"

"Harlan, maybe it's just that I know there is no water in that well. So why bother? I could pump Wes for satisfaction until I'm blue in the face, but you can't make someone into something they're not. So I take my satisfaction where I can find it."

"Like where?"

"Well, there's my granddaughter . . ."

"Oh, please. She's barely out of diapers." I scowled at him and he said, "Look, I know you adore Holly. *I* adore the pictures of her and just the sound of her voice . . . well, it sounds like music, doesn't it? Maybe *someday* I'll get to meet her. But, shugah, I want more for my sister than that. Momma would too! And you haven't been happy for so long. You don't even know it! I can't bear it."

"Oh, Harlan. You and I know each other too well, and it's pretty obvious that you're running a campaign for me to dump Wesley."

"Not really. I just want you to be happy."

"Thanks, sweetheart. Look, I meant it when I said I don't want to spend every weekend for the rest of my life with a bunch of home-wrecking whores disguised as nice young women who make me feel like an old frump. I want to have fun and be happy!"

"Well, thank goodness for that!"

"And what happened in Edinburgh was terrible, but it wasn't really grounds for a divorce, either. I guess I have a lot of thinking to do. It's not like Wesley has given me a concrete reason to divorce him."

"And it's not like he's given you one to stay, either, has he?"

"Except that it might have been nice to know we had twenty-two million dollars to our name."

"Again, you didn't know it because he didn't want you to know it. You need to think about that. How many other secrets does he have?"

"Other than that? I think he's pretty transparent. Maybe he's hiding new golf clubs or something, but he's not a womanizer—at least not in the past ten years. Well, not that I know of."

Except maybe for a possible escapade in Atlantic City, but I kept that to myself. This fire didn't need any more fat.

"I rest my case," he said. I looked up at him and he added, "Temporarily. Now there's one other matter of business we have not discussed."

"Which is?"

"Did you love seeing Jonathan Ray ogle you to death last night?"

"Oh, come on. You know it's always wonderful to discover an old friend again, isn't it?"

"Don't be coy with me, honey bunny. I saw you two eyeballing each other. Hmmmm?"

"He's just an old dear friend, Harlan, who said he'd be happy to take care of my arm for me while I'm here."

"I'll bet he wants what's attached to that arm as well!"

"Harlan! What a scandalous thing to say!"

"You know what, Leslie? Maybe a good scandal is exactly what you need! And a pair of diamond stud earrings. Why don't you take yourself over to Croghan's Jewel Box and get a big old sparkly pair? Let Wes see *that* on the Visa card. That might wake him up."

"You're a devil, sweet brother." It wasn't a bad idea.

"Hmmm. Maybe sometimes, but I'm gonna tell you something."

"What?"

"You only have one life, Leslie. I think you've sacrificed too much for too little in return. Charleston is our birthplace, our heritage. As they like to say around here, it's the blood-soaked land of our ancestors, people who gave everything they had for freedom. There's a lot to be learned from it, especially when things don't seem so clear."

"Oh, Harlan, I know you mean well but . . ."

"Hush, Sister, and let me finish. Why don't you take some time and just look at the women who have gone before you in this town? The Pinckney girls, for example—Eliza Lucas Pinckney, for sure, but Miss Josephine Pinckney most especially. You're walking the same floors she walked, for heaven's sake. You know?"

"Okay. I'll do that."

"Promise? They both faced worse horrors than Wesley."

"Such as?"

"Redcoats! Yankees! Seriously, Eliza Lucas practically put the indigo crop on the map. She was an absolutely amazing woman. Really. Read her letters. She ran three plantations simultaneously." He stepped out to the sitting room and took a volume from his shelves, handing it to me with a flourish. "This is a treasure."

"I will treat it like one," I said. "Thanks. I need a diversion."

Then we laughed in some kind of relief, and I hugged him with all my might. Maybe he was right. Maybe I needed a deeper understanding of my real feelings so I could make better decisions about my future. At that moment I couldn't even imagine a future. And I didn't have emotions that incited me to real anger or raging grief— just something that felt like utter frustration. Maybe the Pinckney girls could shed a little light. Coming to Harlan was the smartest thing I could've done. Ever since we were kids we went to each other over every problem we had. He was my rock.

"But Josephine is still a mystery to me," he said.

"Why's that?"

"Well, her novel *Three O'Clock Dinner* sold almost a million copies. Maybe more. I mean, that was a *huge* number in the 1940s! Think about it—no Barnes & Noble, no Books-A-Million, no e-readers. Did you ever read it?"

I shook my head.

"To be honest, Harlan, you've been throwing her name around for years, but I've never even heard a single thing about her. I mean, I hate to sound like a dimwit. I know we've got Pinckney *this* and Pinckney *that* all over Charleston, but I've never heard a peep about Josephine. Besides your dog, that is."

"That's my point exactly! She sold millions of books. She got the highest advance ever paid back in the day for a book-to-film deal. MGM gave her something like a hundred and twenty-five thousand dollars. And we're all saying Josephine who? How does a woman with this drop-dead historic pedigree and platinum résumé just vanish into obscurity?"

"Good question."

"Well, sweetie, we don't want it to happen to us, either. She should've written a book about a Gullah-speaking vampire dog that's into erotica. There'd be a statue of her in Marion Square right next to John C. Calhoun!"

We laughed at the thought of it. Would Charleston really tolerate one of its aristocrats writing such a thing? Well, it sort of had! Josephine Pinckney allegedly had courage in spades.

"What's this world coming to?"

"I don't know, but somewhere in her papers is the answer to her obscurity. Maybe you can figure it out with women's intuition, because I sure couldn't."

A challenge. All our lives we had challenged each other on various things: Who starred in what movie? (Harlan always knew the answers.) Who made the best lasagna? (Me. Hands down.) Gumbo? (Harlan—his was divine.) Who had the prettiest garden? (Well, it depended on the season.) An outsider might have accused us of sibling rivalry, but we viewed these contests as legitimate competition with winners and losers and then we laughed about it for ages. And truly, who cared? If Harlan made his famous gumbo and I got to eat it, how did I lose?

Harlan left for Rome with his group from the college on June eleventh. I stayed on in Charleston. We agreed it would be good for me. I still had not spoken to Wes. He knew where I was and didn't care as long as I wasn't dead.

Harlan called me on the house phone when he arrived and got settled.

"Hey! How was your trip?"

"Too perfect for words," he said. "Everything okay?"

"Everything is just fine. How's Rome?"

"Ah, R-r-r-oma!" he said, rolling his *R*. "The Eternal City! So gorgeous! Every time I come here I just want to throw on a toga and rush to the Colosseum! All I can think about is Tony Curtis in *Spartacus*. How wild is that?"

"Very. Please don't pull the sheets and make a toga. Better to call room service for a plate of pasta."

"I'm sure you're right but the temptation is fierce."

He promised to call every few days.

Yep, so back in Charleston there was just me, my lurking dilemma I was trying to ignore, and Harlan's pup. She really was a darling little thing, but *spoiled rotten* didn't begin to describe her personality. When late afternoon rolled around and the sky began to turn red at the horizon, she positioned herself in front of the large window on the second floor in Harlan's study from where you could see the sunset. As soon as the day faded into darkness, she'd run from the window and bark at her wardrobe closet. She didn't stop barking until I brought down her pearl pink quilted satin dressing gown with the marabou trim and fixed it on her little twelve-pound body. She even stood on her hind legs to make it easy to put her front legs through the armholes. When she was satisfied that she was appropriately dressed for the evening, she'd hop up into her Marie Antoinette–style bed and curl up into a ball. This was only good for as long as she didn't need to be given a moment in the moonlight with nature, which was usually just before my bedtime when she barked to remind me to open the door. There was little doubt as to who was really in charge. Maybe I needed a dog. But then did I really need another thing to boss me around?

I had only been in Charleston for a few days, and let me tell you, they were the longest days of my life. All my routines were broken and I was on the lam, sort of. But what was I doing? Had I really left

Wesley? At that moment I didn't want a divorce, but I also didn't want to go back. I just couldn't see myself in that life anymore. And for the life of me, I surely could not see Wesley changing the smallest detail of his habits or his personality. Wesley's truth was the only truth that mattered. If he thought he was fine, he was fine.

And here's a terrible thing to consider. Even if he decided to give up golf, would I really, truly, and honestly want to spend an entire Saturday or Sunday with him? What would we do? Play Scrabble? Chitchat? On top of my growing pile of complaints, now that I knew the truth about our financial situation, everything was changed. I was furious with him in a way I didn't know I could be furious with anyone. What a colossal liar he was. How could I ever trust him again?

I finally turned my cell phone back on, and the first person's call I returned was Charlotte's.

"Mom? Are you okay?"

"I'm perfectly fine," I said. "How are you? How's Holly?"

"We're all fine, Mom. So? What's going on?"

"I'm watching your uncle Harlan's house for him while he's away."

"Oh. So when are you coming home?" I could hear the veiled annoyance in her voice.

"I'm not sure. Why?"

"Well, I need you, Mom. Dad needs you."

"Oh, I'm sure y'all are managing just fine without me."

There was a long silence.

"Mom? Did you and Dad have like a terrible fight or something?"

"Not at all."

"Well, it's just so weird for you to pick up and go to Charleston without telling anybody."

"I wanted some time off."

"From what?"

"Oh, I don't know. Cleaning the house with my arm in a sling?"

"Oh. Wait. Don't you have what's her name? Martha?"

"Twice a month."

"Well, Mom, that's ridiculous. If you need her more, just call her."

"It requires an act of Congress to adjust the budget. You should know that."

"Yeah, Dad's pretty tight."

"It's easier to be here for now."

"Yeah, I'll bet it is. Charleston's gorgeous. Can I come and visit?"

"Of course you can. Just let me know when you might like to come so that I don't make other plans, okay?"

"Plans? With who?"

"Honey, you seem to forget that I still have a few friends in Charleston."

"Oh, I'm sure you do."

"So how's the world of real estate going?"

"Well, it's kind of hard to work when I don't have *child care.*"

"Ah," I said, and let it go with that.

"And the housing market is in the tank, you know. Everyone wants like the Taj Mahal with a media room for under two hundred thousand. Ain't happening. People are so unrealistic."

"That's *true,*" I said, hoping that I might strike a chord with her conscience, which I may have done.

There came another silence, one where I could hear the wheels in her head churning with frustration. She knew I didn't think much of her business acumen, and she suspected I didn't think much of her mothering skills either. But she probably inherited the latter from me.

"Mom? Come on. What's going on? Are you having an affair?"

"What? Don't be ridiculous. And remember, missy, just because you think you're an adult doesn't mean you can ask your mother such a rude and personal question."

"Well, stranger things have happened in this world, you know."

"Really?"

We hung up a few minutes later and I thought, So, it would be that strange if I had an affair, would it? *Good old Les!* Your father thinks it's fine to cavort with whoever strikes his fancy and his friends have new wives who are half their age, but women like me never had affairs? Or worse yet, it would be a modern-day miracle if someone actually wanted a woman like me? Wait a minute! Did I have an expiration date stamped on my forehead? What was that old story about how women had a better chance of being abducted by aliens than they did getting married after forty? Was that it? Hell, I couldn't remember the details, probably due to *my* age. So shoot me. If Charlotte came to Charleston, I was going to give her a piece of my mind.

I still had only spoken to Wes once, that unfortunate occasion when I hung up on him. There were at least a dozen messages from him the first day and then none after that. I guess he thought it was up to me to call him and it probably was, but to be honest, I didn't feel up to his harangue. He would try to outargue me and convince me I should come home with my tail between my legs. No way. My desire to face him, even on the telephone, was nil. Part of me felt that by day five, he should've been doing some huge soul-searching and then upon his self-realization that he was, in fact, an ass of gargantuan proportions, he should've been sending me flowers—buckets of them. But then an hour later I'd realize if I was going to wait for him to come to me on bended knee with his arms flailing apologies all over the place, I had better find a comfortable spot for my pity party slash self-righteous indignation to camp out. Wes never apologized for anything because in his mind he was *never* wrong. *Ever.*

On my stronger days, I was actually enjoying my time alone,

listening to classical music, which of course Wes despised. I scanned Harlan's shelves and naturally, in addition to an entire library of books on art history, he owned a signed first edition of everything Josephine Pinckney had ever written. I had begun *Three O'Clock Dinner* and was enjoying it enormously, surprised by how contemporary it felt even though it was published in 1945. Class struggle still thrived even in 2012.

Walking from room to room, I had to say that Harlan had himself one helluva house. I thought about the burden of living in a historic home, one owned by an ancestor of Governor Thomas Pinckney, one of America's first ambassadors to Great Britain, and Charles Cotesworth Pinckney, who signed the Constitution. Oh la dee da, my inner cynic said. But it was true that being a Pinckney was a far heavier burden to carry than being a Kennedy, Johnny-come-latelies, our mother always said as though our family had hopped off the *Mayflower*. But Harlan insisted that Jo Pinckney, as she was known to her friends, was a truly modern aristocrat, and always looked forward, not the least bit encumbered by her heritage or by the memories of the Civil War, of which her own father was actually a veteran. If anything, he said, she used her name to great advantage, gaining entrée into the most sophisticated literary circles up and down the East Coast when women were generally excluded. She was ambitious and serious minded, beautiful and talented; and any way you shook it up, so far my reading proved that she was a very interesting writer. Perhaps by the time Harlan returned I'd have an answer.

The weather had been gorgeous. The temperatures were still below ninety, and if I walked the Battery Wall, the breezes were saturated with the fragrance of so many different flowers and the salt of the sea, it was enough to get you drunk. In fact, Jo Pinckney's first book, a volume of poems, was named *Sea-Drinking Cities,* which I thought was a brilliant title. I took long strolls with Miss JP through White Point Gardens and thought about the real Miss Jo, and of course, I thought of Wes and Charlotte and I wondered if my little Holly was missing me. I wondered what Josephine Pinckney would do about Wes if she was in my shoes? Then I had to laugh. As far as I could tell from what I'd read, a man like Wes would've bored her to death. He was far too pedestrian for a woman whose great friends were the likes of Amy Lowell, Laura Bragg, and Edna St. Vincent Millay. No, she'd take *all* his money and walk.

Harlan said that if I wanted to get an idea what life was really like in the forties and the fifties that I should go across the street to the South Carolina Historical Society and read Josephine's papers. Maybe I would if we got a rainy day. Heaven knows the history of anyone else's life was more exciting than mine.

Apparently Jo Pinckney never married or had children, but she enjoyed the company of two prominent gentlemen for long periods of time, both of whom *were* married with children. I'd bet the Charleston tongues wagged a gale force wind about that! Harlan quoted her saying, "Few people realize how much courage it takes in a community like ours to ignore the established taboos."

I liked the idea that she had the courage to thumb her nose at the social conventions of the day and find a port in the storm. Charleston's genteel citizens must have believed that her extreme creative bent combined with her undeniable pedigree allowed them to overlook her passions of the flesh. Still, she must've been a very brave woman, I thought.

Ah, Wesley! Why are you such a Neanderthal? I know him so well and I could see him in my mind's eye, standing in front of his sink in the morning while he shaved and saying something like *She'd better apologize for this!* Well, I wasn't apologizing. And the longer I didn't hear from him, the more I was convinced that my absence was only a frustrating inconvenience. He obviously didn't miss me one bit except for the duties I performed that facilitated his everyday life. He probably had our housekeeper there every day. Let's be honest, if I could be replaced by my own housekeeper, what did that tell me?

On other days, I wept. I would torture myself over every detail I could remember from all the years of our marriage and how I might have steered things in another direction for our children if I'd only had the courage. But Wes was always so volatile. He argued with me over every single thing! The least little thing would cause him to bellow. Go bellow in hell, I thought. Go bellow in hell. Look at the two fine messes we have for children. I did everything your way, Wes, and look at them. Look at us. I hope you're happy.

And then Jonathan called. Just as I'm daydreaming about the lovely prospect of Wes yelping, dodging Satan's pitchforks, Jonathan calls. *Hello, Trouble?*

"Hey! How are you?" He sounded so warm and nice.

"I'm good," I said, completely surprised. "How are you?"

"Well, if I waited around for you to call me, Christmas might come and go!"

"Was I supposed to call you?" I said and remembered he had given me his card.

"If you want to spend the rest of your life with your arm in a cast, that's your prerogative."

"Ah, yes. My arm is still in that dastardly cast. It sure is. Well, how do you like that?"

"So why don't you come around to the office about four tomorrow and let me have a look at it. I mean, you have instant access to the greatest sports medicine in the country. You may as well exercise that privilege."

I thought about this quickly and decided that there was absolutely no reason to believe that his call was anything more than a friendly gesture to help out an old friend in need. But, Lord, he sure did have a big head.

"Well, thanks. I'm getting pretty tired of this business."

"You probably don't even need that sling anymore, but let's see."

I wrote down his office address and said, "Thanks, Jonathan. I'm in such a fog over here, I hadn't even thought about it."

"Well, let me do the thinking on this one. See you tomorrow."

"Great. Thanks."

It was true that I had spent the week sort of wandering around in my head, befuddled, and definitely not making any forward progress. The only conversation I'd had of any real satisfaction was with Danette, who called to say she didn't see a single thing wrong with coming to Charleston for a while. This was before Harlan verified the money situation and when I was thinking that leaving Wes would mean I'd most certainly spend my old age in poverty.

She said, "Shoot. Wes and Harold go on business trips all the time. So maybe you need a little time away for the business of your life! What's wrong with that?"

"Exactly!"

It was more than just a little time away and we both knew it, but I wasn't sure how to articulate it. Besides, Danette had never been the kind of friend who would try to push me into saying things I wasn't fully ready to discuss. I was grateful for her patience and to know she was in my corner.

When I had told her the story of Cornelia and Lisette getting into a brawl at the golf club, she sighed deeply.

"I have to say, I view these reports as validation that Harold is certifiable."

"The whole world has gone mad," I said. "It was like some tawdry reality show."

"I don't blame you for walking out," she said. "Wes called me, you know."

"No, but that's okay. I didn't call you because I didn't want to put you in the middle of it."

"I appreciate that. Damn it, Les! Do I have to buy a beach house down there so I can still have my best friend around?"

"Maybe? I don't know."

Now I wished she was next door so I could tell her about Jonathan and my arm and get her opinion.

So I called her.

"Got a minute?" I said.

"Sure! What's going on?"

"Get comfortable. This is kind of a long one."

I told her all about Jonathan and what we had meant to each other all through high school. I was a student at Ashley Hall and he went to Porter-Gaud. He came to my class plays and I went to his football games. We spent so many lazy summer days on Sullivans Island at his grandmother's house at Station 22, eating egg salad sandwiches, drinking iced tea, walking the beach, waterskiing on the Intracoastal Waterway all the way up to Capers Island. We had the classic, idyllic teenage love affair. And then I went away to college in Atlanta. And he went to Duke undergrad and then medical school. Unlike everyone's expectations, we drifted apart and married other people. Then I saw him at Harlan's party.

"Good Lord, Les. Get your hair blown out, put on some lipstick, and go see him. What could be more benign? He sounds darling!"

"He's way beyond darling, which makes me think he'd never take a second look at me—especially now. I'm sure he's just being nice."

"Okay, so he's being nice. What's wrong with *that*?"

"You're right. It's just that what could be worse than being rejected by your first boyfriend?"

"What does that mean?"

"You know. What if he thinks I'm an old cow?"

"He didn't reject you the other night, did he?"

"No. But it was dark, and alcohol was involved. Isn't this kind of the ultimate litmus test for whether or not to crawl into a cave and gnaw on your arm until you stop living?"

There. I'd said it, more or less. Jonathan was the *one that got away*. But was I *his* one that got away?

"Girl? Please don't be so insecure. Put a smile on your face, get yourself moving, and call me afterward, okay?"

The next day I arrived at Jonathan's office on the stroke of four and announced myself to the receptionist, who was well into her seventies, had a perm tight enough to hold a dozen Bic pens, and was quite plump. The name tag on her bow blouse read CAROL ANNE, a double name I actually liked.

"I gonna take you right in, Mrs. Carter." She all but jumped from her seat to open the door for me. "You must be a very important patient."

"Why's that?" I said and followed her down the long hallway.

"Because you can't find neither hide nor hair of Dr. Ray on Fridays after four!"

"Oh, well, I'm just an old friend from a million years ago."

"That's so nice!" She stopped and turned back to me, whispering behind her hand. "He could use a friend, old or new, if you know what I mean?"

"I'll remember that," I said. Good Lord. Some people sure like to work their jaws, I thought.

I went into the examining room and put my purse on the chair next to the examining table and concluded it made absolutely no sense for me to perch myself up there like I was here for a Pap smear. Perish the thought! Almost immediately, the door opened and there stood Jonathan, in his white coat over his blue-and-white seersucker suit, white shirt, and adorable red foulard bow tie. The sight of him was so cute and wholesome, all the way down to his white bucks, that I laughed in delight.

"What's funny?" he said with a huge smile.

"Nothing! You just look so, so . . ."

"Madam, have you forgotten that this is the standard that sets the gentlemen of Charleston apart from the rest of the world?" He pulled back his jacket and snapped his skull-and-crossbones braces against his chest. "I wore these just for you."

"Wonderful!" I said and laughed, shaking my head. "Dr. Killer! You are too much!"

"Hmmm," he mused. "Now let's see that arm."

I held it out, and he carefully undid the Velcro fasteners and removed the cast. My arm was as white as a fish belly.

"I remember these freckles," he said.

"You do?" Now, why that remark sent my thermometer up is anybody's guess, but it had been a really long time since anyone said anything remotely personal to me. "I need a tan."

He smiled. "And I want an X-ray of this pretty little arm of yours. Let me call our tech." He picked up the phone and asked for Betty. "I'm pretty sure, just by the way you're moving, that you don't need the cast, but I want to be sure. Any discomfort?"

"Zero."

"Good sign."

Twenty minutes later the X-ray of my arm was on a light box and we were looking at it together.

"Clean break, no displacement . . . looks very good to me. I'd say you can safely dump the cast and sling. Just take it easy for a week or two—no handsprings, okay?"

"Gee, just when Cirque de Soleil called me back for a second audition? Rats."

He looked at me and chuckled. Unlike Wes, who rarely got my sense of humor.

"Want to go to the rooftop bar on East Bay and get a martini?"

"Why not?"

So just like that, I walked out of Jonathan's office with him, slingless and castless, deciding on the spot that there was nothing wrong with having one drink. Even if there was, I was doing it anyway.

CHAPTER 10

Wes Isn't Happy

So it was Sunday morning and I had a late tee time. I was relaxing, listening to my boy Sinatra and reading the paper, drinking my second cup of coffee, and the phone rings. Was it my lovely absentee wife? No, it was my daughter.

"Daddy? I need a huge favor! Please say yes!"

"Whaddya need, princess?"

"I need you to take Holly for a couple of hours. There's a huge open house this morning, and if I can sell this house, it could totally change my life."

I thought about it for a minute. First, I'd have to cancel my golf game, but so what? I probably play enough golf. Second, nobody understands the value of work more than I do. If she's got a chance to make some money, she should do it. Third, it would give me a chance to spend some time with my granddaughter, who's finally old enough now to talk to like a real person.

"Daddy? Are you still there?"

"Yeah, I'm just thinking, that's all."

"Oh . . ."

"Okay, I'll cancel my golf game. You bring her over. I'll take her out to lunch or something."

Well, she must've been calling me from the car because as soon as I hung up with Harold, I heard her coming through the door.

"Pops!"

"Holly Doodle!" I called back and squatted to catch her. She broke into a tear, flying down the hall, and threw herself into my arms. I swung her around and planted her little feet back on the ground.

"Upside down!" she squealed, grabbing my hands and starting to walk up my legs in her sneakers—they had blinking lights in them—so she could do a backflip.

So I flipped her over a couple of times while Charlotte watched from the doorway.

"She'll throw up, Daddy. You'd better stop."

Charlotte smirked at me, and I winked at Holly.

"Your momma doesn't know that we do the magic flip that does not make the flipper barf, don't we?"

Holly thought about it for a second. "Not gonna barf," she said to Charlotte and reinforced her words with a deliberate nod in the affirmative.

"You go on about your business," I said to Charlotte. "Holly and I will be fine. What time do you think you might be back?"

"Around three? Is that okay?"

"Sure! That still leaves me time for nine holes before dark."

Charlotte gave me a kiss on the cheek and left. I closed the front door of the house and turned to face Holly.

"Want to watch the Golf Channel?" I said.

"What's a Golf Channel?" she said.

"Oh, sweetie! It's the most important thing on television! Come on, let's get a bag of cookies and watch it!"

"Okay!"

"Wait! Did you have lunch?"

"Nope."

"Well, come on then. Pops will make you a peanut butter and jelly sandwich! How does that sound?"

"And bananas and Nutella too?"

"Why not?"

She clapped her hands and followed me to the kitchen. Skipping. So I skipped with her. I'm sure we looked ridiculous, but who was watching? You really do have more fun with your grandchildren than your own children. I don't think I ever skipped through the house with Charlotte or Bertie. And I sure as hell never skipped anywhere with Leslie.

I picked Holly up and sat her on a bar stool at the island in the middle of our kitchen. Just for the record, this is an English country kitchen, and what that meant was that Les hired some decorator who convinced her she needed all new cabinets and all kinds of stupid things like a pot filler. I mean, eight hundred dollars for a pot filler? A stupid faucet that comes out of the wall over a pot on the stove? Do you know how much spaghetti you'd have to eat to break even on that? A boatload, that's how much.

"You comfy, sweetheart?"

"Uh-huh," she said and bobbed her head up and down.

"Don't fall off, okay?"

I made a peanut butter and jelly sandwich on whole wheat and a Nutella and banana sandwich on white bread, cut them in half, and put them on a plate. I did it just like I'd seen Les do it at least fifty times. That wasn't so hard, I thought.

"Would you like a glass of milk?"

"Can I have Coke?" she said.

"Wellllll, you should probably have milk, but what the heck? This is a special day!"

"It is? Is it your birthday?"

"No, no. It's special because you're here!"

"Oh!"

I poured her some in the little Coca-Cola glasses Les used for juice because Holly's hands were too little for a regular glass. Maybe I didn't do this kid stuff all the time, but that didn't mean I wasn't paying attention. Not much got by me.

"Here you go, Holly Doodle," I said and put the knife and small cutting board in the dishwasher. "So what's new in your life?"

She drank her Coke straight down without taking a breath.

"What's new in *your* life?" she said, parroting me.

"Not much. You need some help with that sandwich?"

"Can I have more Coke, please?"

"Sure!"

I refilled her glass. She pushed her plate toward me, and I took a piece. It was delicious. No wonder kids ate peanut butter and jelly all the time. The Nutella wasn't bad either.

"Where's Gammy?"

"Oh, Gammy took a little trip to see her brother."

"Oh," she said and looked pretty sad.

"Hey! No Gloomy Gus, young lady! As soon as you finish your lunch we can go watch the Golf Channel and eat Oreos!"

"Yay!" She began to stuff her sandwich in her mouth and wash it down with the remains of the bottle of Coke she picked up from the counter as soon as I stepped away.

I looked in the pantry for the bag of Oreos and the bag of potato chips I bought at the gas station earlier in the week. They were no-where to be found. Could they be in the bread drawer? They were not. Where could they be? Wait! Didn't Martha have a teenage kid, a son who drove her back and forth to work every day now that I needed full-time, thank you, Leslie? Would her boy take food out of my house without asking? I couldn't even ask Martha if he did because Martha didn't speak ten words of English! How in the world did Leslie deal with her? Now what? I promised Holly a special treat, and the treat I had promised simply wasn't there. Okay, I thought, this is a desperate moment. I would have to break into my special stash of Twinkies. And maybe even the Devil Dogs. They were behind the cans of tomatoes and boxes of broth in the pantry, hidden where I couldn't take them out without some effort. At least they were there, I thought as I brought them out to the counter.

"Well, it's not Oreos," I said. "But this is very good stuff! Come on, Holly Doodle, the Golf Channel waits!"

She climbed down from the counter on her own and wiped her hands on her dress. Needless to say there were some pretty impressive grape jelly stains on her clothes.

"Come over here and let's wash your hands," I said, thinking she'd get food all over the sofa.

I pulled out the small step stool Leslie kept in the kitchen to help her reach the high shelves and put Holly on it.

"Okay," I said, squirting some liquid soap into her palms, "hold your hands under the water and rub 'em like crazy."

"Pops?"

"Yep?"

"I know how to wash my hands. I'm almost four, you know. I'm not a baby!"

"Good grief! What was I thinking? Of course you can! You're probably going to college next week!"

"Ha-ha-ha! You're funny, Pops!"

I made big eyes at her and she laughed some more. See? I told myself, I can do this! How smart did you have to be to watch a kid? I wiped her dress with a damp paper towel and most of the jelly came off.

So we got on the sofa and I clicked the remote, bringing the beautiful seventh hole on the third nine of Baltusrol into view. I love that course. It is a par seventy-two, one of the more forgiving courses of the top one hundred, and on a side note? I intended to play them all before I went to Glory.

"See that, honey?"

"What?" Holly didn't seem too enthralled.

"That's Springfield, New Jersey. Isn't it pretty? Want a Twinkie?"

"Yeah!"

Now I had her attention! Holly made short order of her Twinkie and asked for another one. I thought it probably wasn't such a good idea to give her so much sugar, but then I remembered that when I was a kid I could eat six of them. No problem. And wash it all down with a quart of milk!

"Have all you want, baby! But eat slowly! Be sure to chew slowly! Isn't golf great?"

She looked over at me and in all seriousness said, "Pops? You watch TV. I'm gonna go color."

"Oh? You want me to find your crayons for you?"

"No, I know where they are!"

She scampered away with a third Twinkie in her fist and I thought, Boy, this is great! She's getting more and more independent every day.

The next thing I know it was almost three o'clock, and there was no sign of Charlotte. I called her cell phone and it went right to voice mail. I waited fifteen minutes and tried her again. I got her voice mail for the second and then for the third time. I started getting pissed.

Finally I gave up and called Harold. "Well, I don't know where my daughter is and I can't go off and leave my granddaughter, you know?"

"Don't sweat it! We've got eighteen holes in the morning. Why don't you meet us at the club later on? We can get a good steak and have a few laughs. Paolo and Lisette are coming."

"Sure. Sure. I'll let you know."

A few minutes later, Holly appeared in the doorway of the family room.

"What's the matter, sweetheart?"

"I wanna go home. My tummy hurts."

With that, she threw up all over her dress, her shoes, the carpet, and God knows, there were intermittent events of exploding vomit in a trail behind us as I rushed her to the bathroom. She began to wail and I struggled to get her clothes off.

Is this what Leslie dealt with?

An hour later, Holly's stomach was finally finished lurching and pitching, and I had her in one of my T-shirts, tucked into her usual bed in the guest room. She was sleeping like a lamb and her clothes were in a plastic garbage bag by the door. Poor kid. She shouldn't have eaten so much junk! It took an entire roll of paper towels to clean up the mess, and then I discovered her artwork. She had drawn red and purple flowers and orange suns with smiley faces all over the bottom cabinets of the kitchen. They were ruined. Wasn't Holly too old to be drawing on the walls? Apparently not. I called Charlotte again, a number of times, and she still did not answer my calls.

Seven thirty rolled around and I was wildly pissed with Charlotte. What was the matter with her? Didn't she think I had to eat dinner? I was starving! She did this exact same thing all the time to Leslie. But it was different! Leslie was her mother and she didn't have the same social responsibilities that I did. Finally, at right before eight, I saw her headlights through the window as she pulled into the driveway. I felt like wringing her neck.

I went to the door and opened it, waiting for her to get out of her car.

"Just where the hell have you been?" I yelled to her.

"Daddy! Daddy! I'm so sorry! I didn't know my phone was off! I should've called you. I know, I know."

She walked past me and into the house. I closed the door and followed her, jabbing my finger into the air between us.

"Do you know your little girl has been throwing up her guts *all afternoon*? *No*! Of *course* you don't because *you* don't have enough *sense* to keep your *phone* on!"

"Oh, please! Kids throw up all the time. I look at her and she throws up. It's no big deal, Daddy."

"Really? Wait till you see what she did to your mother's custom-made kitchen cabinets!"

"Come on. Show me."

"And another thing, Charlotte. Where's your consideration of my time? I had a golf game this afternoon! People were *waiting* for me!"

"I thought you said you weren't playing, Daddy. That's what you said."

"No, ma'am. It is not what I said. You said you'd be back by three and I said good, I'd still have time for nine holes! Remember now?"

"Well, I'm sorry. I really am. Wow! She really did a number on Mom's kitchen, didn't she?"

"It's probably gonna cost twenty thousand dollars to replace them and who's supposed to pay for that?"

"Oh, Daddy, they're washable markers. Do you have like Windex or something? I can wipe it right off."

"Oh, sure you can! How should I know if we have Windex? Look under the sink. Good luck with that." I knew the cabinets were ruined, and I was almost disappointed when Holly's artwork disappeared in minutes as though it was never there. When it was all spotless, I started to calm down.

"So what did you feed her?"

"Feed her? Um, well, she had a peanut butter and jelly sandwich and then half of a Nutella and banana sandwich and some Coca-Cola and then later on while we were watching television she had a couple of Twinkies and I think one Devil Dog."

"Are you trying to kill her? You want to know why she got sick? Jesus, Daddy, what were you thinking?"

"Don't criticize your father. Didn't you ever read the Bible?" I knew she was right, but what was the point in admitting guilt? What was done was done. So I wouldn't do it again.

She was staring at me with that same face of indignation her mother had from time to time, standing there with her hands on her hips.

"So, Charlotte, did you sell the house?" I knew that would get her.

"Oh, please! It was just an open house, Daddy. It was fifty brokers eating chicken salad sandwiches and gabbing their heads off. But I think I have a buyer who would love it. We'll see. I'd better get Holly home. She's asleep?"

"Yeah, like an angel."

"So maybe I should just pick her up in the morning? I don't want to disturb her. You don't know how hard it is to put her back to bed."

I just stood there wondering for a moment if she was serious. Was this how she manipulated her mother? No wonder Leslie was fed up with her all the time.

"And I sort of made plans to meet some friends for drinks. What do you think?"

"I think you go and get your daughter, take her home, put her to bed, and act like a mother should. If it's hard to get her back to sleep, that's your problem. If you'd been on time, you could've put her to bed at her normal time. In her own house."

"Wow, Daddy, you're really pissed, aren't you?"

"Yes. Yes, I am. You took advantage of me, now you want to take advantage of me some more, and I don't like it. Now, move yourself before I really lose my temper."

"Oh, come on, Daddy. I said I was sorry."

"Sorry? Really? Maybe this kind of behavior is why your mother's in Charleston! Did you ever think about that?"

"Blame me? You want to blame *me*?"

Charlotte flounced out of the room and came back inside of a minute with a sleeping Holly thrown over her shoulder, headed for the front door.

"Daddy," she said, "you want to know why Momma's in Charleston? Look in the mirror."

She slammed the door and was gone. Boy, she had some lousy temper.

The phone rang. I picked it up and knew from the familiar crackle that it was Bertie calling from Kathmandu.

"Bertie? Is that you?"

"Hi, Dad! What's happening?"

"Don't tell me you're calling for money! Not tonight! I can't take it!"

"Actually, I have some good news."

"I'm all ears," I said and sighed.

"I sold three images to *National Geographic*. They're going to be in a special issue on Bhutan and Tibet."

"Well, that's good news, son! How much does it pay?"

"Well, only six hundred dollars and I don't get paid for thirty days. So do you think you could help me out just one more time?"

"*NO!*" I slammed the phone down as hard as I could.

I was going to the club. I was going straight to the bar. I was going to have a double vodka martini straight up, dirty not filthy, with two olives. I couldn't get there fast enough.

In the car on the way there, I thought about Charlotte and Bertie. No wonder Leslie was always on edge. Our kids were a damn disgrace. But singing along with Dean Martin cheered me up.

There was no valet that night, so I parked and went inside to the crowded bar. Harold and Cornelia waved me over. Lisette was sitting at the long teak bar with Paolo, but she was wearing sunglasses and a hat. Very odd, I thought. It was dark outside.

"Hey! We've been waiting so long we were giving up hope!" Harold said.

I ordered my drink, gave Harold a slap on the shoulder, and smooched Cornelia on her cheek. "How are you, gorgeous?" I said to her. "Sorry, guys, my daughter was late and then my son called." The bartender handed me my martini and I said, "Cheers!"

"Drink up!" Harold said. "We're way ahead of you."

"What's the news with Bertie?" Paolo said.

"Well, he's actually sold some of his work," I said. He was wrong to keep asking for money, but it probably wasn't nice for me to slam the phone on his ear. Oh, so what?

"That's wonderful!"

"Yeah," I said, "thanks! So Lisette? What's going on, darlin'? Setting a new fashion trend or something?"

She took off her hat and sunglasses. There was no hair where her bangs should've been, and she'd obviously been on a crying jag.

Paolo leaned into me and whispered. "My girls? Well, they aren't so sweet on my marriage as you know and they did something stupid . . ."

"Stupid?" Lisette wailed. "Wes? They put *Nair* in my shampoo bottle! It's *criminal*! I just wanted to freshen up my bangs! Then the phone rang and I got hung up in a conversation for like fifteen minutes and then my hair came out in the sink! Thank God I didn't wash my whole head!" She started crying again.

Lisette was a card-carrying airhead, but she made Paolo happy.

"Oh, honey," I said and thought, *Holy shit!* Wasn't *Nair* that smelly stuff women used to get rid of hair? Yeah, and obviously it worked. "That's terrible! Why would they do such a thing?"

"Because they hate me!" She really began to blubber in earnest.

"Come on now, sweetheart," Paolo said and put his arm around her.

I reached for my handkerchief and realized I didn't have one to give her. Another thing Les always took care of for me. Thanks, Les! I can't play the gentleman because of *you*!

"Wait, wait! Y'all? There's more," Cornelia said in a drawn-out drawl, one that might come from Scarlett O'Hara herself. "They also cut the crotch out of all her panties. Nice, huh?"

"Good grief," I said and thought, Good God! That's disgusting! "Well, they can be replaced. It's only money."

Now, since when did I feel like that? It's only money? I'll tell you, since Leslie took off, I was seeing the world in a whole new light.

CHAPTER 11

Leslie on a Slippery Slope

One of the first things I did Saturday morning was to call Danette, not because there was so much to discuss. I guess I was just lonely for my old friend and wanted to hear her voice. Talking to her might add some note of normalcy to my day.

"Hey! You busy?"

"Hang on! Let me turn down the television. Now where'd I put that darn clicker? Oh! There it is sticking out from under the bag of celery. This kitchen looks like a bomb went off. I'm making chicken stock and veal stock. Been up for hours." I could hear her television blasting in the background of her kitchen and her cook's clogs thumping across the floor. The noise subsided and she resumed our conversation. "So what's going on? How's Jonathan? Hmmmm?"

"Well, I don't have to sew big red *A*s on all my clothes, if that's what you're asking. What're you watching? *Barefoot Contessa*?"

"Of course I am. And of course that's what I'm asking! What happened last night?"

"Ah me, last night, last night . . . It was all very nice, I'm sorry to say. First, we went to a very swank rooftop bar on East Bay Street to have a glass of wine."

"Which one? I'm trying to visualize this. I don't have all day here."

Danette had obviously swallowed more coffee that morning than I had.

"The one that's above a steak house called Grill 225, which by the way, is mind-blowingly good. Anyway, we ordered some wine and talked about the state of the world, you know, reminiscing about the old days. It was great. And I got my cast off."

"Good about the cast, but cut to the chase, please."

"Well, we watched the sun go down and the lights of the city come up. It was very beautiful."

"*Ahem!*"

"What?"

"And *then* what? Do I have to drag it out of you?"

"You know, hon, you might need a caffeine intervention?"

"Sorry. It's just that I want to hear the story!"

"Well, we wound up going downstairs and having a steak and a nitrotini, which is a martini that's smoking because it's infused somehow with nitrogen? I should've taken a picture."

"Who cares about that? Please! And then?"

"And then he walked me home." I giggled.

"And *then*?"

"And then we said good night, but along the way he said some really sweet things to me."

"Such as?"

"Oh, I don't know. But one thing stood out. He said something like being with me made him feel so young again. I felt the same way. Energized, you know? I mean, probably just because we were talking about being teenagers and all that stuff. But when I looked in his eyes? I swear to you, Danette, there was the same eighteen-year-old boy I used to love hiding behind all those little crinkles. He was right there."

"That's pretty sweet, Les. And there you were all worried that he'd treat you like an old bag."

"Yeah. I know. Stupid, right? Well, anyway, like you, I haven't been out with another man since the Russians launched Sputnik. In fact, I've never even *looked* at another man since my wedding day, except for George Clooney. He doesn't count."

"No, he doesn't count."

"Listen, Jonathan makes me very nervous. It's weird, you know?"

"Of course, I know! So did you feel like a wicked little slut? Ha-ha!"

"Only for about two seconds. It was practically totally harmless." I laughed too. "No, it wasn't. It wasn't even close to harmless. But it wasn't exactly dangerous, either. Does that make sense?"

"Yes. It's called the mating dance."

"Jesus God, Danette. And I mean that as a prayer. Mating dance?"

"Yeah. You know, he struts a little, watches your reaction, and retreats a bit until he thinks you're ready? Then he zeros in!"

"Gross!"

"*Pounce!*"

"*Stop!*"

"Whatever! So let me ask you something. Did you kiss him?"

"God! Danette! No! Decaf!" I gasped, feigning offense. "Okay, but just a sort of drive-by kiss."

"What the heck is that?"

"Like I kiss my granddaughter. You know, a smooch."

"How dull. Okay, but could you see yourself with him?"

"Dan, I can't see myself with *anyone*. How's that?"

"Know what? Me either. I mean me, not you. I can't see myself with anyone either. I've got this smoking-hot landscape architect from down the street supervising his crew as they're digging up my backyard. He's giving me the eye and I'm giving him the eye, but when it's cocktail time, I pretend I've got to rush out the door to meet somebody else."

"Wait? Is he asking you to have drinks and you're saying no?"

"Yeah, sort of. It's just too awkward. I don't know. I'm just not ready or something."

"Why not? What's one drink? At least that's what I told myself when I wound up spending the *entire* evening with Jonathan."

"Right? Well, he's a bit younger."

"How much?"

"I don't know. I think a lot—maybe ten years? Maybe more?"

I giggled. "And your problem is?"

"I know. You're right. I'm like you. But the whole business of having sex with someone new gives me the heebie-jeebies."

"Who said anything about sex? *Sex?* What's *that?*"

"Exactly. My magic garden has dried up from drought."

"Magic garden, indeed. So what's our alternative? If I leave Wes? Are we going to wind up a couple of old biddies going on cheap Caribbean cruises with a bunch of other old biddies? I can see us now, standing on buffet lines, eating twelve kinds of layered Jell-O salads and gray meat loaf, killed under heat lamps. Then we'll drink too much cheap sangria and flirt with Danish cabin boys who could technically be our grandsons?"

"What a picture! Hell, no! That will *never* be us!"

She laughed like crazy, but I was dead serious. If I left Wes, where was I really headed? Down Lonely Street to the Heartbreak Hotel?

"You know, Danette, I think I've had it with my marriage."

"Yeah, I know. It's okay. It really is, you know."

"And Charlotte and Bertie too."

"Well, your children aren't even close to who they're going to become yet. So you can't really say something terrible like that about them and mean it."

"Maybe. I hope you're right. But you know what? Wes *is* who he has become and I can't say I'm too thrilled with him. Not thrilled at all. Oh God, I feel sick inside my heart. I mean, Danette? If you ask one of those guys who makes up actuarial tables? I'm gonna be dead in twenty years. How do I want to spend them? What do I want?"

"What do any of us want?"

"I don't know. I mean, I think . . . I think, I just don't want to feel like I'm *already* dead. Do you know what I mean?"

"Yes. I know *exactly* what you mean. For me? I really hated the idea of everything already spelled out before me—predictable everything—and all I was doing was walking this lonely path toward the grave, retrieving Harold's golf balls from our shrubbery and putting them in a bucket in our garage. If Harold hadn't left me, there wouldn't have been a single surprise left in my life."

"God, at one point in your life all you *want* is for life to be predictable. And then you wake up one day, you feel like a zombie, and you can't *bear* all that predictability for another second."

"I tell myself that if it wasn't for Molly's wedding, I'd be out there having fun every night. I feel like I have to remain nunlike until after the big day so she doesn't have to stress about another thing. I mean, she hasn't said it, but I'm sure she worries that I'll show up with some man she doesn't know and embarrass her like Harold did when he showed up married with Cornelia at her engagement party and upstaged the whole night."

"And don't we women always put everyone else first? Anyway, Harold's a dope and you staying home in the convent is ridiculous. If you want to go out with this guy—what's his name, by the way?"

"Nader."

"What kind of name is that? Where's he from?"

"I don't know. Iran, I think. His mother is from some little South African country and his father is a retired diplomat. He's interesting. Speaks a dozen languages. Studied law at Harvard. He's very cool."

"Wow. I'll say. Cooler than Wes and Harold."

"Well, that doesn't take much."

"To be sure. Well, listen, Danette, you're divorced, and neither one of us is getting any younger. I think you ought to do what you want and don't worry about what Molly thinks."

"Probably. I'm thinking about it. So how are you doing, you know, in your head?"

How was I doing? Not so hot.

"I'm scared, Danette. I'm scared like hell."

"Oh, my sweet friend. I know." I heard her sigh long and hard. "Change is very frightening at this age. Look, for me? Harold made this brilliant decision to get a divorce, not me. He just walked out. He had Cornelia waiting in the wings. At first, you know I was devastated. But I can tell you that once I got my brain wrapped around the fact that it was over, I got on with my life pretty quickly."

"Well, parts of it."

"True. So Mr. Tall, Dark, and Handsome will have to wait a little. And tell me to mind my own business, but have you talked to a lawyer?"

"No. Because I'm not sure I really want a divorce. I'd just like to be away from everyone for a while—you know, time off for good behavior."

"Who would blame you?"

"I really sort of hate Wesley right now. And Charlotte needs somebody to give her a good throttling, something I should've done a long time ago. But divorce? I think it would be wise for me to get over my anger first. Then I can decide what I want to do."

"Yes. Absolutely. You're right. It's never a good idea to make big decisions when you're angry."

"And this may sound cosmically irrational, but I just don't feel like I belong in Atlanta anymore. You know? There's nothing for me there. Wrong vibe."

"What do you mean?"

"I mean just exactly that. When I think about Harlan coming back and my going home, I get this huge lump in my throat, like I'm suffocating. But when I think about staying here in Charleston, I want to cry my eyes out."

"Girl? That is screwed up. Tell me why you want to cry."

"Because it was all a mistake. Thirty years of one mistake after another. I feel like a miserable failure. I failed at marriage and don't get me started on motherhood."

"Look, I can understand why Charlotte and Bertie get your motor going, but I don't see where *you* failed. Honest to God! I don't! You did *everything* for them!"

"I sure tried."

"True enough! I was there! I remember the hours you spent driving them all over the place."

"If I could just have the time I spent in the car line back, I'd be thirty-five again."

"You, me, and every other mother on the planet! Look, Les, people, even very young people, make choices that impact their whole lives. Like to study or not to study. But they have to live the life they want to live, don't they? And where did you fail in your marriage?"

"Are you kidding? I let Wes manipulate me into every single choice we made over the smallest details in our lives. I should have stood up to him more."

"Oh, please. Good luck with that! Stand up to Mount Rushmore? Yeah, I'd love to see that."

"I know. I married a damn bully. And you know what? Maybe I don't want to be bullied anymore."

"Well, who'd blame you for that either? Now let's talk about the fun stuff. When are you seeing Jonathan again?"

"Tonight."

"Whoo-hoo! Girlfriend? You'd better shave your legs!"

"Oh, please. I haven't seen a hair on my legs in the last ten years!"

"Or maybe you just can't see them. Shave anyway!"

I was glad we had changed the subject. I'd check my legs out later.

We hung up, with me promising to call her back in the morning to give an update on Jonathan. I attached Miss JP's leash to her collar and took her outside for a walk in the park. She pranced down the street, stopping to sniff and looking up at passersby as though she understood them when they remarked on how adorable she was. I could've sworn that dog was smiling. Her red-striped sundress was more or less accidentally coordinated with my red pants and striped shirt. As silly as it may seem, I had a thought that it was too bad I didn't have red framed sunglasses. Then we would've looked like we belonged to each other. Maybe I'd look around at Target for some inexpensive ones for the fun of it. How long had it been since I'd done anything just *for the fun of it*? People would think I'm peculiar. I liked the notion of having a bit of an eccentric reputation. Why not?

When she had deposited her calling card in the border grass, she tugged on her leash in the direction of Harlan's house. Mission accomplished and she was ready to go home. I picked her up and nuzzled her neck and she rewarded me with a lick on my nose. It was my first kiss from Harlan's baby. I was suddenly aware of how much this little dog depended on the reliability of others, and I was glad she seemed to appreciate me. At least somebody did.

I had not told Danette about the money. She would've fainted on the floor and then got up to say she wasn't surprised, that I should divorce Wes and buy myself a new black Mercedes. The two-seater with white leather interior all piped in black—all in the name of sweet revenge. She'd say we should ride by his house and blow the horn and she'd holler through a bullhorn that I bought it at sticker price just to drive him crazy and Wes would shiver and break a sweat that lasted for weeks.

But the fact was that I hadn't told her. I loved Danette to death, but truly neither one of us was wired for revenge. I didn't want money to become the focus of why I should divorce Wes when it was the fact that he lived in another world that really cut my heart into little pieces. I would tell her when the time was right. But I have to say that the thought of a sporty little Benz was pretty nice.

Every time I gave any real office space to Wes keeping our millions a secret I wanted to backhand his smug face with all my might. And now, when I'd lie awake at night thinking about Edinburgh, I wanted to knock *his* teeth out! But it wasn't just those one or two facts that were breaking what was left of my heart. All the years of lies and embarrassments and slights and being overlooked and taken for granted and unappreciated and, yes, unloved had suddenly surfaced and brought me to this state of mind. I was not a cherished woman. Not even a little bit. Wes had never treated me the way I treated him. Nor had he ever looked at me as if he was in love, at least not in decades.

I could remember brushing my hair and putting on something fresh and pretty, waiting for him to come through the door at night. How many times did my heart skip a beat? So many. I'd made his favorite soup or roast and I couldn't wait to serve it to him because I knew it would make him happy. That was all I wanted to do. I wanted to be a good mother and a good wife and I tried as hard as I could to be both of those things. Somewhere along the line, it stopped being enough.

I'd look up to see a blank expression in his eyes. Was a *Gee, I'm glad to be home with you* glance or some iota of affection too much to want?

They say you only have so many breaths in your lifetime, and I think disappointments might be the same. After a certain number of tries, I began to eat my dinner with the kids and then later on with Holly and just leave something for Wes on the back of the stove. If he didn't care, why should I? Why should I?

Who could I say really loved me? Well, my brother did and so did Danette and my sweet little Holly. But gosh, that was a short list. The love my children and husband professed looked like a lot of lip service to me now. They surely did not *act* like they loved me, and didn't actions speak louder? And did I love myself? Maybe *that* was the problem. I had not worried enough about my own happiness to secure its future. In some really naive way, I think I had always believed that if I took care of my husband's needs, he'd take care of mine in return. Boy, in retrospect? That was stupid. Really stupid. And now I had to figure out *what* exactly I wanted and what I thought *would* make me happy.

I decided a good soak in the tub on the third floor with *Three O'Clock Dinner* would suffice for that day, and dinner with Jonathan would be a thrilling episode to wind it all up. I told myself to quit sulking around and snap out of it. I had many blessings to count, not the least of which was a gorgeous place to go when I needed to run away.

I slipped into the steaming tub of mint-scented bubbles and was soon lost in the world of Charleston society during the 1940s, when who your *people* were determined your social position. It was a time when you could be shunned for generations for some sin committed by a long-dead distant relative. I'd had enough trouble with the living ones. And the dead of my immediate family had not been of much help.

I began to wonder why Pinckney had written a story so clearly defining and then blurring the lines of class struggle when it was something that should never have concerned her for one second. With her background she could have traveled in any circle she pleased. But maybe the fact that some could *not* fascinated her, and perhaps the reason she wrote about it was to understand it. Harlan said that she was a great rule breaker. Like our mother? Is that why Harlan loved Jo Pinckney so much? Besides her illicit affairs with Wendell Willkie and others, what rules had she broken? Well, she never married. Just like our mother never remarried. But as I understood it from Harlan, the reason Josephine never married was because her mother chased away all her suitors because she thought they weren't good enough for her. Her mother was nicknamed Camilla the Gorilla and she sounded like Wes. Another bully. And our mother never remarried because her tattooed lover was so completely and totally inappropriate—and hairy like a gorilla too. Maybe I had something in common with her after all.

I toweled off and pulled the belt of my robe around my waist. It was cool in the house, but I knew the night would be damp and sultry. My hair was guaranteed to rise up like cotton candy once I went out into the evening air, and no doubt we'd stroll over to whatever restaurant he had chosen because walking everywhere was the great advantage of living downtown. It was time for some makeup and a new updo and something to wear without stockings, so I went to work digging in my closet and in my cosmetic tool chest. In both places the pickings were slim.

I twisted my hair up in a pretty silver clamp encrusted with pearls and pulled some wispy pieces down around my face so I didn't look too severe. The last thing I wanted to do was to come off like a dust bowl schoolmarm. In the far reaches of the closet, I had found a pastel floral sundress with little tucks all down the front that was feminine and pretty but didn't make me look like a cat on the prowl. It was something I'd bought for an outdoor ladies' luncheon at the club. Not exactly what a harlot would wear. Within an hour I thought I looked presentable. I began to pace, waiting for Jonathan to arrive. *Was* I a cat on the prowl? Secretly in my heart? No, I was just excited to have something positive to be excited about. And, by the way, it was the first time in three decades that I was planning to go out at night in a dress without panty hose. Wasn't I the wild one?

Okay, that's not entirely true, what I said about not being a cat on the prowl. But if I admitted to myself that I was excited to see Jonathan again, then my behavior would be only marginally better than Wes's when he was in Atlantic City and spent his evening with a professional escort.

I looked in the mirror at myself and wondered just how immoral it was for me, a married woman, to have a third encounter with an old boyfriend. I could excuse the first time because it was just a serendipitous event that rolled out without much forethought or intention on either side. Our first evening together after Harlan's party had been so unexpected and chaste that I wouldn't have been the least bit embarrassed if Wes's boss had walked into the restaurant. I could have introduced Jonathan with a completely clear conscience, explaining away the fact that I was dining with a handsome man from my past and drinking copious amounts of wine by merely claiming the coincidence of our being together as a fluke. *Aren't flukes wonderful?* I would've said that. But now what? If I ran into Harold or some other friend of Wes or someone from work or the club, what would I say? That this was a second fluke? That this man I was with said really nice things to me and my husband never did? That he was my orthopedist? That I was trying on singlehood the way most people try on shoes? That I had maybe sort of left Wes and I was probably going to get a divorce but maybe not because (a) I wasn't sure what I wanted to do with my life but I knew I couldn't take it anymore as it was with all the bimbos and manholes and (b) I was pretty much convinced that Wes didn't love me anymore anyway so why stick around and wait to croak? And I probably wouldn't mention (c), which was the secret money, because who would believe it?

Any way I sliced this devil's food cake, I was a married woman fooling myself that another evening with Jonathan was perfectly socially and morally acceptable. I was going to have to talk to him about some ground rules. He was going to have to understand that I wasn't thinking of sex. Oh, sure. Now how was I going to phrase that total and complete lie in a delicate fashion that I hoped he'd ignore so the onus for anything that happened of an intimate nature would be on him? Oh, brother. I wished I could see six months down the road so that I could know where I was headed. Indecision made me nervous. My heart was racing. I felt my face flush like I had a fever. I trembled all over. I'd never done anything that was really wrong in my whole life, and guilt was rising up in me with a fury. My skin felt itchy.

The doorbell rang.

I was instantly jettisoned out of my mental wreck of a purgatorial daydream. There stood Jonathan, as innocent as a choirboy, in a brown-and-white seersucker suit with an armful of flowers. Stargazer lilies. My favorite. A sense of calm washed over me, as though I was a lonely, marooned debutante and my escort had just appeared through the mist to take my hand and dazzle the world with our elegant waltz to the live music of the Charleston Symphony Orchestra. Yeah, boy. I was in deep merde.

"Hi!" I said and stood back so he could come inside. "Don't you look handsome?"

"Well, thanks, ma'am! I brought you these and by the way . . ."

"Thanks!" I was suddenly nervous again. When was the last time someone brought me flowers?

"You look beautiful, Leslie," he said.

"Aw, come on! I've got to find a vase. These babies need water." I buried my nose in the flowers and inhaled deeply. "Gee! They even smell pretty!" My face was as hot and red as it could be. *Smell pretty?* I looked at him and he didn't seem to mind that I was so awkward. In fact, he was grinning. So I tried to regroup. "Would you like a glass of wine?"

"Sure!"

I turned to go to the kitchen and I could feel his eyes as he followed me down the hall. I was in hot water—like the hot water in a hot tub on the expressway to hell.

"Is white okay? There's a bottle in the fridge and glasses over there. In that cabinet."

I spotted a vase while passing through the dining room and brought it along, thinking it would be just the ticket to show off the magnitude of the bouquet in my other arm.

"Sure! White's great."

I filled the vase with water, took the kitchen shears from the drawer, and started trimming away the bottoms of the stems, trying to appear nonchalant.

"So how was your day?" I said. My heart was beating pretty fast.

"Great, great," he said and pulled the cork. "I love Saturdays. You know I get up and read the paper and putz around the house. Then I do errands, maybe read or exercise, grab some lunch. It's relaxing." He filled two glasses with reasonable portions and handed one to me. "How about you?"

Oh, I wanted to say and did not, *I spent the entire day obsessing over you and what it would be like to be seduced by you. Madly, wildly, and completely seduced. Legs in the air. Hanging on to the headboard. You know, the*

whole shebang, so to speak? And while you're at it, would you mind making
Wesley disappear? Thanks.

Instead I said, "I love the weekends too, although every day has
been like a Saturday since I've been here . . . on this, you know, sort
of vacation I gave myself."

"Is that what it is? A vacation? I mean, for all the talking we've
done, we've only skirted the whole business of what's going on with
you and you know, *him*. That guy with the stupid name?"

"Cheers!" I said and touched the rim of my glass against his.
"Well, that's the million-dollar question, isn't it?"

"I guess so." He smiled at me, and I felt like the rest of the world
didn't matter very much at all. "But we have a six o'clock table at
McCrady's, so we'd probably better start hoofing it in a few. And
your personal physician would be happy to help you sort out your life
over dinner."

"Ah, Jonathan, I think I need a big fat shrink for this one."

"Nah. They're all a bunch of nuts. By the way, how's your arm?"

"Great. Not even a twinge of anything."

"Good, but no circus shenanigans, okay?"

I took a large sip and put my glass down on the counter.

"Got it, boss. Let me close up the house so we can go." I called
out for Miss JP. "Come on, sweetheart! Let's go outside!"

Miss JP, wearing her dressing gown, scampered into the kitchen,
through the den, and directly to the terrace. Jonathan took a sip of
his wine and shook his head.

"Is that dog really a dog?"

"Yeah, and she's great company, as long as you pay the right
amount of homage."

She trotted herself back inside and headed for her daybed in the
corner of the dining room, this one upholstered in the same red
exotic floral chintz as the curtains.

"I've always thought it would be hard to be in a bad mood with a dog in the house. This one would be a laugh a minute!" he said.

"Oh, no! No laughing! Make no mistake about it. If you laugh at her, she'll get her revenge. The other day I snickered at some doggie-diva thing she did and I couldn't find one of my shoes for hours!"

"And people think dogs don't understand humans? Amazing. Come on, let's go."

We turned off most of the lights, locked the doors, and stepped out into the warm late-afternoon air. He looped my arm through his and we made our way toward the restaurant, chatting about every innocuous topic of the day—the weather, Spoleto, the tourists this year, which seemed to have doubled over last year . . . and, of course, he said at least twice how nice it was to see me again.

I decided I was in very safe waters and that all my naughty thoughts would probably never come to fruition, which was undoubtedly for the best. Unfortunately. But he had brought me flowers, had he not?

"Ah! Dr. Ray! So nice to have you with us again!" the maître d' said and shook his hand. "Table sixteen," he said and handed two menus to one of the hostesses. "Please follow Jeanine. She'll show you to your table. Have a wonderful dinner!"

"Thank you, John," Jonathan said.

"Wanna dance?" I said and quietly hummed the opening bars of an oldie we all used to dance to in the seventies. Jonathan just shook his head. "Can you still shag?"

For the uninformed, the shag—in Charleston and indeed all over the Carolinas, Georgia, and Virginia—is not a haircut or a sexual act. It is a dance, and shagging like a native is a passport to your southern authenticity. The shag is also the state dance of South Carolina.

"Madam, you know that I can still cut a rug with the best of them."

"Maybe I'll get to see that sometime." I slipped into my chair, and Jonathan pushed it in for me.

"Well, you may find this hard to believe, but there's actually a shag club in Charleston and I go now and then, just to be sure I'm not getting rusty. When's the last time you went dancing?"

Dancing? I thought about it for a second and quickly decided that dancing between Wes and me was nothing more than an obligatory thing—a spin around the floor at a club dance or a wedding. We had not gone out for an evening of real dancing just for the fun of it since the children were born.

"A long while," I said.

"Hmmm." Jonathan was running down the extensive wine list while the sommelier stood by. He ordered a bottle of white wine and said, "We can start with white and depending on what you'd like to have for dinner, I can order some red too."

"Sure," I said.

"So? A long while, huh? Doesn't Wes like to dance?"

"Not really. He likes to play golf."

"I see."

The sommelier returned and opened our bottle. Jonathan tasted it and nodded for the pour.

"A toast," he said.

"Sure," I said, "to what?"

"More dancing!"

"To more dancing!"

Over a dinner of frisée salads with perfectly poached farm eggs, a rack of lamb with fingerling potatoes and minted peas, and finally pecan pie with some concoction of a ginger whip, I laid out my marriage for Jonathan. He listened like a good friend would, stopped me now and then to ask a question, and nodded when he agreed. And I told him about the money, which pretty much sent his eyebrows to the ceiling.

"So that's where it is, and those are all the reasons I'm here," I said at last. "What would you do?"

"Well, I'm not quite sure. I have to give this some thought. But I know one thing for sure."

"What's that?"

"I don't like seeing you in this conundrum. A gorgeous woman like you ought to be a lot happier than you are."

CHAPTER 12

Lonely Wes

I took myself out to the golf club almost every night. Les's Martha couldn't cook anything except red beans and rice and chicken with enough garlic to kill you. Apparently, the people in wherever she came from never heard of plain string beans or steamed spinach or God, I don't know, but I couldn't take her cooking anymore. I mean, Les was no four-star chef, but at least her cooking didn't fight me all night long. Suddenly I was living on antacids and longing for salad from a bag with lemon juice and olive oil, the way Les always fixed it.

So, as I was saying, I was at the club in the grill room studying the menu and who walks in? Cornelia!

"Hi, Wes!" she said. I stood and she gave me a peck on the cheek. "Sit! Sit!"

I continued to stand. "Well, good evening, Mrs. Stovall! Where's Harold?"

"Oh, he's home in a funk and I figured you might be here."

What in the world? Trouble in paradise *so soon*?

"Well, come join me! This eating alone business is getting old!"

"Are you sure? I don't want to intrude."

I moved around the table to pull back a chair for her. "Don't be ridiculous! Sit! Join me! I haven't even ordered yet!"

"Well, if you're sure . . ."

"I'm positive."

She lowered herself into the chair with a practiced and singular hip-swiveling movement reminiscent of Hollywood bombshells from movies made in the 1930s. You know, it was like watching Lana Turner or Rita Hayworth swing their gorgeous haunches into a sports car without touching a thing. That Harold was some lucky dog.

I took my seat again and snapped my napkin over my lap and motioned for the waiter to bring us another setup and menu.

"Would you like a cocktail? I was just thinking about ordering a martini."

"You know what? Yeah! I'd love a martini."

"Vodka or gin?"

"Vodka, dirty not filthy, straight up with two olives."

"That's just how I like mine!"

"Really? Wow! I had no idea!"

So I ordered our two martinis, and they were there in almost under a minute and we touched the edges of our glasses. A speedy bartender is essential to a good club.

"What are we toasting?"

"I don't know. Let's drink to Thursday night! It's still Thursday, isn't it?"

"Yes, ma'am! It's still Thursday. Here's to it!"

She drank half of it in one sip and I thought, Wow, young people must have cement guts or something.

"That's delicious!" she said.

"Yeah, the guys here make a mean drink." We were looking at the menus. "I'm thinking pork chops. How about you?"

"Pork chops sound great," she said. The waiter arrived and Cornelia looked up at him demurely. "Mr. Carter can order for me." She smiled and handed her menu to him.

Now, in the South and perhaps elsewhere, it was customary for a gentleman to order for a lady, but in the privacy of your own club? It seemed unnecessarily formal. I mean, Les knew all the waitstaff forever and they knew that she liked the Dover sole with the mustard sauce on the side. So if she said she felt like fish or how's the fish, they took her order.

"Well, it looks like we're having pork chops," I said. "Pink on the inside, but not rare."

"They will be perfectly done to your taste," said Diego, who'd worked at the club longer than I could remember. "Would you like another?" He lifted Cornelia's empty glass.

"Why not?" she said.

Why not, indeed? Maybe because you might roll out of your chair and pass out on the floor? But I wasn't saying a word about it.

"So what's going on with Harold? Why's he in a funk?"

"Because, because . . . oh, Wes! Harold can't . . . you know. . . . perform!"

"Oh, Lord."

"Wes? Aren't I too young to face the rest of my life with no more sex?"

Aw, sweet Jesus! Did I really want to know this?

"Um, sweetheart, that's really none of my business, but you know . . . there are pills?" I was whispering because the last thing I wanted was to be overheard.

"He can't take them. They goof up his heart or something."

The pork chops arrived and I realized I was starving. We began to eat.

"Wow. I didn't know. I'm sorry."

"I mean, my whole marriage is just a mess. I broke up his marriage with Danette and she hates me, which is too bad because she's really supposed to be a nice lady."

"She is. She's great. So you feel bad about coming between them?"

"Sort of. The wedding is going to be awkward as hell. But, I mean, I never put a gun to Harold's head, you know."

"True."

"I'm not ever gonna get laid again and oh, Wes, don't you have any advice for me?"

I sat back and wiped my mouth. What could I say? "Honey, if I was that smart, Les would be sitting here right next to me."

"But, Wes? You're the smartest man I've ever met. Surely, you can help me figure this out. Please?"

She put her hand over mine and squeezed it and I thought, Oh, boy, this is way more than I bargained for.

CHAPTER 13

Les Infatuated

The next morning I walked Miss JP to White Point Gardens and back, or maybe I should say we went together and, pardon the pun, stretched our dogs. At home we shared scrambled eggs and toast on the terrace in the fragrant and cool morning air. A good long stroll and breakfast had become our new habit, weather permitting. And Miss JP was such a good listener.

"So, my little furry friend? What do you think I should do about Jonathan?"

She looked at me and turned her head to one side. She seemed to be waiting for me to tell her more, as though how could she offer a worthy opinion when she didn't have enough facts?

"It's kind of a mess, isn't it? A woman my age running around with an old flame? Is that really ever going anywhere? Should I call my husband and see how he's doing? No? You're right. He's probably at work, and we *know* he hates personal phone calls at work."

My relationship with Miss JP was evolving quickly. She looked at me intently then and stood on her hind legs, her front paws landing in my lap as if to say, *Well, I don't think you have to report in to that son of a gun anymore!*

I would have sworn that dog was smiling.

"Come on back inside with me," I said. "It's time to get dressed, and I think today I'm going to exhume Josephine Pinckney's past!"

As Harlan suggested, I decided to knock on the door of the South Carolina Historical Society to see what they had in their collections that pertained to her life. I'd enjoyed *Three O'Clock Dinner* very much, but I wanted to put it in the context of her own life and time. All the things that were so shocking in her day—cross-dressing, lesbians, women smoking, infidelity—had become commonplace in mine. But I wondered, did she view them as commonplace in hers? She came of age in the Roaring Twenties, after all. But she was a founding member of the South Carolina Poetry Society. I couldn't reconcile flappers reading Emily Dickinson. But the changing world around Jo Pinckney must have influenced her behavior because she wrote about infidelity with such authority. Harlan was right to say that she was a bit of a wild child, but I wanted to know it for myself.

Karen Stokes, the researcher who answered the door, was extremely cordial and invited me to come in and have a seat at a table in any room as though I was an old friend coming for a visit to her house. She said she would gladly bring me a box of Josephine's letters.

"We only ask that you sign in here and pay a small fee . . ."

I was happy to comply.

"You have an interest in Josephine Pinckney?" she said.

"Yes, sort of. I'm actually staying in her house across the street."

"At Harlan's?"

"He's my brother."

"Oh! My goodness!" Karen said. "Well, we're so happy to have you here! Harlan is just an amazing friend to the Historical Society."

"Harlan is amazing period. He's the greatest brother in the world."

"I'll bet. Wait! Look at your eyes! I see the family resemblance. Aren't genes funny?"

"Sometimes. Not always."

She stopped and looked at me, probably thinking about some crazy relative she'd been forced to endure out of a sense of duty. One that should've been locked in the attic but that very same one insisted on sitting on the front porch. In her nightgown. Harlan and I had a few of those. Didn't most families? Well, Charlestonians did—it was all that lead that lined the old cisterns that made our grandmother's generation batty.

"Boy, are you ever right about that. Let's get you settled."

I took a seat in one of the two-hundred-year-old rooms that were filled, from the heart pine floors to the sky-high plastered ceilings, with historical reference books on the old oak bookshelves. Over the next few hours, I shuffled through her correspondence with Amy Lowell, Edna St. Vincent Millay, and Alice B. Toklas. There were letters from Prentiss Taylor and Dorothy and DuBose Heyward and plenty of letters from her publishers over the years. But in terms of understanding who she was? I was getting nowhere. I got up to stretch, and Karen Stokes reappeared.

"Can I bring you another box?" she asked.

"No, I think I'm all done for today. I'm not really finding what I want."

"Well, tell me what you're looking for, and maybe I can zero in on something."

"Well, you know Harlan. He's consumed with all things historic, and he adores Josephine Pinckney."

"I know. I've met his dog." She covered her mouth with her hand and giggled. "She's the best-dressed dog in Charleston!"

"I know. I'd kill for her pearls." Then I giggled too. "Anyway, I'm trying to get a sense of who Jo Pinckney was, if she was satisfied with her success and why she sort of disappeared from the spotlight. I mean, I *grew up* here and never even heard of her."

"Ah!" Karen said. "Okay. Look, if you're not here to do scholarly research to produce some new learned opinion on Josephine Pinckney's life, you should read Barbara Bellows's biography. She actually did all the scholarly research. It took her years! It will tell you plenty! Stay right here. I'll get you a copy."

She slipped around the corner and came back with *A Talent for Living*. "Hold on to your hat," she said, handing it to me. "Josephine had some life."

"Thanks."

"You know, we usually don't do this, but you can borrow it if you like, since you're Harlan's sister and all. Besides, it's a contemporary book and we have about a dozen copies."

"Wow! Thanks! I'll return it, I promise."

"Oh, you don't exactly look like a flight risk to me. Anyway, Ms. Bellows spent *years* researching Josephine Pinckney, and I'd say her book is definitely the quintessential book to read to get a good, clear picture of Pinckney's life."

"You've read it?"

"Yep. Twice."

"So what do you think?"

"Well, I loved it."

"This is probably a stupid question, but has Harlan read it?" I began to flip through the opening pages.

"Isn't he thanked in the acknowledgments? I think she gave him his own paragraph. Toward the end?"

She took the book back from me and pointed to Harlan's name.

"My brother! He's something else, isn't he?"

She agreed. I decided to go back home, walk Miss JP, make lunch for myself, and curl up somewhere comfortable to read the Bellows biography.

"Thank you so much," I said to her at the door.

"Are you kidding? I'm so happy to have met you!"

I walked across the street and down the block feeling great. I'd been given a doorway into something and someone who mattered to Harlan, and I'd have the chance to form a reasonable opinion on Miss Pinckney without a dozen years of research. After all, I could be dead of natural causes at any minute.

To my surprise, when I came home and into the kitchen, there was a sandwich wrapped in waxed paper sitting on a plate. I had not made a sandwich. I did not use waxed paper. I unwrapped it and looked inside. It was sliced ham and lettuce on buttered white bread. Every hair on my body stood on end, and a current ran through me as though I accidentally touched a bad wire. There was no ham in the house. I never used butter with ham.

I ate it and it was delicious.

After lunch and a brief escape with Little Miss JP the hound, I settled upstairs on the third floor in the sitting room opposite my bedroom. After I'd skimmed about half the book, I came to realize I was reading about Josephine in the very room where she wrote all her novels. No wonder I kept getting chills. What an eerie feeling!

The house phone rang, shaking me out of my fog. I looked at the caller ID and saw it was Harlan. A relief, to be sure.

"Hey! How's Rome?" I said.

"We're in Florence today and, honey, it is too grand for words! I mean, we were just in the Basilica di Santa Croce, standing next to Galileo's crypt. Can you believe?"

"Awesome!" I said.

"You know, the pope du jour thought he was a heretic and threw him in the clink."

"Didn't they think everyone was a heretic?"

"Practically! So how's the house and my dog?"

"Perfecto! Guess what? I'm reading Barbara Bellows's biography of the real JP."

"And?"

"Well, her momma was a pain in the butt."

"Camilla the Gorilla. That's what they called her."

"So you said. Well, wasn't she just a little bit like our mother? Interfering in our love life every chance she had?"

"I hadn't thought of that."

"And she, like me, never finished her undergraduate degree."

"Hmmm!"

"*And* she had one brother. Like me."

"So are you channeling Josephine Pinckney? Are you her reincarnation?" Harlan laughed.

"No, but there's definitely something weird going on in this house. Last night my nightgown was on my bed when I got home."

"Oh, that's just Victoria Rutledge. She puts out my PJs all the time. She was Miss Jo's baby nurse who stayed with Jo forever."

"Does she make ham and lettuce sandwiches on white bread with butter and wrap them up in waxed paper?"

"Yes! Oh my word! She must really like you, Leslie! It's only when she decides she likes you that you get fed."

"Great. Scare the liver out of me. Go ahead."

"Eat the sandwich."

"I did."

"It's totally harmless. In fact, I think it's kind of nice. Anyway, that house was built in 1836. Only the good Lord knows how many people that house has seen. In the Lowcountry, you're never alone! But you're right. It's haunted like all hell."

"Who's here besides Victoria Rutledge and Jo? Or should I say what's here?"

"I'd go with whom. Let's see. There's Jane Wightman, who built it, and the whole Benjamin McInnes clan, not to mention my Leonard and God knows who else! Wait till you find supper waiting on the stove. Or a whole smoked ham on the sideboard. Apparently, Old Vic was a helluva cook. Leonard still makes cocktails."

I thought, Oh, brother, have you lost your mind? But maybe I was on the edge too.

"Harlan, the day a ham appears on the sideboard? You'll find me at Charleston Place Hotel, okay?"

"Hmmm, well, I'm just saying, don't be surprised. Just because you don't believe in something doesn't mean it's not true."

"I'll let you know. Meanwhile, I'm loving this book. It puts her life right into perspective."

"Well, when I get home, we'll discuss. So now tell me, how's Jonathan?"

"Oh, Lord. He's a wonderful man, Harlan, he really is."

"Is he putting the moves on you?"

"Oh, please. On me? Be serious."

"You listen to your brother, honeybun. Just like Jo Pinckney kept all the boys guessing all the time if she would go for it or not? Well, Jonathan isn't going to play the celibate gentleman forever. The South will rise, if you know what I mean."

"Dear Holy Mother, Harlan Greene! Go wash your mouth out with soap!"

"Or maybe a glass of a great Barolo! I'll call you in a couple of days! Ciao!"

It was pretty hard to get the smirk off my face for the rest of the day. Harlan was so naughty and so hilarious. I needed more Harlan in my life. That was one certainty. How had I allowed Wesley to deny me his company? And maybe I needed more Jonathan too.

Was Wes calling? No.

It was around four in the afternoon and time to start thinking about what I was wearing that night. I decided my simple black dress would do, no matter where we were going. I went back to the Bellows biography, and all the time I was trying to concentrate on what I was reading, I kept thinking about my own mother. She knew Wesley was wrong for me. But I was so stubborn that I married him anyway, because I was pregnant and couldn't see my way to any other choice. But why had I stayed in such an unsatisfactory marriage? Why had I settled for so little? I couldn't help but wonder what my life might have been if I had been smarter about birth control. I might have had a life of romance and real adventure like Pinckney. She'd had lovers galore—married ones, single ones, Lord knows, you had to admire her optimism! She'd apparently even tried to make it happen with a *confirmed bachelor* or two. Shouldn't I have at least one? Straight lover, that is. And, so we're all clear about this, back in Jo's day, *confirmed bachelor* was code for men who preferred their own team.

It was a big world out there, and since marrying Wesley Albert Carter IV I hadn't seen much more of it than Las Vegas, Edinburgh, the Bahamas, and the Piedmont Driving Club. Sorry, it just wasn't enough anymore. I wanted romance and adventure too, and by golly, I was going to have it. I wasn't dead yet. I still wanted to see Italy and France and Switzerland and Napa, so many places. Instead of coming to some conclusion about reconciling with my husband, I found myself becoming more determined to end it. The time and distance away from Wes made it all seem completely ridiculous. I decided to send him an e-mail, a cowardly move but it was all I had the strength for.

I booted up Harlan's computer and clicked on his e-mail program to open it.

Dear Wesley, I wrote, and then I stared at the blinking cursor for a solid five minutes. What was it I wanted to say? Did I want to tell him that I quit? No, I didn't have the courage for that. Not yet. Did I want to say that I needed time? No, because I was taking time and no one was telling me it was past curfew. What I really wanted to say was that he should consider himself to be separated until further notice. But those words seemed too harsh and he wouldn't know what I meant by that. Wesley wasn't guilty of anything except being himself. A brutal, pushy, lying, philandering, manipulating, selfish, cheap bastard. I'd be an idiot to go back to that. So I began to type again.

> I'm not coming back. I'm sorry to tell you this in an e-mail, but I just don't feel like hearing you scream at me ever again. Ever. When I hear you in my head yelling like I killed somebody because the dry cleaning bill went up or I want to give a lunch for my dearest friend's daughter's wedding, my heart starts to pound and I feel like I'm going to be ill. I can't take it, Wes. Not for one more day. I'm sorry. Leslie
> P.S. Please remind Martha to water my topiaries. Thanks.

I reread it ten times. There I was, apologizing when he's the one who should've been apologizing. Was I really sorry that I didn't want any more abuse from him? What was the matter with me? I hit the send button. My marriage was beyond ridiculous.

Jonathan arrived at six on the nose. This time I had put out some pâté and cheese with crackers in the den behind the kitchen. The den was more discreet than the parlor in the front of the house where anybody walking down Chalmers Street could peep through the windows and see me with him. I mean, it wasn't that we had anything to really hide, but still. And it was nice to have the terrace at our disposal too. We could step outside from the den and enjoy Harlan's tiny garden.

There was still at least two hours of daylight left, but I had switched on a couple of small lamps so that when we got home it wouldn't be pitch dark. Coming into dark houses made me nervous for some reason. Maybe a few lights would keep the ghosts at bay. Anyway, there stood Jonathan, wearing a multicolored striped seersucker suit, and he smelled like something so delicious it was all I could do not to bury my nose in his neck.

"You smell so good!" I said. "Come in!"

"Thanks! And you look beautiful!"

"Well, thanks! Do we have time for a glass of champagne? Or something else?" Like a big make-out session?

"Why not? Our table's at seven. What are you grinning about?"

"Oh, nothing! I was just wondering how all your seersucker will fly in California?"

"Good question."

We smiled. "And where are we headed tonight?"

"FIG. Very groovy restaurant on East Bay. All the groovy people go there. It seems that if the restaurant has just one name, it's a groovy place. You know, like Cypress, Husk, McCrady's, FIG, Fish . . ."

"That's the dumbest thing I've ever heard you say because you also love the Restaurant at Charleston Place and Grill 225 and Rue de Jean and High Cotton and need I go on? And they're all pretty cool, if you ask me, Dr. Groovy. Now, about that drink?"

He smiled at me and said, "Hmmm. I think I feel like a vodka and tonic. It's been so muggy all day."

"That sounds great! You know where the vodka is. I'll dismember a lime."

I could see him smile in my peripheral vision.

"You do that," he said.

He filled two highball glasses with ice from the door of the refrigerator and pulled the vodka and a bottle of warm tonic from the liquor cabinet. Jonathan went about fixing our drinks, and I squeezed two wedges of lime into the glasses.

"So how was your day?" he asked.

"Awesome. Yours?"

"Two torn Achilles and a bunch of sprained wrists and ankles, but wait! I did have a chance to give an opinion on four, count them, four knee replacements! Ain't nobody on the planet who can do a knee like me!"

"Four different patients?"

"Yep! Pretty exciting, those knee replacements. Not as interesting as shoulders, but better than hips. Cheers!"

"Cheers. Would you like a little pâté?"

"Sure! So what made your day awesome?"

I walked over to the coffee table in the den and spread some pâté on a cracker and handed it to him. "I spent the day reading a biography of Josephine Pinckney." *And I sent an e-mail to Wes telling him it was over. And a ghost made me a sandwich.*

"So Harlan made you drink the Kool-Aid too? Thanks."

"I guess. But, heck, this was *her* house. Seems rude not to care, doesn't it?"

"You see, this is what I always loved about you."

"What?"

"That you care. You actually honestly and truly care about other people besides yourself to the point you'd remark on how to be considerate of a woman who's been dead for how long?"

"Early 1950s."

"That's over sixty years. Can I help myself to another?" He cut a piece of pâté and spread it on a cracker.

"Sure! Yeah, but not when you read about her life. Seems like she could just walk in here from another room, and she'd fit right in with everything in 2012."

"A woman ahead of her time."

"*Way* ahead of her time." I stopped and watched him drain his glass. He was staring at me. "What are you looking at?"

"I'm looking at you."

"Why? Is my mascara running?" I wiped under my eyes, but my fingers were clean. "Do I have lipstick on my teeth?"

"No, you silly girl! You're perfect. I was just thinking about messing up your hair."

Well, here we were at the moment of truth. Harlan was right.

"Don't you dare! Do you know how long it took to blow it out?" I was playing dumb for the moment. I looked at my wristwatch. "Whoops! It's getting on to six thirty! We'd better start going, right?"

He looked at me with one of those male confident smiles that said, *I've got the hook in you, my little tuna, and I'll reel you in when I'm ready.*

"Sure, let's start moving," he said and laughed a little.

I took the last sip of my drink and handed him my glass. Wait, wasn't it less than an hour ago that I said I wanted romance and adventure? I decided that therein lies the difference between dreams and reality. Dreams made your eyes sparkle over the possibilities of doing something new and exciting. Reality made the rest of you break a sweat in panic. I was terrified.

The restaurant host took us to our table right away, and to my surprise we were seated next to the mayor of Atlanta, Kasim Reed, sitting with Mayor Joe Riley of Charleston and six other men. I wondered what Mayor Reed was doing here. It probably had something to do with tourism. Somehow, Charleston seemed to ooze a feeling of well-being and prosperity, despite all the reports of economic reversals around the country. And there was so much to do here it boggled the mind. Perhaps most important, the city was organized around every kind of activity a tourist could want—golf, tennis, water sports, fishing, eco-tours, plantations, shopping, museums, and historical events—the list went on and on.

"What do you think he's doing here?" I said to Jonathan.

"Maybe he's just here for dinner," he said. "The food is really great."

"Very funny," I said.

We ordered our meal. I was having the rutabaga soup and the tilefish, and Jonathan ordered the scallops and the fish stew.

"This calls for a hearty white or even a light red. Do you have a preference?"

Did I have a preference? When on earth was the last time someone asked me about my personal preference?

"Oh, why don't you just choose something?"

"Well, do you feel like California or Italy?"

"To be honest, I've never been to either place."

He lowered the wine list and stared at me. "Really?"

"Yes. I know, pitiful."

"Do you hate to fly or something?"

"Not at all. And I'd love to go to California and see the wine country and to Italy to see, well, thousands of years of history. Maybe throw a coin in a fountain, eat a bowl of pasta, ride a Vespa?"

The sommelier came over and stood at Jonathan's side waiting patiently.

"We'll have a bottle of the Luigi Ferrando," Jonathan said.

"That sounds so great! Do you know that wine?" I said.

"Nope. I just picked the one that had a name I could pronounce."

We had a good laugh at that. I loved that he wasn't so pretentious.

"You are so adorable," I said.

"I'm going to whisk you away to Italy and to California too."

"Okay. Let's go!" I giggled at the thought of it.

The sommelier returned, Jonathan gave the *Chateau Whatever He Ordered* a sniff and a sip and a nod. The sommelier poured two glasses for us. I sat back, sipping and dreaming about traveling all over Italy with Jonathan. Why, I *knew* I'd have a wonderful time! Wonderful! When had I ever said that?

"You have the funniest look on your face! What are you thinking about?"

Having crazy sex all over Italy with you. Which I did not say. I simply said, "Oh, nothing. You know, Italy, I guess. And how much fun we might have."

"How much fun we *will* have!" He raised his glass. "Cheers! So tell me some more about our Miss Pinckney."

This is what I loved about Jonathan—he remembered how I had spent my day. He actually wanted to hear about it. Wes would have harrumphed and looked to Harold to discuss the Braves or some golf course he had heard about and wanted to play.

"Well, I'll tell you this much. She was predestined for infamy," I said.

"How so?"

"To begin with, she was the very first student enrolled at Ashley Hall."

"Your alma mater."

"Yes. But she also started their literary magazine—she was just a young girl."

"Why is that so unusual?"

"Well, because she stood up for what she wanted when she was merely fourteen? And later on, in only her twenties, she became a founding member of the Poetry Society of South Carolina. However, she spent the next fifteen years fighting to maintain credit for that and many other things she did. In those days, the gentlemen had a tendency to swallow up the accomplishments of the ladies."

"Not so in today's world. At least not in my practice. And you know what? Sometimes women make better doctors, especially when the patient is a child or geriatric. Women just naturally have more compassion."

It was a slightly sexist remark, but I ignored it. If anything, Jonathan was always well intentioned.

"I agree, but it's how it was then. Anyway, at some point she broke away from the Poetry Society and began to travel with her mother all over the place. She spent a lot of summers in Massachusetts, and she got her heart completely broken by a fellow her mother adored and was dying for her to marry. His name was Dick Wigglesworth."

"That's some name."

"Yes. Unfortunate. Old Boston family, he was the seventh-generation Harvard Law School graduate. His mother's brother-in-law was Oliver Wendell Holmes. I mean, we're talking about some seriously pedigreed Yankees."

"I have to imagine there were and still are more than a *few*," Jonathan said, laughing.

"There are scads of them, and we both know it."

"Yes, but would our *grandparents* have admitted it?"

"In a pig's eye, honey. Anyway, she takes old Dick out . . ."

"What a curious string of words."

"Jonathan Ray! Hush your mouth! In a *canoe*! A *canoe*! Let me rephrase! She goes for a canoe outing one day and she suggests they elope."

"Oh, I see."

"Please! So he said something terrible to her like *he felt unable to screw up enough enthusiasm for something so, so* . . . what was the term he used? *Irrevocable!* That's it!"

"Jeez. Not the most sensitive way to put it. She must've been pretty unhappy to hear about his lack of enthusiasm!"

Our appetizers arrived. "This looks delicious! Well, of course, but wait; he moved to Berlin with some government job and came out of the closet."

"That must've been a shock."

"I'll say, but you see, that's the whole thing. She didn't have the greatest judgment in the world when it came to men. And the parade of men was impressive in its numbers. More than a couple of them were married, and there is a long list of her short-term affairs. But the one man she was really serious about, besides Dick Wigglesworth, was Thomas Waring."

"From the *Post and Courier* newspaper?"

"Yes. Even though he was married and they made every effort to be discreet, their love affair was pretty well known among their friends. It went on for years until he died."

"Love affairs are *supposed* to be discreet when you're married."

"What are you telling me?" I said, caught off balance. *Does he think we're lovers?* "Aren't we discreet?"

"Are we having a love affair?" Jonathan was now grinning all over in delight.

For whatever crazy reason I had, I decided to take the leap and be bold.

I said, "Yes, although it's kind of an Abelard and Heloise business at the moment, I'd say we are!" And then I mumbled, "Sort of."

We both laughed then, and he leaned across the table, covering my hand with his.

"Listen, I know you're still married. I don't want to mortify you by being too forward. But I am going to tell you this. As much as I swore off any more commitments of a romantic nature years ago, I'm not letting you get away again. But I'm not in a hurry, either. You have a lot to sort out. I want to be the one you lean on."

"Oh, Jonathan, thank you . . ."

"No. This isn't about thanks. I'm not doing you a special favor. I happen to love being with you. Just like when we were kids, I feel so great when I'm with you. And when I'm not with you, all l can think about is seeing you again. I'm like a twenty-year-old idiot! I mean it, Les. I'm going to get you through whatever you have to do to be free of Wes, and then, well, I guess we'll see how we feel. I mean, come on, so far this is pretty wonderful, isn't it?"

"Yep. It sure is."

"And you'd come visit me in Napa, wouldn't you?"

"Of course!" Was he really going to do this?

The people at the table with the mayors started taking pictures of one another, and some of the guests hopped over to them to get a picture with the mayors too. I looked back at Jonathan and thought for a moment about all the things he had just said to me.

"Yes, but while I'm so uncertain about many things, I know this much for sure. We're here together for a reason. Fate, call it what you want. Wasn't it Fate that threw me in a manhole in Scotland to wake me up from my stupid life?"

"I'd say so."

"Horrible. Anyway, I think that sometimes opportunity is awfully hard to recognize. Because isn't timing important? How's our timing?"

"Well, if our children were still little, I'd say lousy. But I think at this point, we're old enough to do what we want to do. Would you like dessert?"

"No, no. Rarely touch the stuff. Why don't we go back to Harlan's and have a nightcap?"

"That sounds like an excellent idea."

We walked back to Chalmers Street arm in arm, our gait perfectly matched, and the night air was as sweet as mortal sin. When we got home, Miss JP went flying to Jonathan. I took this as a good sign. I let Miss JP out into the garden and while I waited for her to do her best, Jonathan poured us a little cognac in Harlan's gorgeous Waterford snifters.

He brought me mine, put his arm around my waist, and I knew I was about to be kissed. But he started with my neck (which as you might imagine was practically virgin territory) and, sugar, that's all I'm saying. It was like an episode of *The Young and the Restless* com-

bined with the Old and the Determined. I perspired. I have not perspired in a bed since I had the flu ten years ago. Even Miss JP ran
inside and up the stairs. We found her the next morning in Harlan's
room under his pillows curled up with a pair of his socks.

"How old are we?" Jonathan asked me over coffee, looking
shameless and happy.

"Old enough to do whatever we want," I said and smiled like
Mona Lisa.

Maybe I'd move to Napa, too.

CHAPTER 14

Wes Is Jealous?

It was the tenth e-mail from Cornelia that day. She was driving me nuts. I didn't like her sending me e-mail to begin with, and second, I sure didn't want them on the company's computers. Didn't she know that? No. She was young and impulsive and undisciplined and Harold sure had his hands full. No, I told her, I didn't want to talk to her over lunch at the Ritz in Buckhead where they had two hundred bedrooms upstairs and she'd have a key, which I would never ever use. We'd be seen eating a hamburger and Harold would hear about it and he would think the worst. I say that only because if I was in his position, I would think the worst. But let's get this straight. Even if she did have a head of thick copper-colored hair that drove me crazy, a face like the Madonna, and a gorgeous body to boot, I wouldn't screw my best friend's wife for all the money in this world. I mean, I was a man of principle.

Poor Harold. Impotence is bad. Very bad. Especially when he has a young wife. But there has to be something he can do about it. If he couldn't take the pill, there had to be other ways. I started researching it on the Internet and found a medical site that had all sorts of information on a surgical procedure that seemed to have a very high rate of success. It was some kind of a pump. "Oh, yeah," I said to the thin air. I remembered some guys in the locker room talking about that.

The intercom buzzed.

"I've got Cornelia Stovall on line two for you?" said Gina.

"Ah, jeez. Okay. Put her through."

"Wes? I'm sorry to bother you, but . . ."

"Cornelia? I've got about two seconds for you this morning. I'm very busy."

"Wes, I'm really, seriously thinking of leaving Harold, and before I pull the trigger, I just wanted to talk to you about it, that's all."

"Where are you?"

"In the lobby of your building."

Great, I thought. This is just great. I hit the print button on my computer.

"Well, then, come on up." Just what the hell was I supposed to say?

Minutes later, in she walked all decked out in some kind of dress the female meteorologists wear on television—short and tight with way too much cleavage. Gina's eyes were as big as dinner plates as she led her into my office. I didn't grow up with women who dressed like Cornelia during the daytime. But Cornelia's breed of cat didn't seem too concerned over whether anyone thought they were a lady or not.

"Hi, sweetheart! Come in! Can I get you a Coke?"

"Hey, Wes." She kissed my cheek. "Do you have a Diet Coke? In those little bottles?"

"Gina? Can you . . . ?"

Gina's eyebrows were scraping the ceiling. "Sure! Right away."

Gina closed the door and Cornelia turned to me.

"Well, she's pretty."

She leaned her head in the direction of the office door, like she was suspicious that I was up to no good with my secretary. I wanted to say, *Listen, honey, you don't poop where you eat,* but since she and Harold had done exactly that, there was no reason to insult her. No reason whatsoever.

"Aw, come on. She's just a kid. Anyway, let's sit over here." She sat on the sofa and I sat in an armchair opposite her. "Make yourself at home and tell me what's going on."

Gina returned with a glass of ice and an opened bottle of Diet Coke and placed it on the coffee table in front of her.

"Thanks, Gina," I said.

"No problem," Gina said and left, only to return seconds later with some papers. Her face was a deep red. "You printed this?"

I looked at all the pages of information on penile implants and thought, Oh, boy, this is gonna fly around the office like pollen.

"Excuse me for a moment, Cornelia," I said and took Gina by the arm out to the hall. As soon as we were out of earshot from Cornelia I whispered to her, "That stuff wasn't for me."

"Not my beeswax, Wes."

Poor Gina was looking in every direction except where my face was.

"It's for her husband, my friend in there, who she's thinking of divorcing because they've got a problem, if you know what I mean."

"Do you mind if I take an early lunch?"

"No! Of course not! Go. And Gina?"

"What?"

"It's probably best if this news doesn't travel."

"I got it, Wes. Don't worry. I like my job."

"Good girl. Just send my calls to voice mail, okay?"

"Sure thing."

See? That's why I liked her so much! She understood discretion. And she's right. Because if she started a rumor about me, I'd throw her out so fast she wouldn't know what hit her. She knew it too.

I went back in my office and sat down, placing the papers on the table, facedown so Cornelia couldn't read what they were about.

"Okay, so talk to me. What's going on?"

"Well, Wes, as you know, things aren't good."

She turned on the waterworks, and her tears began to flow. Big. Crocodile. Tears. Aw, God. I didn't have the time for this. I reached for the tissues and put the box in front of her.

"I'm sorry."

"Things in the bedroom are an utter failure . . ."

"Come on, Cornelia, let's dry your eyes now. I've been doing a little research on alternatives for Harold and look what I found on the Internet." I handed the papers to her.

She sniffed loudly and blew her nose and began to read. "I sure as hell don't see him getting a pump sewn into his you-know-what." She put the papers back on the table.

"So what are you saying?"

"I think Harold wants me to leave. He's so humiliated. I think we'd be better off." She started to cry again.

"Oh, Cornelia honey, I'm so sorry." I held the tissue box out for her.

"Thanks. It wasn't supposed to work out like this, you know?"

"Yeah, I know." The poor girl. I felt very bad for her. "So where are you going to go?"

"I don't know. Paolo and Lisette have enough trouble with his kids, and I don't have any money. And I don't want to ask Harold for anything. And I don't even have a job anymore, never mind a place to lay my weary head. Oh, Wes! What am I going to do?"

Then she looked at me through her tears and her big blue eyes, and she sat up straight, pulling in her stomach and accentuating her best features, and she waited. OH. MY. GOD. She wanted to come to *my* house.

"Look, Cornelia, Harold has a legal and a moral obligation to take care of you, even though you haven't been married for so long. I've known him almost all my life, and he's not the kind of man who would throw you out like that. You have to talk to him."

"Wesley, I was just thinking that with Les being gone and all, y'all have room, don't you?"

"Yeah, honey, but not for a scandal."

"Oh my God! You don't think I'm coming on to you, do you?"

"Frankly, Cornelia, no." Yes, she was. "But if anybody heard about you sleeping under our roof, I'd never reconcile with Leslie."

"You must love her a lot," she said.

"We've been together since we were in college."

"Wow. Amazing. How's she doing down in Charleston?"

"Well, to tell you the truth, we're not speaking at the moment."

She looked at me with the strangest expression and said, "Wes? What makes you think only marriages like mine can pop like a bubble?"

"What do you mean?"

"Look, Les is a nice-looking woman, for her age, I mean. And she's dignified."

"And?"

"And if I'd been her after that night of the catfight at the club? Honey? That was all so stupid. I'm just saying I would've walked out too. You were yelling at her. For what? She didn't do anything except take an elegant step back and let us all look like the fools we were."

"Really?"

"Yeah, really. If y'all aren't speaking, I think I'd go pay her a visit and see what's up before it's too late. Take her flowers."

"Oh, she'll come around. You don't know my Leslie. She can't live without me for too long."

"If you say so."

"Look," I said and stood, indicating this meeting was over. "You go on home, Cornelia, and talk to Harold. Ask him what he wants you to do. I think when he learns that you were thinking he wanted you to leave, you'll be very surprised. Harold loves you, don't you know that? Besides, we're talking marriage here, which is way more important than just living together or something. Pretty soon we'll all be back at the club together and laughing about this."

She looked at me, shook that hair of hers, and nodded. Finally, she stood. "I hope so, Wes. I hope you're right."

I walked to the door and opened it for her. "If I can do anything, just call me, okay?"

"You're a sweetie," she said and gave me a kiss on my cheek.

I watched her walk down the hall to the elevators, and every muscle in my body relaxed. Disaster avoided! I could've had her panties off in five minutes.

I could hear my cell phone ringing back in my office. I picked it up when I got back and read the caller ID. I had missed a call from Charlotte. I hit redial and she picked up right away.

"Dad?"

"Yeah, honey? What's going on?"

"You see the *Atlanta Journal Constitution* today?"

She didn't know I read the *Wall Street Journal*? Didn't she grow up in my house?

"Nope. That's not my paper. I read the . . ."

"Yeah, I know, but you might want to pick up a copy and check out the front page."

"Why's that?"

"Business section. Check it out. Then call me back."

"Okay."

I hung up. What now? I didn't have time for some Mystery Tour. I'd already blown half the day with Harold's problems. I stuck my head outside my office and spotted a copy of the newspaper on Gina's desk. Did she say front page? Of what section? Business? Yes, business.

Okay, I had it and all right, our mayor was there in Charleston with a bunch of guys . . .

Wait! Was that Les in the background? I needed a magnifying glass.

There was one in my office. I went back in, laid the paper across my desk, and examined it. It was Les all right. Plain as day. There was a man with her. What the hell? I could feel my blood pressure going up. Here I was warding off a toss in the hay with Cornelia like she's got some kind of a terrible disease and Les was down in Charleston living it up with another man! Well, screw that! I didn't like this picture one little bit.

I called Harold.

"Harold? Hey, it's me, Wes. I'm taking the day off. Want to play a round?"

"Sure! Why not?"

"See you there in an hour."

"Sounds great."

Gina was returning to her office just as I was leaving mine.

"Hi, I'm out of here for the rest of the day. Got some things to take care of."

"Oh, sure! Is everything okay?"

"Of course! I'll be on my cell if anyone needs me. Just text me, okay?"

"You got it!"

I drove to the club and Harold was there in the locker room, changing his shoes.

"You talk to Cornelia?" I said. I swapped my street shoes for my golf shoes, pushed the locker door shut with a thud, and sat on the bench next to him to do the same.

"Not since breakfast. Wes, this whole thing is turning into a nightmare."

"Yeah, I got that. I got that in spades. She was in my office this morning, bawling her eyes out."

"Aw, man. I *told* her not to bother you."

"Yeah, well, who's she going to call? I'm your closest friend." I took off my shirt and tie and traded it for the knit shirt I had in my duffel.

"I guess. But what a mess, huh?"

"Every guy over sixty has this happen once in a while. It's not about desire. It's about blood flow. And it's fixable!" I unzipped my trousers and tucked in my shirt.

"Women. Come on. Let's go hit a bucket of balls."

We picked up our clubs from the starter's room, walked out to the driving range, and hit about a hundred balls. Neither one of us was swinging worth a damn. I kept hooking mine into the trees, and Harold couldn't get more than a hundred and twenty yards on his.

"What do you say we stop killing birds and embarrassing ourselves and go get lunch?"

"You see what I'm doing here?" Harold said. "Good grief. Couldn't hit the broad side of a barn today."

"So," I said after we ordered our food. "There's a picture in the *AJC* of Leslie in the background of a photograph of our mayor and the mayor of Charleston. She's with another man."

"You're shitting me."

"Nope. And she's smiling."

"Holy crap. What are you gonna do?"

"I don't know. I gotta tell you, Harold, I was shocked right out of my shorts. Shocked."

"Didn't you tell me that you got a rather strong e-mail from her that she wasn't coming back?"

"Yeah. She said that."

"Didn't she say something to the effect that you should consider you two to be separated?"

"Yeah. But I didn't think she really meant it like that. Harold! That was *my* Leslie in that photograph smiling and enjoying the company of another man in a restaurant nice enough for two very important mayors!"

"Well, now, Wes? That's an interesting comment. Are you pissed because she was smiling because another man made her smile or because he took her to a really nice place, which implies he's trying to impress her? And one other thing. She's not exactly *your* Leslie."

I thought about that while the waiters put our food down in front of us.

"Yeah, I guess she's really not. Harold, you know what?"

"What?"

"I miss her. You can't believe how hard it is to get along without her. I have to take my shirts to the cleaners, I have to fix my own breakfast—I mean, it's damn lonely. Can you pass the mustard?"

"Yeah. Here. Wes, I don't know what to tell you. To begin with, I have a really hard time thinking about Les and some other guy."

"How do you think I feel?"

After lunch we went out to play nine holes, and the afternoon sun was bearing down on us something fierce. Still, we played some of the best golf we'd played in ages.

Every other shot Harold would say, "Women."

And I would reply, "You're telling me?"

"You know what, Harold?" I hit my ball a clean two hundred yards, and it landed right in the middle of the fairway. "I was just thinking about something."

"What's that?" He hit the ball with a clean *thwack,* and it landed close to the pin.

"Nice shot! You put that baby right up there on the dance floor!"

"Thanks. Now what are you thinking about?"

"Well, you don't really want more kids anyway, do you?"

"Whaddya out of your cotton-picking mind?"

"What if Cornelia gets pregnant?"

The look on Harold's face was beyond horror. I thought he might faint.

"You know, my momma used to say, marry in haste, repent at leisure. She sure had my number. I'm really starting to think this marriage was a mistake."

"Well, she is young."

"Yeah, *too* young. Are you really going to divorce Les?"

"Nah, I'm gonna make her beg to come home. Why should I spend the money until I have to?"

"So you're not all that upset about her being with that guy in the restaurant?"

"I don't love it, but isn't she the one who said I should consider us to be separated? I'm saving this nugget for later, if I need it. Wouldn't you?"

"Oh, man. I'm the litigator, and still, I wouldn't want to be on the other side of the table from you."

"Thanks. Now let's get outta here before we drop dead from this heat and the women inherit everything."

"Wes? I gotta tell you this, you ought to convince her to come home. She's a good woman."

"Probably should. It would sure make my life a lot easier."

"And think of all the money you'll save. I know these shrinks who run a very high end business. They save all kinds of marriages."

"Well, let me have the number."

We hit the showers. The soap and hot water felt so good. And then I was afraid my luck had run out. I felt a lump. This could not be a good thing.

CHAPTER 15

Les Dances

It was the last week of July. Jonathan and I were having our daily midmorning chat. I told him that I thought it was high time I made dinner for him, and he seemed delighted by the idea. The man had been spoiling me to pieces. We'd been to every restaurant in the city, west of the Ashley and east of the Cooper. We'd had take-out Chinese, Japanese, and Thai at his house on Sullivans Island and Harlan's at least twice a week. It was high time I stepped up and cooked. The sling was long gone.

"What's your favorite meal of all time?"

"Whatever you're in the mood to fix," he said.

"So if I made fricassee of calves' liver and onions stuffed in the spleen of an iguana with boiled Brussels sprouts on the side, you'd be thrilled?" It was the weirdest combination I could think of at that moment.

"I'd eat mud pie made from real mud if you put it in front of me."

"You're so full of it!" I laughed.

"Yes. Yes, I am. In any case, give me a clue on the menu and I'll bring the wine."

"Deal. I'll call you after I shop. But I was thinking mousse of sole or whatever whitefish I can find, with a lobster sauce, little potatoes, and a nice salad, and maybe some kind of fruit for dessert? How does that sound?"

"It sounds like a lot of work. I don't want you to go to so much trouble."

"Jonathan? I'll throw burgers on the grill another night. You've taken me out to dinner so many times that I need to put on the dog for you. Besides, my brother's kitchen has every gadget you can think of, so modern inventions will be doing most of the work."

"Well, this dog appreciates it. I'm already starving. Look what you've done to me. It's only ten thirty and my mouth is watering for lunch."

"Okay, my dear. I'll call you in a bit."

"Great! I'll talk to you later."

I got my things together and made a list for the grocery store. Just as I was pulling my phone off the charger, it rang. It was Wes. I had not heard from him since I e-mailed him I wasn't coming home, which was further proof to me that I shouldn't be married to him. Since I'd told him I didn't want to hear him scream ever again, I thought, Well, if he's calling me now, he's probably not going to scream. So I answered it.

"Wes?"

I thought I heard a man sobbing on the other end of the phone. Was it Wes?

"Wes? Talk to me! Are you all right? Is Charlotte okay? Dear God, nothing's happened to Holly! Wes! Answer me!"

"I have cancer," he said with huge gulping sobs.

"Oh, my God! Wes! *What* are you telling me?"

"I have to have an operation."

He sobbed some more, and I said, "Oh, Lord, Wes. I'm so sorry. Do you want to tell me what kind?"

"Testicular. I'm scared, Les! I might die!"

"You're not going to die, Wesley. You're going to be fine." I didn't know that obviously, but my reflex was to reassure him. "Did your doctor say it spread?"

Wes cleared his throat and regained control of himself. "He's not going to know until they take out the tumor, and I guess some tissue around it?"

"Who's your doctor? I mean, are you sure it's the best guy?"

"Yeah, he is. This guy is Harold's client and he's the top urologist in Atlanta for this kind of thing. Don't worry, I checked him out too. He's the one to get. Jesus, Les." He sighed so powerfully I could almost feel his breath. "I wish you'd come home and take care of me."

I knew that was coming.

"When's your surgery?"

"August thirteenth. It was the first date I could get."

"I'll try, Wes. Let me think about it."

There was dead silence. Then he exploded.

"*Think* about it? Really? Well, *that's* nice! I'm your *husband*, Les! You're *supposed* to take care of me!"

"Excuse me, but I'm no longer taking orders from you!"

"Really?"

"Yes, really! And lower your voice or I'm hanging up."

"You don't tell *me* what to do either!"

"Hey, Wes? Why don't you ask Cornelia to come sit with you like you asked her to sit with me in Edinburgh?" I couldn't believe I'd said that to him, but at least he quieted down.

"Let me ask *you* something, Leslie. Just who's the man you're having a nice cozy dinner with in the picture I saw in the *Atlanta Journal Constitution*?"

Oh! My! God!

"What? Oh, please. He's just an old friend I grew up with. Besides, he's got nothing to do with you and me." When did I learn to lie like that?

"Okay, Leslie. Have it your way. Your husband's got *cancer* and you'll *think* about whether or not you want to see him through major surgery. Very nice. Sorry I bothered you."

The phone went dead.

I collapsed in a chair, practically breathless. It wasn't like I hated Wes or *anything* remotely close to that and I *was* really sorry to hear his news. But I really didn't want to walk back into that life, get trapped in the quicksand of it, and disappear. I just didn't want the anxiety of being there or of leaving again. I didn't need it, and to tell the truth, I was so happy in Charleston, the happiest I'd been in years. Why would I throw it all away? To go home to a screaming maniac? I don't think so. What *was* I going to do about Wes?

For the moment, I was going to put it all out of my mind and concentrate on making the most beautiful dinner I'd ever prepared. I needed to get my bearings again.

"I'll be right back, Miss Jo! Just going to the grocery store."

I would swear on a stack of bibles that the dog speaks English. She practically nodded at me and hopped on her dining room bed.

Of course, it was ridiculous to think I could temporarily ignore Wes's phone call. It was all I could think about. I drove Harlan's crazy car down to Harris Teeter, and as I went up one aisle and down the other, dropping things into the cart I'd never eat, I thought about how frightened Wes sounded. He probably really *was* scared. On the other hand, we weren't on the phone for two minutes before he was yelling and pushing me around again. And what did I know about testicular cancer? Nothing except that it was pretty rare. I'd google it. I'd ask Jonathan. I wondered what he would say when I told him the news. I paid for my groceries, pushed the cart outside, and starting loading the bags into the trunk.

My cell phone rang and I looked at the caller ID. It was Charlotte. Even though cars were backing out and pulling in all around me, I answered.

"Hi, sweetheart," I said. "I'm just at the grocery store in the parking lot. It's one hundred degrees in the shade. I'll be home in five minutes. Can I call you back?"

"Mom! Don't hang up! You know Daddy has cancer, right?"

"Yes, I spoke to him this morning."

"Mom! This is a *very* big deal!"

"Of course it is! Did you hear me say it wasn't?"

"He told me you weren't even coming home for his surgery!"

"Charlotte, listen to me. Don't get involved with this. It's between Daddy and me."

"Mom! Even Bertie is flying home from Kathmandu!"

"Which your father probably demanded?"

"I don't know, but Dad's terrified. You've *got* to be here!"

"Guess what? I don't need you to tell me what I have to do. I told him I'd consider it."

"Oh, nice. I bet *that* made him feel better."

"It is no longer my job to make him feel better. Or to take any lip from you. Is that clear?"

Silence.

"Mom? What's happened to you?"

"Charlotte? What newspaper do you read?"

"The *AJC,* like everybody else. Why?"

"Who do you think might have called your father and told him to check out a picture with Mayor Reed in the foreground?"

Silence.

"Did he tell you I told him?"

"No. He did not. You just did."

Pause.

"Mom? Look, I probably shouldn't have told him, but I did because I think the two of you are in trouble. You're my mother . . ."

"I'd still be your mother if I moved to Mars."

"Daddy is so short tempered and miserable since you've been gone. I don't care what he says or how he acts, he loves you, Mom. And now he's got this horrible cancer. You can tell me to mind my own business if you want, but I really think you ought to come home. I mean, *please* come home because if anything happens to him I couldn't take it if I didn't have you to help me get through it."

"Charlotte? I never told him I wouldn't come. I said I'd think about it. Okay? And nothing's going to happen to him. He's going to be just fine."

"Mom, I know Dad's being very dramatic about this and I'm sure you're right, but what if the anesthesiologist gives him too much juice and his heart stops?"

"Now who's being dramatic?"

"That's how Jim Henson died, you know, the guy who created the Muppets? If it could happen to *him* . . ."

"Charlotte, come on now. And besides, Jim Henson died from pneumonia."

"I'm just saying a million things can go wrong. People die in hospitals all the time. There's this disease called MRSA? And there's C. diff?"

"Let's talk later, okay?"

We hung up and I looked at my phone.

"You're just like your father," I said, threw it in my purse, and got in the car.

So Bertie had been guilt tripped into getting on a plane and coming home. As I was driving back to Harlan's, I thought, Wes must have really laid it on thick. But if Wes knew anything, it was how to work your gizzards until he got what he wanted. And he had to have an audience. Why had it taken me so long to see that? In any case, it would be awfully nice to lay my eyes on my only son. I had not seen him in almost a year. But there was also nothing to stop Bertie from making a side trip to see me in Charleston, was there?

I brought all the groceries inside the house. Someone had set the table, and it was set perfectly as though they already knew what I was going to prepare.

"Thank you!" I called out to the thin air. "I wish you would iron." Then I laughed.

My mind was still glued to Wes. I put everything away as quickly as I could and booted up Harlan's computer. I googled *testicular cancer* and got thousands of sites offering information in seconds. Memorial Sloan-Kettering had tons of information and I felt much better after I read it. The odds were that Wes was going to be fine. But still, the Big C was scary like all hell.

I called Danette while I sliced and diced. She answered on the third ring.

"Hey!" I said. "Did you hear the news?"

"What news? I was just going to call you!"

"About Wes?"

"No. What?"

I told her the whole story about Wes's cancer and she said, "Why in the world didn't Harold tell me?"

"Because he's probably focused on his life. Anyway, I have to figure out whether or not I'm going to come back and get Wes through his ordeal."

"Well, I probably would if I were you."

"Really? I guess I probably will."

"Yeah. You have to. I mean, who's he got? Charlotte? Harold? Paolo? Look, if you decide to come to Atlanta, you know you're welcome to stay here with me. And I think I heard they do that surgery practically on an outpatient basis. It's pretty routine."

"Unless it's spread," I said.

"Let's hope not. Meanwhile, on a lighter note, I've got a hot date tonight."

"How's that going?"

"Um. My coat's shiny."

"Girl?"

Then we *really* laughed.

"Well, I've got to run too. Jonathan's coming for dinner, and I've got a ton of things to do."

"Poor Wes. I'll say a prayer for him."

"Wes sure needs prayers. Lord knows he does."

I took a shower and blew out my hair, and threw on a sundress with my most comfortable sandals. The problem with cooking was that you stood on your feet while you cooked and then you stood some more while you served and then you stood again while you cleaned up. By the time the night is all over, you're so tired and your legs hurt so badly that you could lie down and die. Did I mention my lower back? Hence, the comfortable shoes. God, was I middle-aged or what?

But I was smarter that night than I normally was, perhaps because the fuel of family conflict put my brain in high gear. Everything was quickly put together, and all the prep dishes were washed and put away except for the bowl of salad and the platter of fresh fruit in the refrigerator. And the fish mousse was chilling in an oiled mold, ready to slip into the water bath in the roasting pan in the oven. The lobster sauce was in a saucepan (I was using premade lobster bisque that I reduced—much easier!) and only needed to be warmed up, and the potatoes were in another pot, ready to boil. My parsley was minced, and I was ready for a lovely night with Jonathan. This was one of those menus that looked hard but wasn't.

I hadn't made a meal like this in eons, but Jonathan was more than worth the effort. It was pretty obvious to both of us that we were more than old friends, but I still had these moments when I felt like we really shouldn't have been fooling around in the sack until I got divorced. *If* I divorced Wes, that is. But on the other hand, what was Wes going to do? Send me to my room? Jonathan was so nice and so smart, he had gorgeous manners, he was attentive, and he made me feel beautiful. Did Wes offer any of those qualities? No, he did not.

I opened the French doors and Miss Jo scampered past me, running around the courtyard and garden as though she had been held in captivity for days. She was so joyous! Once I figured out what I was going to do with my life, I was definitely going to get a dog. Maybe I'd get a rescue. I liked the idea of an older dog that was already broken in and just needed a loving home. The irony was, that wasn't too different from how I was feeling about myself.

It was only four o'clock, so I decided to finish Barbara Bellows's biography on Josephine Pinckney, as I only had thirty pages left to read. When I turned the last page and put the book down, I was left with an odd combination of admiration for Pinckney's long list of accomplishments and sadness too because I felt like she was a lonely woman in many ways. Although her relationship with Tom Waring was satisfying in many ways, he never married her. She was always left a little bit out in the cold, and ultimately, she wound up alone with no children. And worse than that, she faced the hour of her death alone. Was that where I was headed? What if I divorced Wes and Jonathan moved to California and I never saw him again?

"How terrible," I said, as though Jo Pinckney herself was there in the room and I was sympathizing with her. Something gave me a chill.

By the time Jonathan arrived, I was teetering on the edge of a funk. Between Wes and Charlotte and poor Jo Pinckney, I felt pretty blue. Jonathan appeared right at seven with a bottle of white wine and a bottle of red. Miss Jo raced to the door and jumped up, walking on her hind legs, waiting for Jonathan to acknowledge her.

"You never called me, so I just brought one of each. Hey, princess!"

Miss Jo yipped and Jonathan handed me the wine and leaned down to scratch her behind her ears. She hopped into his arms.

"Oh, Jonathan, I'm sorry. It's just been a crazy day."

He gave me a peck on the cheek and then stood back and looked at me seriously. "Okay, what's going on with you?" he said. "I sense an aura of annoyance or something slightly darker."

"Today the world is proving to be far more sinister than I hoped," I said, following him and Miss Jo to the kitchen where he put her down and took the corkscrew from the drawer. "I'm all right. Really."

"No, no. I know you, Leslie. What happened today? Red or white?"

"Red. Save the white for dinner. Well, Wesley called to tell me he has testicular cancer. That was the first bummer. He has to have surgery and he screamed his head off at me to come home and take care of him." I slipped the fish in the oven and set the timer.

"Wow. That's too bad. Did they stage it? If he wants to send over his tests, I can get a second opinion from the head of urology at MUSC."

"No. Wes probably won't want any favors from you because he also saw a picture of us in the newspaper. Remember that night at FIG? Apparently, we looked too happy for his blood."

"So one of those pictures made it to the paper. Great. Well, I can understand why he was in foul humor. But one of the reasons you're here is to be happy, isn't it?"

"Yes, it is. But my happiness makes Wes unhappy. And then my daughter called, accidentally revealing that she was the one who brought the picture to Wes's attention."

"Nice. Kids are overrated, I think."

"There ain't no *I think* about it.

Jonathan smiled. He'd been accused of causing narcolepsy back in high school. But after talking to Wes? Please. Maybe Jonathan was too reserved sometimes, but he was sane, a greatly undervalued quality in Wes's world. I'd take his brand of reliable, dependable, and predictable sanity any day over Wes and his screaming.

"So you've had a helluva day. How about some music?" he said. "Harlan always has such great music playing whenever I'm here."

"That's a wonderful idea. The CD player is sitting on a shelf in the den, and all his music is in the cabinet underneath it."

"Great! I'll dig around and find something."

Soon the sounds of Johnny Mathis crooning "Chances Are" filled the house and I thought, Oh, boy, I remember parking on the Battery and steaming up the car windows with Jonathan in like 1970 or something to this exact same song, sung by Johnny Mathis on an oldies station.

"Remember this?"

"And your daddy's Chevrolet?"

"It was a Pontiac. With very long bench seats."

"Now, how could a girl forget something like that? We had no idea what we were doing."

"What are you talking about? We knew *exactly* what we were doing! It was the intense exploration of your body that made me interested in medicine!"

"Good grief," I said, and my face turned red.

"No need to be embarrassed. Your young and supple body was a lot more interesting than the cadaver they gave me in medical school."

"Well, *that's* nice to hear." I giggled.

"Her name was Susie Q. We all named our cadavers. Would you like some more wine?"

"Thank you. Yes. And a straw."

He refilled my goblet, I took a big sip, and then he took my glass away, putting it down on the kitchen counter.

"Dance with me."

He took my hand and we danced slowly, moving together the same way we had in high school. It was lovely and I felt young and alive. And excited. I was falling in love with Jonathan again, wondering why I had wasted all those years with Wes. Jonathan and I were as perfectly designed for each other as two adult humans could ever be. When "It's Not for Me to Say" played, he held me tighter; and by the time "Wonderful, Wonderful" came on, well, let's just say Harlan's den sofa got a hot and steamy workout and Miss JP was howling at the moon. We only relented and decided to have dinner when the shrill, insistent ringing of the oven timer had to be quelled.

"Johnny Mathis is dangerous," he said.

"So are you, Dr. Ray."

"I'm famished," he said.

"I'm going to feed you like a king," I said and laughed.

The dining room table looked gorgeous. Harlan's celadon plates against the white fish mousse sliced over a bed of pink creamy lobster sauce and those tiny little potatoes all glistening with butter and sprinkled with parsley were a very pretty sight. I almost pulled out my phone and took a picture, but I decided it was better to appear cool. Oh yes, that was the new me, the coy one.

"This is delicious, Leslie. If I'd known you could cook like this, I'd have swept you away from Wesley years ago."

"Thanks! And we'd both weigh nine hundred pounds by now."

"Oh, this isn't the low-cal version?"

"Um, no. Well, if you take out the cream and the butter and the egg yolks, it's low fat. But listen, we don't eat like this every day. Would you like some salad?"

"Yes, but first I want more fish. Should I just help myself?"

What did he do? Inhale it? I guess he liked my cooking.

"No, hon, I'll get it for you. You sit."

I'd left everything on the stove to keep it warm. I refilled his plate and came back to the table.

"You may address me as King Jonathan."

"Your Majesty," I said and put the plate in front of him. "Poor Wes. As much as I dread even the sound of his voice, I feel sorry for him. Cancer of any kind is very frightening."

"Yeah, it is. So what are you going to do? Are you going to take a trip to Atlanta and see what you can do for him?"

"I don't know. I guess I should, but I really don't want to. What would you do if your ex-wife called you with something like this, asking for your help?"

He was quiet for a moment, clearly thinking of an answer. "I'd probably go see what I could do. I mean, she's the mother of my children, you know? It would be weird, but I'd go."

"And he's the father of mine. Or the tyrant. Jonathan, I know I sound like a shrew, but I just don't want to leave Charleston. And I don't want to leave you."

"Les, I'm not going anywhere, and neither is the Holy City. You go and do what you think you should do. But don't be gone for too long."

"I won't. Can you watch Miss Jo?"

We looked under the table and there she was, asleep on Jonathan's feet. She liked me well enough, but she adored him. So did I.

CHAPTER 16

Wes Is Scared

I was sitting in the family room watching television with my son, Bertie, who had grown dreadlocks. I couldn't even look at him. I guess he thought his hair made him look like an artsy-fartsy photographer. I thought it made him look like a bum. I mean, if anybody ever interviewed with me that looked like *him*? Please. He'd never get past Human Resources in the first place, but if he did, I'd ask him kindly not to waste my time. And he wondered why the world didn't take him seriously? Really? How about let's start with some basic grooming, like a shower? Everything about him had this funny smell. Even Martha, after smelling his laundry, expressed her disgust in her native tongue and quit. Les wouldn't be too happy about that, if she came back here to live that is.

Les should've arrived already. Maybe her flight was late. Who knew? But it was getting late. I had thought there for a while that she wasn't going to come, but she relented in the end. I think the fact that she heard me choke up did the trick.

Charlotte was in her old room putting Holly to sleep. Yes, Charlotte had moved back in because business was so terrible she couldn't make her rent. I really didn't care too much because it was a little lonely being without Les and all, and I loved having little Holly's arms around my neck. But in the long run I didn't think it was the best situation.

It was after ten and I heard the front door open. Les was here. I got up to go greet her, which I thought was the right thing to do even though this was her house, and old Bertie, wiped out from his long flight, didn't budge. Hadn't seen his mother in a year and he couldn't be bothered to get off the sofa. Nice. I felt like giving him a swift kick, but I ignored him and went out to the hall. You can't go to war over everything.

"Hey! You're here! How was your flight?"

"It was okay. How come no one picked me up at the airport?"

Oh, crap. Did we forget? Wait, I wasn't going there.

"Because you never told me when your flight was."

"Oh. I guess you're right."

She put her roll-on bag by the stairs and dropped her purse on the hall table where she always had. "So how are you?"

"Nervous. I have to be there at six thirty in the morning."

"Oh, you'll be just fine, Wes."

"I can't eat or drink after midnight."

"That's standard. Is Bertie here?"

"Yeah, he's out back in the family room. Draped across the sofa, and don't be too shocked when you see him. He's got braided hair like a Rasta man. And his feet are encrusted with something—probably dirt."

"Oh dear," she said.

"And Charlotte's moved back in. Can't make the rent, it seems."

She looked at me with that *How could you allow something so impossibly stupid to happen?* look of hers. I just shrugged my shoulders and kept walking toward the den.

"Bertie! Get up and say hello to your mother!" I said.

Bertie unfolded himself and stood, placed his hands together, and looked at his mother. "Namaste," he said.

"Namaste, my ass," I grumbled.

"Oh, Bertie," she cried, like the Dalai Lama had dropped in for a slice of blueberry pie. "Come let me give my boy a hug!"

Then Bertie hugged Les like he hadn't seen her in forever, and she hugged him back with all her might. I guess that old saying about mothers and their sons was true, although my mother never hugged me like that. But then, my father never believed in showing children too much affection. He said it made them weak. Maybe it was coincidence, but it appeared my father was at least partially right.

"How's Nepal?" she said.

"Well, we didn't find the Yeti yet. Ha! Ha!" Bertie said, just like the half-wit I suspected he was. "But Kathmandu is awesome. I took some pictures out in Pashupatinath last week I want to show you. Monkeys everywhere, even a funeral pyre. Really amazing."

If I had a dime for every time he's said *awesome* and *amazing* in the last twenty-four hours, I could buy Charlotte a two-bedroom condo. And furnish it.

"Oh, my sweet boy!" Les said, and her eyes actually filled with tears. "It's just so wonderful to see you. My goodness! Look at your hair! Is this really your hair? It looks dusty!"

"It's the dust of the Himalayas and a thousand bodhisattvas."

"Boddis—who?"

"Saints, Mom. Hindu saints, enlightened ones."

"My goodness, Bertie! I didn't even know they had saints over there!"

"Awesome," he said.

I thought for a moment Leslie had really come home to see Bertie and taking care of me was the price to pay. But then I said to myself, Why are you jealous of your own son? That's stupid!

"Yeah. My hair. Pretty crazy, huh?"

"I imagine it's normal in your realm," Les said.

"Hey, Les," I said, thinking, You can marvel over his dirty hair some other time, "why don't you and I sit down for a moment? I just want to go over some things about tomorrow."

"Sure. You want me to make a pot of coffee?"

"Nah, I gotta be asleep in an hour. Let's get a nightcap, and then I'm gonna turn in."

"Okay. Feel like a snack?"

"I ate. You didn't get supper?" I went to my office to get my extraspecial twenty-five-year-old single malt whiskey, something worthy of this occasion. It cost me a pretty penny, let me tell you. I kept it under lock and key. Otherwise my daughter would be putting ice and diet soda in it. Sacrilege! No, no. Since Charlotte came home? I keep the bar stocked with an array of bargain-priced white wines and she's not complaining.

"No. But I'm not famished. I'm just going to make a tomato sandwich unless you're saving this one for something?"

Was she asking permission to take a tomato from her own kitchen? Why would she do that? Or maybe she didn't feel like it was her kitchen anymore?

"Help yourself!" I called out and then rejoined her.

Before I could say another thing to her, here came Charlotte with Holly on her hip.

"Gammy!" she said and threw her arms out to Les. "I miss you!"

"Hey, Mom," Charlotte said and gave Les a peck on the cheek. "She wouldn't go to sleep until she got to give you a hug."

It seemed to me that Les and Charlotte were a little chilly to each other and I wondered what that was about. Maybe I was imagining things. In my present state of mind, I mean with me facing the knife and all, anything was possible.

"Come here, you sweet little darlin', and give me some sugar!"

Leslie took Holly in her arms and Holly threw her skinny little legs around Les's waist and her arms around her neck, squeezing her as hard as she could.

"Now, you go to bed, young lady! It's very, very late!" Les said.

Holly whimpered and hung on tighter. Charlotte pried her away, and Les and Holly blew kisses to each other until she was out of sight.

Les refocused on her lettuce and tomato sandwich, which was looking very good and I was thinking then that I might like one too.

"Sure you don't want one?" she asked, reading my mind.

"Well, okay," I said, "it might be my last. You want a glass of wine or something?"

"Sure. A glass of white wine would be nice."

She put my sandwich together, sliced it in two big triangles and put it on a plate, sliding it across the table to where my drink waited. She sat in her old chair, and I put a glass of white wine in front of her. For a moment, it seemed like nothing was out of order, like she had never left. I sat down and raised my glass to her.

"Cheers!" I said. "Thanks for coming."

"Cheers," she said. "Good luck tomorrow."

"Leslie, we have to talk."

"About what?"

"I've had a premonition, Leslie. I have this horrible feeling that something is going to go wrong tomorrow and I'm going to die."

"What's the premonition? A bad dream or what?"

"No, it's just a feeling. Leslie, I'm so scared."

She looked at me with her most solemn face and said, "Wes, I think what you're feeling is pretty normal. I really do. I mean, when's the last time you were in a hospital?"

"When I took that stress test for the insurance company? But here's the thing, they got me taking a statin for cholesterol, something else for blood pressure, an aspirin, a diuretic . . . what if those meds get mixed up with the anesthesia? I might have a stroke or something terrible. Actually, I quit taking my aspirin a week ago because it's like a blood thinner and I might not clot. I mean, can you imagine how awful it would be to bleed out through the balls? What would my obituary say about that?"

"Wes? That's gross, and it's not going to happen. I'm going to drive you there in the morning and we're going to fill out all the ten pounds of paperwork and then they're going to put you to sleep . . ."

"Will you keep my wallet and my wristwatch?"

"Of course I will. And then I'm going to stay until you're out of surgery and then I guess we'll see what the doctors say. Either you'll come home or you'll stay overnight."

"Listen, if the worst happens, the key to my files is taped under the center drawer of my desk. In my files are my will and all my insurance policies and everything you'd need to bury me."

I started to cry. I couldn't help it. I didn't want to leave this world! I still had so much to do!

In a moment of kindness, she reached across the table and put her hand over mine and squeezed.

"Come on, Wes. You're going to be fine. They do this surgery all the time."

I knew this was a stupid thing to say, but I said it anyway. "You know, Leslie, this is going to cut back my sperm production like crazy."

"Excuse me," she said. "Do you really want more kids? You're kidding, right?"

And then we started to laugh, laugh like we had not laughed since college. Leslie had such a great sense of humor. Why did I always tell her it was lame?

"Oh, God! That was good, Les. Can you imagine more of *them*?"

"Seriously. I look at these families that have five kids or more and I just wonder how much the parents drink."

"If there was ever anything that could drive you to the bottle, five children would do it."

"No kidding. Can you imagine the laundry?"

"And the expense! Whew! I feel better. I do. Thanks. You're funny, you know?"

"Good. Look, why don't you get yourself upstairs to bed," she said. "I'll close up down here."

"You're a gem, Les. Thank you for everything. I'll see you in a bit?"

"Wes, you just go on to bed and go to sleep. You don't need me tossing and turning and kicking you if you snore. I'll stay in the guest room tonight."

And suddenly it hit me. She wasn't coming home to be with me. She was doing this out of some sense of duty, not because she loved me. I'd lost her.

"You're never coming back, are you?" I said.

Quiet hung in the room like something dark and terrible, and I really didn't want to hear her answer.

"Oh, Wes, right now we're going to take care of you. We can talk about us when this is all over."

"Les, if I come through this, there's someone I want us to go and see."

"Let's talk tomorrow."

I realized then that everyone in the house had hugged and kissed her except me, yet it felt awkward for me to touch her.

I stood and put my glass and plate in the sink. "You're probably right," I said. "We can talk about everything later. Please say a prayer for me, Les."

"You know I will, Wes. Now, stop worrying and go get your rest."

"Okay," I said. "Thanks, Les."

"For what? The sandwich?"

"For everything."

She got up and said, "Come on, you old bear, let's have a hug."

I felt so much better. It was awesome and amazing just how much better I felt.

CHAPTER 17

Les the Nurse

I woke up at five and dressed quickly. It wasn't like I'd had the best night's sleep anyway. Every time I rolled over and realized I was back in Atlanta, sleeping in my own guest room no less, I felt my chest tighten with anxiety. For as determined as I was to be kind to Wes and our children, I was completely annoyed with them all. Forgive me if this sounds petty. It wasn't just Wes who dropped his plate and glass in the sink, it was that Charlotte and Bertie too had been leaving their dirty dishes in there all day long. Now, did they not know that the dishwasher was strategically located *exactly* next to the sink? Just who was supposed to clean it all up? Had they left it for me? Obviously, they had.

Last night on the way upstairs with my bag that neither Wes nor Bertie had bothered to take up for me, I opened the door of the laundry room and immediately wished that I had not. There were wet towels, sheets, and clothes piled up to the sky. Who was supposed to wash, dry, and fold this mountain? Well, since Martha's unfortunate departure, it was waiting for me! Was this to show me how much I was needed?

But it was a new day, and I had other priorities. I'd get Wes through his surgery and then I'd raise hell. I started a pot of coffee and began to empty the loaded dishwasher. As soon as I finished putting everything away, I poured myself a cup of coffee and went upstairs to wake Wes.

"Time to shake a leg, Wes."

"Okay, thanks. How much time do I have?"

"Twenty minutes."

"Okay, I'll meet you in the kitchen."

I went back downstairs, turned off the alarm, and went outside to see if the newspaper had arrived. It had not, so I walked around to my backyard to see how it was doing. It did not appear to have suffered very much from the heat or my neglect. Amazing. I had thought the July heat would have fried it to a crisp, but it looked pretty good. At least our landscaper had not jumped ship. The flowerpots looked a bit dry, and the edges of my hosta were brittle. If I had time I'd get out my shears and clean it all up. Then I thought, Why, this isn't my garden anymore!

I heard the familiar slap of the newspaper as it slid across the bricks of our front walkway, so I went back around front and picked it up. *The Wall Street Journal*. No *Atlanta Journal Constitution* except on Sundays.

"Not necessary," Wes used to say. "We don't need two papers. Waste of money."

Okay, Wes, I thought. Why didn't you ever care about what I might enjoy? Truth? I bought the *AJC* and the *New York Times* every day for years and threw them away before he got home.

Charlotte had practically avoided me last night, which was fine with me. She probably thought I was permanently angry with her for telling Wes about the picture in the newspaper of Jonathan and me smiling and having dinner. Well, I *wasn't* happy about that, but that wasn't it, really. I could not have cared less if the entire population of the earth saw it. What bothered me was that in my mind I saw Charlotte riding the prevailing winds, thoughtful to placate her benefactor. With me out of the picture, she'd apparently do anything to ingratiate herself to the one who would provide her with what she needed. A babysitter, a roof over her head, spending money . . . It was a pretty pathetic state of affairs. I was not angry. I was just deeply disappointed in her behavior. Daughters were supposed to stand by their mothers. Charlotte had chosen sides.

And Bertie? What was that *smell* in his clothes and his hair? Well, I'd fumigate him and then we'd see. It was time to have a serious talk about his future whether he wanted to have that talk or not. Actually, it was long past time to talk to both of them.

I went back inside and there was Wes, pacing the kitchen floor like a two-hundred-pound cat.

"You're ready?" I said.

"As ready as I'll ever be."

"Here's the paper. Are the kids coming?"

"Thanks. They said they'd come down around ten. I should be dead by then."

"Wes! Stop! Read the paper to take your mind off this. Now, did you pack a little bag in case they want you to stay over?"

"If they don't kill me, I'm coming home. I hate hospitals."

I paused for a moment, deciding the lemon wasn't worth the squeeze. Either one of the kids or I could always run home and get him a pair of pajamas.

"Okay. We can always take care of that later. Now, are you sure you have your medical insurance cards?"

"Yeah, you want to drive? I'm too nervous."

"No problem. I'd planned to drive you anyway. Just go get in my car and relax. It's all going to be all right, Wes. I promise."

"Okay." He sighed over and over. "Thanks."

Surprisingly, there wasn't much to do to have Wes admitted, or at least it didn't take as long as I thought it would. He gave me his watch and his wallet and stowed the rest of his clothing in one of the lockers they provided for same-day-surgery patients. I stayed with him while he crawled up on a gurney in his skimpy hospital gown, paper shoes, and shower cap. They started his IV, and I felt so sorry for him then. His surgeon came in to say hello and see if Wes was ready to go. Naturally, Wes pretended he was fine and his surgeon looked Wes square in the face and told him not to worry.

"I do a dozen of these a week," Dr. Chen said. "No problem!"

"And I thought it was so rare," Wes said.

"Atlanta's a big town, and, besides, people come to us from all over the Southeast."

"Yep," said the orderly who was there to roll Wes down to the operating room. "Dr. Chen's got the magic touch."

"You ready to go, Mr. Carter?" Dr. Chen said.

"Yeah, in a minute. Hey, Les, come over here. I wanna tell you something."

"What, hon?" I leaned down to him.

He whispered in my ear, "You're a wonderful woman, Leslie. I've been a foolish man not to realize that. I've missed you a lot. Please don't leave me."

Big strong Wesley Carter reduced to a mere mortal by fear. I stepped back a little and brushed his hair away from his forehead.

"Don't worry, Wesley. I'll be right here when you wake up." I squeezed his hand and watched them roll him down the hall.

I knew he was asking me to stay with him for the rest of his life and I wished with all my heart that I could, but I let him think his request wasn't clear. Only Wes would ask something like that in this very dramatic moment. I knew in my heart he was trying to work me.

"The poor thing," I said to no one and went to find a spot where my cell phone would work.

I called Jonathan. "Well, they just took him off to surgery," I said.

"Look, I'm almost one hundred percent sure he's going to be fine, but I'm guessing he's nervous. You're awfully good to be there."

"It's probably a really good thing I am here. The house and the kids were pretty discombobulated. And I think me being here makes it somewhat less frightening for the kids and probably for him too."

"Well, hang in there. When are you coming home?"

I loved that Jonathan called Charleston home or maybe he just meant *back to me,* which was even better.

"I think I have to stay as long as he needs me."

"That could be forever."

"No," I said. "I'll call you soon."

Then I called Danette.

"So I'm in the cell-phone area down at Emory and they just took Wes in."

"Oh, Lord. How's he doing? I'll bet he's a mess."

"He's a wreck. Nobody's a big shot when you're lying in a hospital bed."

"Boy, is that ever the truth. But I'd bet the ranch he was glad to see you."

"Yes, he was. You were right. All those years together? I couldn't just leave him to go through this alone."

"I'm sure it's very emotional."

"Yes, it is. You know, I'm here with the kids and Holly, all of us together to see about Wes and I keep worrying that I'm making a huge mistake. Anyway, Bertie's here and I never get to see him. Maybe you could come by?"

"Of course I will and we'll talk! I have to see you, and Lord knows I haven't seen Bertie in ages. Let's see how Wes does. Call me when he's out, okay?"

"Will do. He's going to be fine. So can you give me Harold's cell? And Paolo's? Wes wanted me to call them to remind them that he's going *under the knife* this morning."

"Oh dear! High drama, huh?"

"Men make terrible patients. Big babies. We both know that. I'll call them as soon as he's in recovery."

She gave me their numbers, and I promised to call her back too.

"If you want me to come sit with you, all you have to do is squeak," she said. "I feel terrible not to be with you especially if you're feeling, you know, uncertain about things."

"Oh, thanks, babe, I'm okay. It's just hard. He should be out of recovery by noon or one, I'd think."

I settled down with a magazine and began thumbing the pages. An hour or so passed. My cell rang. It was Bertie.

"Hi, Mom. We're on the way, and we wondered if we could bring you anything?"

Really? They must've sensed my discontent when they saw the sparkling clean kitchen.

"I'll have whatever y'all are having. Thanks, son. Dad just went into surgery."

"Okay, good to know. See you in a few."

About twenty minutes later, Charlotte and Bertie arrived with Holly in tow. They'd brought bagels and cream cheese, still warm. And hot coffee.

"Well, this is nice," I said as I lifted Holly right up and onto my lap. She weighed considerably more than she had in May. And she was taller. "I think you've grown!" I said to her.

"Yep! I know! I've got a cinnamon one," she said. "Want a bite?"

"No, no, honey. But thank you," I said.

"Yeah, she's grown almost a whole two inches! Do you want pumpernickel or onion or plain?" Charlotte asked.

"How's Dad doing?" Bertie asked. "I'll take onion. This is one thing I sure missed. You can't get decent bagels in Kathmandu."

"I'm sure. I'd guess Dad's still in the operating room," I said, and I reached over to take a cup of coffee from the cardboard tray. "We should hear something soon. I'll take half of a plain one?"

"Here you go, Mom," Charlotte said, handing it to me on a napkin.

"Thanks, sweetheart."

The wall clock went from ten to eleven, and closer to noon, Dr. Chen appeared. As if on cue, we all stood.

"Mrs. Carter?" he said to me. "Your husband did just fine. We're reasonably sure we got it all."

"That's wonderful," I said.

"We had to remove one testicle and we took some lymph nodes. They appear to be clean. Of course, we have to send them out to pathology and they'll give us the definitive answer in a few days, but I wouldn't worry. It was a seminoma tumor, stage I, and it does not appear to have metastasized."

"Thank God!" I said. "When can I see him?"

"Well, he's still sleeping right now."

"Can I take him home soon?"

"Actually, we decided to admit him for one night, just for observation. His blood pressure has been bouncing around. He's in no danger, but he's probably safer here."

"I see. So when can I see him?"

"As soon as he starts coming around, I'll send someone right out to get you. Just remember to tell him to take it easy when he gets home tomorrow. We'll give him something for pain. No driving for a week and no heavy lifting for at least two."

"Great. Well, I'm so glad he came through it okay. Thank you, Doctor."

"Yes, thanks, Dr. Chen," Charlotte said.

I noticed that Dr. Chen wasn't wearing a wedding ring. I also noticed that Dr. Chen noticed Charlotte and that she noticed him. He also appeared to have not even *noticed* Bertie was with us. Well, I had to admit, Bertie no longer looked like our tribe.

"So who wants to go get your daddy's pajamas and a toothbrush?" I said.

I stared at their blank faces.

"Fine," I said and sighed. "I'll be back as quickly as I can. I'm sure your father will be happier to see your faces than mine when he wakes up anyway."

"Oh, fine!" Charlotte said. "I'll go! Come on, Bertie."

One bag of bagels does not a life change make. And here I had thought they were off to a grand new beginning.

When the elevator door closed, I sighed again and dialed Harold.

"Harold? Hey, it's me, Les. How are you?"

"I'm doing okay. But we miss you, Les, you know?"

They did?

"Thanks. Wes just got out of surgery and he did fine. He wanted me to give you a call."

"Good. Glad to hear it. I saw him yesterday and wished him good luck. He's got the best doc in the country."

"Thanks to you, I understand. Okay, then."

"Let me know if I can do anything, okay?"

"Sure. Thanks."

Harold sounded funny, like something was wrong, but he didn't say and I didn't ask.

I dialed Paolo next. My call went straight to voice mail so I left him a message.

"Hi, Paolo, it's Les. Just calling to let you know that Wes is out of surgery and he's fine. Give me a shout if you want the details."

I settled back into *People* magazine, thinking I had no idea who

I was reading about and further, I wondered why the idiotic antics of these lunatics were news. The whole celebrity magazine thing seemed like reports from the zoo. Pretty young people go and do something outrageous, like tattoo their children or overdose or get married in a tree in the jungle, the paparazzi combs their garbage, finds some juice, and sells it. Then an incredulous Dr. Phil reads them the riot act, they go on all the talk shows, and eventually some crazy publisher gives them a book deal. They write a memoir with a ghostwriter and go on Oprah's show, and she calls them all a pack of liars—and she's right, by the way. Then their story is picked up by Lifetime and made into a movie. A few months later, they walk the red carpet in borrowed gowns and win an Emmy. All that and I still don't know who they're talking about and why they're worthy of all this attention. Nonetheless, in no time they're a spokesperson for their own line of pots and pans or jewelry for JCPenney or Target. This, my friends, is a multibillion-dollar industry. Go figure.

"I love this country," I said to myself and looked up to see an orderly staring at me.

"Mrs. Carter?"

I stood. "Yes?"

"You can follow me now."

We went through several sets of swinging doors to the recovery area, and there was Wes, groggy and drifting in and out of sleep. I took his hand in mine.

"Wes? Wes? Can you hear me?"

He nodded his head and then drifted off to sleep again. I stood there for around twenty minutes until a nurse came and checked his blood pressure.

"We're going to move him to a room now. Room 129. We'll meet you there?"

Another nurse or orderly appeared, and the next thing I knew, Wesley was rolling down a hall again.

When I reached the cell-phone area, I called Charlotte and gave her Wes's room number. I found his room, and just as I arrived, so did he. They transferred him from his gurney to the bed and tucked him in neatly. I watched him as he slept and thought about all the trials and tribulations we'd been through together over the years. The truth was there was much more we'd gone through separately. He had not been a particularly attentive father or husband, traveling as he did for business and playing golf when he wasn't traveling. Maybe things might have turned out differently if he'd been around a little more. If he'd been more interested in us, our home might have been happier. But it wasn't fair to blame Wes for the children's performance in life any more than it was fair to blame myself. The *children* were no longer children. Maybe they had not enjoyed an idyllic childhood, but it wasn't so bad. They were well educated and well fed, they had excellent health, and I had always believed that they were good people at heart. Maybe they just needed to be sent to their rooms. Wait, they *were* in their rooms.

Wes slept for another hour, and then I saw his eyes flutter a little.

"Hey, there," I said. "Everything's okay. You're gonna live."

"Les? I love you, Les."

Oh dear, I thought. He was drugged. If only he would say he loved me when he wasn't.

"You just rest now. I'll be right here until the kids come back. They just went home to get your pajamas."

He didn't hear me. He was already sleeping again.

Soon Charlotte and Bertie came in with Wes's things and took a seat.

"Where's Holly?" I said.

"She's playing with the little girl who used to live next door to us. I told her mother I'd pick her up when we leave."

"Well, that's good. She needs to be around other children," I said. "Look, as long as both of you are here, I'm going to go home for a while. Dad's fine so far. Maybe I'll catch a nap."

I could see that Charlotte was about to object, but then she looked at me, suddenly remembering I'd been up since the crack of dawn.

I guess my age must have been showing on my face because she said, "Don't worry, Mom. You look beat. If anything changes, I'll call you right away."

"Yeah, definitely," Bertie said. "Get some rest. We'll call you."

"If he starts to moan or toss and turn, go get a nurse, okay? Oh, and here's the key to his locker? Maybe one of y'all could go collect his things."

"No worries," Bertie said.

Charlotte rolled her eyes at him and I smiled.

Walking down the halls of the hospital, I thought about them again, my two offspring. At the very least, they had some kind of camaraderie. There was the normal push-pull of siblings, but there also was a sweetness between them that I hoped they wouldn't let expire. Someday when I was gone and Wes was gone, they'd only have each other and maybe a spouse and another child or two. That was not exactly a life crawling with relatives and people who ought to love you. Before I returned to Charleston, I'd remind them to cherish each other. And I'd tell them if and when they married, to marry wisely.

When I got home, I couldn't help but be disheartened by the state of the house. How could I sleep? I decided to put in a load of sheets and whites and change Wes's bed. He didn't need to come home to anything but a spotless and completely sanitary bedroom and bathroom. Especially with an incision to heal in such a tender place, an infection was the last thing he needed. So I went to work, wiping down every surface with bleach. I wanted to flip the mattress, but I didn't think it was a good idea to try to do it with my arm, as it was still tender sometimes. I needed Martha. I called her and used my horrific Spanish.

"Martha? Señora Carter aquí. Por favor, Señor Carter es en el hospital."

"Hospital? No está bien?"

"Sí, no muy bien. Y la casa es terrible. Por favor? You come?"

"Sí, sí. En una hora, okay?"

"Oh! Gracias! Gracias!"

Well, praise God and all his saints. I was so relieved that I put my bones on the guest room bed and fell into a deep sleep. I never even heard her arrive. When I woke up two hours later, I could smell the dryer and what I thought was a roasted chicken. I found her folding towels in the kitchen with Danette. Danette was speaking very animated and loud English. Martha was speaking animated and even louder Spanish or some version of it, and the two were having a wonderful time.

"Hey, you!" Danette said. "I brought supper!"

I gave my friend a hug.

"Oh, gosh! Thank you! And Martha? Thanks for coming."

"Señora Carter loves Martha," she said and laughed. "But Martha no love Señor Bertie and Señorita Charlotte and Señor Carter. Too much trabajo!"

"Sí! Es verdad!" I said. "They're too much work. What's cooking? Chicken?"

"Yep, chicken, stuffing, gravy, carrots, and a salad's in the fridge. And there's a chocolate cake for dessert."

"You are the greatest friend in the world." I said. "I'm exhausted. You want a cup of coffee?"

"Sure," she said.

I set up the pot and clicked the start button to let the water drip. As best I could, I explained to Martha what I wanted to do to Wes's room and bathroom. She said *sí* and *no problema* about twenty times, gathered up what she needed to clean, and went upstairs. Soon I heard water running, toilets flushing, then the vacuum sucking the last bits of life out of our old carpet and I knew everything was going to be done exactly as it should.

"So, Wes is okay?"

"Yeah, there was some fluctuation in his blood pressure, so they just wanted to keep him to be sure he's stable. I'm bringing him home tomorrow after lunch."

"That's great. And how long are you staying?"

"Until he's steady on his feet. End of the week, I think." I poured two cups for us and put the half-and-half on the table. "Think we could sneak a slice of that cake?"

"You have to have cake with coffee."

Danette got up and brought it to the table. I took two plates from the cabinet and forks from the drawer. My cake knife was miraculously right where I'd left it. I lifted the cover of her cake carrier. Her carb bomb was completely covered in pecan halves. It smelled so darned good.

"Danette! This is gorgeous! Are you sure we should cut it?"

"Oh, no," she said, in a bad-girl voice with her hands on her cheeks. "Let's save it for the others."

"Right," I said and sliced two healthy pieces for us.

"When are Bertie and Charlotte coming home? I'd love to catch a glimpse of them."

"Soon, I'd imagine. Charlotte has to pick up Holly from a playdate and give her supper. She's moved home again, you know."

"Oh, dear. Wes can't be happy about that."

"Who knows? He probably loves it. Anyway, I guess this real estate market is tougher than it looks. All their stuff is piled up in boxes in the garage and I'm sure that works his nerves. You know how territorial he is." I sat down and put a forkful of cake in my mouth. It practically melted. "Jeez Louise! Where'd you learn to bake like this?"

"Duncan Hines." She giggled. "But it's good, right?"

"Yeah, it is! It's delicious!"

"Ha-ha! And how long is Bertie staying?"

"Who knows? I just got here late last night. There hasn't really been any time to talk."

"Well, I know you're glad to see him. Molly asked me to see if he might like to be a groomsman if he'll be here in September."

I burst out laughing. "Wait till you see him. He's got dreadlocks down to here."

"Good grief! Dreadlocks? Maybe he just needs to meet a nice girl."

"Danette? What in the world would a nice girl want with a boy who looks like Bob Marley?"

"I don't know? A walk on the wild side?"

"Hmmm. I don't like to think about things like that. So what else is new?"

"Well, things are fabulous with Nader."

"He's great, right?"

"Yeah, he's *really* great. He's smart like anything and he's a gentleman. He's wonderful company, and he tells me I'm pretty."

"What else could you ask for? I can't wait to meet him."

"You'll like him."

"If you like him, I will too. Now, would you like to split another slice of this devilishly good mortal sin?"

"Oh, no. I've got to go home. He's coming at six for dance class tonight. We're learning to tango."

"Tango? Has Molly met him?"

"She loves him! She invited him to the wedding herself!"

"Wonderful! I knew it! That's why you're taking tango lessons?"

"Why not? And cha-cha!" She stood up and picked up her purse. "Tell the kids I'll see them tomorrow."

"You're too good!"

"Thanks, Les. So are you."

I watched her car back out of the driveway. She tooted her horn twice and waved and then she was gone. I turned around and walked back inside my house. Every room was like a museum, every object some reminder of the past. When I returned to Charleston, was there anything I wanted to take with me? Maybe some pictures of the kids, taken when they were young, and the few pieces of my mother's silver I had inherited. Maybe clothes. And my car. Other than that? Wes could have it all. It was just stuff. The only antiques we had of any value were his desk and the rug on his office floor. That figures, I said to myself.

Martha appeared and said, "Finished, Señora."

I gave her all the cash in my purse and a hug. "Señor Carter no es tu responsibility, Martha. Muchas gracias."

"Sí, pero, sick? Diferente. If Señora Carter come back, I come back. No come back? I no come back."

"Sí, sí. Comprendo. Gracias."

Martha left and I thought I didn't blame her for one second. This house had been a pigsty, and now it smelled like lemon wax. Even Bertie's clothes didn't even smell too bad at all.

Soon everyone was home and ready to eat. I set the table and poured milk for Holly and tea for us.

"How's your father?" I said as we sat down.

"Sleeping like a baby," Charlotte said.

"Did you wash your hands?" I said to Bertie, without really meaning to insult him.

He looked to the ceiling for guidance and patience.

"I washed mine," Holly said. "Gammy says you *have* to wash your hands to come to the table."

"They're clean enough," Bertie said.

I didn't say one word.

"I'm gonna take a quick trip over there after supper just to check on him," I said.

"No point in that," Charlotte said. "They've got him so drugged he won't even know you were there."

"Exactly," Bertie said. "Can I have some more gravy?"

"Help yourself," I said. Bertie gave me a funny look. Did he think I was going to hop like a bunny to serve him? "That's *precisely* why I'm going. Just for your future reference? You should never leave someone alone in the hospital when they've just had surgery. Anything can happen. Especially if they're still unconscious." I made a mental note to never put my children in charge of my health care.

"Gee, I never thought of that," Charlotte said.

I just looked at her and hoped she could read my telepathic message, which was, *There are so many things you've never given thought to.*

"Dinner is really good, Mom," Bertie said.

"Danette brought this chicken for us and everything else too, including a delicious chocolate cake."

"Wow," Charlotte said, "that was supernice. How's the wedding coming?"

"We need to send a gift, you know. And I want to give a brunch for her the day of the wedding." I was going to say, *and I hope you'll help me arrange it,* but I didn't want to lay another expectation on her that wouldn't be met.

"When's the wedding? Maybe I'll stick around," Bertie said. "Hard to believe Molly Stovall is getting married. I still remember her as a kid; you know, freckles and pigtails?"

"Well, for heaven's sake, she's nearly thirty. She's not too young," I said.

"She's not a kid anymore. That's for sure," Charlotte said.

"Listen, she's marrying a very talented doctor, and they're going to have a beautiful life."

"Depends on what you think is beautiful, Mom," Bertie said.

"Lately, Mom's all about money, little brother."

"Money is the root of all evil," Bertie said.

"Solvency is a *good* thing, son. Don't let your sister *ever* convince you otherwise," I said.

"Can I have cake, please?" Holly said. "I cleaned my plate!"

"Of course you *may*," I said. I took her plate to the sink to rinse it. "You're a very good girl!" I cut a piece of cake for her and put it on a small plate.

"And I'm not a good boy, Mom? Is that what you're saying?"

"Oooh! Somebody's sensitive," Charlotte said.

"Look, we can have this discussion now or later. You choose. But at some point before I go back to Charleston, we're going to talk about what you're doing with your life, son."

"I think this is my cue to put Holly in the bathtub," Charlotte said.

"Yes, and then you can avoid the dishes," I said.

"Mom! Why would you say something like that?" Charlotte said.

"When's the last time you ever washed a dish when I was in this house? Or run a load of laundry?"

"I'll be back," Charlotte said and got up. "Come on, Holly."

Holly licked her fingers and wiped her mouth on her napkin.

"What do you say to Gammy, Holly?"

"Thanks for the cake?" she said.

"Go get your bath like a good girl," I said.

"In Tibet they only bathe once a year," Bertie said. "The air's so thin you can't smell anything like body odor."

"That's what you think," I said. He was stoking the coals of my furnace.

There was a long pause, and then he said, "You've had it with us, haven't you?"

THE LAST ORIGINAL WIFE / 229

"Yes, in a way, and in a way, no. You're in the middle of an MBA program, which we're paying for, and you drop out and head out to the other side of the world without a penny to your name. Then you call your father for money at least once a month because you can't earn your own way? You come home filthy dirty from head to toe and smelling like hell. Am I supposed to be thrilled to see you like this?"

"Wow."

"Wow, you say? Molly Stovall is marrying a brilliant doctor. My daughter? Only wants to go out with her friends to bars and drink wine. Can't sell one house. Can't support her child. Neither one of you seem to be able to pick up after yourselves. I own the bragging rights on my two kids, and do they care about pleasing their parents? I don't think so."

"Chill, Mom! You shouldn't take this stuff so personally."

Now I was pissed.

"Chill? You tell your mother *to chill*? You've got some nerve, young man! I want you to remember this conversation when I'm dead and gone. *Where is your pride?* Why don't you want to stand on your own two feet? God forgive me, but you are as *lazy* as the day is long."

"Sorry."

"And I shouldn't take your failure to join the human race as an adult *personally*? Let me tell you something, Wesley Albert Carter V, go look in the mirror and take a good whiff! You smell like a pack of goats!"

"For real?"

"Yes, you really do. You look like a goatherder or a homeless person. Every other child on this whole blooming earth in every single culture wants to make their parents proud except mine. Shame on you both!"

"Wow," he said. "This is heavy."

"Mom? What's going on? Holly wants to say good night."

Charlotte was standing in the doorway. I didn't know how much she had heard, and I didn't much care.

"Fine," I said and passed her on the way to Charlotte's old bedroom. I said to Bertie, "Talk to your sister." I couldn't remember the last time I'd raised my voice to them. I probably scared them half to death. So what?

"She's totally pissed," I heard Bertie say.

It took a little effort to calm myself, but by the time I reached Holly's room, my breathing was normal again.

I pushed open the door that was left ajar and there was my little Holly in her summer nightgown with the unicorn on the front. She was playing possum, and for a fleeting moment I remembered Charlotte when she'd been this young and innocent.

"Hey, sweetie!" I said, using that bedtime voice that's louder than a whisper, the one reserved for putting children to bed. "I'm just coming to tell you I love you and to have sweet dreams!"

I sat down beside her and she rolled over and opened her enormous blue eyes.

"Gammy?"

"What baby?"

"Know what I want to be when I grow up?"

"A ballerina?"

"Nope. I want to be a Gammy like you who takes care of everybody."

"Oh, sweetheart!" I leaned down and kissed her forehead. "You go to sleep now, okay?"

"You smell so good, like flowers. Not like Mommy. She smells like the stuff she puts on my boo-boos."

Alcohol. I had now reached the absolute limit of what I would tolerate silently.

"Good night, sweetie, don't let the bedbugs bite!"

"Bugs?" She yawned widely, her little head probably already filled with lovely little girl dreams that waited.

"Just an old saying," I said and pulled the sheet over her shoulders.

I returned to the kitchen, and with every step I took I knew my sharp-tongued daughter was waiting with some sassy retort. I was wrong. I found her there in tears, Bertie holding her hands, consoling her. The dirty dishes were still on the table. They were sharing a bottle of wine.

"Why are you so mean?" she said.

"I am not mean. Almost thirty years I gave this family and *this* is what I get in return? I walked in here to a filthy house and a veritable mountain of dirty laundry? All of it was just waiting for me because my children are too lazy to lift a finger? It's a disgrace!"

"Is that all you have to say?"

"No. Your little girl says you stink from alcohol. How does that make *you* feel because *I* surely don't like hearing it! I'm going to check on your father, and I'll be back later. Put the wine away, wash the dishes, take out the garbage, and clean up this kitchen. Both of you! Start acting like adults! Don't wait up. Shame on you both."

I left them there, stunned. I'd always made excuses for them because Wes screamed and yelled enough for both of us and, frankly, I didn't like confrontations. But the time was long overdue that they heard it from me too. Maybe they thought they could still be children themselves until someone, me, told them their behavior was beyond absurd.

I picked up a box of chocolates in the lobby of the hospital and delivered them to the nurses' station on Wes's floor. You could never be too nice to the nurses.

"Hi, this is for y'all so in case my husband snores too loud tonight y'all won't suffocate him?"

The head nurse on duty took the box and said, "Well, thank you! Who's your husband?"

"Wesley Carter. Room 129?"

"Oh, that man? He's sleeping like a little lamb," the nurse said and turned to the others. "Y'all want a chocolate-covered caramel?"

"Just keep an eye on him for me tonight, please?" I said.

They became as one voice, a Greek chorus of comedy and appetite.

"You know it, shugah! Come in here bringing candy? We gonna take extraspecial care of Mr. Carter! Isn't that right, ladies?"

"Uh-huh. I'm gonna watch him close!"

"Me too! Is that a chocolate-covered cherry?"

"Get your hands off that nougat! That's mine!"

There was a flurry of thanks and assurances. I smiled and went to find Wesley.

True to their description, Wesley was asleep, snoring softly and looking so calm and peaceful, if I hadn't known it was him by his pajamas, I might have thought someone switched bodies. I pulled a chair right up to the side of his bed and held his hand in mine. I was leaving him and without actually saying it, we all knew it. We all knew it.

CHAPTER 18

Wes the Patient

Les drove me home. The minute I opened the door from the garage I could sense the difference. The house smelled good. Les had been cooking. The kitchen counters didn't have crumbs all over them, and the garbage can wasn't overflowing. There were even some flowers on the table—probably from the grocery store—a nice touch. I stopped for a moment to catch my breath.

"What are you making?" I said.

"Lasagna," she said.

"That's my favorite," I said.

"I know. And I'm making beef stew and chicken soup."

"We don't need all that food," I said. What I should have said was *thanks*, but it just rolled off my tongue. It was probably the medication mixing up my manners.

"I'm making it to freeze."

"Oh," I said and realized she meant that she was cooking for us so we'd have something decent to eat when she left.

She still intended to leave. What could I do to make her stay? It was so damn nice to have her here. All at once I was bone tired and sore as hell.

"If you can just help me upstairs, I think I'm gonna take a nap," I said.

Les said, "Bertie? Help me, son."

"What?" Bertie looked up from the den where he was watching the Nature Channel or something. "Oh, yeah, sure. Come on, Dad. Easy there."

"Are Charlotte and Holly here?" I asked Bertie.

"Birthday party for some kid," Bertie said. "Back by five."

So they couldn't be here when I came home from the hospital.

"Seems like they should have been here," I said.

"Wes? You were barely gone for twenty-four hours," Les said, reading my mind.

"Whatever," I said.

I limped up the steps, leaning on Bertie and pulling on the rail. Then when I pushed open the door to my bedroom, I was pleasantly surprised. Everything was as clean as a whistle and a fresh pair of pajamas was laying on the side of the bed. I undid my belt and zipper and let my pants slide to the floor. Then I sat on the side of the bed, kicked off my loafers, and wiggled my legs free.

Les said, "Here, I'll get that."

"Thanks," I said.

She picked up my trousers and folded them lengthwise along the crease just as she'd done for the past thirty years. Then she took my loafers to the closet, and I'd bet every last dollar to my name that she put the shoe trees in them before she put them back in their place. My closet was kind of a mess because since she'd been gone I just wasn't as diligent about those things.

With her help, I eased myself under the covers and drifted off to sleep, but it wasn't really sleep. I could hear them talking, but I couldn't understand what they were saying. They closed the door and I thought they were still in the room but they weren't. The next thing I knew it was after five and I had slept away the entire afternoon. It was my cell phone that woke me up. I reached over and looked at the caller ID. It was Paolo. I answered it.

"I'm still alive," I said and chuckled.

"This is good news. So how'd it go?"

"I don't know. Okay, I guess. I had this Oriental surgeon, you know. Harold got him for me."

"I'm pretty sure they say *Asian* now but who cares? In general, they're smarter than everyone else anyway."

"Yeah," I said. "Walk in the park."

"For him maybe. You got any pain?"

"Not too bad. Not great but not impossible to deal with. Okay, it hurts like hell."

"Aw, man. Can I do anything for you? You want gelato?"

"Gelato? You Italians and your gelato. I love it. No, I think I need a martini, but I can't drink any booze with the medicine."

"Now *that's* terrible! What did they give you?"

"Hell, I don't know. Some antibiotic. Something else for pain that's blocking the road in between me and the vodka. So what's up with you? Heard from Harold?"

"Yeah. He's good. Anyway, so when can we hit the links?"

"A week. Maybe ten days. I'll get the green light from this Dr. Chen and let you know."

"Sounds good. So, no chemo or radiation?"

"Nope. Not so far."

"I'll call you tomorrow."

"Paolo?"

"What?"

"Coffee gelato is my favorite."

"You asshole."

It was good to hear from him. It was good to be alive! I knew it didn't pay to fool around with young girls like Cornelia and Lisette. Well, fool around maybe, but marry? Not in a million years! Here I was in my bed and my sheets smelled so good, and that never would've happened if Les was thirty. The best news of all? I wasn't going to die. Not yet anyway.

Les opened the door.

"I thought I heard you talking," she said.

"Yeah, Paolo called. You know, to see how I was feeling. Can you help me up? I want to go to the bathroom."

"Let me call Bertie. He's much stronger than I am. *Bertie!*"

"I'm so glad you're here, Les. You just don't know."

"Thanks," Les said kindly. "So how are you feeling? It's time for your pills."

"I'll take the antibiotic, but I don't want that other pill. Makes me too groggy."

"The doctor actually said you could try Motrin if this other pill made you itchy or anything like that."

A martini!

"We got any Motrin?"

Bertie came in.

"Ready, Dad?"

"Not quite." I rolled over on my side and propped myself up on one elbow. Slowly, I pushed myself up into a sitting position, but when I tried to stand, it pulled so badly in my groin that I thought I might topple over. Bertie grabbed me under the arms. "Maybe I'll take that pain pill."

"Yeah, I'd think you'd want them for the first couple of days," Les said. "After that Motrin might do the trick. The whole story with pain management is to stay ahead of the pain."

"I guess I'm stiff from lying down."

"Stitches pull too."

"Yeah," I said. "I want to go downstairs."

"For what?" Les said.

"To sit in my recliner and watch the Golf Channel."

"It's easier to bring a television to you, Wes."

"You can stream it on my laptop," Bertie said, helping me across the room.

"I don't know about streaming, but if I don't get in that little room soon . . ."

We made it there, and Bertie just kept standing around.

"I'll call you if I need you, son. Thanks."

"Okay, I'll go get my laptop. Be right back."

Streaming from a laptop. It was a whole new world, wasn't it?

I took my pills from Les, and Bertie set me up with actual live television on his computer. For the record, the computer did not smell. So I was all propped up and Les came in with a bowl of chicken soup and some buttered toast on a tray. Now, this was living!

"I thought you might be famished," she said.

"You know, now that you mention it, I am." It smelled delicious.

She moved the computer aside and put the tray on my lap.

"Call me when you're done, or I'll just send Charlotte or Bertie up to get it."

"Les, you're the best! Isn't it wonderful to be here with all of us together?"

"I think the pain medicine has gone to your brain, Wes. Really."

"Well, thanks for the soup."

She left the room and I thought, Oh, boy, this isn't going to be easy. I reached for my cell phone and called the house. Les answered.

"Why are you calling the house?" she said.

"Because it hurts too much to call out for someone. Can I talk to Bertie?"

"Sure. *Bertie?*"

"What's up, Dad?"

"Get your sister and come upstairs."

"Uh, okay."

A few minutes later here came Bertie and Charlotte.

"I brought you a slice of chocolate cake and a glass of milk," Charlotte said. "It's pretty good."

"It's hard to get good chocolate cake in Kathmandu," Bertie said.

"I'll bet. Thanks," I said. "Sit down."

They sat and looked back and forth at each other.

"Okay, what's wrong with your mother?" I took a bite of the cake. It was delicious.

"Good question," Charlotte said. "She gave us total hell last night."

"Yeah, we weren't going to say anything about it with you being sick and all, but she totally talked to us like we were a couple of losers," Bertie said.

"Well, is she wrong? Do you think you're big winners?"

Charlotte stood to leave. "You know what? I liked it better when you and Mom didn't agree on anything."

"When was that?" I said and didn't know what in the hell she was talking about.

Bertie piped in. "Yeah, she always used to defend us but not last night. I mean, she was really pissed. She went into this whole speech about how we're the only two children on earth who aren't obsessed with pleasing their parents."

"What's the matter with pleasing your parents?" I said. "Tell me because I'd like to learn something here."

"It's obsessive behavior that's a problem for me," Bertie said. "Man, that's sick."

"I see," I said.

"If I were you?" Charlotte said. "I'd look out. I'll bet you're next on her list."

"She's been nothing but nice to me," I said. "Ask her to come up here. Here, take this with you, please." I handed her my tray.

A few minutes later, here came Leslie. I put on my best face, under the circumstances.

"Come sit down, sweetheart, talk to me."

"You okay?" she said.

"Yeah, yeah. I'm fine. So I just wanted to say thank you for everything you've done, Les. You really saved me, you know. I mean, the house is all organized. You cooked all this great food. I'm just so happy to have you back. I'm really hoping you're going to stay."

"I'm not staying," she said.

Just like that. She said, *I'm not staying* just like she was saying *Pass the peas.*

"Why not?"

"Are you kidding me? Listen, Wes, ever since I walked in this door I've been cooking and cleaning. No one lifts a finger around here. When I got here, this house was so filthy that I called Martha and had to *beg* her to come back and help me. And she's not coming back unless it's a life-or-death situation. I was so tired I almost fell on my face."

"We need you, Les. I need you. You're the only one I trust."

She was as cool as a cucumber as she delivered the lethal blow.

"Trust? You listen to me, Wesley Carter, and hear me good. For thirty years I've been your personal slave, swallowing more nonsense than every dumb goose in Canada. I've scrubbed, cleaned, scrimped and saved, driven old cars, shopped sales, and all the while you've been sitting on twenty-two million dollars! How do you think I feel? I feel like a fool, that's what."

Oh my God! Wait! She knew!

"I thought I told you to use the key only if I died!" Now I was angry.

"I didn't touch your stupid key. When you get out of bed, go check the tape. Shame on you, Wesley Carter. Shame on all of you. I wish someone in this house could give me just one reason to stay. Just one."

"Because we need you?" I said.

"Need? You know what? You could've said you *love* me or *please stay because if you left it would break my heart!* But not you. You say stay because *we need you*. Get another maid, Wes. I'm going back to Charleston."

"What are you saying? Are you telling me you want a divorce?"

"No. No, I'm not saying that. I just don't want to be here until I'm all used up, Wes. There's precious little joy in this for me. Who in this house cares about my happiness?"

She walked out of the room and I thought, Oh my God, I am so screwed.

I called Harold as fast as my fingers could dial his number.

"Hey, Wes! You feeling okay?"

"No. Leslie just told me she found out about the money. She's very angry."

Silence.

"Bubba? You'd better calm her down, or it's gonna cost you half of everything you own. It's equitable distribution in Georgia. That's the law."

CHAPTER 19

Les Returns

By the time I left, there were thirty-six one-pint containers of various soups, stews, and pastas stacked up in the freezer, all labeled and dated. The atmosphere did not improve a whole lot except that Wes was being *extremely* nice. He wasn't kidding me. Not anymore.

Thursday night I *served* chicken piccata with a mushroom risotto and a green salad. Wes was able to dress and come to the table unassisted, so as far as I was concerned, my responsibilities to take care of him *in sickness* had been fulfilled.

"So you're really leaving in the morning?" Charlotte said.

"Where're you going, Gammy?" Holly said, picking the mushrooms out of her risotto.

"Back to my brother's house," I said. "You'll have to get your mother to bring you down to see me and I'll take you to the beach. We can make a sand castle and hunt for seashells and all sorts of wonderful things. Don't you like mushrooms?"

"I like 'em separate. You bring me, Mommy?"

"Sure," Charlotte said.

"This is absolutely delicious," Wes said.

"Yeah, it's totally awesome," Bertie said.

"Thanks," I said. "But I've made this dish exactly the same way for as long as I've been cooking."

"Well, it's more delicious than I remember," Wes said.

I wanted to slap him right across his disingenuous face. I sighed instead.

"So when will we see you again?" Charlotte said.

"I'll be back for Molly's wedding, but Harlan is coming home and I'd like to spend some time with him."

"That's an excellent idea, Les," Wes said. "Please give him my very best regards."

I looked at him and thought, Now it's time to knock his teeth out. But I sighed again, doubly hard. It was the very first congenial thing Wes had to say about Harlan in twenty years or maybe ever. And there was no possible way that he meant that or any of the overblown compliments and platitudes he was hurling around like Frisbees.

"Do you need a ride to the airport?" Charlotte asked.

Suddenly I had a chauffeur?

"No, but thank you. I'm going to drive back to Charleston," I said.

"How come?" Wes said and wiped his mouth with his napkin. "Do you think I can have another piece of that delicious chicken? Is there enough to go around for everyone to have seconds?"

"There's plenty. Charlotte, please give your father another piece of the delicious chicken." Obviously Wes had gone off the deep end. "Because I need a car there, and I want to take some things with me. It's not that long of a trip."

Charlotte got up without a word and fixed Wes another serving of everything on his plate.

"What are you taking?" Wes said and resumed eating with theatrical relish. "My God! This is unbelievable chicken!"

Where were my hip boots when I needed them?

"Are you worried that I'm taking the silver?" I asked.

"No, of course not, Les," Wes said. "The silver! Isn't your mom funny? Ha! Ha! Good one, Les!"

Charlotte and Bertie exchanged nervous looks.

"I'm taking some more clothes and a few other things I'd like to have with me."

"Well, then take my car," Wes said. "The tires are newer, and it's got roadside assistance if you get a flat or something, God forbid!"

The Almighty Benz? Did Wes grow a giant brain tumor overnight?

"But, Wes, I've never driven your car," I said.

"That's because *no one* drives Daddy's car," Charlotte said. "Unless they want to die."

"Charlotte, don't be silly! Leslie? I insist! Drive it around the block while the kids do the dishes. You're taking the Benz and I don't want to hear another word about it."

The *kids* were going to do the dishes? What did he say to them?

"Wes? What if something happens to it?" I said.

"Oh, don't worry. It's leased."

How could I forget that? How? Really? Easy. Because I didn't want *to remember* that he leased a new Benz every three years so he could get all the latest gadgets like fanny warmers and massagers. I drove an old Audi that I bought used that was leap years behind in technology. It was so old it didn't even have a GPS, much less satellite radio or backup warning sensors.

"Well, if you insist," I said.

"I insist. The key is in the ashtray of the car."

After dinner, the kids actually cleaned the kitchen, and I took Wes's car out for a spin. I have to say, it was pretty much like heaven to drive. I thought, Well, you know what? Maybe I'll dump my old

Audi and lease one of these for myself! Why shouldn't I have a nice car, one as nice as his? Maybe even one slightly newer!

The next morning I packed the Audi. I didn't want Wes's car. Then I went into Wes's files with the secret forbidden key to look for the title and I found it in the folder named *cars*. Then I pulled a dozen checks from our joint checking account register that I had never used and put them in an envelope in my purse. I was all done with Wes Carter deciding who got what when and how much. I left the key in the center of his desk. Naked, waiting for an inquisitive pair of eyes.

No one was awake except Holly, and she was in the den fully occupied by an episode of *Sesame Street,* eating dry Cheerios with a juice box. Charlotte kept those things on a lower shelf in the pantry within her reach. This was parenting in 2012? I gave her a kiss and a hug and told her she was a good girl. She smiled like an angel and told me she loved me.

I had a cup of coffee and looked around, picking up a few things— pictures of my parents, the children, and Holly; a paperweight my father had given me; a small clock that I'd always loved. Its chime would remind me of Holly's sweet voice. In a shoebox, I packed up my CDs of Mendelssohn, Schubert, Bach, and Vivaldi that no one would miss. And I took my seldom used rice steamer. After all, if I was to have a new life in Charleston, it couldn't be a proper life without a rice steamer. I'd take my mother's silver at another time. If I moved out bit by bit, no one would even notice.

I was about to leave when Bertie stumbled into the kitchen, wiping the sleep from his eyes.

"Hey, Mom. I'm glad you're still here," he said. "We got coffee?"

"Yep. A whole pot."

"Sweet." He poured himself a mugful. "So I've been thinking about what you said; you know, the other day when you read me and Charlotte the riot act?"

"What about it?" I said.

"Well, I just think you have to accept us for who we are, you know? I mean, we accept you for who you are, don't we? It's important to be tolerant of others and celebrate our differences."

It was really much too early in the day for murder.

"Bertie, here's my problem with that reasoning. When people see you, they think *this* is who you are." I waved my hand from his head to his feet. "But the truth is that this whole costumelike persona is only one tiny aspect of who you are. There's a lot more on the inside than you can see on the outside. So as long as you look like this, people will judge you unfairly."

"Mom, I look like all the guys my age in Kathmandu."

"But you're in Atlanta. Take a bath."

"I see your point."

"Look, I've got to get on the road or else I'm going to sit in rush-hour traffic for hours. I'll see you in a few weeks if you're still here for the wedding."

"Yeah, I think I'm gonna stay for a while. Dad needs help getting around, and it's pretty nice here at this time of year."

"You might think about gainful employment," I said, and he gave me a look. "It's just a thought."

"Mom! Wait!"

It was Charlotte.

"You didn't have to get up," I said. "We said our good-byes last night."

She threw her arms around me and hugged me hard. Then she stood back and looked at me with such an odd expression I thought she was going to start crying.

"Taking Dad to the doctor. Checkup this morning."

"Good," I said.

"I'm sorry, Mom. I don't blame you for being frustrated with us. We suck."

"Yeah, at the moment you both sort of do, but life's long and there's time yet for you both to amount to something spectacular."

"I'm going to do better. I swear," Charlotte said.

"Me too," Bertie said.

"That's a start. But I'd rather see y'all shoot higher than to merely be *better*—go be brilliant! Now, I'll call y'all when I arrive, okay? Tell your father I said so."

There were the perfunctory kisses all around and one last hug from Holly, who had traipsed in to see what was going on.

"Love you, Gammy," she said. "Don't go."

I didn't want to leave her either, but the only way Charlotte was ever going to be the kind of mother Holly needed was if she had to.

"It's okay, Holly Doodle, I'll be back before you know it."

They followed me to the garage, watched me squeeze through the narrow space between my car and the wall to get in my car, because Wes insisted on the better one, and only then did they realize that I wasn't taking the Benz.

"Hey!" Charlotte said. "I thought you were taking Dad's car!"

"Nah," I said. "I decided to get a Benz of my own when I get to Charleston. You can tell that to your father too if you want."

"Righteous," Bertie said and smiled.

"Oh, shut up, Bertie," Charlotte said. "You've never even surfed one day in your whole life."

"Bye, y'all!" I said, raised my window, and backed out of the garage. Wes was in my rearview mirror, dressed for the day and holding *The Wall Street Journal*. I stopped and rolled down my window again.

"Les? Can you turn the car off? I want to talk to you for a minute."

Every hair on the back of my neck stood up. Instinctively, I knew Wes had something up his sleeve. Had he already discovered the missing checks? And that I had taken the title to the Audi?

"Sure," I said and put the car in park.

"Want to get out so we can go sit on the porch?"

"Okay," I said, turned the car off, and got out. "What's going on, Wes?"

"I've been thinking, that's all, and I just want to talk to you about something."

I sat on one of the wrought-iron benches that stood on either side of our front door, and he sat on the other.

"You know, I don't think we've ever sat on these at the same time," I said, and it was true. They were awfully nice, but mostly decorative.

"You're probably right. So, Les, I've been thinking. We can't do this like this."

"Do what how?" I said.

"Almost thirty years together and boom? It's not right. I think we owe each other more than this, you know, to at least try and figure out what we're doing here."

"What do you mean?"

"Well, remember I told you that I got the name of someone I wanted us to go and see? They're these supershrinks who manage to rehab all kinds of relationships, and I think we ought to go and see them. You know, give it a stab? In fact, I've already set up a couple of crisis sessions with them for the week after next. Normally, it takes weeks to get in, but I convinced them . . ."

"You *what*?"

"Yeah, I did. I knew you wanted to go see your brother and all that, which is fine. So go see him, have fun, but please if you can, come back next Sunday so we can make our Monday appointments?"

I thought about it and came to a quick conclusion that it was hopeless.

"I don't know, Wes. I don't know."

"Look, I never asked you for much," he said. "I think this is critical."

I just looked at him and cocked my head to one side. Was he kidding? Never asked me for much? He saw it on my face.

"Okay," he said, "maybe I asked for a lot. But you're walking out of here and busting up our family like this? I just think you owe it to me and to all of us to make sure this is the right thing to do."

Now what was I supposed to say to that? Frankly, I didn't feel like I owed him a damn thing. It was quite the other way around. But he had gone to the trouble of trying to get us to at least talk it out with a professional. Maybe that meant something. Maybe his experience with cancer had made him reconsider his behavior.

"Okay, Wes. I'll go to one session for you, but that's it."

"Well, I booked more than one, but we'll see. Thanks, Leslie. I just don't want you to have any regrets."

"I'll see you Sunday," I said and started the car. "E-mail me the information, okay?"

"Sure. Drive safe."

Wes was really going to lose his mind when he discovered the missing checks. He was going to need CPR. I smiled the whole way out of Atlanta. I knew the only reason he wanted to see those psychiatrists was because he didn't want to give up one dime he had to his name. It had nothing to do with love. But what if it did? It was true that different people loved in different ways and that they showed it differently. What if all the nice things Wes had been saying to me were his way of trying to show me how much he cared? It was easy to leave Wes when I was convinced he didn't give a damn, but I didn't want to hurt anyone. That wasn't the woman I'd ever been. But they all made me so angry! What would life be if I went back to Wes? Horrible! It gave me chest pain to even consider it. But was I ready to walk away from *all* of it? My *children*? *Holly*?

I drove for several hours and finally began to sense the Lowcountry. I passed over the Edisto and other smaller bodies of water, over which hung the enormous branches of live oaks and long sheers of Spanish moss. Those haunted trees had graced the banks of these same rivers and streams from the days the Catawbas, the Sewees, and the very first fathers and mothers of our country walked the land. At one point in South Carolina's history over twenty tribes of Native Americans lived here. In my mind's eye, I could almost see them silently moving down the water in canoes or making their way through the woods. The water, glassy and pristine, reflected every dock and boat and tree in a perfect mirror image. How did I always forget how powerful the Lowcountry was? Because I had lived the past thirty-plus years of my life in Atlanta, lost in the needs of Wes and the children when Wes had never cared about mine. It was so beautiful here you could lose yourself in the landscape.

Actually, I thought to myself, that's kind of a funny point because what *were* my needs? I'd been so consumed by Wes and the children I'd never had time to develop any personal desires. I gardened, true, but mostly out of a sense of duty to the house. Okay, I'll admit I got some pleasure out of the results, and the work itself was a great way to relieve stress. But the only passion I really ever had, my love of chamber music, had been squelched by Wes's aversion to it. Well, things are going to be very different from now on, I told myself. Very different. Maybe I'd indulge myself in endless concerts, learn all about it. Maybe I'd grow fruit trees and wire gorgeous music into the garden of wherever I wound up living.

As soon as I passed Orangeburg and changed counties, I opened my windows and let the edges of the Lowcountry rush inside. It's just a fact of life that the air around Charleston is sweeter and thick. I wanted to drink it. I called Jonathan when I was about thirty miles outside of the city. He didn't pick up, so I just left a message that I'd be home soon.

Just as I was coming into the business area on the outskirts of Charleston, my cell phone rang. It was Harlan calling from Milan. I pulled into a gas station to talk to him.

"Ciao, bella! Come stai?"

"Tutto bene!" I said, using all my Italian in one exchange. "When are you getting home? I have so much to tell you!" I pulled over into a filling station.

"Tomorrow afternoon. Is everything okay?"

"Yes. Everything is fine."

"Where are you? Do I hear the roar of traffic?"

"Yes, you do. I'm in an Exxon station. As you know, it's against the law to hold a phone and drive an old beat-up car at the same time. I'm just coming back from Atlanta."

"It's a bad idea anyway, never mind the law. Why did you go to Atlanta? A conjugal visit?"

"Heavens, no! No, this is terrible, but Wes found out that he had testicular cancer, so I went to Atlanta to get him through the surgery."

"Testicular cancer? Holy Mother Church! *That's terrible!* Is he all right?"

"He's totally fine. They don't think he'll even need chemo."

"Well, good, I guess. Now, more important, how's my Miss Jo?"

I giggled. I couldn't blame Harlan for not caring too much about Wes's well-being.

"She's been staying with her uncle Jonathan while I was away, and I fear he's spoiled her rotten."

"Impossible. She couldn't be any more rotten than she is."

"Well, we're all in love with her. That's a fact."

"I brought her something she's going to love," he said, in a voice that told me whatever the gift was that it was something ridiculous.

"Okay, tell me," I said. "What extravagance did you manage to find?"

"Matching father/daughter Prada raincoats and hats." He started to laugh. "You know Leonard adored anything Prada."

"Oh, Harlan, there's no excuse for you!"

"And a great handbag for her auntie too! You'll love it!"

"Oh, Harlan! You are too much, brother. I'm going to make a feast for you!"

"If you'll just throw away all the catalogs and junk mail, that will be sufficient, thanks. Hey, how's Jonathan?"

"Jonathan's great. He's probably the kindest man I've ever met."

"Hmmm. Sounds lukewarm to me. Don't settle for lukewarm, Les."

"Hey, Harlan? I'm not settling ever again. Don't worry about that. See you tomorrow. Safe flight!"

Was my relationship with Jonathan lukewarm? Hardly. His kindness is what brought me back to life and made me feel like a woman again. Harlan would see that when he got home. But Harlan would also see that I wasn't ready to jump into another committed relationship with anyone. Besides, Jonathan kept talking about moving across country in perhaps as soon as a year.

By the time I pulled into Harlan's driveway, I had spoken to Jonathan. He had a plan. He was picking me up at six, we were driving out to the beach, and he was making dinner for me.

"Nothing fancy," he'd said, "but at least you won't have to cook on your first night home."

I'd told him I'd be ready and I was. I brought all my things inside and placed the pictures I'd brought all around my bedroom and the sitting room. I put a small one of Holly right by my bed. I was excited to see Jonathan. God forgive me, but the few hundred miles between me and Wes felt so good. I'm sorry to say it, but it just did. I was already dreading going back for the wedding.

I had this crazy fluttering in my chest, and the closer it got to six o'clock my pulse picked up speed. But true to his punctual habits, six o'clock rolled around and the doorbell rang.

"Hey!" I said. "It feels like I haven't seen you in a month!"

It was true.

"Hey, yourself!" He gave me a great big hug and a bunch of silly, noisy smooches all over my face that made me laugh. "I missed you!"

"I missed you too. You've got Miss JP in the car?"

"She's out at the beach. I can tell you with authority that she doesn't like the sand at all."

"Well, of course not. She's got tender little princess paws. That mean old sand gets very hot."

"I can't believe Harlan doesn't have little sandals for her," he said. "In eight colors."

"I know. It's abusive. He'll be home tomorrow. I'll bring it up with him."

"Tomorrow? Great! I hate to admit it, but I'm not cut out for dogs," he said.

"Really? I thought you loved Miss Jo."

"I do. If you could potty train her, I'd love her a lot more. Come on, let's get going. I'm too old to pick up poop."

He held open my car door, and I slipped in the car next to him.

"Potty train a dog?" I said. "I know they can potty train cats, but I'm too old to share a bathroom with anyone."

We got to Jonathan's house and pulled up in the yard. I could hear Miss Jo yipping on the other side of the door. She was excited, and when we opened the door, she literally jumped with joy.

"Come here, you darling little girl!" I said, and she flew into my arms, licking my face in a frenzy of dog kisses. "My goodness!"

"Can you imagine what she's going to do when she sees Harlan?"

"She'll pass out cold!" We laughed. Miss Jo was now on the floor, on her back, tongue hanging out with happiness while I rubbed her tummy.

"Feel like a glass of wine?"

"Are you kidding? You cannot believe the week I've just had."

He poured me a goblet of wine, and he had one for himself.

"I'll bet. Come on outside and let's catch the breeze."

We walked out to the porch, and the breeze blew my hair all around. It felt like a baptism then, as though the damp salty air cleansed me of all my sins. It was telling me I was home and I was safe. I inhaled, exhaled, took a sip of my wine, and looked at Jonathan with the sparkling ocean and the white dunes and the crazy sky shot with so many colors, all behind him in a panorama of what heaven must look like.

"I love the way you look," I said. "I love the way your eyebrows grow and the shape of your nose and how you listen with your eyes and ears. You're just wonderful. Do you know that?"

"Where have you been all my life?"

"Darlin'? I've been in the wrong church, in the wrong pew, at the wrong service. The air smells so good out here."

"Yes, it does. So tell me how it went."

"Where to start? Wes's surgery was textbook and he's fine, still waiting for the lab report but we're pretty sure he's rid of the cancer, but that doesn't mean it wasn't high drama. My daughter and son? They're another story. They almost drove me insane, and for the first time in forever, I gave them both a piece of my mind."

"What's the matter with them?"

"My daughter just has this awful attitude. She thinks I live to wait on her like a personal maid. And she's pushy. And she's lazy. My God, she's lazy! She can't even wash a spoon! Can't support her child. And she drinks too much. Only to be outdone by her brother, who looks like a shepherd from the days of Moses. He can't earn a living either. And he smells."

"Look, my kids gave me a run for my money too, but you can

never give up on them. Ever hear the old saying, every flower blooms in its own time? They just haven't bloomed yet."

"Well, my two are sure taking their sweet time."

"Hmmm. Listen, just remember; don't give up on them. How old are they?"

"Old enough to act like adults."

"Maybe now they will. You put the fear of God in them and walked out? I'm sure you gave them a lot to think about."

"Honestly? I think they were more insulted than put in their place. I hope you're right. I guess a lot remains to be seen."

"Always. Be thankful that life's long. You hungry? I've got a bowl of steamed shrimp in the refrigerator. And some kind of avocado, tomato, mozzarella salad they were selling at Whole Foods."

"That sounds like exactly what I want."

He had set the table in his dining room, but in the end we decided to eat at the table on the porch. The air was too delicious to ignore and peeling shrimp was a messy business anyway. We talked and ate until the island was covered in darkness, and then we lit some hurricane-covered candles and talked some more.

"So I promised him I'd go to this therapy with him, which I'm sure will be a complete waste of time and money."

"Most therapy is a narcissistic exercise," Jonathan said.

"Honey? You think Wes Carter is in this to justify his exemplary behavior and have a professional agree with him? Heck, no. He's trying to keep control of every single asset. It's all about control. He thinks a therapist can make *me* see the error of *my* ways, as though this will help me calm down and spend the rest of my life making Wes's breakfast. Ain't happening. You should've heard him. He said he set this all up for *me* so *I* wouldn't have any regrets."

"Good grief. The subtle manipulation. I hate head games."

"Me too. The only regret I have is that I agreed to go back."

"Well, a few sessions with a shrink are one thing. But I can't imagine you going back to that life. I mean, it's your decision. You have to do what you think is the best thing for you."

"Don't worry. I'm never going back. This visit convinced me of that more than ever."

"You're not stringing me along, are you, Leslie?"

"Why in the world would you say that?"

"Therapy makes me nervous. A clever therapist can make you believe a lot of things."

"I'll be on guard."

In the morning, Jonathan dropped me and Miss Jo off at Harlan's and then went on to work. It was so easy to be with him. As much as I proclaimed that I wasn't going to get into a serious relationship with anyone, I could slide right into Jonathan's life like a hand slips into the perfect-fitting kid glove. We both knew it. The truth was that Jonathan was as much a friend as he was a lover and maybe at this point in my life, that was what I needed. Maybe as you aged, what you wanted from a relationship changed too. Yes, I could see that. It wasn't so terrible to get older if you could be with someone who had a good sense of how much you wanted and if how much you were willing to give was enough for them. No, Jonathan and I were in a comfortable groove.

I thought about this as I rushed around, tidying up all the rooms, putting fresh flowers in the dining room and a small vase of roses right from the garden next to Harlan's bed, but there was already one there. This house was making me a wreck. I lifted the vase and inhaled. They smelled delicious enough to eat. His e-mail said he was arriving at three, and I still had tons to do to prepare for his home-coming. I fluffed his pillows and changed his towels, which were probably dusty from sitting there for a month, and I checked the liquor cabinet, making a list of what to replenish. Then I shopped, deciding to make rack of lamb for dinner with mashed potatoes and those little French string beans. Comfort food. And I made an apple tart. Harlan loved apples. Okay, I used a premade crust, but the house smelled fantastic and I knew Harlan would be so happy.

All the while I flitted from room to room, Miss Jo was on my heels, following me everywhere. Every time I said, *Daddy's coming home,* she wagged her tail and barked. It was as though she knew Harlan was on his way back to her. Finally, at around three, she sat in front of her wardrobe closet and barked like mad. She wanted a new outfit. I didn't blame her. She'd most likely been wearing the same dress all week.

"I'm with you, girl. Jonathan's a great guy but all that seer-sucker? It doesn't scream fashionista, does it? I think it's time to resurrect the martini dress and the Barbara Bush pearls. What do you think?"

Soon, I was pulling into the Charleston Airport with a coiffed Miss Jo. Now, I'm not saying she knew *exactly* what was going on, but she recognized the airport as a place where people came and went. We parked, went inside, checked the arrivals board, and waited in the baggage claim. His plane had just touched down.

Minutes later, here he came. Miss Jo was so excited she wiggled her way out of my arms, jumped to the floor, and strained against her leash until he reached her.

"Yes, yes! My sweet! Daddy's home! Hey, Les!"

"Hey, Harlan."

I couldn't stop laughing. It was the sweetest thing I ever saw. Miss Jo was wild with enthusiasm. Wild! She sat, she held out her paw, she walked on her hind legs, she rolled over, and she sat up to beg. She performed all her tricks to show Harlan how happy she was that he was back. Finally, he picked her up and cuddled her, and only then did she begin to calm down.

"Thank the Lord I only have one dog!" he said, and we laughed.

"Let's get your bags," I said. "Are you exhausted?"

"Beyond! All the trustees came home yesterday with our travel person, but I stayed an extra day. At least I didn't have to be the tour guide and lead all our folks through customs and all of that."

I nodded my head. "So it was great, huh?"

"What can I say? Italy? It's incredible. Just boggles the mind. Even the dirt is more beautiful than ours. Plus, it's porcini mushroom season. Grilled, with a little olive oil and coarse salt? I ate them for lunch and dinner every day until my tongue turned black. Then I gave them a rest."

"That was probably for the best. Are those your bags?"

"Yep. Adesso! Andiamo! Let's blow this pizza parlor."

"Am I going to be subjected to Italian metaphors for the foreseeable future?"

"Sì, signora."

"Good! I'm so happy you're home. I really am, Harlan. I missed you like mad."

We threw his bags in the trunk of my Audi and slammed the lid closed.

"There's nothing in the world like a great sister!" he said.

"I'm assuming that means me," I said and gave him another sisterly hug.

Over dinner, I told Harlan the whole Atlanta story about Wes, his surgery, the kids, and the proposed therapy, and he was as attentive as he could be given how tired he was.

"Sounds like insanity. So, by the way, how are things with Jonathan?"

"Comfortable. Wonderful. But you know, I'm not divorced, and I haven't even decided if I'm going to go through with a divorce. And he's talking about moving to California to be near his kids."

"Plans change." Harlan paused and then said, "Well, sugar, if you don't know what you want to do, therapy is an excellent idea."

"You don't think it's a waste of time?"

"Maybe, but look. Thirty years is a long time, and I wouldn't throw that away until I'd satisfied myself that it was truly over."

"I think this is about the money. He knows I know."

"How did he handle that revelation?"

"Ballistic on the level of a Chinese New Year's firework display? In Beijing? At the Olympics?"

"I bet. Well, look, I think you have to go back. Then you can tell yourself you gave your marriage every chance you could."

"Harlan? Do you think it's possible to sell my Audi and lease a new little red Benz before I go to Atlanta? I brought some checks with me."

Harlan nearly spit his mashed potatoes across the table, and then he began to laugh this uproariously crazy laugh. I hadn't heard him thunder like that in twenty years. Then I began to laugh with him. This went on for what seemed to be a very long time. We got up from the table, and Harlan hugged me with all his might.

"She's saved!" he cried. "Oh, Leslie Greene Carter! You're alive! It would be my greatest pleasure to handle that for you myself!"

"Can we get one that comes with diamond stud earrings?"

"I'm certain that we can."

PART THREE

Therapy Continues

CHAPTER 20

Wes—The Joint Session

"So the way this is going to work," said my leggy therapist, Dr. Jane Saunders, "is that I'm going to lead this two-hour session with Wes for almost half the time, and then we'll have a break for ten minutes. After the break, Dr. Katz is going to take over and we'll hear from Les. If at any time the other party wants to make a comment, please feel free to do so. I know that the two of you are not terribly hostile toward each other, but I want to remind you that the more civil you are with each other, the more success will be had. All right?"

"Sure," I said.

"So, Wes?" Dr. Saunders said. "I believe you've had some news from your company, is that right?"

"I've been offered an early retirement package, and I think I should take it."

Les said, "Really? Are you ready to retire, Wes?"

"Well, it came as kind of a surprise, but it made me think. I have to retire eventually, and I don't want to wait until I'm too old to enjoy it."

"I know how you feel," Les said.

Both doctors made a note of Les's remark. Did Les mean that she wanted out of our marriage as though she was retiring from a corporate job and with that she could take *her* retirement package and just go do what *she* wanted?

"What's that supposed to mean, Leslie?" I said it nicely, but her remark certainly did sound insulting.

"Look, Wes, what have your retirement plans always been?" she asked.

"To play the top one hundred golf courses in the United States. I've said it a million times. They're located in some very lovely places that even you might enjoy."

"Such as?"

"Well, all up and down the California coast, but there's also a great one in Ardmore, Pennsylvania, and there's another one in Frankfort, Michigan, and one in Roland, Arkansas. Don't forget Ooltewah, Tennessee."

"Wesley? Do you really think I have any interest whatsoever in seeing those golf courses? I mean, I'm sure those are perfectly nice places populated with lovely people, but I wouldn't get excited to have dinner with even the likes of Tiger Woods unless he came to my house. Even then I'm not so sure. *I don't* care about golf. *You* care about golf."

"So what does *that* mean, Leslie? That if I want to hold my family together I have to give up golf in my golden years and sit home with you on the sofa watching you *knit*?"

"First of all," Leslie said, "I don't want you to give up golf. You love it! You live for it! And I don't knit. This is not about holding our family together, Wes. The kids are adults and ought to be living on their own. But Charlotte and Bertie will *always* be my children *and* yours. This is about us. We just want different things."

"Do you want to tell these nice relationship counselors what you did when you left Atlanta the last time? What you took? And what you bought?"

"I took ten checks from an account in my name that Wes has hidden from me for the entire span of our marriage. That account is in my name as well. It has twenty-two million dollars in it, and I never knew it was there."

"Because you would've gone crazy and spent it," I said. "Look at how much you blew in the last month!"

Dr. Katz interrupted. "Leslie? Have you ever been fiscally irresponsible in the past?"

"Never in my life," she said.

I wasn't letting them get away with this. "And what did you buy yourself with those checks, Leslie?"

"I leased a little Mercedes-Benz and I bought a pair of diamond stud earrings for three thousand dollars," she said, without one single solitary trace of remorse.

"See?" I said triumphantly. "That's why I never gave her access to that account! The first thing she does . . ."

Then Saunders piped up. "What kind of car do you drive, Wes?"

"Well, it's a Benz, the big one, but in my line of business, it's important for a man in my position to have the right car. It says something about my position in life. Leslie doesn't need a Mercedes to go to the grocery store, does she?"

"Wes?" Leslie said. "I wanted one. That simple. I wanted one, we have the money, you have one, now I have one."

"So you think you're getting even with me or something? For what? What did I do?"

"Nothing, Wes, and that's part of our problem," Les said.

"What is that supposed to mean?" I was getting plenty pissed now.

"It doesn't mean anything, Wes. We've been through all this, how many times?"

"Well, tell me this. What in the hell are you doing going around buying yourself diamond earrings? Who are you trying to impress?"

"Wes, almost every woman I know has at least one piece of good jewelry. It's my sixtieth birthday soon, and I've always wanted a pair of diamond studs. We have the money. It's not like I called up Cartier and told them to send over the biggest diamonds they have."

"Your sixtieth birthday isn't for two years." What? Now she's going to let the world know I forgot her big birthday was coming?

"Actually, it's next week. Would you like me to show you my driver's license to prove it?"

"It is?"

"Yes, it is."

Shit! She had me! I must look like a pathetic idiot. Can't even remember my wife's birthday? No. That looks very bad.

"But you look so young? How can this be? Is it true? You're sixty?"

"Yep, next week."

"I'm so sorry, Les. I guess I've been so worried about my cancer and all and now they want me to retire. Can you imagine how *I* feel?" Everyone in the room was quiet. "Well, wear them in good health, Leslie. You deserve them if that's what you want. I just wish I'd given them to you, that's all. A woman shouldn't have to buy her own diamonds."

Dr. Saunders spoke up. "All right, let's take a break now and meet back here in ten minutes?"

Leslie stood up and said, "Great! Then perhaps we can talk about Wes and his hookers?"

This was not going well.

CHAPTER 21

Les in Therapy

Now it was Dr. Harrison Katz's turn to lead the discussion.

"So, Leslie, you've taken up residence with your brother in Charleston, South Carolina. Is that right?"

"With her brother, Harlan. Who is a cream puff," Wes said, for no good reason at all except that Wes's homophobia was a disgrace to the twenty-first century and all humanity.

I thought Katz and Saunders were going to collapse. Katz turned red, and Saunders turned white.

"It's precisely this kind of cruel prejudice and Wes's lack of respect for my family that led me to take up residence with my brother. And, for the last time, Wesley, if you insult my brother once more? You'll regret it," I said.

"Oh, please," Wes said and rolled his eyes to the ceiling.

"Look, Wes, I'm not the same girl you married."

"Boy, I'll say," he said and sort of coughed.

I wanted to grab him by his shoulders and shake him to make him stop.

"There's no reason to be insulting, Wes," I said. "Listen to me. The purpose of this therapy was for you to satisfy yourself that leading separate lives is the best thing for us to do. I think it is, and with every day that passes, I believe this more and more. I'm not angry with you, Wes. And it's not that I don't care about you, because you know I do. We just want different things in our lives at this point, and I think we ought to be able to pursue those interests. Look, maybe we have twenty years left before we're dead. Shouldn't we do the things we want to do?"

"Well, *I* intend to," he said. "And what do you want, Leslie? Some stud like Danette's got herself?"

"Actually, no. I want to travel all over Europe, Wes. I want to hear an opera at the Vienna opera house and La Scala too. I want to learn about wine and cheese in France and Italy, and I want to go to all the great museums. And I want to listen to chamber music in my house, morning, noon, and night, until I have memorized every single quartet, sextet, and octet ever written, and I want to recognize who's playing them. And I want to laugh, Wes. I want to laugh and have fun. I have earned it."

"This is about that man I saw you with, isn't it?" Wes turned to Katz and Saunders and said, "I saw a picture of my wife with a man in the background of a photograph in the *AJC*. Nice, huh?"

"The man was Jonathan Ray, an old high school friend, and he has absolutely nothing to do with this entire ordeal."

It was true.

"You view this as an ordeal, do you?" Wes said.

"Because it is. What about your hookers, Wes?"

"Hookers don't mean anything. It's just sex. It's not like Harold and Danette."

I turned to Saunders and Katz and said, "The idea of my husband picking up hookers is completely revolting to me. It's still infidelity. And, Wes, you cannot possibly compare their marriage to ours."

"Maybe, but you're right; we're not like them. And right again, I hate chamber music. It's like funeral music! And I'd rather take a bullet than sit through an opera—cats screeching! Apparently, we *don't* want or like the same things anymore."

"I'm not sure we ever did."

"So this is it? You want a divorce?"

"No, I don't. Not today or in the foreseeable future either. I just want to do what *I* want to do in the same way *you* want to do what *you* want to do."

"Oh, I see, what's good for the goose is good for the gander?"

"If it helps you to understand my feelings, then yes. Look, I have a proposal for you that won't make the lawyers rich."

"Well," Wes said, "I'm all ears for that."

"I've been spending a lot of time thinking, Wes. A lot of time. And I want whatever happens between us to be fair. Maybe this is too modern for your blood, but how's this? You keep the house and everything in it except for my mother's silver and my personal belongings like my clothes and so forth. I'll find a house of similar value in Charleston, and you'll buy it and pay the cost to furnish it. Not with period antiques and all that, but with reasonable furnishings."

"Wait a minute. Since when did I say it was okay for you to go buy another house? Did you earn the money?"

"Wes. Wake up. Thirty years of marriage. I don't need your permission to do anything."

"Fine." Wes exhaled deeply enough to muss our hair. "Continue."

"Half the bank account is mine, except for the Coke stock you inherited. So you keep that and put half of the rest of the assets in my name. Then we rewrite our wills to say that whoever dies first will inherit the other's estate. I remain your executor, you remain mine, and you'll keep me covered with medical insurance. Then we go our own ways. Should the time come that we want a divorce, we'll get together and discuss it. Meanwhile, we will let our respect for each other be obvious to our children and friends and continue to watch our family grow. If you need me for anything, just call me."

"But, Leslie, if I deduct the furnishings of this new house of yours from my share, then you wind up getting more."

"Then get a lawyer, Wes."

He was quiet for a few minutes.

"You've really thought this through, haven't you?"

"Yes, I have."

Saunders and Katz were completely silent. I knew that they thought Wes was a horse's ass. The bigger question was, would Wes ever realize it? And given his Ebenezer streak that was as wide as I-95, Wes had to realize this arrangement would save him a fortune in legal bills.

"Let me sleep on it," Wes said.

"You do that," I said. "You have one week to decide."

"You're threatening me now? What if I don't?"

"This is not a threat, Wes. If you have a better idea, I'd like to hear it."

"No, I don't. And yours is pretty fair. I just don't like you telling me I only have one week. You're not in charge."

"And neither are you, Wes. Those days are over."

He looked at me with the strangest expression, like he was seeing me for the first time.

"And what if I don't get back to you in a week?"

"I'll hire a divorce lawyer that will find the five dollars your aunt Teresa gave you for your fifth birthday and anything else you have stashed away someplace. And I'll take much more than I'm asking for now, Wes. So you sleep on it. Okay? How's that?"

For the first time since Charlotte announced her unplanned pregnancy, I saw that little vein next to Wes's left eyebrow begin to pulsate.

"Since when did you get so ballsy?"

"I finally learned to love myself, Wes, and I just want what's mine."

"What about the wedding, Les? If we don't go together, everyone will talk."

"Wesley, for God's sake, people are *always* going to talk. Who cares?"

I looked at my watch and realized our time was up, so I stood and gathered up my purse and scarf.

"Well," said Jane Saunders, "I think we're all done here for now. You two don't really need us at this point."

"I think that's right. Thank you," I said. "Thank you for everything."

"You're welcome," Saunders said.

"Yes," Dr. Katz said, smiling. "You call us if you need us. You have my card, don't you?"

"Yes, thank you," I said. "I do."

It was a little bit like getting the Good Housekeeping Seal of Approval. Our work was finished. I felt an enormous sense of relief. And I was very proud of myself.

Wes followed me out to the garage. I clicked my key in the right spot and the lights of my new car flashed. I opened the door to get in, tossing my purse across to the passenger seat.

"You're really leaving me, aren't you?" he said.

"Pay attention, Wes. I already did."

CHAPTER 22

Wes—More Hell Breaks Loose

I stopped by my office after our last session with the shrinks, and I have to admit I didn't know what to do with myself. The thought of not coming here to my office every day was very destabilizing. True, I wanted to play golf all over the country, but what if I got bored? And would my mind go to mush without all the challenges in business that shaped my life?

Even though I was driving again in the past few days and I felt fine, the pathology report still had not come in yet. But bad news traveled at the speed of light, so I kept telling myself I was cancer free. And because I had taken off so much time from the office, there were no messages and nothing really to do, except read sales reports. I could do that at home. Les would already be on her way back to Charleston. I still couldn't believe I'd forgotten her birthday. I'd send her flowers or something.

I called Harold and gave him the rundown on Les's proposal.

"Should I get a lawyer?" I said.

"Nah, at this stage, you should get a martini. How are you

feeling? Why don't we meet in the grill room for an early supper? How's six?"

"I feel great. Dinner sounds like a plan. Yeah, call Paolo, will you? I haven't seen him in a while."

"Sure thing. I've got a story to tell y'all."

"Tell me now," I said.

"You're worse than a girl, Wes. This story needs alcohol and face time."

"Okay."

Hell, I'd had cancer, my career was at an end, and I was losing my wife and half my assets. What could Harold possibly have to tell us that could top that?

I decided to take a walk down Peachtree Street and stop at the first decent restaurant I passed to have a little lunch. I needed to clear my head. It was Friday afternoon and hot as all hell, so most of the executive floor was empty, except for the secretaries. I threw the stack of sales reports in my briefcase and took the elevator down to the street. I left my briefcase with Charlie at the front desk so I wouldn't have to carry it in the heat.

"Charlie? Where's the nearest coffee shop that you like? Or a deli where I can just grab a sandwich."

"If you go out and make a right, go down two blocks and cross the street there's a Greek restaurant on that block. Athena's Café or something like that. They make a great chicken salad with those stuffed grape leaves? I eat there all the time."

"Right! Athena's! I always forget about that place. Thanks, I'm sick of our cafeteria food. And I need to stretch my legs. I'll be back in about an hour."

"By the way, Mr. Carter? There was a redhead here about twenty minutes ago who wanted to come up and see you and then she changed her mind."

"Same one who was here a while back?"

"Yeah, I think so."

"Cornelia? Cornelia Stovall?"

"Yeah, that's the one. I'm pretty sure. Funny, she asked me for a lunch place too. I sent her to Athena's. You might bump into her."

"Thanks for the heads-up, Charlie. See you soon."

What in the world did Cornelia want with me now? I may as well find out and deal with it. I made my way down the street, not thinking about much more than reaching air-conditioning and what I felt like eating. I wasn't sure I had the strength for Cornelia. Maybe she had just gone home. But the doctor said it was good for me to walk, so I was following doctor's orders and sweating like a workhorse. I pushed open the heavy door of Athena's Café and into blessed cold air. Who did I spot in a booth, reading a menu? She took off her sunglasses. Her eyes were swollen and red.

"Cornelia, sweetheart! What's the matter? Mind if I join you?" I sat down on the bench seat opposite her.

"Oh, Wes! I'm so glad you're here! I've got a *huge* problem."

"What's the matter?"

"Harold wants to kill me and Molly wants to call off the wedding, and they both hate my guts!"

"Why? What in the world has happened?"

"Things were going so well between Harold and me after the last time you and I talked. You know, things were working? In the bedroom?"

Was she going to tell the whole blooming world?

"Ssssh! Yes, I understand!"

"And now . . . I don't think we can put this one behind us, Wes. I think we're really done now."

She began to cry. I thought, Wow, I've seen more of Cornelia's tears in the last few weeks than I ever saw of Les's in years.

"Tell me what's the matter, Cornelia? If you don't tell me, I can't help you."

"Okay. Well, Molly? The one I thought I could be such great friends with? She's marrying Shawn, right? Well, you won't believe this but I used to . . . well, *date him*?"

"*What?*" Was she kidding?

"Yeah. Apparently, Molly doesn't like the idea that her stepmother slept with her future husband." She took a tissue from her handbag and blew her nose.

This took a moment to compute. The waitress approached and handed me a menu.

"Can I get you something to drink?" she said.

"Another Diet Coke," said Cornelia, sniffing.

"Same for me," I said. Then I whispered to her. "Wait a minute, you slept with her fiancé?"

"It was a long time ago, and it only happened once. Okay, maybe more than once. Okay, maybe we hooked up a lot. But for God's sake, why did he *tell* her? Isn't that the most stupid thing you've ever heard?"

"It's out there, all right." The whole generation of kids from Charlotte's age to Cornelia's were royally screwed up. "My father used to always say that discretion was the better part of valor." I felt a thousand years old and removed from Cornelia's generation by light-years.

"Yeah, well, that stuff was before Facebook."

"Are you telling me this fella put the intimate nature of your relationship with him on *Facebook*? What in the world is the matter with him?"

"No! *She* put it on Facebook! That's how I found out that she knew. I mean, she said it in a roundabout way, something like *What would you do if you found out your future stepmother used to hook up with your fiancé?*"

That wasn't *a roundabout way* in my book.

"Holy whopping hell!" I felt almost the same distress that she did. "What did you *do*?"

"Well, we're Facebook friends, so I denied it! What would you do?"

"I'd deny it too! Without a doubt! Great God! I've never *heard* of such a thing!"

The waitress returned, put our drinks down, and said, "Want to hear the specials?" Without waiting for a *yes, please,* she rattled off the specials anyway. "We've got Greek chicken and moussaka for entrées and soup of the day is vegetable, which personally it seems too hot for. But that's up to you. Y'all ready to order?"

"I'll just have a big Greek salad, no anchovies, please," I said.

"Me too," Cornelia said. After the waitress left, Cornelia continued, "So first she unfriended me, and then she called Harold and pitched a fit the size of Texas and then Harold called me a slut and then I didn't know what to do, so I grabbed my purse and got in my car. I almost came up to your office, but then I decided you might not even be there and you've had enough going on without another pile of crazy from me and Harold. And now I'm here and Harold's home and pissed and we're drinking Diet Cokes. Have a nice day, right? So how are *you,* by the way? You feeling okay?"

Nice of her to take a moment out of her own soap opera to realize she wasn't the only person in the world with issues, I thought.

"Yeah, I'm fine. Cornelia, I'm sorry, honey. You have to talk to Harold. It's not like he didn't sow his oats when he was young."

"Everyone does, don't they?"

"Well, some more than others, I'd have to say. But you know, they say time heals all wounds, doesn't it?"

"Look, I don't know about that. Molly is off the wall. And even I'll admit, it's a *bit* awkward."

"Yeah, well, if Les was here, she'd say you have to forgive your-self and move on."

"Forgive myself for what? *I* didn't do anything wrong! I wasn't married to Harold yet and Molly wasn't even dating Shawn yet! What did *I* do?"

I came from a generation where women were busy trying to remain virgins until the altar. And if they weren't, they lied about it. With this generation, virginity seemed irrelevant, that it was a given that they had a busy sex life unless something was wrong with them.

"You're right, of course. On the other hand, it is a bit of a sticky wicket."

"Whatever *that* is! According to Harold, Molly's going to break her engagement and call off the wedding. And naturally, if she does, that will cause a huge war with Harold, who'll say I broke his daugh-ter's heart and then he'll definitely dump me." She took a deep sip of her Coke. "Oh, Wes, it wasn't enough that . . . you know, what I told you before about his . . . us in the bedroom? But now this? What should I *do*?"

"Yeah, this is pretty rough all right. I think you have to let this play itself out because there's nothing you can do. I mean, you might try talking to Molly? You know, say you're sorry this very pecu-liar thing *happened,* which is not *apologizing* for it happening exactly. Then you can save face? Do you know what I mean?"

I looked at Cornelia, who was staring off into space, and imag-ined her mind was wandering the universe, planning her next move. The waitress put our salads down and left.

"Oh, Wes! I never even *thought* of the possibility of Shawn show-ing up in my life again." She picked at her salad. "Especially not as my potential stepson-in-law! Jesus! In a city of four million people, what are the odds on that?"

"I sure couldn't have called it. As far as Shawn goes, I can have a little talk with him, if you'd like." I took a huge bite of the lettuce and cucumbers and thought it was pretty good. After nonstop soup and Jell-O since my operation, I relished the crunch.

"Oh, sure! Like that will do any good. What would you say?"

"I'd tell him to have some respect, that's what I'd say. Of course this is awkward, but it's also 2012 and it's time to get over this and put it in the past where it belongs if he's going to be a part of the family."

"Yeah, that sounds good, but the reality is that I slept with him—a lot. Molly knows it, Harold knows it, and Shawn probably has a smirk on his face as wide as the Mississippi. He's known I was Harold's wife since *New Year's*. Why did he wait until *right before the wedding* to tell her? In fact, why did he tell her *at all*? *Idiot!*"

"That's a good question. Maybe it was a last-minute confessional thing, you know, laying all the cards on the table before they tie the knot? Anyway, you're not to blame if they're fighting." I said that, but inside I was thinking, Whoo boy! If she didn't give our club enough to talk about before now, just wait until the wedding! She was pretty, but brother, was she trouble! And wait till Les heard about this.

"Wes, look, if I'm around and so is Shawn? We all know that it's *always* going to be awkward. One of us has to go. This should be a really happy time for the family, but Molly wants everyone to think the wedding's ruined all because I'm in the picture."

"Her age is showing. And she's just being, well, stubborn. She needs to understand . . ." Actually, Cornelia was right. It was one thing to have a trophy wife, but it could be very inconvenient in certain situations. Truth? They'd all be better off with Cornelia gone. "Oh, wait and see; she'll come around."

"Never. She never will, and I'm not so sure I would if I was in her position. How do you like that?"

"Women."

"It's how we are. Look, I love Harold, but he's so mad at me I don't think he will ever forgive me for this even though I didn't do anything wrong."

"Hey, I'm having an early supper with him at six. I'll talk to him."

"Go ahead. But I think I should just pack up and go this time. Let them have the wedding and everything and call me horrible names for the rest of their lives."

"Do nothing of the sort. Let's see what Harold has to say."

"Once again, here I am: no job, no money, no place to go . . ."

"Look, as I told you before, Harold's not the kind of guy who would hurt you. Let's see what he says. And if it comes to that, I can probably find you a job with my firm. We have offices all over the world."

She only slightly paused before she blurted out, "Wow. I've kind of always wanted to see Hong Kong."

I wondered if Hong Kong would be far enough away.

At six that evening, when I got to the grill room at the club, Harold was at a table, polishing off what I assumed was his first martini and reading the menu. If I had been in his shoes, I'd be on my third. I wondered how he was going to deal with the bomb about Cornelia, Molly, Shawn, and the wedding.

"Hey, my man! Don't get up!" I said and nodded to José the waiter. "The usual."

José nodded back. Relief was on the way.

"What? Now I have to stand up for you like you're a girl?"

"Up yours," I said, laughing, and took a chair. "What looks good?"

"They got lobster tonight and monster rib eyes," he said. "Want to get a two-pounder and split it?"

"Sounds great. Want to split that cowboy rib eye too?"

"Hell, yeah. So Paolo bailed on us."

"How come?"

"He's home getting whipped."

"He's got nothing but grief with those two daughters of his. By the way, I had an accidental lunch with Cornelia today. You should praise God that you only have one daughter."

"So you know then?"

"Yeah. She told me everything."

We were both quiet until José appeared with fortification.

"So what do you think? Do I call my daughter's bluff and tell her to call off her wedding?"

"What are you *crazy,* man? She's about to marry a *doctor*! She'll be cash flow positive!"

"Hmmm," Harold said. "You're right."

The waiter put a plate of crudités in front of me and a basket of bread in front of Harold.

"Yeah, just think about it, never mind all the money you've probably already spent for this extravaganza. You'd lose all that too, you know. Nonrefundable deposits?"

"Never mind Molly's gown for ten thousand. Yeah, but then what? I gotta go through another divorce? Can I have a stick of celery?"

"Help yourself." I put the plate in front of him and took the bread, helping myself to a roll. "Look, Harold, I've been thinking about this all afternoon. The larger question is, Do you love Cornelia so much that you would jeopardize your relationship with your daughter for the rest of your life?"

"Good question. Good question. I don't know. I mean, but won't it be very weird whenever Molly and Shawn get together with us? What about the holidays and all that stuff?"

"Exactly! And when the babies start coming? Forget about it! Molly's gonna be sitting there staring at Cornelia, sending her daggers while Shawn's smirking his guts out. But I have to ask you, these are all sophisticated young people. Why can't they just put this unfortunate coincidence in the past? I mean, *I* couldn't do it, but young people today? Doesn't everyone have friends with benefits or something like that?"

"I don't know about friends and benefits. Anyway, it's just too nasty for Molly to accept, and it's very uncomfortable for Cornelia, and frankly, I don't like it either."

"Well then, my friend, you have your answer."

"Cornelia's got to go. Damn it. You want another martini?"

"Definitely." I looked around and made eye contact with José. We gave the nod and he understood. "Look, it's probably best for everyone involved, Harold. Let's be honest here; it's cheaper to dump Cornelia than to support Molly for the rest of her life if she doesn't marry the doctor!"

I didn't want to say *I think Cornelia's leaving anyway.* I had just wanted to prepare Harold with a little exercise in logic.

"You're right about that. I gotta get this divorce done and fast."

"I think my firm's got a suitable job for Cornelia in New York, if you're interested. Maybe even Hong Kong."

"Wes? That would save me. Getting her out of town would be the best thing. You're right. I can't ask my child to sacrifice the only man she ever loved. It isn't right. Besides, I'm an old man."

"You're not an old man. Thanks, José." I took a sip of my second silver bullet. "Yeah, Cornelia could be a brand ambassador. She'll do all these public appearances—she's perfect for the job and she'll love it."

"You're a great friend, Wes."

"Hey, this is what friends are *supposed* to do for each other. Anyway, Harold, you and I both know, you can love more than one woman in this world."

"Yep. I'm living proof of that. And thank the good Lord for the generous supply. Still . . . it's not going to be pleasant to tell Cornelia."

We ordered dinner.

"Just let her down easy, my friend. Let her down easy. Say you're the shit. Tell her you take full responsibility."

"Don't worry. I've got the perfect excuse."

"What's that?"

"My willie died again. And now it's really dead."

"Aw, *Jesus,* man! What are you telling me?"

"I'm not kidding. Ever since I heard this about Cornelia and Shawn? It's as dead as a doornail."

"Take a pill."

"Can't. Blood pressure meds and all this other stuff I take? Makes my pulse race."

"Right." That was exactly what Cornelia had told me. "Look, there's this surgical procedure?"

"Yeah, yeah. The pump. I know all about it. I'm probably going to get it, but I have to get used to the idea. My doc said it's that or nothing, so I guess it's going to be the pump. But the thought of somebody cutting on my best friend? I don't know, Wes."

"I'll go to the hospital with you. Don't worry. They do this all the time. You'll be fine."

"You're the best, Wes. I don't care what anyone says."

"Thanks." I shook my head, smiling.

José put our lobster in front of us. It was huge. We looked up, and there stood Paolo. He had been standing there listening. He pulled out a chair and sat down with us.

"Well, it looks like we're all in the same boat."

"What do you mean?" I said.

"Lisette says she's done. She can't stand it anymore."

"Ah, Jeez! José?" José nodded. "One more."

"What happened?" Harold said. "You want some lobster? This thing is big enough for six people."

"Sure. It looks great. Oh, you know my girls, right? Suzanne and Alicia put all Lisette's dry cleaning in the washing machine with bleach and ruined, I don't know, a couple of thousand dollars' worth of clothes."

The waiter put another setup on the table and filled Paolo's water glass. Harold and I passed him pieces of lobster.

"Can we get some more butter and lemon here for Paolo?" I said to the waiter.

"And a glass of sauvignon blanc?" Paolo said.

Harold said, "That's terrible!"

"Man, those girls of yours are a couple of hellcats! What did you do?" I said.

"I gave Lisette the American Express card and told her to go replace everything. What else could I do?"

"No! I mean, what did you do to the girls?" I said.

"Doesn't she have her own card?" Harold said.

"Hell, no! What did I do to the girls? I told them I was very dis-appointed in them and made them apologize to Lisette. And I told them their mother would be deeply disappointed in them, which they didn't believe for one minute." He dipped some lobster into the warm butter and popped it in his mouth. "This is amazing!"

"Right? I haven't had lobster in ages. And Lisette is still steamed and the girls didn't mean a word of what they said, am I right?" I said.

"Correct," Paolo said. "It's a very sad day when a father can't dis-cipline his girls, you know, make them feel bad for the terrible things they do. They have no remorse."

Then the lightbulb came on. With Lisette *and* Cornelia out of the picture, there was no longer any reason for Leslie to ever leave me! I knew then I could talk her into coming back. The wedding was just a couple of weeks away. I was going to romance her home.

"You're right. It's disgraceful. I don't know what's wrong with young people today," Harold said. "This is like the best dinner I've had in months!"

"You know, sometimes I think the girls do these things to honor their mother's memory."

"Tessa wouldn't have approved of this kind of foolishness," I said. "You know? We should do this more often."

"So true," Paolo said.

"So where's Lisette going to go?" Harold said.

"I don't know. I suggested we just get Suzanne and Alicia their own apartment, but Lisette's already out and staying with her old roommates. She says she doesn't feel safe sleeping under the same roof with my girls."

"Humph. Understandable, unless you're there all the time," Harold said. "So you heard about Cornelia?"

"Harold? I heard and I am stunned. My God, what next?"

"All of us—bachelors!" Harold said.

"Maybe you assholes are bachelors, but I'm going to get Leslie back. Watch me."

"So are you not going to act on Les's proposal?" Harold said.

"What proposal?" Paolo said.

"Wes will tell you later."

"Nope, I'm going to ignore it for now," I said. "But here's what I still don't understand?"

"What?" they said.

"Look at us! Three supersuccessful men in the prime of our lives, and we all just got dumped! What the hell did *we* do? Where did we go wrong?"

CHAPTER 23

Lowcountry Les

I packed my pretty little car (which left them all slack jawed) with some more clothes and small household items that meant nothing to anyone but me, said good-bye to my children and Holly once more, and began the long drive back to Charleston. Now that I had a car that could sync to a phone I could talk while driving, but for most of the trip there were no cell-phone towers nearby so it didn't really matter because I couldn't get a signal. When I reached the Columbia area, I had service galore, so I called Jonathan, and to my disappointment, my call went to voice mail. He was probably with a patient, so I left a message that I'd be in around four. "Let's have dinner!" I said and hoped he was free.

When I got back to Harlan's, he wasn't at home but, always considerate, he'd left a note to say he was out running errands and he'd meet up with me after five. Miss Jo or Miss JP, the dog with two names, met me with a wagging tail and lots of kisses. She was wearing a new monogrammed blue oxford cloth shirt. I'd bet anything that Harlan was too. It was so nice to have a happy dog to come home to, some ten pounds or so of happiness, eager to see you.

"Come on, sweetheart," I said. "I bet you'd like a breath of fresh air."

I let Miss Jo out through the French doors in the den to visit the garden and poured myself a glass of iced water. It was a hot and very humid day. I watched her prance around, sniffing every blade of grass. Even in deep summer Harlan's garden was still fragrant and beautiful. She scampered back inside and I closed the doors to keep the heat and bugs at bay.

The next project to tackle was to relocate my roll-on bag from the foyer up to my room to unpack. I began lugging it up the steps, wondering why I took so many heavy shoes from Atlanta when I knew the dastardly stairs were waiting for me at the end of my trip. Those priceless stairs I once adored were now mocking me with their steep pitch. Harlan seriously needed an elevator. We weren't getting any younger, and I decided right then and there that any house I bought in Charleston would have one or else the house would have to be all on one level. There was no sense in dropping dead from steps. I wasn't Rocky Balboa, for heaven's sake.

I couldn't help thinking over and over how terribly sad it was that my marriage was coming to an end. But it was. Everything on this earth had a life span. Wes and I had simply outlived the life span of our marriage. In fact, the time for it to groan to a close was long gone. It was so hard to walk away, especially because my future was so uncertain and I wasn't so young. The reality that I was actually planning my final act hit me again. I wasn't leaving Wes to run to Jonathan like Harold had flown to Cornelia. I was leaving Wes because I just couldn't live in that dead horse life for one more day. Worse than everything, I had a nagging going on in the back of my brain that I needed something larger than a dead horse to justify leaving. My personal unhappiness and deep feelings of unfulfillment didn't seem important enough. But wasn't that how women of my generation had been programmed? The good woman, the exemplary mother and wife put the needs, happiness, and dreams of everyone else before her own. We were at the disposal of our family around the clock throughout the year until we drew our last breath. Therein lay my guilt. I reminded myself to love myself more, especially now.

It was probable that for a long while or maybe for the rest of my life I would mourn the surrender of my house, and I knew it. In every corner there was a memory of something—the children, Christmas trees and turkeys, and all the birthday and cocktail parties we used to give. Dinners around our table, all the nights I snuggled up on the sofa with my children watching movies, sleepovers and Halloweens and Easter egg hunts. I was so proud of that old house that had sheltered us through everything life threw our way. It certainly wasn't the grandest home in Atlanta, but our fingerprints were on its every square inch. Maybe Wes would give it to Charlotte. If he did, maybe I'd will my yet-to-be-found house to Bertie. What I'd miss the most was seeing Charlotte and Holly practically every day. But as I've said before, the only chance Charlotte had of becoming a devoted mother would be if I wasn't so available to her. I really believed that with all my heart. It was too easy to put Holly in my care, and I had such a terrible time saying no.

And maybe I was feeling melancholy at the moment, but, weirdly, I felt like I'd even miss Wes. Not in the sense of how I'd miss a red-hot lover, someone who'd broken my heart, leaving me for a prettier girl. But Wes and I were friends in an odd way. At least I liked to think we were. And there had been some good years. I had already decided that if Wes got sick again, I'd go back to Atlanta and help him if he wanted me to. And I was going to walk into Molly's wedding by his side, sit with him, and be polite to him. There was no reason to steal one bit of thunder from Molly's special day. But the miser owed me a phone call to give me his decision on my offer. He had six days left, and I wasn't playing around on this. I couldn't or else things between us would revert back to how they had always been with Wes calling all the shots. That would force me to file for divorce.

I opened my suitcase to unpack but then decided to call Danette to catch up. I'd been so busy in Atlanta with the therapy marathon that I'd not had the time to touch base. I went to the kitchen for another cold drink and dialed her number.

"So what's new?" I asked.

"Do you have a seat belt on and an oxygen tank nearby?"

"No, why?"

"Well, girl? *Set yerself* down and get comfy cozy. You ain't gone beeee—lieve . . ."

When Danette used her supercharged teeny-tiny Southern town twang, I knew I was in for some juicy headlines.

She rolled out the story of Cornelia and Shawn. I was absolutely aghast. Then, after a minute or two of being properly horrified and blustering with indignation, we nearly died laughing.

"Holy hell! What did Harold do?" I said. "I can just *see* his face!"

"Molly said he threw a conniption fit with Cornelia the likes of which could light Atlanta in a blackout. I've never heard him go crazy like that, not in all our years. I didn't even know he *had* all that fury in him! Anyway, Molly was out of her *mind* with anger. It was awful for her, the poor thing."

"Do you blame her?"

"Of course not! But listen, here's what really frightened me. She was about an inch away from calling off the whole wedding. I sat her down and said, 'You listen to your mother. You and Shawn are perfect together. Don't let your daddy's whore ruin your life. Besides, this whole nasty business happened a long time ago, so get over it!' "

"Excellent advice. Tell her that her auntie Les said to take this story, put it in a box in her mental attic, and never open it again."

"You're right. Women have to forget a *whole lot* of things if they want to stay married, and not just from husbands. There are about a thousand boxes in my attic. Anyway, the latest poop is that Cornelia has moved out."

"Well, that's probably the first noble thing she's ever done in her worthless life, bless her heart."

"Amen. I mean, we're as modern a family as there ever was . . ."

"Come on. *Really?*"

"Okay, we're not so modern. Truth? Once that dreadful cat was out of the bag, it was just way too awkward for my blood."

"I completely agree. And the good news is that you don't have to look at her at Molly's wedding."

"Thank heavens! In her miserable size two dress."

"Girl? Speaking of? You haven't even told me what you're wearing!"

"Oh, please. I've got about ten different dresses laid out in the guest room and every day I change my mind!"

"I'll bet! Well, I'm wearing a little navy blue dress if that's okay. The MOG isn't wearing navy, I hope."

"No, she's wearing burgundy. So, I told Harold, I said, 'Honey? If you lay down with dogs, you get up with fleas.' He didn't want to hear it."

"No, I imagine he didn't. I love that saying."

I could hardly take a breath without laughing again.

"And the other fast-breaking news is Lisette packed up *her* little red wagon and . . ."

When Danette was finished with *that* story, I could hardly take it all in.

"Danette? Stop! This is like winning the lottery of all gossip! I need to catch my breath! My Lord, Paolo's girls are something else. I live vicariously through them for Tessa's sake."

"Me too. And of course, Suzanne and Alicia are both in the wedding. Gotta love those two."

"I *do*! Well, listen, more to come on them all, I'm sure, but in the meanwhile I have a few things to tell *you*."

I told Danette about finding the money and the therapy and that for the foreseeable future, I'd be living in Charleston, riding around in my new Benz. Wearing diamond earrings. I thought she would die laughing all over again and that I would too. However, I didn't tell her the details of the offer I'd made Wes. It didn't seem like the right time. When Wes and I had everything worked out, then I'd tell her. Besides, Danette, as anyone would expect, was in wedding overdrive.

"So I don't want you to worry about the bridal brunch," I said. "I've booked it at Loews in midtown. The New Wes is happy to pay the bill."

"You must have scared the absolute devil out of him."

"I did. Therapy was pretty much an exorcism. But believe it or not, he's still half clueless. Anyway, Loews has a great-looking restaurant called eleven. Check it out on the web. Does eleven to two sound good for a time?"

"Perfect! All the out-of-town guests are staying there because it's so close to the club. I'm putting together hospitality baskets for all the rooms with all the information they need for the weekend and of course some treats and a bottle of wine. And the hotel is giving us a hospitality suite where people can meet and talk."

"Great. Don't forget to give them corkscrews! And I'd throw in a peach, a Vidalia onion, and a Coke!"

"An onion?"

"Yeah, with a recipe on how to fry onion rings! Give them a packet of the White Lily mix?"

"Oh, gosh, I miss you, Les. You're so funny."

"And I miss you. But I'm going to see you soon, and your beautiful daughter is going to be queen for a day! I can't wait. Now, how are those tango lessons going?"

"Fab. I'll tell you. Les, a younger man? Oooh-weee, baby. He's something else. And wait until you see my yard! It's beyond anything

I could've imagined. We're having the rehearsal party here. I found beautiful red and yellow paper lanterns to hang everywhere all above us in the trees. It's going to be a gorgeous party, if the weather holds, that is."

"Sounds amazing. And how are the groom's folks?"

"Shawn's mother is a living doll and his father too. They're so relieved they don't have to do a thing except pay the caterer, the florist, and smile."

"Well, didn't we say months ago that a big party is too hard to manage from a distance, especially if you don't know the town? Wait! They don't know about this business with Cornelia, do they?"

"I see no reason to tell them anything, do you? If Shawn didn't tell them, why would I?"

"Heavens, no! I wouldn't tell them either. When you get a head count for the brunch, let me know, okay? I'll get the invitations in the mail as soon as you send me a mailing list. If you have e-mails, I can do evites too. Maybe we should just add the brunch to the itinerary for out-of-towners? We don't want the Yankees wandering around eating out of vending machines when they could be eating eggs Benedict with us."

"Excellent idea. I'll e-mail you the list this afternoon. I think we're about fifty."

"Great!"

Wes was going to choke.

We talked for a few more minutes, and then we hung up, promising to speak in the next few days.

So Cornelia and Lisette were back on the streets and had to stake out new victims, did they? I'd bet they were already waxing their southern climes and making cupcakes for some poor women's unsuspecting husbands. Wow, I thought again, Cornelia had an affair with her almost stepson-in-law? That wasn't even redneck—it was downright nasty! Did Wes know this? Of course, he must! Why hadn't he told me? I could just see him at the club with Harold and Paolo, all of them consoling themselves with big steaks and lobsters and martinis. Laughing. I'd bet they were laughing and having a good time. Oh, so what if they were? I needed to make sure I didn't fall into that trap of thinking they all had a better deal than I did. And there wasn't a single thing I missed about any of them beyond some nostalgic twinges of our shared past in better days. I went back upstairs to unpack. My clothes were all put away.

"Thank you!" I called out.

Later on, downstairs, I checked the refrigerator to see what there was that I might rustle up for dinner and there wasn't more than some cheese, olives, and pickles. I could pull together some finger food for cocktails, but other than that, we were going to have to go out.

My cell phone rang and I answered it without checking the caller ID. It was Jonathan.

"I knew you were back!" he said. "Suddenly the sun's brighter and I'm in a better mood for no good reason at all."

"Thanks! Boy, it's good to hear your voice! Can we have dinner?"

"I can come by late, after dinner. We've got a department meeting tonight. Usually they cater in something like bologna sandwiches, which are darned hard to resist. All that yellow mustard and mushy lettuce."

"Sounds delish. Sure, just call me first, okay? I'm a little tired from the drive and all."

"Yeah, you must be. So how did it go?"

"How did it go? The therapy? You know, I think it went well, given all the issues. Wes is probably of another opinion. But anyway, at least we know where we stand with each other and coming to an understanding is very important."

"So what's the understanding?"

"I may not know where or exactly how I'm going to live out my days, but I'm certain it won't be with him. It's very sad. Anyway, want to go house shopping with me?"

"You bet! I love snooping around other people's houses and seeing how they live. You know, check out their medicine cabinets for what they take and bedside table drawers for who knows what? To see how they get crazy in the middle of the night!"

"Jonathan! Naughty boy! I never knew that about you!" The devil!

"Ah, madam, I have many surprises in store for you. Stick around!"

"I will! So call me later?"

"Yep. Count on it."

I had a few stories to tell him too.

As predicted, at five o'clock Miss JP barked, the front door opened, and Harlan was home. I was in the den reading *Splendid in Ashes* by Josephine Pinckney. It was terrific.

"I'm back!" he called out.

"In here!" I called back.

I got up and met him in the kitchen. He gave me a hug and scooped up Miss Jo, who washed his face with kisses. And, yes, they both wore monogrammed blue shirts, but Miss Jo's had short puffed sleeves.

"All right now! That's enough!" he said. "So how was your trip?"

"There's a lot to tell. Want to go to Magnolias? There's not diddly squat in the refrigerator."

"I know. I'm on a diet. I gained eight pounds in Italy. Can you believe? But sure, let's go have supper. Where's Jonathan?"

"Department meeting. He might stop by later."

"Great. Let me just put away my dry cleaning and all this stuff and we can get out of here. Want to walk?"

"Definitely. Just leave it by the stairs. Victoria Rutledge is in an unpacking mood!"

Minutes later we were walking up East Bay Street until we

reached the ancient building that housed Magnolias, one of our favorite restaurants in the city. It was early, so they were able to take
us right away and we were seated at a small table in the front room.
There was a fever of pouring water, bringing menus and bread, did
we want a cocktail and wasn't it hot today? Vodka and tonics with
extra limes would be great, and before you could say Robert E. Lee,
we were sipping away. This was why we loved Magnolias. Great service, friendly, beautiful, and casual, all at the same time. Not to
mention delicious.

"I'm possessed. All I can think about is shrimp and grits with bits
of chorizo and tasso gravy," Harlan said, reading the menu. "I should
be eating broiled fish with lemon juice. *If* I had any discipline."

"And you could get hit by a truck tomorrow," I said.

The server approached the table.

"Y'all ready to order?" she said.

"I'll have the shrimp and grits," Harlan said, adding with a
straight face, "because I could get hit by a truck."

I giggled, and Harlan looked sheepish.

"Yes, sir," the server said. "And for you, ma'am?"

"Oh!" Harlan said. "How rude of me! I should've asked you to
order first, Les, but I knew if I didn't just go for it, I'd change my
mind."

"I'll have the same thing," I said. "Don't worry, Harlan. I'll
always be your partner in crime."

"Our poor cholesterol," he said. "Now tell me about your trip."

"Wes is such a knucklehead it's unbelievable."

"This is not news, little sister. Tell me something I don't know."

"Okay."

For the next thirty minutes, I told him about what I had offered
Wes as a deal and he said he thought it was very smart.

"If you're not ready to file for divorce and go through the whole
discovery process, this is a brilliant deal and more than fair."

"Well, he's got a week to agree, and if he doesn't, I guess I'll have to retain a lawyer. And then there's wedding news."

For another thirty minutes, I told him about Molly, Shawn, Cornelia and Harold, and Paolo and Lisette. I threw in an update on Danette, Nader, and their tango lessons.

"I hate weddings. Truly I do," he said. "But I'd pay money to go to this one."

"You don't have to. All you have to do is get in the car."

"And have Wes go crazy?"

"Screw Wes. It's not his party. Listen, you haven't seen my children in years. And you've never met Holly. Don't you think it's time? I'll call Danette. She'll be thrilled! You can stay with me in the hotel. I've got a junior suite with two queen-size beds at the new Loews. And I'm hosting the bridal brunch. You can help me."

"I've heard it's gorgeous, and I *did* just pick up my tuxedo from the cleaners . . . are you *sure*?"

"Positive. We'll have a wonderful time!"

We scraped up our remaining spoons of grits with the last biscuits and smiled over how bold we were.

"Do you want dessert?" I said.

"Absolutely. Let's split the strawberry shortcake . . . as long as we're going to hell, we may as well make it worth it."

"I agree. Then they can roll us home."

Harlan's laundry was still in the foyer when we got back to the house.

"She didn't put your stuff away," I said, stating the obvious.

"One should never assume when dealing with the dead."

It was around nine when the house phone rang. We were watching a PBS special about the Metropolitan Opera. I thought it might be Jonathan. Harlan picked it up.

"Hello?" he said. "Who? Oh, Wes!" Pause. "Fine, thank you. And you?" I muted the television, and Harlan made the crazy symbol on

the side of his head with his free hand. "Of course. She's right here."
Pause. "You too, Wes."

As he handed me the phone he mouthed, *What's wrong with him?*

"So much," I whispered and took the receiver. "Hello, Wes? Is
everything all right?"

"Oh, yeah. So you got back okay?" he said.

"Yes. Thanks. I texted Charlotte. She didn't tell you?"

"No, but that's okay. So I have news. My doctor called. I'm fine."

"Oh, Wes! That's wonderful. You must be so relieved."

"Yeah, it was on the voice mail when I got home. And guess what
else?"

"I couldn't begin to guess."

"Your daughter has a date. With that Oriental guy? Dr. Chen,
my surgeon?"

"You must be kidding."

"Nope. Bertie offered to babysit. And are you sitting down?"

"No, but I will." I sank into the armchair where Harlan had been.
"Okay, I'm sitting."

"Bertie has a job interview with CNN next week."

"With CNN?"

"Yep. They're looking to fill some kind of a job called deputy
photo editor, whatever *that* is. But you have to be a photography
expert and he *is* that. He sent in his résumé and they called him back
right away. They want to see his portfolio."

Charlotte had a date with a *surgeon,* and Bertie had a *job* interview.

"Wes? Did you slip something in their food?"

"Les, if there was a drug that could make this happen, we
would've given it to them a long time ago."

"Well, Wes, we finally agree on something."

"Yeah. Maybe things are going to turn around with those two.

And if it does, all the credit goes to you. I see now what hell you've been through with them."

"Thanks. I guess it's a wait-and-see game now, right?" My cell phone was ringing in my purse. "Okay, Wes, I'll talk to you later."

"Is that another phone ringing I hear? Isn't that your cell?"

"It's Harlan's cell," I lied. Whoever was calling me was none of Wes's business. "Well, I'm really glad to hear about your results, Wes. That's the most important thing."

I motioned to Harlan to answer my phone, which he did. He mouthed *Jonathan* to me. I motioned to him to talk to him for a few minutes. He nodded and took the phone out to the dining room.

"If you don't have health," he said.

"You don't have anything," I said, finishing the old but true saying.

Then I simply got quiet to indicate I'd said all I wanted to say.

"Okay then," he said. "We'll talk later."

Sensing that I was frantic to get off the phone with him, he let me go.

"Okay, then. Bye."

Harlan came back and handed me my cell phone.

"Jonathan?"

"Hi! Is it too late for a nightcap? Or I could just whisk you out to the beach with me and we could have a glass of something under the stars."

"I'm pretty tired, babe. Why don't you just stop over for a short one. I want to see your face."

"I'll be there in about ten minutes."

"Great," I said and clicked the end button.

"It's raining men, hallelujah!" Harlan sang and danced a little spastic disco.

"Stop!" I said, laughing.

"I've got to practice up for the wedding. Honey, if anybody else signs on the Leslie bandwagon, we're gonna have to put a switchboard in the house!"

"Hush! Is there a cold bottle of white wine in the fridge? I have to pour *something*."

"Make vodka tonics in insulated traveler cups and take him for a walk on the Battery wall. It's almost a full moon tonight."

"That's a great idea!"

"Leonard and I used to do that all the time. The cups are in the pantry closet. There's a lonely lime in the hydrator."

"Thanks!" I wondered if Harlan would ever find another partner. He rarely spoke a word about his personal life. Everything was all about work.

A few minutes later, the doorbell rang. I went to answer it, and there was Jonathan in patch madras trousers and a navy blazer. He pulled me to him and hugged me something fierce.

"You are too adorable," I said.

"And you are more beautiful every time I see you."

How could I not love this man? He came in to say hello to Harlan.

"Hey!" Jonathan said, and Harlan stood and shook hands with him. "I haven't seen you since Italy! How was it?"

Miss Jo jumped from her bed and then danced and yipped all around Jonathan's feet, trying to get his attention. Jonathan picked her up, and she licked him all over his chin.

"She's been cheating on me all over town," Harlan said. "Italy is the most glorious place in the world. I had a truly wonderful trip."

"That's great! Okay, you little minx, I'm putting you down now!" Jonathan put Miss Jo on the floor, where she promptly stood on her hind legs, begging to be picked up again. "I keep telling your sister that I'm going to take her to Italy whenever she wants to go."

Miss Jo was relentless in her dancing.

"*Miss Josephine Pinckney!*" Harlan said, and the lights flickered all over the house. "Where are your manners?" The lights flickered again and Harlan added, talking to the thin air, "I mean my dog, not *you!*"

"What am I missing? Do you need an electrician?" Jonathan said.

"Maybe," I said and winked at Harlan. "Come on, I've got a treat for us. And I need to walk off some butter."

I screwed the tops on the cups, handed Jonathan one, and put the house key in my pocket. Jonathan followed me up Chalmers Street until I looped my arm through his and touched his cup with mine.

"Cheers!" I said. "It's a light vodka and tonic."

"Cheers! Great!" he said. "So talk to me."

"Oh, Jonathan, it's been quite the soap opera this week."

We walked until we reached the Battery, and then we strolled along the elevated wall. I told him about the therapy sessions.

"You were right," I said. "Wes never heard almost anything I said."

Then I gave him the lowdown on Cornelia and Shawn.

"You've got to be kidding me," he said. "Run that one by me again, please?"

"Yeah, is that the most hideous coincidence ever?"

"You know, Atlanta is the fast lane of the South, well, next to the Big Easy, but here in Charleston? We're like the Chinese, eating rice and worshipping our ancestors. Very conservative. Although I'm certain a fair amount of illicit screwing around goes on, I'm usually not privy to the details. All that being said, that is *some* story, all right. Wow. Don't you need your personal physician to be your escort?"

"Oh, Jonathan, I already invited Harlan. I'm sorry."

"And no doubt Wes will be there, right?"

"Yes, this is his best friend's daughter who's the bride. We've known them since they were born."

"Then you don't need any more excitement than you've already got. You'd better make sure you video it. I can only imagine. Wow."

"Yeah, the word 'wow' was invented for a situation like this. That's for sure."

"My God. When's this wedding?"

"Weekend after next."

"I can't wait to hear every detail. By the way, next Wednesday? Don't make any plans, okay?"

"Oh, Jonathan, that's my . . ."

"Birthday. I know. You think I'd forget my first true love's birthday? I've thought about you on that day for the last forty years. When's mine?"

"January twenty-fifth," I said and smiled. "And I have too. Thought about you, that is."

"You don't have plans, do you?"

"Actually, no. I don't."

Some public display of affection ensued, right there on the Battery for everyone to see.

"Good. I've got something special planned."

And Wes wasn't even sure when my birthday was or how old I'd be.

"We need your daddy's car," I said. "That Chevy."

"It was a Pontiac. Come on, let's get you home. I have to do rounds at seven."

"Appalling hours," I said. "Appalling."

"True. You look sleepy too, sweetheart," he said.

We began walking back to Harlan's.

"What did you just call me?"

"Sweetheart."

"That sounds so good coming from you."

"I've called you that before," he said and squeezed my shoulder.

"Yes, but it never sounded so good."

On the morning of my birthday, I smelled bacon cooking. I went downstairs and there was Harlan, frying bacon and making waffles. He handed me a cappuccino.

"Hey, birthday girl! How do you feel? Old and decrepit like me?"

"Thanks! Right. You're like a thousand years older than me! Ha! Ha! Gosh, I love cappuccino."

"Leonard used to draw things in the foam, like smiley faces or Christmas trees."

"You must miss him, Harlan." I stirred the foam a little and scooped it up on my spoon. "This is like a really airy coffee meringue!"

"I miss him every minute of every day."

"And you don't see yourself with anyone else?"

"Honey, anyone else would be such a step down that I couldn't deal with it. And I sort of like being unencumbered by all the complicated rules of a relationship. You know?"

"I like it too. I don't miss Wes's endless demands one little bit."

"I'm sure. But you don't think Jonathan thinks that he's in a relationship with you?" He opened the waffle iron and pulled off two perfectly toasted waffles. "Come, let's sit."

"Oh, we are, but it's not *encumbering,* at least not yet." I sat at the kitchen table with him. "Mostly we're just great friends."

"Hmmm. Really? Well, here's to you, little sister. Happy birthday to my favorite girl!"

He held up his juice glass and touched the edge of mine. "Cheers!"

"Thanks, Harlan. This is a beautiful way to start my sixties."

"You're welcome. But I have to tell you, I think Jonathan thinks y'all are more than just great friends."

The doorbell rang and Harlan got up to answer it. He came back a few minutes later carrying a vase of red roses.

"Here we have one whole dozen half-dead roses jammed in a cheap vase filled with Styrofoam being strangled by, God save us all, baby's breath and sword fern all tied up in the cheapest ribbon money can buy. Who do we think this vile thing is from? Two guesses."

"Is there a card?"

"Here it is." He pulled it off the clear plastic stick and gave it to me. It read, *See? I didn't forget! Happy Birthday! Love, Wes.*

"What can I say? It's classic Wesley Carter."

"Dr. FTD strikes again," Harlan said. "He really shouldn't have."

"Where should we put them?" I said. I started pulling out the baby's breath, and I untied the ribbon. They looked better right away, but honestly, I didn't think they looked that bad.

"I don't know. Somewhere where they won't disturb us? These flowers are giving me anxiety."

"Harlan? You are so bad!"

"It's a simple matter of taste, Leslie. And Wes has so little."

It was true, unless you were talking golf, martinis, or steaks. I couldn't begin to count the cheap leather purses I abandoned in Atlanta.

It was seven o'clock that night when Jonathan picked me up. I could just as easily have driven myself out to the beach, but he said no, this was a special occasion and he wanted to be every inch the gentleman.

"So how was your birthday so far?"

"It was great! The kids called, Holly sang to me, and then they all sang to me again in a video Bertie e-mailed to me. And Danette called and we talked for an hour. She's excited to see Harlan at the wedding."

"You didn't hear from Wes?"

"He sent some flowers."

"Aren't you surprised he sent anything at all? Maybe there's a last-ditch effort in store for you when you go to Atlanta."

"Last-ditch effort for what?"

"To regain your affection?"

"It's not possible, but even if it was, it would take a lot more than a bunch of roses packed in Styrofoam in a vase. With baby's breath. Which I now don't like because Harlan said it's gross."

"I'm making a mental note—no baby's breath. Ever!"

"And no Styrofoam," I said and giggled.

As we crossed the Ravenel Bridge that spanned the Cooper River, I looked down at a cruise ship that was in port, docked there among all the container ships. It looked so pretty with all its white lights that stretched from its bow to its stern.

"Now, tell me why the cruise ships are such a problem, Jonathan. Apparently if I'm going to resume living in Charleston, I'm going to have to form an educated opinion."

"Let's see. Well, they dump their sewage too close to shore. Nasty. The smokestacks blow sticky black ash all over the historic district, which makes them unpopular with the South of Broad set. In addition, the passengers seem to wander around South of Broad, peering into the windows of our citizens like a tribe of Peeping Toms. And worst of all, their passengers don't really seem to boost Charleston's economy because they eat their meals on the boat. Maybe they buy some trinkets in the market, but that's about it."

"And I should like them because?"

"Well, Charleston's entire history is all tied into being a port. And because we are reputedly the most desirable tourist destination in America, that should include those who travel by water. We have to hope that the cruise ship owners will work out their problems with the town fathers. Theoretically, they should be good for our local economy and behave as guests should."

"Can't they make them follow some environmental regulations? You know like, if they blow ash or drop sewage, they have to pay a fine?"

"You would think you didn't have to legislate common decency, but since these ships are usually registered in some foreign country, they are far out of the jurisdiction of Charleston and are not bound by law to comply. Or something like that."

"Well, that stinks."

"Yeah, it really does."

"You know, I look at those cruise ships and even the container ships and I wonder where they're going and where they came from. They're so dramatic."

"Yes, they are. See the *Yorktown* down there?"

We were just passing over Patriots Point, where the decommissioned battleship the USS *Yorktown* was permanently docked and open as a museum to the public.

"Speaking of drama," I said, "can you imagine leaving here to go into combat on one of those? Holy cow. Those poor boys must have been terrified."

"No, I can't imagine it. Have you ever been on a cruise?"

"Jonathan, I am the most undertraveled woman you know. I don't even know if I would get seasick, but I think I might like to go on a cruise if it was a smaller boat that didn't roll."

"We should look into it. In fact, I'll do that. I'd like to see Croatia and the Dalmatian Coast. It's very popular."

I didn't tell him, but I wasn't even sure where Croatia was, and the Dalmatian Coast? Was it populated with dogs?

CHAPTER 24

Les Goes Red

The morning after my birthday, Jonathan took me home and, needless to say, I was smiling from ear to ear. We had a wonderful night.

"Want some toast?" Harlan said, calling out to me from the kitchen.

"Sure!" I dropped my tote bag at the bottom of the steps.

"How was your evening?" he said. "There's coffee. Help yourself."

"Thanks."

"You know, if staying over at Jonathan's becomes a habit, I might have to talk to you about birth control."

I giggled and said, "You might have to talk to me about *self-control* but birth control? Probably not." I sat down across from him and stirred a drizzle of half-and-half into my coffee.

"Oh dear, look at you." Harlan smirked at me and then smiled wide. "What on earth did you *do* last night? Your hair is a fright, and your eyes are all puffy!"

"It was *wonderful,* and that's *all* I'm going to say."

"My word! Well, did he bake a birthday cake?"

"Harlan? He made a whole Italian dinner of veal marsala and

some sautéed escarole and little potatoes, and he made a cake. Yes, he made a cake. It was delicious. Yellow cake, chocolate icing. From a mix but it was absolutely delicious."

"And how much red wine did you drink?"

"What makes you think we drank wine?"

"Because there's a rather impressive red wine stain on your blouse?"

"Oh." Sure enough when I looked down, there it was. "Just one bottle, I think? Anyway, guess what?"

"What?" Harlan said, wiggling his eyebrows. "He tried to have his way with you?"

"Oh, please. No! He gave me a trip to *Italy*! And he's coming too, but only if I say so, which I will. He just doesn't want to push me. And of course, we need you to help us plan it. But it's only valid if we go before my next birthday. Isn't he great?"

"He sure is. Did he buy tickets yet?"

"No, he wants me to tell him when I want to go and then he'll buy tickets. Yep! I'm finally going to Italy. Isn't he marvelous?"

"Yes, he is. That's *fabulous*! Absolutely fabulous. I've always liked Jonathan. Well, I got you something too. I was going to give it to you yesterday, but I didn't have the paperwork yet." Harlan got up from the table, picked up an envelope from the kitchen counter, and handed it to me. "Here. It was the best gift I could imagine for the woman who now has everything."

I opened the envelope and inside was a picture of a magnificent Havanese surrounded by puppies.

"What's this?"

"This is Miss Jo's sister and she's just had another litter. I've reserved you a male. His name is DuBose. We can't have him until he's weaned. Eight weeks—and I'll housebreak him."

"A puppy? Harlan? Have you lost your mind?" I started laughing.

"No, and whenever you and Jonathan want to go off on a trip to Madagascar or some crazy place, DuBose can stay with his uncle Harlan! We can go to the tailor together. When he's fully grown, I'm going to have a white dinner jacket made for him."

"Oh, Harlan! You are too funny!" I got up, hugged him, and kissed him on his cheek. "You are simply the most wonderful brother in the world."

"True enough. *And* I've got a broker to help you find a house. When you're in the mood to shop, that is. I mean, you could just stay here and we could become one of those famously weird families that wind up in Southern gothic novels. I could call you *Sister* and you could call me *Brother*."

"Probably better if I get my own place." I giggled.

"Probably," he said.

Being with my brother had become a great source of lighthearted happiness for me. It was wonderful to share a space with someone who held you in the same regard in which you held him. I wanted to see that Harlan was happy and he constantly went out of his way to do the same for me. The fact that Wes worked so hard all those years to deny me Harlan's splendid company and that I had allowed it? It made me sick inside. Those years were gone and I'd never get them back. But I'd spend the rest of my life being the greatest sister I could manage to be. That was the best scenario I could envision.

The following Thursday, Harlan and I dropped an excited Miss Jo off with Jonathan for the weekend and tore up the road in my sporty new car, heading for Atlanta. The car was packed to its last square inch, and both of us were eager to get there. Harlan had loaded the CD player with beach music and chamber music.

"Harlan? Do you still like to dance?"

"Yes, but usually when I'm alone. And after a martini. You've seen me dance!"

"Think you might dance with me at this wedding?"

"If you let me lead. As I recall, you always liked to lead."

"Harlan, the only dancing I've done since high school is *the walk around*."

"And what, may I ask, is the walk around?"

"Wes held one of my hands and put his other hand on my waist and we walked around the dance floor."

"Dear Mother. I don't know if that's more pitiful or tragic. All those years you could've been doing the watusi and the limbo." He snapped his fingers in the air. "Gone!"

"That's the old Les. Danette tells me they've hired an outrageous band. The new Les intends to dance her way into old age. I'm excited!"

"Well, hoochie coo, I'd be glad to help." He was quiet for a minute and then spoke again. "Not to bring up a sore subject, but does Wes know I'm coming?"

"Yes, he does. I called him the other day because he had not called me with his decision about the division of our assets, which, by the way, he said he wanted to talk to me about this weekend. And if he thinks I'm interested in discussing my financial future in the middle of a wedding, he's out of his mind. I told him you were coming, and he actually apologized for his prejudice all these years. He's trying to change. At least that's what he says. Somebody must have dressed him down."

"He's such a stupid man," Harlan said in a matter-of-fact voice.

"And foolish," I said. "Very foolish. But like Josephine said, I'm going to row my own boat in the future."

We were quiet for a few minutes.

"Good for you! So we've never really talked about Josephine Pinckney. What did you finally decide about her?"

"Well, I read *Sea-Drinking Cities* and *Three O'Clock Dinner* and part of *Splendid in Ashes,* which I hope to finish when we get home. But then I read the Bellows biography and got a whole insight into her life that made her fiction make a lot of sense. I guess I think a lot of things. For one, she was way ahead of her time."

"Agreed. She was probably the original liberated woman, if you don't count Julia Peterkin, of course."

"Now who's Julia Peterkin?"

"Oh my word! She was the only woman from South Carolina to ever win a Pulitzer, that's all. And she was and still is probably twice as controversial as Jo Pinckney."

"Oh. Gosh. There's another one I don't know a thing about. But I imagine you'll bring me up to speed on her sometime?"

"You know it. But back to Jo?"

"Well, I feel like her overbearing mother sort of ruined her prospects of a husband and family. But I'm not certain she was ever interested in having children anyway."

"But she sure liked having a man in her life," Harlan said, "even if his availability or his proclivities were dubious."

"You said it. She had as many men as she liked, but you know when she was young I think she was more interested in having a career and making a name for herself. And she was so close with Amy Lowell, who was a great mentor for her. When she was older, she was attached to that fellow Waring, who, like her own father, was so much older than she was. And to be honest, who knows what really went on there?"

"Probably not much."

"Exactly! And then Amy Lowell died young, DuBose Heyward died so young, and then her mother and Waring and her old nurse, Victoria Rutledge, all died; and I think death terrified her. Each one of those deaths had a profound effect on her. It was almost as though she couldn't believe they were really gone or that they had left her. Except for her mother, whose death liberated her even more."

"And then she winds up dying herself, alone in a hospital room in New York at sixty-three years of age. Her worst nightmare."

"Everyone's worst nightmare."

"But this doesn't answer the question of why she slipped into obscurity," Harlan said. "She wrote wonderful poetry and fascinating fiction and helped found the Poetry Society of South Carolina. She traveled like mad, knew and ran around with all the important people of her day, and yet . . . you had no idea who she was. Why?"

"I don't know. Maybe poetry fell out of fashion and people started watching television? Maybe because she never got her movie made."

"And I think there was a general change in the taste of the public too. After World War II, Hollywood became more serious. All that Ginger Rogers and Fred Astaire stuff seemed frivolous in light of the times. Maybe."

"It doesn't matter," I said. "I loved her writing."

We became quiet, and as soon as the music changed from the Four Tops to Vivaldi, Harlan put his head against the window and drifted off to sleep. I began to remember our childhood. While he dozed I wondered how many indignities my sweet brother had endured because of his sexual orientation. I remembered then how he was bullied in school and for the longest time I was too young to understand it. Once when I was about eight years old, some high school kid, Tommy Something, called Harlan a terrible name and I kicked him in his shins as hard as I could. That got me in hot water with everyone except my mother, who thought I was pretty wonderful to do it. After that, the kids at school never called Harlan names or teased him in front of me. But when I was pregnant with Bertie and had to marry Wes, well, after that Wes dictated every aspect of my life. I was glad I remembered then because it strengthened my resolve that leaving Wes was the only way to salvage what was left of me. I'd never ever be in that kind of a compromised position again.

At last we pulled into the drive of the Loews Hotel in Atlanta after crawling along in traffic and gave the car to the valet. We quickly registered, and the bellman took us up to our room. He opened the door for us and began turning on lights. We entered a large living room with a wet bar and a half bath. There was a beautiful sofa and two club chairs, a table with four chairs and a large flat-screen television. The bedroom had two queen-size beds and a beautiful low and long chest of drawers on which stood another television.

Harlan peeked in the bathroom and said, "There's a swimming pool in here."

I looked, and sure enough, the bathtub seemed like a small swimming pool to me too.

"Can I get y'all anything else?" the bellman said as he brought in our bags and placed them on luggage racks. "Ice?"

"No, we're fine," Harlan said and walked him to the living room door. I heard the door close and then Harlan called me. "Les? Come here!"

I walked out to the living room, and there on the coffee table was a vase of *two* dozen red roses packed to death with baby's breath.

"How did we miss *this*?" Harlan said.

"I'm afraid to ask, but is there a card?"

"Dare we open it?"

I took it from the plastic stick and opened it.

"It says, *Meet me for a drink tonight? Love, Wes.*"

"He really went all out, didn't he?"

"Mother Machree," I said. "I guess I have to do this?"

"No, you don't," Harlan said. "You don't have to do anything you don't want to do ever again."

"He's never sent me two dozen roses in my whole life."

"He's never had to give anybody this much money in his whole life either. I mean, I'm sorry to be so blunt, but . . ."

"No, no. You're right, Harlan. Whatever he has to say to me, he can say it over the phone."

"Absolutely. And you might remind him that this is better than going through lawyers. He *knows* that. In fact, this is such a transparent effort to get you back in his fat clammy hands, I'll even guess that he'll go along with whatever you propose. Watch. Call him right now and watch what happens."

My stomach cramped and I felt slightly nauseated. "What do I say?"

"Girl? Where's your spine? You just tell him that you're busy and what does he want to talk about, that we've got plans for tonight and that's it. *Soooo, what's up, Wes?*"

"Harlan? I love you but don't push me. But you're right. Damn it. I may as well do it and get it over with."

"That's the spirit! I'll be in the other room. Call me if you need me."

"Okay. Thanks." I reached into my purse, took out my cell phone, and thought, I really didn't ever want anyone to tell me what to do, but Harlan was right. I pressed in his number. Wes answered on the second ring.

"Leslie? Is that you?"

"Yes, Wes. It's me."

"Did you get the flowers?"

"Yes, thank you. You didn't have to do that, you know."

"Please! I just wanted to welcome you home, that's all. So where should we meet? Want to come by the club around six? We can get a nice corner table and talk about things."

I didn't say, *This is no longer my home* or *The last thing I want is for you to put me in a corner ever again.*

Instead I said, "Well, first of all, I have plans and as I told you the other day, there's really nothing to talk about, Wes. I've said all I have to say."

Harlan stuck his arm into the living room and gave me a thumbs-up gesture. Then he came in the room and whispered, "Is everything okay?" I shushed him away.

"But *I* haven't," Wesley said.

"You can tell me right here and now, Wesley."

"Well, it's just that . . . I don't know, Les. Things aren't the same without you."

"This is how it is now, Wes. I'm sorry, but this is how it is."

"Yeah, I know, but the difference is that I really miss you, Les. I do. In fact, it's become sort of stunning, this hole you left in my life when you walked out. I don't like it. I'm not happy."

"Well? I don't know what to say to you except I think for the sake of our old friends, we should attend this wedding as two civilized adults who love *them*. This weekend is not about us. It's about Danette and Harold and Molly. And I hate that this may sound so cold, but I think you need to write me a check or hire a lawyer. Sorry, Wes."

"I see. So, there's no, um, changing your mind? I mean, Les, have a heart."

"That's the whole problem, Wes. I do have one and you broke it."

"And there's nothing that can put it back together again?"

"Not that I know of, Wes. I'm sorry, but I'm really all done."

He didn't say anything.

"Wes? Wes?"

I heard silence. Wes had disconnected me.

"That son of a bitch," I said.

"I heard your every word," Harlan said rushing in. "You sounded very nice, given the stress of the situation. But what did *he* say?"

"It's not what he said but what was unsaid. He never apologized or said that he loved me. Not once." I felt so disgusted and abused.

"He's really a dope," Harlan said.

"Not exactly revelatory, Harlan. But why do you say that now?"

"Because for a woman like you who devoted her entire life to him and your children, that's about all he *would* have to say and there's a fair chance he might have won you back. That he doesn't *know* it makes him a huge dope."

I hated to admit it. Harlan was right. I might have gone home if Wes had only said he was sorry in the sober light of day and that he loved me. How pathetic was I?

"You don't understand, Harlan. Wes is never, *ever* wrong."

"Well, he sure is now," Harlan said.

"Yep," I said and burst into tears.

"Oh, sweetheart, I'm sorry! What did I say?"

"It's just sad, Harlan. It's not your fault. What you said is probably *true*. And it's going to cost him an awful lot not to love me."

"It can't cost him *enough*, if you ask me."

I smiled then. I smiled and thought how lucky I was to have Harlan and how lucky I was to have another chance to be happy.

"I'm going to take a shower," I said, "and then let's go out and paint the town."

"That sounds like an excellent idea."

While I showered, washing away the remnants of my conversation with Wes, I wondered how many married people were out there who hated each other but couldn't afford to get a divorce. They simply couldn't pay for two households. I'd bet there were more than a few. And would I really go back to Wes if he had said he was sorry and that he adored me? I decided it didn't matter anymore. If I ever went back, all the same problems I had with our marriage that made it unbearable would still be there waiting. Wes would still be so cheap he squeaked, there would be no romance, and he would never look me in the face and really like what he saw. He'd never value my intellect, humor, or resourcefulness. No, I had made the right decision. I was completely certain of it.

Over cocktails Harlan said, "Are you feeling better now?"

I said, "Harlan, the reason I got upset this afternoon was not because I'm sorry I left Wes or because I'm still in love with him or anything like that. It was because it's painful and embarrassing to realize how little affection I was willing to live with for all those years. I talk to him and it's more than a little startling that he thinks that tossing *me* a crumb will be a life-changing event for *him*."

"Well, he's going to regret losing you for the rest of his life."

"But he'll never know why it happened, Harlan. That's what bothers me about him. The crumbs bother me about myself."

"God, sister, you would've made the best psychoanalyst in the world."

"Thank you, brother, but I prefer to plan a trip to Italy."

"You know, Leslie? I have great admiration for you."

"Why's that?"

"Because you're smart, you're beautiful, and we know this but lately, I guess ever since you've made this momentous decision to redesign your life? Well, you seem like my kid sister again. And I've missed my kid sister something fierce. The one with the guts."

"Ha-ha," I said. "Y'all better look out, world! She's back."

"Good news for me! So tell me about tomorrow night."

"Danette is hosting the rehearsal party for Shawn's family. I imagine Harold will be there, definitely without Cornelia, and I think Danette said that her friend Nader is coming. That should be very interesting. But it's mostly out of-town guests like us and the wedding party. So Charlotte will be there with Holly and I imagine Bertie too. I can only hope that Bertie will have washed."

"Hmmm. I never thought about it, but now I'm wondering how does one shampoo his dreadlocks?"

"I have no earthly idea. He must've cleaned up his act somewhat because he had a job interview this week."

"Well, let's hope it went all right."

We ate dinner at the hotel. I didn't feel like getting the car out and dealing with any more traffic, and Harlan didn't care where we ate. So we picked some appetizers from the bar menu and shared a bottle of wine.

"What's the dress code for tomorrow night?" Harlan asked.

"I spoke to Danette earlier just to let her know we're here. She's pretty excited. Sport coats for the boys and something nice for the ladies."

"And for the wedding?"

"Black tie. You brought your tuxedo, didn't you?"

"Of course. I hope you're not wearing that black dress again," he said.

"Why not? It cost a fortune!"

"Hello? So what? You're rich, remember? Let's go to Neiman's first thing tomorrow and buy you an outfit that will make Wes lose his mind!"

"Really? Oh, Harlan, who cares what he thinks?"

"I haven't given two hoots what Wes thought in a thousand years, but the part of you that wants to make him see the difference in you wants a new dress. And that's that."

"You know what? You're right!" I smiled, thinking I completely agreed.

By ten thirty the next morning I was standing in front of a mirror in a dressing room at Neiman Marcus trying on every even remotely appropriate dress in the store. By noon we had narrowed it down to three. A flesh-colored dress with bronze metallic trim that made me look naked, or so I thought. An aqua silk dress with silver beading that made me look like a mermaid. And a red crepe dress with cap sleeves and a sweetheart neck that I thought showed too much cleavage but made me feel like a movie star. It had a tight waist and a full skirt and reminded me of a Doris Day movie from the sixties.

"Les? I love the flesh-colored dress. It's *dazzling*! Dazzling is good."

"I think it's immoral," I said.

"Okay, then, how about the blue one? That color reminds me of the water around Bermuda. It's beautiful with your hair."

"It makes me feel old, like a great-grandmother."

"But you don't feel like a vamp in the red one?"

"Yes, I do, and I think vamp is good." I looked at the price tag and nearly gagged. "I need shoes too."

"Black suede?" said the salesperson. "What size?"

"Eight medium," I said.

While we waited for the shoes, Harlan began to hum "Hard Hearted Hannah (the Vamp of Savannah)."

"Put that red dress on again. I want to see it with the shoes."

"Okay. Shoo!"

Harlan left the dressing room and I put it on. Was this going to turn heads? When was the last time I wore a red dress? When I was a girl? It was time. Time for red. I wondered if I could get someone to put my hair up in a French twist after the brunch tomorrow. Or maybe I'd just do it myself.

The saleslady returned with several pairs of shoes and I chose the plainest ones, thinking I could always use a great pair of black suede pumps. And she had a large circular brooch for the shoulder of the dress that appeared to be made of rubies and diamonds. We pinned it on.

"Okay, so what do you think?" I said. "I think it looks very real."

Harlan was sitting on a chair in the waiting area. He inhaled and when he exhaled, he whistled long and low. Then I twisted my hair up and held it.

"The new you. It's absolutely perfect. Wes is going to go into convulsions."

"Let's hope."

Danette's party was gorgeous and the weather was fine, although they were predicting rain. Impending storms brought the temperature down, which was a good thing, because the day had been a scorcher. Harlan and I got there a little late because of traffic and had to park way down the street. There was a small steel drum band playing and we heard the music long before we saw the first guest. The air was suffused with the smells of flowers and roasting meat, and there was laughter. Lots of it. Danette had outdone herself. Her back porch and garden were filled with young people laughing and talking and eating different foods all served on little bamboo skewers.

"She's going to be picking skewers out of the bushes for the next two years," I said.

"I think this looks like a really fun party," Harlan said. "Wait! Is that Danette with the short hair?"

"Yep, that's her!"

"She looks amazing! I'm going to say hello. Can I bring you a drink?"

"No, I'm fine," I said and scanned the crowd.

I spotted Charlotte first and noticed that she was in fact with Dr. Chen. There seemed to be more than a passing familiarity between them and I wondered if she was sleeping with him. Then I told myself she was a grown woman and that was her own business, not mine. And Wes was standing by the bar with Harold and Paolo. They were drinking some amber-colored drink, which I assumed was alcoholic. They looked very somber. Well, I thought, they sure had plenty to commiserate about.

And there, by the roasting pig turning on a spit and a long buffet spread of every kind of island food, was my Bertie, talking and laughing with Suzanne and Alicia. He had them charmed. They held their plates and ate like little birds. His dreadlocks were tied back with a leather string, but other than his weird hair, he looked rather nice in his chambray shirt and khakis. I praised all things holy that he was wearing shoes and not sandals. He must've taken a series of showers and soaks. Even my wild child still had some regard for decorum. And, as it turned out, one of the groomsmen had taken a nasty spill and broken his arm, so my Bertie, dreadlocks and all, was filling in for him. Danette said that Molly was delighted to have his hair in her wedding pictures, and I told Danette that this was yet another bloodcurdling indication that I was definitely getting extremely old.

Molly and Shawn moved through the crowd, thanking everyone for coming. Molly looked radiant, which was a relief, because I couldn't look Shawn in the face without thinking of Cornelia. It appeared that the Cornelia disaster was behind them and that they had decided to forgive, forget, and move on.

Young love, I thought and sighed heavily.

I spotted Holly at the end of the crowd, in the deepest recesses of Danette's yard, wearing a beautiful dress with a bow in the back, running, playing some kind of a game with a little redheaded boy around her age. I assumed he was the ring bearer. They were so darling, a snapshot of childhood. I couldn't wait for Harlan to get to know her.

The lanterns overhead moved with the breeze, and it was a beautiful sight.

"You look lost," a male voice said. "Can I get you a drink?"

"Oh!" I was so involved in taking the scene all in that I was surprised.

"Oh, I'm sorry! I startled you!"

I'd never seen him before. He was younger than most of us but older than our children. He was very handsome, with a deep olive complexion and the most beautiful smile. And, let me tell you, he was spraying the yard with testosterone through every single pore in his body. I knew at once who he had to be.

"Nader?"

"Yes, I'm Nader Tavakoli, Danette's friend. How did you know?"

"I'm Leslie Carter. I'm so happy to meet you! It had to be you because Danette's told me all about you."

"I hope all good?"

"Only good," I said and giggled like a fool. "But you are even more handsome than she described!" What was I saying? It sounded like I was flirting! "Not that she didn't say you were . . . handsome, that is."

He laughed too. I liked him immediately.

"Come, let's get a drink," he said and took my elbow.

We walked toward the bar. Danette grabbed my arm and introduced me to Shawn's parents and his sister and his old-maid aunts from Tennessee.

"Why don't I just bring you something?" Nader said.

"Any kind of sparkling water would be great," I said. "Thanks."

Shawn's aunts were lovely. In typical Southern fashion, we chatted away about Shawn, stories from when he was a mere lad. And I threw in a few stories about Molly and how my children had grown up with her and the bridesmaids. Forgoing wine, I sipped my glass of sparkling water, in deference to the dress I had struggled to zip, and I ate only protein tidbits. They moved away to talk to someone else and there I stood. A target for Wes.

I couldn't avoid him so I spoke to him.

"Hi," I said.

"Nice party," he said.

"Yes," I said. "It is. Danette did a beautiful job."

"Looks like she's herself got a boyfriend, although he looks pretty young for her."

"I think he's just right," I said and looked at him.

I was thinking he had some nerve to make a crack like that when he was in her home and on the receiving end of her hospitality.

"Harold's not too happy about him being here," Wes said.

"Tough noogies for Harold," I said and smiled.

"Oh, I get it. You're saying what's good for the gander is good for the goose?"

"I'm saying nothing of the sort. I think Nader is a lovely gentleman and Harold might lighten up. He should be glad she's found someone who makes her happy. Would he rather have an ex-wife who wanted to torture him for the rest of his life? God knows, she's got grounds."

Wes looked at me, obviously surprised by my direct remark. "Really?" he said.

"Yes, really. What's the matter with you, Wes? Is your memory really that short or do you fellas get together and rewrite history?" I said and walked away.

Maybe it wasn't the nicest thing to say, but he could not possibly have expected me to support Harold.

The night went on, people eating and drinking and taking endless pictures of each other until the young people peeled off to go to a club. Holly, who was enthralled with her new uncle Harlan, climbed up in his lap and went to sleep. We were a small group then, Danette and Nader, who mingled; Harlan and I, who listened; Paolo, Wes, and Harold, who clustered and blustered; Charlotte and Dr. Harry Chen from Shanghai, who told wonderful stories about his family and their Chinese weddings.

"So the grandmothers always have to outdo each other, and the aunties fight over everything else . . . food, music, who will design the flowers. All families are a little bit crazy," he observed with a solemn face.

"Oh, Harry," Danette said. "You have *no* idea how true that is!"

"Someday I'll tell you stories," Charlotte said.

"It was a wonderful night," I said to Danette. "Thank you."

She nodded her head in appreciation and agreement.

"I'm so tired, but I'm so excited too. And golly, it's just so good for all of us to be together for this."

"Yes. Yes, it is! And I'm excited too," I said. "Come on, Harlan. Big day tomorrow."

"Righto! Why don't I go get the car so you don't have to walk on the road in the dark?"

"That's sweet! Thanks! The key's in my bag over there."

Charlotte gave me a kiss on the cheek and said, "See you tomorrow, Mom. I've got to get this little flower girl to bed."

Charlotte seemed different then, as though having Holly and treating her with lots of motherly attention made her more attractive to Harry Chen. I hoped I was right.

"See you, honey. Y'all be careful going home, okay?"

Harry Chen smiled and said, "Don't worry! If anything happens, at least she's with a doctor!"

I smiled at them.

"Got 'em!" Harlan said; he tossed the keys in the air, caught them, and left with Charlotte and Harry.

"He's so great," Danette said.

"Yeah, he really is; he's a wonderful brother. Hey, if I can do anything for you tomorrow, I'm here, okay?"

"Oh, please! You're giving the brunch and that's enough. It's a pretty small wedding so I'm hoping it will go off without any major calamities."

"I'm sure it will be perfect."

I was reasonably confident that it would be perfection. After all, Molly was Danette's only child.

Our brunch was lovely. People came and went because hair appointments and so forth interfered slightly with our timing, but I had figured it might be that way. It was more like an open house than a seated meal. And actually the casual atmosphere put everyone at ease. After several hours of mimosas and Bloody Marys, omelets and salads, our guests began to leave, thanking me, saying it was so nice of us to provide such a lovely meal and that they were excited to see what the rest of the day would bring. The ceremony was at six.

Harlan looked at his watch. It was almost three.

"Wow," he said, "that was easy."

"Yes, it was. I just paid the bill with Wes's credit card. He's going to have a cow when the statement comes at the end of the month."

"No, he won't. He's terrified right now."

"Really? How do you know that?"

"Because I could see it in his face last night. He was looking around at Paolo and Harold, and it was as clear as anything that he doesn't want to wind up like them."

"Our marriage was nothing like theirs," I said. "Tessa died and Harold ran around."

"It doesn't matter. Wes doesn't want to die alone."

"Who does?" I said.

CHAPTER 25

Wes—The Wedding

Everybody has their own point of view about things. Last night at Danette's party, and I would never say this in a thousand years, I thought Harold was pathetic. There he was looking like a fool to everybody who knew the story on Cornelia. Everything about him said he was the classic lonely guy—his slouched posture, his pained expression. And I'd never admit this to Les, but she was right. Harold had no business to even entertain the idea that he was calling the shots in Danette's future. He should've put on a happy face and slapped Nader on the back and told him thanks and good luck or something. But what did he do? He sulked. It made him look juvenile. Worse than that? I knew, because he told me, that he was still seeing Cornelia on the side.

Next we have Paolo, who also looked like a dummy. There were Alicia and Suzanne, as beautiful as two young women could ever be, flirting with my crazy-ass son, Bertie, who may not be so crazy after all if he could hold their interest. And Paolo? He was still mad with his girls, but I know—because I saw him having lunch at the Ritz—

that he's already dating another girl and this one's even younger. Meanwhile, he's still plotting like the CIA for how he's going to get even with his daughters.

I said, *Gentlemen, gentlemen, this is no time to quarrel!* Les was right about this too, that this was Molly and Shawn's wedding and we should all rally to make sure this is a happy memory for all parties involved. Harold should be grateful to Danette that she pulled all these festivities together and Paolo would be well advised to realize his girls were going to despise anyone he dated who seemed the least bit inappropriate.

And I saw the crowd at the brunch today and figured the bill is probably at around eight to ten thousand dollars if it was seventy-five dollars a head, which it probably was because I glanced at a menu and did some quick math. You know what? Suddenly, I didn't even mind. Les was right again. She and I are Harold and Danette's oldest friends, and it's absolutely the right thing for us to host a nice party for them. After all, what's money for? I couldn't take it with me, but if today didn't go right, Les might take it with her! And even if she didn't, was I supposed to leave it all to the kids? That made no sense! Nah! Better to enjoy it a little.

I almost missed the whole wedding because of traffic and because I couldn't find my studs, but I got there just in time. Everyone was already inside a private room having cocktails and chatting away. I slipped through the bar to take a shortcut to the party, and to my utter and complete shock, there were Lisette and Cornelia sitting up at the bar drinking some kind of pink cocktails in double martini glasses. Cosmopolitans, I think. They were dressed in provocative short dresses and high-heeled shoes, but this was nothing new for them. However, this could only mean one thing—trouble. Cornelia caught my eye, and I knew I had to say hello.

"Well, hello, ladies! What a surprise to see y'all here today!"

"Hi, Wes," Cornelia said and offered her cheek for me to peck, which I did.

"We still have signing privileges," Lisette said, and I pecked her cheek as well.

"And why not?" I said. Hell, it was none of my business who signed on Harold's and Paolo's accounts, but Les was right that Lisette was a dimwit. What a thing to say! "But you do know that Molly's wedding is in the ballroom in just minutes?"

"Of course," Cornelia said. "We just wanted to take a sneak peek and then wish her well, if there's a moment that seems like it wouldn't cause a stir."

"The last thing we want is trouble," Lisette said. "Right, Cornelia?"

"Right," Cornelia said and bobbed her head in the affirmative. "I just love weddings. That's all."

"No, I didn't mean to imply *anything*!" I said and thought, Yes, I did. I thought I may have detected a slight slur in their speech. Nah, I told myself, they're nice girls. They're not really going to start any kind of nonsense, are they?

"Listen, how's this? I'll let Molly and Shawn know y'all are here and I'm sure they'll come out and say hello. Anyway, I have to rush or Charlotte will kill me if I miss Holly going up the aisle. See y'all in a bit?"

"Sure!" Cornelia said and waved her fingers in a toodle-ooo.

Oh no, I thought. Now, I was no psychic, but I knew when something bad was afoot. How could I stop them from crashing the wedding? That must've been why they were here! Why *else* would they be here? To sell Avon? No, they were here to start trouble and they were gassing up on vodka to fortify their nerve. Is this what the world had come to? Great, just great. There was no dignity anymore.

Harold, Danette, Molly, and Shawn were all sequestered with the rest of the bridal party, which included Bertie, Charlotte (to overlook Holly), Suzanne, and Alicia. This was the last thing they needed to hear at that moment. I hurried along, and as I got to the room where the cocktails were being served, people were leaving to go to the room where the service would be held. Paolo was nowhere in sight.

I hurried to the chapel and searched for Les and Harlan, spotting them almost right away. I rushed down the aisle to them and entered the row, taking a seat next to Les.

"Doesn't the room look beautiful?" Les said.

"I don't know. It looks like a wedding. Where'd you get that dress?"

"I bought it."

"Oh. Well, it looks really nice."

"Thanks."

I looked her over. "And that pin? I hope it's fake."

"It is."

"Well, it looks good. Listen, Les, I think there's trouble on the horizon."

"What's the matter?" she said.

"What's going on?" Harlan said.

Oh, now he had to know everything too? But wait, I told myself, be nice to Harlan.

"Maybe I can help in some way?" Harlan continued.

"Cornelia and Lisette are in the bar getting hammered." I said this in a low whisper and I was pretty sure no one else heard me besides Les and Harlan. "We can't let them ruin the wedding."

The crowd continued pouring in like molten lava, moving quickly until nearly all the chairs were filled.

"Oh, dear!" Les said, obviously disturbed. "But what can we do?"

"Did you tell security?" Harlan said.

"No. That's an excellent idea!" I said. "I'll be right back."

"Wait," Les said, "too late."

As I got up to leave, the music rose and Shawn, his best man, and the minister appeared on the makeshift altar, which was surrounded by thousands of white flowers. (Glad I didn't have to pay *that* bill!) And it was that kind of music I hate with a purple passion—all fruity violins and a flute. Then here came Shawn's mother on the arm of a groomsman, walking slowly with Shawn's father behind them. Next Danette walked slowly up the aisle on the arm of my Bertie, of all people, with Nader trailing behind her. I remembered right then that Bertie had an offer from CNN. But as far as the angry women who were perhaps about to do something disastrous? It was too late. I couldn't stop the wedding procession. I took a deep breath.

"Right after the ceremony," Harlan said, "and I'll go with you. Don't worry."

I thought, He doesn't give a rat's fanny about this. He just wants to get his money's worth out of this wedding like an old yenta. Well, actually, so did I. Maybe Harlan wasn't so bad.

"Que sera sera," Les whispered. "Now, calm yourself down or you'll give yourself a stroke."

I saw Les smile out of the corner of my eye, and I hoped it was because she was proud of me. It was good for her to see me attempting to do something heroic. Well, maybe heroic is too strong a word, maybe gallant is better. As soon as this ceremony was over I was going to find security and tell them the situation. It would be okay. I felt better.

"You look good in red," I said to her.

"Thanks," she said. "Are you flirting with me?"

"Maybe," I said.

We stood when the music swelled, and here came the brides-maids followed by my little Holly Doodle walking very slowly, dropping rose petals and smiling. When she passed us, Les had tears rolling down her cheeks. She loved Holly so much. So did I. And our little Holly was so pretty. I took Les's hand in mine and squeezed it. She didn't jerk it away, which I took as a good sign.

Finally, the moment arrived and here came Harold with Molly on his arm. The father of the bride looked terrific. And Molly looked like an angel.

"I've known her since she was just a little girl and now she's all grown up," Les said as she continued to quietly weep.

I handed her a tissue. Since she'd left I'd had to use tissues.

I leaned over to Les and Harlan and said as quietly as I could, "He's doing pretty good considering he just had surgery."

"Oh, no! What happened?" Les said and Harlan leaned in to hear.

"He had a pump sewn into his, you know, his um . . . johnson."

"Good grief!" Les said in a normal tone of voice, and half the guests turned around. Then she whispered. "Why?"

"I'll explain it to you later," I said. I forgot that Les didn't know about the world.

"If I'd known, I would've sent flowers," Harlan said, deadpan.

Even I had to chuckle at that.

CHAPTER 26

Les—The Bare Truth

I was so embarrassed by what Wes told me that Harold had done to himself I thought I would pass out right on the floor. What was the matter with these men? We could talk about *that* until the end of time. Instead, I concentrated on Molly and what a magnificent bride she was, a confection of tulle and lace as she floated up the aisle and on Holly, my little treasure, carefully dropping rose petals right and then left. It was all simply magical, the bridesmaids in gray silk with pearls and pink flowers in their hair and pink and white bouquets. The groomsmen, so young and handsome in their tuxedos, wondering which of them would be next. And the profusion of flowers cascading everywhere, and everything and everyone glowing in the pale gold warmth of a thousand candles. It was very traditional and classic and simply spectacular.

As Molly and Shawn said their *I do*s, her voice quivered with emotion and his was strong and firm, as though he couldn't wait to let everyone know he intended to marry her forever. It was a very moving ceremony.

As soon as Molly and Shawn were pronounced man and wife, Wes and Harlan slipped out through the side aisle in search of security before the newlyweds even came back down the aisle. I sighed in relief. Where was Cornelia's and Lisette's pride? How could they show their faces here and on this day especially? Wes was right. They were up to no good. I couldn't help but wonder what evil they had cooking in their tiny little peanut-sized brains.

I moved slowly along with the throng as we all made our way to the ballroom, thinking it was the sweetest wedding I had been witness to in years and certainly the most beautiful. Suddenly in that moment, I felt maternal pangs. All I wanted then was for Bertie and Charlotte to find someone to love. It wasn't about getting married necessarily, although I would love for Holly to have a stepfather. I just didn't want my children to be lonely. Loneliness leads to despair and then depression, and I just couldn't stand to think about my children feeling so blue or having no partner for them. Though I liked the way Harry Chen and Charlotte deferred to each other. Maybe something would come of it. And I thought it was curious that both of Paolo's daughters were flirting with Bertie. You never know. I loved my Bertie like a wild woman, but with that hair of his? Well, the old saying about beauty and the eye of the beholder had never been truer. Ironically, I had just discovered that being alone didn't necessarily mean you'd be lonely and now I was wishing for committed relationships for my children. Motherhood rots your brain.

As soon as we all reached the ballroom, everyone picked up the little cards that indicated our seating assignments, but I put ours back on the hospitality table so Harlan and Wes could find me without a problem. We were all seated at Table Five, which was just opposite the long table that had been set up for the wedding party and the parents of the bride and groom.

The band was playing and Danette was right—they were incredible. And this wasn't a band—it was an orchestra. There was even a horn section and they were playing "The Way You Look Tonight." For some reason, every time I heard that song my eyes welled up with tears. But I'd already shed a few tears during the ceremony, and I wasn't going to shed any more and ruin my makeup. Maybe I was particularly sensitive because my own marriage was evaporating.

I didn't hate Wes and I wasn't really angry either. Exasperated but not angry. And, in the interest of full disclosure, Wes and I had not been like man and wife in years, except once on Valentine's Day a few years ago when he realized that he forgot to buy me a card when I gave him three, stashed in his medicine cabinet, his sock drawer, and under his coffee cup. Maybe he thought a five-minute mattress mambo was a worthy substitute? I'd rather have had roses. Even from the grocery store and with a gaggle of baby's breath. Oh well. It didn't matter anymore anyway. I'd told him to go on about his life and consider us to be separated and I'd meant it.

I took a seat at the table and unfolded the napkins to my left and right and draped them on the back of the chairs so the other guests at our table would know those seats were taken. Two young couples approached and sat down. They politely introduced themselves as friends of Shawn and said that they had all gone to medical school together. Four doctors at one table.

"My goodness!" I said. "If anyone has a heart attack tonight, they can be saved!"

"I'm actually a dermatologist," the doctor to my left said, "and my wife's a psychiatrist, but we'll do our best."

"Yes, ma'am," the other male doctor said, "and we're both ob-gyns but we can help too!"

We all laughed at that, and I looked up to see Wes and Harlan coming toward the table.

Charlotte and Harry were seated at another table with the ring bearer's parents, on the other side of the bridal party so that Charlotte could keep an eye on Holly.

"So how did it go?" I asked Wes.

"Well, first of all, security can't remove either one of them because Harold and Paolo never rescinded their signing privileges. But they said they'd keep an eye open."

"Great. Harold and Paolo probably haven't had the time," I said.

"Yeah, well, Harold doesn't want to and Paolo doesn't care," Wes said.

"Those two are pretty liquored up," Harlan said. "And I don't think they fully appreciated the poetry Wes offered them. In fact, I'm afraid they might have taken some offense."

"What did you say, Wes?"

"What? *Me?* Look, I just said what was obvious, which was that they seemed a little over the edge for so early in the evening and that they might want to pace themselves a little bit. That's all."

"Actually, Wesley, that's not the story in its *entirety,*" Harlan said.

"Then *you* tell it, Harlan," Wes said, with patently obvious annoyance in his voice.

It was that old familiar tone Wes used when he was right on the verge of pulling the pin on his hand-grenade tantrums. I recognized it and Harlan sensed it, so we both became very quiet, giving Wes a moment to compose himself. This was another example of why I didn't miss living with Wes.

The waiters began pouring wine and champagne and they couldn't have arrived a moment too soon for me.

"Cheers!" I said to the whole table and raised my glass. "To Molly and Shawn!"

"Cheers!" they all said. Wes mumbled something that sounded like *harrumph.*

"So, Wes?" I said with a smile. "What do you think they are up to?"

Wes was now placated because I skipped over Harlan's version of the story to soothe Wes's very delicate ego. Wes took a long drink of his white wine and put the glass down.

"I think that Cornelia somehow wants to embarrass Molly and Shawn and that she needs a lot of vodka and her sidekick to find the nerve to do it," Wes said and looked around. "I just said to her, 'Look, sweetheart, I know you caught the short end of the stick on this one, but give Harold a little time. Don't go showing your weaknesses. Always deal from strength.' Isn't that what I said, Harlan?"

"Yes, and then you added something to the effect of 'It's not like Harold has any other children,' and she said, 'You mean so that if he had another child get married, he'd have to throw me out of the house again?'"

"For some reason she took issue with that," Wes said.

"Well, honey, I guess she did," I said.

"Why? What did I say?"

"Wes?" Harlan said. "What you basically said was that she was unfit for family celebrations. At least, that's how she took it."

"Aw, come on. Really? Cornelia knows me well enough to know I wouldn't go out there and insult her! *I'm* the one she's been crying to all along! She *knows* me."

"She's probably pretty unsure about everyone in Harold's world at this point, Wes."

"Maybe," he said.

"Those two make me nervous," Harlan said.

Wes said, "I agree, Harlan. They make me nervous too."

The orchestra announced the first dance, and Shawn and Molly took the floor, dancing a lovely waltz. We all stood and applauded, and then all the parents joined them. A few moments later, Harold tapped on Molly's shoulder and he danced with his daughter while Shawn danced with his mother. And then in a moment of generosity,

Danette changed partners from Nader to Harold and Molly danced with Nader. Eventually the entire Nicholls family was on the dance floor with all the Stovalls and all the bridesmaids and groomsmen. And our little Holly? She held the hands of the ring bearer in a tight grip and led him around the floor, pausing every now and then to spin him around. The photographer and the videographer were everywhere, capturing the entire moment for posterity. I couldn't wait to see all the pictures.

The dance floor got busy as the waitstaff put the first course on our table. It was two large grilled shrimp over a mixed green salad. Not very imaginative, but then it was club food. And most people liked simple straightforward meals.

"Not bad," Harlan said, taking a bite.

"And the wine's not too terrible either," Wes said.

"It's actually quite nice," I said.

"This club is the greatest," Wes said. "They really know how to throw an event."

"Yes, they do," I said.

We passed the bread baskets around, ate, and made small talk with the other guests at our table, watching the bridal party dance. Holly ran over to us several times, once to announce that when she grew up she was going to be a princess like Molly except that her dress would be covered in sparkles, another time to tell us that she was the only person in the whole room who was getting chicken fingers and French fries, and finally to ask Wes to dance with her. Wes said, *of course,* got up and led her on the dance floor. She stood on his shoes and he took her all around the room. The sight of them was priceless. When the music ended, Wes walked her back to her table and then came back to ours.

"There's a reason why young people have babies," he said.

"Yes, because it takes every bit of strength you've got!" I said.

"Yeah. I wish they'd play some Sinatra," he said.

The salads were cleared away and replaced by plates of individual beef Wellingtons or Cornish hens stuffed with mushrooms and rice. They both contained a million calories, so I decided I might as well have the beef.

"I'll have the beef as well," Harlan said.

"Me too," Wes said.

The poor little tenderloin had been cooked hours earlier and was killed off completely when it was reheated. It was shoe leather. We all took a few bites, looked at each other, and stopped eating.

"I should always take the chicken," Harlan said. "Pretty hard to wreck a chicken."

"True," I said and shook my head.

"Want to dance?" Wes said as the orchestra played a slower tune. "That's Streisand."

The band was playing "The Way We Were," and I thought, Oh, boy, here we go.

"Why not?" I said. Separated or not, there was no reason not to be civilized to each other.

Harlan smiled and winked at me. "I've got the next one."

"That's a deal!" I said and walked out on the crowded dance floor with him.

We began to do the walk around, and Wes held me closer than usual.

"You smell good," he said.

"Thank you, Wes," I said. "So do you."

"You know, Les, with Cornelia and Lisette gone now, there's no reason why you can't come home."

"Come on, Wes, we've been through this. Those stupid girls were only one aspect of what made me so unhappy. You know that."

"I think we should try again, Les. We can show the world how to make a marriage work. And our kids. We can be an example."

"I don't think that my being in Charleston sets a bad example. At all. And I'm not saying that I want a divorce. There's no point in making a bunch of lawyers rich. We've been over this, Wes. We want different things and we're going to be dead, maybe soon. Who knows?"

"Well, my cancer scare sure taught me about looking the grim reaper in the eye."

"And you've still got eighty-something golf courses to play, don't you?"

"I guess. Yeah, you're right. It's time." Suddenly, Wes pushed me back and stopped dancing. "Oh my God!"

His eyes were riveted to the main entrance. I turned around quickly to see Cornelia and Lisette sashaying their way across the ballroom with a pronounced swing of the hips, and neither one was too steady on her feet.

"Oh no," I said.

They stopped in front of the bridal party's table and leaned over to their ankles as they pulled up their dresses to reveal their bare bottoms. I saw Harlan whip out his cell phone and start snapping pictures, as did the photographer and everyone else with the dexterity to quickly get their phones aimed at the moons. As if this wasn't bad enough, Lisette's heels were so high that they compromised her center of gravity. By the time she reached her ankles, she toppled over, and she took Cornelia to the floor with her. The orchestra stopped playing, the room began giving consecutive gasps, and Harold and Paolo rushed to Cornelia and Lisette to get them off the floor. As we moved back toward our table, I could see something was written on their backsides. Every time they tried to get up, they fell to the floor again.

Harlan was almost having seizures, suppressing a tidal wave of laughter and trying to appear properly horrified at the same time.

"What do their butts say?" I asked, and the question sounded so funny that I started to laugh. I couldn't help it. I mean, did they have vocal cords back there?

Wes said, "Yeah, I saw something like . . . it was maybe written with a Sharpie?"

Harlan, seizing the übercrescendo of the night, showed us a picture he took on his phone.

"The redhead must've written on the little one, and the little one must've written on the redhead. But what's so funny is this!"

He enlarged the picture so we could see that *Kiss This!* was written on Lisette's backside, but Lisette had written *Kizz This!* on Cornelia's, spelling it wrong.

"I always said she was stupid," I said.

"Oh, dear God," Wes said. "Can you e-mail that to me?"

"Sure. It's probably already on Facebook. This town's too fast for me," Harlan said. "I'm going home to put on my jammies and watch *Ozzie and Harriet!*"

Molly remained in her place, perfectly cool but laughing like crazy. Shawn didn't move, except to take Molly's hand. He was more upset than she was. The bridesmaids sprang from their seats and clustered around Molly, giggling like schoolgirls. The groomsmen waved their fists, making manly gestures of support for Shawn. There was no doubt in my mind that everyone at the head table knew every single detail of the Cornelia affair. And everyone in the ballroom watched in horror as Harold and Paolo, after what seemed like an hour, finally got the two wretches off the floor and led them, staggering and laughing, out and away.

"I'll bet their signing privileges are revoked now," I said.

"Wow," Wes said, "I gotta go see what's going on." Wes followed Harold and Paolo outside.

It was so like Wes to run to the boys that I decided to run to my friend too.

"Let's go check on Danette," I said.

Harlan and I found her standing near Charlotte and Holly.

"Can you believe?" she said to me. Danette wasn't smiling, but she wasn't hysterical either.

"No. Are you okay?"

"Les? It's merely confirmation of what I've always said. Hopefully, Harold and Paolo will choose more wisely the next time. Honest to God! And listen, Molly thinks the same thing. If she's not upset, I'm not. As long as Molly doesn't feel that her wedding was ruined, I surely don't either."

"Amen, sister," I said. "What did Nader say?"

"Nader? That devil? He said this is the best wedding he's ever been to."

"It was certainly more exciting than having a tarot card reader," Harlan said.

The band started playing again, and the music for the remainder of the evening was upbeat and easy. Harlan and I danced and danced, and I even did a few more walk arounds with Wes. We had decided many things, Wes and I. At long last he admitted he never should've been so secretive about our assets and that he should've been more generous with me. He even admitted that playing golf in Edinburgh was probably not a good call. But we both knew there had been way too many disappointments to ever patch things up between us.

"I've been such a fool, Les. I see that now."

"We're all fools, Wesley. But forgiveness is what life's all about."

"So you forgive me?"

"Yes, of course I do. If you forgive me."

"Forgive you for what?"

"For wanting my own happiness to matter, for putting myself first now, for finding so much fault with you and the children."

"But here's the thing, Les. You're right about it all. You were right about it all."

Epilogue

Looking at houses can be very emotional, the whole business of trying to envision your life in someone else's space and how could you change it to make it work for you? After seeing a half dozen of them downtown, two in the Old Village of Mount Pleasant and at least ten on the islands, I was exhausted. I had even considered a house on Logan Street, the same street where Harlan and I grew up, but coming literally full circle did not appeal to me. I liked the concept much better that life moved in an upward spiral. Which place felt like it gave me the biggest spiritual boost? And, as this was a question of where I might like to spend the rest of my life, it also meant I was having the occasional passing thought about the end of my life, which I hoped would never come because I'd never been so happy.

"Take the cottage on Sullivans Island, the one with the Meyer lemon trees; then I can have a beach house!" Harlan said.

"Yes, you would," I said and smiled, remembering the breezes and the gorgeous camellias in the yard. That house felt like home. "Okay, I'm putting in a bid."

The three-bedroom cottage, with a tiny guesthouse, that was to be mine was located in a quiet part of the island, near the marsh, but next to the hustle of Atlanta, anywhere on the island would have seemed mighty quiet. I've heard it said before, that Sullivans Island actually *was* a magical kingdom that seemed thousands of miles away from the rest of the world. Downtown Charleston was the only other place I'd ever known that seemed to have the same kind of power, because when I was there, as when I was on the island, the rest of the world just seemed irrelevant. But maybe that was simply all about a sense of belonging. I belonged to Charleston and the island. I always had. I never belonged *to* Atlanta or *in* Atlanta. I wondered then if people from Atlanta felt the same way about other places, and I decided they probably did. In any case, I bought the old cedar cottage with the lemon trees and moved in after doing a little renovation.

Wes retired and was traveling all over the country playing golf with Harold and Paolo whenever his two buddies were able to shake themselves free of work and the Atlanta singles scene for old dudes. I shuddered to think what that might entail. To the best of my knowledge, Wes was not involved with anyone. Curiously, I hoped he'd find someone because Wes truly couldn't take care of himself very well. And I didn't like to think about him being alone. But he had Bertie, Charlotte, and Holly to keep him company, and perhaps that was why he wasn't anxious to meet anyone. This was the news from Charlotte, who was now seeing Harry Chen all the time, and she had sold two houses! Glory be! My fingers were triple crossed for her. And while we're on the subject of children, Bertie did indeed get the job at CNN in spite of his dreadlocks, was putting in some very long hours, and was deeply in love with Suzanne, according to my daughter. Bertie called me to tell me that love was *awesome*. Had he never loved anyone before? But rather than quiz him on his private life (as though boys tell their mothers anything anyway), I told him he was right. There was nothing more wonderful in all the world than love. Bertie and Suzanne had a trip planned to visit Nepal, and I wouldn't have been surprised if we got an announcement that it was going to be a honeymoon. However, far be it from me to predict *anything* because I never would have predicted the life I was living now.

And Jonathan? I wouldn't say we were inseparable, but he was my dearest and closest friend and the mere thought of losing him to California or anywhere would bring me to a weepy state, but the thought of getting married again made me short of breath. I loved him and I was in love with him, but the only aisle I was walking down was on a plane headed to Italy. However, we held hands everywhere we went and my coat? Honey, it glistened like a mink.

Jonathan's house was on the ocean side, and we were only a five-minute walk apart. Many nights we would meet at High Thyme, one of the island's restaurants we both loved. I'd scan the dining room and bar area looking for Barbies, but I never saw any like the ones I'd left behind. Oh, occasionally there were a few divorcées with a carefully calculated look of availability, ambition, and willingness (if you know what I mean), but if the men who frequented the island spots were potential sugar daddies you'd never know it to look at them. Their dress code was super low-key as was their extremely polite manner. Nobody seemed to need the big Benz to accentuate his reputation like Wes had. They all drove SUVs. It was probably assumed that my little Benz came in the nonexistent divorce settlement, which leads me to tell you that Wes lived up to his word and gave me half of everything, and we never went to the lawyers. And my Benz was more like some crazy act of defiance than anything else; inside of a year I'd probably sell it and buy something sensible like a BMW or a Maserati. Just kidding. I sort of wanted a Subaru.

It was almost Thanksgiving and Harlan and I were able to bring my little dog, DuBose, home from the breeder. If I tell you that

DuBose was the sweetest creature I had ever known, it is the understatement of my whole story.

"He's just a black-and-white fluffy ball of love," I said.

"There's nothing more fun than a puppy," Harlan said. "But I have to remember to keep my shoes put away until I find out whether this little devil is a chewer. And I can't wait to see how Princess Jo likes her cousin."

Well, she did not like DuBose one little bit. Miss Jo was so jealous, as if Harlan had cut her loyal heart to the quick, then into little pieces, and fed it to the chickens. So the arrangement that Harlan made with me to teach DuBose where to *do his business* lasted only a week. Suddenly, I had a puppy on my hands.

"He's paper trained," Harlan said, handing him over to me. "Better than nothing."

"I'll manage," I said. "Are you going to be a good dog for me?"

DuBose became my shadow, and in a few days he understood that to go outside successfully brought him a little liver treat, but to use my house as a toilet brought a little scolding and no treat. Problem almost solved.

The children were not coming for Thanksgiving, and I was not going to Atlanta. Charlotte's Harry was on call and Suzanne had promised her father, Paolo, that she'd make a turkey for them. So that meant Bertie wasn't leaving either. Wes, Bertie, and Charlotte were planning to limp through the holiday by letting Whole Foods prepare the meal, and if that was good enough for them, it was certainly okay with me. Of course, it left me to wonder why I had cooked like a slave all those years if letting my grocer cater the meal would have sufficed. Anyway, it removed the awkward part, which would have been what to do about Jonathan? I wasn't ready to introduce Jonathan to them and I sure wasn't leaving Harlan alone.

My children promised to visit separately between Christmas

and New Year's and I said that was fine with me. So I was making Thanksgiving dinner in my new house to baptize it with a holiday, and a holiday about gratitude seemed to be so perfectly matched to this time of my life. I wanted my walls to soak up the happiness we all felt just to be alive and together in that moment. I had all sorts of mums and pumpkins on the front porch and steps, a harvest wreath on the door, and best of all, Danette and Nader were fully ensconced in the guesthouse. Harlan, Nader, and Jonathan were cooking oysters on the Green Egg grill Harlan gave me as a housewarming present, and my turkey was stuffed and roasting in the oven. Danette and I were in the kitchen chopping rutabagas and beets and drinking glass after glass of iced tea. We laughed about the wedding, we laughed about old times, and we whispered secrets to each other like old friends do. We finally came together at the table at around five o'clock, when my little carriage clock chimed. We toasted each other and toasted the day and just as I was about to cut into my plate of food, the doorbell rang. I looked out the window to see a very small car parked in the yard.

"I'll get it," I said, wondering who in the world was visiting unannounced on Thanksgiving.

It was Wesley.

"Can I come in?"

"Of course! Did you eat? What are you doing in Charleston?"

"I'm playing Mid Ocean in Bermuda and I thought I'd surprise you with a trip here . . . you got company?"

"It's Thanksgiving, Wes."

Wes pushed past me and into the dining room. I could hear the sudden silence, and when I got there with Wes, Jonathan, Nader, and Harlan stood to shake his hand.

"Let's see here," Wes said, pointing his finger. "Danette is with you, and that leaves Harlan and you."

"I'm Jonathan Ray," he said.

"Uh-huh," Wes said and then, "are you with Harlan?"

"I don't believe I even know you, sir," Jonathan said.

"Is he your boyfriend?" Wes said to me.

I looked around the table and thought to myself just who did Wes think he was to make a scene in my house, grilling Jonathan as though he had the right to demand an answer from anyone? The audacity! Just barging in like he had!

"So what if he is, Wes?" I said and watched him start to puff up like a blowfish. "Wait! Yes, he is. Jonathan is my dear friend. We grew up together. And I love him."

"You mean, you love him like what? A lover?"

"Yes, Wes, like that. Like a lover." I was shaking all over, worried that he might start a fight or something.

Wes got very quiet, and then he looked me up and down as though he couldn't believe what I'd just told him.

"Wow. Okay, then." He was very calm. "I guess I'll be seeing you, Leslie."

He turned around on his heels, walked out of the door, got in his very cheap, minuscule rental car, and drove away. When I returned to the dining room, everyone stood and clapped. We ate and ate, and it was the best Thanksgiving ever.

Harlan raised his glass and said to Danette and Nader, "Almost, but not quite, as good as Molly's wedding." And then he said to me, "Thank you for this *very* exciting day!" Then I saw him slip a bit of turkey to DuBose.

"Harlan! Don't feed him!"

"He'd starve if it wasn't for me!"

We all laughed, and Jonathan said, "I think it's time for coffee. Cognac anyone?"

"Definitely for me," I said, "but no coffee."

Two weeks later, I was on my way to Rome with Jonathan, but we stopped in Paris for two nights. When Wes left, I decided it was time for me to start really living the whole life I kept saying I wanted. We were having dinner at the top of the Eiffel Tower in the Restaurant Jules Verne. The views were spectacular, the atmosphere was so romantic, and the food was delicious.

After dinner we went up to the observation deck. I said I didn't want to go, it was freezing, that the views from the restaurant were enough to satisfy me. But he insisted we had to go outside to get the full effect. So I went. It *was* cold, and there were only a few people out there. But he'd been right to insist. You haven't seen the world until you've seen all of Paris sparkling in the cold air of a December night. Jonathan put his arm around me.

"I love you, you know," he said.

"I love you too," I said. "I'm going to miss you when you move."

"I'm not going anywhere. My son has decided to move to Charleston and to take over my practice when I retire. Looks like you're stuck with me for a while."

And then a wave of panic swept over me. Was he going to propose? Was that why he brought me here? Oh, please don't! I thought. I'm just not quite ready.

"I bought you an early Christmas gift," he said.

"You did?" Oh, Lord!

He reached into his coat pocket and produced a long slender velvet box. It was not a ring. I breathed a sigh of relief.

"Open it," he said.

I did and inside was a beautiful gold Tank watch with diamonds around the face.

"Oh, Jonathan! It's beautiful! Here! Help me put it on!"

"You really like it?" He fastened it around my wrist.

"Are you serious? It's the prettiest thing I've ever owned!"

"It's too dark to read it out here, but it's engraved on the back."

"What does it say?"

"It says, in little bitty letters, *Take your time. I love you. 12-25-12.* I bought it from Trisha at Croghan's."

"Oh, it's so perfect you don't know."

"Yes, I do. Now kiss me so we can go someplace to get warm!"

I kissed him in Paris at the top of the Eiffel Tower, I kissed him in front of the pyramid at the Louvre, I kissed him in the Tuileries, and I kissed him all over Italy, in a gondola and in one trattoria after another and even in St. Peter's Square, which was probably somewhat of a sacrilege, given the legality of our situation. But while I stood there with all the saints in history over our heads carved in marble in proximity (or not) to the bones of St. Peter, I thanked God for sending me Jonathan with all the fervency I had in me and then rationalized that since I wasn't a Catholic I might not go to hell. This made me giggle.

"What are you thinking about?" Jonathan said.

"Well, I was thinking that we'd better start lighting candles in all the churches to ask for forgiveness for our sinful souls or else we'd better get married."

"How about June the eighth?" he said. "I was looking at a calendar last week and June the eighth seemed like a great time."

"Sounds great. I always wanted to be a June bride." I had actually said yes and so did he.

The day our divorce went through, I called Wes. Old Bear was pleasant and even wished me good luck, saying Jonathan seemed like a nice enough person. I told him I was grateful to him for all the years and for our children and for being so generous in the end, making it all go so smoothly. I knew he resented being replaced by anyone, who wouldn't? I told him part of me would always love him and that if he needed me, he should know I'd come to him, but I'd be bringing a doctor too. Then, in a moment that was so uncharacteristic for Wes, he told me he didn't blame me. He'd known when he barged into my house on Thanksgiving because he could see a kind of happiness on my face he'd never seen before.

"What're you going to do with yourself down there in Charleston all day long?"

"Well, I'm looking into volunteering at the South Carolina Historical Society. I want to learn all about the women in South Carolina's history."

Wes laughed at me as though I had truly lost my mind. "Really? Why?"

"I don't know. I'm interested in history, I guess."

Wes was completely incredulous. "Well, I guess you know what you want then."

"Yes, I do."

So, in a very small ceremony at St. Philip's in Charleston, with Danette as my witness and Harlan as Jonathan's and with my children and their future spouses (yes!) and Holly and Nader in attendance, as well as Jonathan's lovely children whom I was meeting for the first time, I married again and officially began a new life with Jonathan Ray. We would toast each other with champagne and feast on oysters and roasted guinea fowl in the private room at Magnolias and cut a small cake with a bride and groom on its top and make small talk throughout the afternoon while my mind traveled the years. When I thought about the individual births of my children, my chest would swell with joy, and for the moment it seemed that they were finally on the right track. I hoped so with all my heart because I loved them so dearly. They, along with Holly, were my greatest treasures. Little Holly was as completely enamored with Harry Chen as he was charmed by her. Her ambitions had been altered as she announced she was going to grow up and become a doctor. We were thrilled to hear it, every one of us, because we knew what it meant for her to say it.

I looked at Danette, remembering us with Tessa, taking our children to the park, sitting together as we watched them perform in holiday pageants, carpooling and birthday parties—how I missed Tessa then, wishing she was with us, hoping she was somehow with us in spirit. Wouldn't Tessa love to know her daughter would be my daughter-in-law? I had already vowed to be a good mother-in-law to Suzanne one hundred times but just in case Tessa could hear me, I vowed once more.

Harlan tapped his knife on the side of his glass and stood. He was going to make a toast.

"I'd like to say a few words about these two madcap daredevil kids who just tied the knot. First of all, Jonathan, I'm a little disappointed you couldn't find a seersucker tuxedo . . ."

"Next wedding!" he said. "I'll track one down by then! I promise!"

We all laughed and Harlan continued.

"And I want to congratulate my beautiful sister, who has done the most remarkable thing in that she beat her own children to the altar!"

Everyone laughed again and said things like *here, here!*

"But seriously, I want to wish y'all happiness in every single hour of every single day for the rest of your lives and I hope that's fifty years at least. I know it's not possible to have that but I wish it for y'all anyway. So I just wanted to say, and this is what I know is certain . . . love is a gift, it's a noun but it's also a verb. And yet, for all the poets in history and how they throw the word 'love' around like a beach ball, the word 'love' still doesn't cover nearly what we need it to mean. Maybe cherish is the better wish for you. Yes, cherish each other and be happy."

"Awesome," Bertie said, and everyone clapped.

I looked at Jonathan and he looked at me and we gave each other a kiss that wouldn't embarrass the children or anyone, for that matter. He took my hand in his and gave my new wedding band a spin around my finger, smiling, his blue eyes twinkling. I loved the feeling it gave me, to know I belonged with him. I was finally home in the Lowcountry of South Carolina where I was meant to be. At last I was with the man who was the right one. I was surrounded by love, and truly I felt cherished. There was nothing more I would ever want.

ACKNOWLEDGMENTS

Using a real person's name for a character in a book has been a great way to raise money for worthy causes. And in *The Last Original Wife* three generous souls come to life in these pages as my characters. I have never met these folks (actually, one of them is a cat), so I can assure you that the behavior, language, and personalities of the characters bear no resemblance to the actual people. (Or the cat.) My thanks go to Carol St. Clair who supported my old high school, Bishop England, and secured the position of a psychiatrist for her mother, Jane Saunders. To Danette Stovall, who won an auction prize from my grammar school, Christ Our King, and will live on as the best friend to my protagonist. Dr. Harrison Katz is the feline friend of Jennifer Blumenthal, who bought immortality for her cat at an auction to benefit the Hollings Cancer Center. Bravo, ladies! I hope you'll get a kick from seeing these names in print. And Nader Tavakoli is in here as Nader Tavakoli because he's my buddy, and I thought it would be fun for him. He knows this random act of generosity will cost him down the line. Nader? It will. However, he has never met Danette Stovall, and they have never engaged in what happens in this story.

Also, special thanks to Barbara L. Bellows for writing her excellent book on the very interesting life of Josephine Pinckney, *A Talent for Living* (Louisiana State University Press, 2006). If anyone wants to know more about the Charleston Literary Renaissance and all about Jo Pinckney, this really is the book you want. Ms. Bellows is just the most wonderful writer, and reading her book will surely enrich your life. I bow to you, Ms. Bellows, and hope our paths will cross one day.

The following people have no idea or maybe they have a smidgen of an idea that their names are in these pages: Trisha Gustafson from Croghan's Jewel Box, Karen Stokes and Faye Jenson from the South Carolina Historical Society, Shawn Nicholls from HarperCollins, my dear friend Clare Mullarney, the great Gerald Imber, and our dear friend of a million years, Ann Del Mastro.

Special thanks and loads of love to Harlan Greene and Jonathan Ray. In this book they play leading roles, and if you've read this, please know they are even more wonderful and brilliant and handsome in real life. Love y'all!

I'd like to thank my brilliant editor at William Morrow, Carrie Feron, for her marvelous friendship, her endless wisdom, and her fabulous sense of humor. Your ideas and excellent editorial input always make my work better. I couldn't do this without you! I am blowing you bazillions of smooches from my office window in Montclair. And to Suzanne Gluck, Alicia Gordon, Eve Attermann, Samantha Frank, Tracy Fisher, Elizabeth Sheinkman, Colette Patnaude, Covey Crolius, Jo Rodgers, and the whole amazing team of Jedis at WME, I am loving y'all to pieces and looking forward to a brilliant future together!

To the entire William Morrow and Avon team: Brian Murray,

Michael Morrison, Liate Stehlik, Nicole Fischer, Tessa Woodward, Lynn Grady, Tavia Kowalchuk, Ben Bruton, Leah Loguidice, Shawn Nicholls, Frank Albanese, Virginia Stanley, Rachael Brenner Levenberg, Andrea Rosen, Caitlin McCaskey, Josh Marwell, Doug Jones, Carla Parker, Donna Waikus, Rhonda Rose, Michael Morris, Gabe Barillas, Deb Murphy, Mumtaz Mustafa, and last but most certainly not ever least, Brian Grogan: thank you one and all for the miracles you perform and for your amazing, generous support. You still make me want to dance.

To Buzzy Porter, huge thanks for getting me so organized and for your loyal friendship of many years. Don't know what I'd do without you!

And special thanks to Patti Callahan Henry for her details on Atlanta.

To Debbie Zammit, it seems incredible but here we are again! Another year! Another miracle! Another year of keeping me on track, catching my goobers, and making me look reasonably intelligent by giving me tons of excellent ideas about everything. I know, I owe you so big-time it's ridiculous, but isn't this publishing business better than Seventh Avenue? Thank you, from the bottom of my pea-pickin' heart, Deb, for your friendship all these years. Love ya, girl!

To Ann Del Mastro, George Zur, and my cousin, Charles Comar Blanchard, all the Franks love you for too many reasons to enumerate!

To booksellers across the land, and I mean every single one of you, I thank you most sincerely, especially Patty Morrison of Barnes & Noble, Tom Warner and Vicky Crafton of Litchfield Books, Sally Brewster of Park Road Books, and once again, can we just hold the phone for Jacquie Lee of Books-A-Million? Jacquie, Jacquie! You are too much, hon! Love ya and love y'all!

To my family, Peter, William, and Victoria, I love y'all with all I've got. Victoria, you are the most beautiful, wonderful daughter and I am so proud of you. You and William are so smart and so funny, but then a good sense of humor might have been essential to your survival in this house. And you both give me great advice, a quality that makes me particularly proud. And William, my sweet William, my heart swells with gratitude and pride when I think of you and you are never far away from the forefront of my mind. Every woman should have my good fortune with their children. You fill my life with joy. Well, usually. Just kidding. Peter Frank? You are still the man of my dreams, honey. Thirty years and they never had a fight. It's a little incredible to realize it's only thirty years, especially when it feels like I've been loving you forever.

Finally, to my readers to whom I owe the greatest debt of all, I am sending you the most sincere and profound thanks for reading my stories, for sending along so many nice e-mails, for yakking it up with me on Facebook, and for coming out to book signings. You are why I try to write a book each year. I hope *The Last Original Wife* will entertain you and give you something new to think about. There's a lot of magic down here in the Lowcountry. Please come see us and get some for yourself!

I love you all and thank you once again.

BOOKS BY
DOROTHEA BENTON FRANK

THE LAST ORIGINAL WIFE
A Novel
Available in Paperback and eBook

Leslie Anne Greene Carter is The Last Original Wife among her husband Wesley's wildly successful Atlanta social set. But if losing her friends to tanned and toned young Barbie brides isn't painful enough, a series of setbacks shake Les's world and push her to the edge.

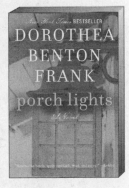

PORCH LIGHTS
A Novel
Available in Paperback and eBook

When Jimmy McMullen, a fireman with the FDNY, is killed in the line of duty, his wife, Jackie, and ten-year-old son, Charlie, are devastated. Trusting in the healing power of family, Jackie decides to return to her childhood home on Sullivans Island. Crossing the bridge from the mainland, Jackie and Charlie enter a world full of wonder and magic— lush green grasslands and dazzling evening skies.

FOLLY BEACH
A Lowcountry Tale
Available in Paperback and eBook

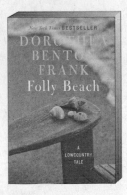

Folly Beach, South Carolina, with its glistening beaches, laidback Southern charm, and enticing Gullah tradition, is the land of Cate Cooper's childhood, the place where all the ghosts of her past roam freely. Now, thanks to a newly deceased husband whose financial and emotional perfidy has left her homeless and broke, she's returning to this lovely strip of coast.

LOWCOUNTRY SUMMER
A Plantation Novel
Available in Paperback and eBook

When Caroline Wimbley Levine returned to Tall Pines Plantation, she never expected to make peace with long-buried truths about herself and her family. Her late mother was a force of nature, but now she is gone, leaving Caroline uncertain of who will take her place.